Blurred Justice

Dennis Jones

ISBN: 978-1-64438-762-7

Published by BookLocker.com, Inc., St. Petersburg, Florida.

Printed on acid-free paper.

BookLocker.com, Inc.
2019

First Edition

DEDICATION

To A, K, J, and M

ACKNOWLEDGMENTS

Thanks to Becky and Dub Narramore who gave me their ideas and opinions and who first said that I might have something. To Dan Botkin of Act-1 Computer who worked his computer magic on the book. And last, to Marion M. Jones who added his insight and reading skills.

ABOUT THE AUTHOR

DENNIS JONES is an attorney, a former District Attorney in Cass County, Texas, and former judge in Kaufman County, Texas. He worked for twenty years in the Dallas County District Attorney's Office as a trial attorney. He was raised in Linden, Texas. Currently, he is retired and lives in Kaufman, Texas.

dennispjones.tx@gmail.com

Chapter 1

"Twenty-five hundred dollars to rent a damn tree mulcher," thought Ramon Garza aloud. "Outrageous." He was still shaking his head as he pulled out of the parking lot of Fast Joe's Rentals. He had never questioned Ulysses Carillo's directives, but he had no idea that this latest one would cost so much. "What the hell," he finally grinned, "we've got money to burn." The money, in hundred dollar bills, had been paid up front. Now Garza was on his way back to Kaufman, the suburban community near Dallas, Texas, pulling the full-sized, gasoline powered limb shredder. As he left Dallas, the traffic was light driving south along Highway 175. Even though the tree mulcher was huge and bulky, the new Chevy pickup pulled it easily. Drug money paid for a lot of things, he thought as he sipped from a can of Miller beer. "Ahh, good stuff," he muttered as he took a long pull from his last beer. The six-pack purchased that morning had been consumed quickly.

"Yeah, but we got money," he nodded smugly. He glanced over the inside of the truck and whiffed the unique smell of a brand-new vehicle. Paying $ 20,000.00 in cash the day before for the truck was routine dealing for Ulysses Carillo, the man Garza worked for.

Checking in the rearview mirror, he saw his cargo was pulling well. Ramon Garza had not been told, in so many words, the specific reason for getting the tree mulcher. Garza had worked himself up the ladder in the drug dealing world and had established himself as Carillo's right-hand man. He knew Ulysses Carillo had not become the largest, most insulated, and most feared cocaine dealer in the Southwest by going easy on traitors. Ulysses Carillo paid well, but demanded extreme loyalty in return. Worship would be more descriptive.

"I told Angela not to cheat him. Ulysses is too smart and would know if someone was skimming money," he thought to himself. Garza slowly shook his head, "She knew better, and now she would have to pay. So piss on her."

The forty-five mile drive seemed to take forever. Although Garza had been there many times, tonight the roads leading to the vacant barn seemed unfamiliar. The secluded wooded area was seven miles from downtown Kaufman, and isolated from the nearby farms and ranches. Shortly before dark Garza's headlights illuminated the building. He instantly recognized Carillo's Mercedes parked in front. Leaving the truck engine running, Garza eased up to the dilapidated barn. As he opened the door and stepped inside, a bright stream of light blinded him. The flashlight's beacon was meant to blind. It followed him as he took a few steps. Ulysses Carillo's voice penetrated the stillness.

"Where in the hell have you been? You've been gone almost four hours." The voice rose. "Where in the hell have you been?" Garza still could not see, and the smell of soured liquor blew into his face. "We have business to take care of, and we don't need you fucking off." The flashlight was lowered from Garza's face and soon he saw the setting and characters that he had anticipated.

Garza thought for a second before answering. "I had to go all over east-fucking Egypt to four different rental companies before I could find one that would lease the damn thing. It was five o'clock before I found one. And it took another hour for them to get the fucker to work and show me."

"I know how to operate the damn thing," Carillo butted in. "I've been around these things before." The sharp anger in Carillo's voice faded fast, and just as quickly a smile spread across his face.

Garza knew what Carillo meant. That previous incident was still picture clear in his mind even though it happened a couple of years ago. He had only been working for Carillo two weeks when one of the minor street dealers had tried to take over the operation. The man had had enough of the incessant orders, the arrogant, relentless dictatorship, and the overall operation of the illicit drug-dealing business. The man had often openly ridiculed Carillo, accusing him of being afraid to expand the cocaine trafficking operation. The accusation had hit a raw nerve with Ulysses Carillo.

His competitors knew he was ruthless. Murder was a fact of life and a necessary tool. Carillo's reputation thrived on that. His methods were designed to scare those who had notions of encroaching into his territory. He liked to brag to Garza, telling and retelling stories of violent murder many times. And Ramon Garza believed them, because he knew the man. Ulysses Carillo enjoyed killing. He tortured. He took pleasure in creating a scene that had his signature on it, his personal stamp of death. It had to have flair, he constantly boasted. It had to be repulsive. Ramon Garza believed this trait placed Carillo above everyone else in the world of cocaine dealers. Garza had seen the results. He witnessed first-hand as Carillo walked-the-walk and talked-the-talk. Ulysses Carillo marveled at his own success. A Cuban, born to poor sugarcane-growing parents, had finally made it big.

"Open the door, Ramon, and drive that damn thing inside!" said Carillo. He turned to two other men who were standing in a corner drinking wine. A young, pale girl maybe all of seventeen years of age, sat helplessly on the ground, blindfolded and gagged, with hands tightly bound.

"Don't just stand there!" he snapped. "Get off your butts and help get that mulcher in here. And bring her over here."

Throwing the wine bottle on the ground, Raul and Hector moved quickly. Picking up the young woman and standing her on her feet, they pushed her toward the menacing Carillo. By this time Angela Hinohosa was wide awake. The effects of marijuana and alcohol had long since worn off. The pretty girl began fighting for her life. For a few minutes it was all Hector and Raul could do to hold on to the prisoner. Even with both hands tied, the arching, contorted torso exhibited superhuman strength. Both legs were kicking wildly. There was a will to survive like Garza had never before witnessed. Her head, swaying and jerking, offered no help in her failing hope of escape. Instinct had taken over in this young girl's fight to live. But her screams... eerie, guttural, and deathly real, eventually quieted. Her resistance was now gone. She had exhausted every ounce of energy in her tender body. Her lungs were heaving-- gurgling for air. With her hands still tied, her small frame was rustled next to Ulysses Carillo. The blindfold was jerked off of her head. Strands of her long, black hair stuck to her sweating face. Carillo grabbed both of her cheeks and vehemently squeezed them with his hands. His calm authority was lost. He suddenly started screaming, "You bitch, you don't steal from me! You hear me? You don't steal from me!" With the truck lights helping to illuminate the inside area of the barn, Ulysses Carillo continued. "I don't give anyone a second chance. Now you are an example to everyone else."

Ramon Garza, standing next to the new truck, dared not intervene. He knew Carillo's anger was real. He had seen it before.

Angela Hinohosa's sudden gasp went unnoticed as the sound of the Briggs and Stratton engine reared to life. Her trembling knees made it impossible to stand, but the two guards prevented her from falling. Orders were given to untie her hands. Fear and nausea hit Hector Rincone. Even though he had known Ulysses Carillo less than two months, Rincone already knew the zeal of his boss. But even Hector Rincone was not prepared for this... A fleeting thought crossed his mind to stop what was occurring. To end it right then and there.

But he did not. And as he nervously looked around at the others, he noticed that Ramon Garza was watching him intently and with a threatening look.

The pulverizing sound of the engine beat against the walls. The rickety, wooden planks hardly muffled the sound. Now, Hector Rincone saw that Carillo's eyes were inflamed with rage. Their leader was actually spitting and frothing at the mouth as he continued screaming into Angela's face. But she could not hear a word. With a sudden explosion of energy, she was again waging war in her ordeal to live. Clawing, kicking, slapping and hitting. Both men assigned to guard her were trying to stomp on her feet with their own, and simultaneously hold her swinging arms, hands and head. She could not get away.

"Put her in feet first," said Carillo. Unable to control himself, screaming and shaking he had gone momentarily mad. He watched as Garza and the other two men lifted Angela and placed her into the tree mulcher. After churning for about a minute, the machine became stuck and stalled. Grabbing a loose plank lying on the dirt ground, Carillo used it to poke and eventually dislodge the machine's grinding teeth that had snagged on a body part. Then the grinder started grating again, spewing body fragments and bloody meat against the barn walls. It took about seven minutes, according to Garza's watch, and then it was over.

Chapter Two

Carillo awoke from a heavy sleep around 8:00 a.m. the next day. The sound of house keys of the maid unlocking the front door stirred him slowly. The events from the night before were only a hazy blur to him now. He had driven back to Dallas alone, leaving Garza and the others to clean up and dispose of things. He felt good about the necessary work that had been done. "Word of this will soon get to the streets. Won't take long," he thought, as he drifted in and out of sleep.

Later, as he stepped out of the shower, his phone was ringing.

"Yeah", he answered.

"We got things all tidied up," spoke Garza. We took the mulcher to a car wash and cleaned it all up; then we took it to a scrap iron place and sold it as junk. We watched them as they crushed it. They did not ask for ownership papers or anything. We threw what body parts we could sweep up into the Trinity River. Fish are eating great now!" he chuckled.

"I want you to start spreading the word about last night," directed Carillo. "Take it to the streets. Tell them that no one fucks with me and lives. You know who to speak to."

"Okay, right. I'll spend the afternoon talking the shit and come by to pick you up about six or six-thirty. Don't forget we have a meeting."

"Yeah. Did you make the arrangements like I told you to?"

"Yeah, seven-thirty."

"Bye."

Before Garza made it to the streets to spread the word about the events of the night before, he had to have a bump. A bump was all he lived for nowadays. That was the beginning and the end. However, it had not always been that way. Growing up in East Dallas in the shadows of the Cotton Bowl football stadium, a young Ramon Garza earned money selling popcorn and sodas during Dallas Cowboy football games. After school he worked at a Dairy Queen on a nearby corner.

Esther and Ersantis Garza had moved to Dallas in the summer of 1970, when their son Ramon was only ten years old. The neighborhood, predominantly black and Hispanic, was less than five miles from downtown. His three older brothers did not want to move with their parents so they stayed in Matamoros, Mexico. After living in the United States for five years, the Garza's applied for, and received, the necessary papers making them legal aliens.

Because of school bussing, Ramon Garza flourished at schools in predominantly white, upper-class areas. At Hillcrest High School he had been selected into the National Honor Society, and was voted "Best Liked" by his Junior Class. During his Senior year, the slim, handsome, dark-haired youth had been elected Student Body President. He had a quick smile, showing perfectly-straight white teeth. With a knack to gab, the easy-going Garza became a favorite with the students and teachers. His laid-back temperament coupled with his natural tendency to be funny made him a hit at school. But his popularity did not compare to his athletic ability. Standing six feet-one and weighing one hundred eighty pounds, Garza possessed amazing quickness and agility, the right-handed Garza had been voted the All-Metroplex shortstop by the Dallas Morning News in his last two years of school. Sportswriters statewide had even named him to the All-State team during his last year.

It was a freak baseball accident in his senior year during the last regular season baseball game that ended Ramon Garza's highly promising baseball career.

The next day the newspaper's sports section described the collision between him and the catcher as ferocious. Garza was knocked unconscious. He awoke in the hospital with a compound fracture of the leg. The cast stayed on his leg for three months. The cartilage damage required additional months of therapy. For the first three weeks, the pain in his leg was nearly unbearable so the doctor prescribed a medium-grade painkiller. After the cast was removed, the pain eventually subsided but he continued taking the painkillers anyway. They made him feel good. The lies he told the doctor about his leg pain enabled him to continue getting the prescription refilled. His leg just would not heal properly. A slight limp became permanent. The large number of college baseball scholarships that had been tentatively offered was summarily withdrawn. It was devastating. He had dreamed, like most baseball kids, of playing professional baseball. And he had put in the road work. The body conditioning, running and calisthenics were all directed toward one goal. And he had been good, really good. But now, his dream was gone. His baseball-playing days, he was told, were over. He felt like he had no other talents. Life started and stopped with baseball. There was nothing else. And the sustained "high" that resulted from the innocuous-looking pills became more and more desired. The physician, accurately fearing that his patient was becoming dependent on the drug, discontinued the prescription. However, the youth had only to turn to his street buddies from East Dallas.

East Dallas was once a very stable, middle-income, working-class neighborhood. However, in the past twenty-five years it had deteriorated into outright slums. The selling of every kind of drug was commonplace on almost every street corner. Garza believed that with baseball, he had found his ticket out of there; but his accident detoured him to painkillers. The painkillers led to amphetamines and methamphetamines. Next it was cocaine. Ramon Garza found that he liked them all. Petty stealing became the avenue to get the money to buy the drugs. As the habit increased, more money was needed. Money could be made from dealing.

Four months to the day after Ramon's leg injury, his father Ersantis Garza unexpectedly died of a heart attack. The suddenness and finality of the situation crumbled the life of Ramon Garza even more. After the shock of his father's death, sadness and loneliness set in. Ramon's only response to these feelings was drugs. Drugs to calm him, drugs to make him forget. And drugs to ease the feelings of emptiness. They helped him survive and face the world, or so he said.

Garza quickly learned that he could turn a hefty profit above and beyond paying for his habit. The months slowly slipped into years, and Ramon's initial reaction to a failed baseball career and the loss of his father turned into a job. Although he raked in more than fifty thousand dollars profit the third year after high school, that still made him a strictly minor player in the spurious drug world. His growing labors were more or less confined to the five-square-mile area that the Metroplex labeled, and derogatorily referred to as, "East Dallas."

When Ulysses Carillo arrived from Mexico City four years after Garza's high school graduation, cocaine was the narcotic most in demand. Carillo had intended to continue his trade in heroin but he soon saw that more money was to be made in cocaine because of its heavy demand. In Mexico City, drug dealing had been safe and profitable. The expansion of the business came slowly by design. He had wanted, and indeed had established, a rock solid, impenetrable drug base in Mexico before expanding north into Texas. While some cocaine dealers were making hundreds of thousands of dollars on the streets of the United States, Ulysses Carillo firmly believed he had the wherewithal to make millions once he moved into the United States.

The networking in Mexico had taken two years to formulate. Carillo had established himself as one of the largest heroin dealers in central Mexico. After buying the finished product from Honduras, Carillo and his confederates would smuggle large quantities to the dealers. And since Carillo was three or four people removed from the street vendor, tracing him up the ladder was practically impossible. And, of course, it did not hurt his protection when he paid thousands of dollars to certain members of the "policia" to look the other way. From his heroin connections established in Mexico, it was easy to find the major cocaine dealers in Dallas.

In East Dallas, Ramon Garza was working on expanding his base. His immediate objective was the territory bossed by Lionel Swift. Lean, eager and aggressive, Garza was going to prey on the fat, lazy Lionel Swift. Strung out on drugs most of the time, Swift was getting more and more haphazard in his dealings. Garza let it be known that he was moving in on Swift's operation.

Not wanting to wage war, Swift took the easy way and offered to merge. Such a deal was fine with Garza, since it meant no bloodletting and a larger area to control more quickly. Through this merger, Ramon Garza met Ulysses Carillo.

Carillo had been in Dallas about one month, making the rounds, trying to make his face known. One Saturday, just as the weather was turning cool, he was scheduled to meet Lionel Swift in a beer joint on Harry Hines Boulevard.

Swift was one of the first individuals that Carillo had sought out to engage in the narcotic business. That morning, Swift brought Ramon Garza along.

It took a few seconds for Carillo's eyes to adjust to the dimly-lit tavern. Billiard balls clicking against one another were easily heard. After spotting the short, fat Swift hunkered over a pool table, Carillo walked over and sat on a stool and watched the game. When the game was over, Swift motioned for Carillo to join them at a small corner booth which was already cluttered with empty beer bottles. After some small talk, Carillo stated how much cocaine he wanted, and the degree of purity. Swift responded with the amount of cash required. Garza sat, drank, and listened to the two men talk shop. Garza observed his new business partner strike a deal for a fairly large parcel of cocaine. He then began sizing up Carillo. Garza had previously been told that the man was Cuban and had built up quite a large heroin trade in Mexico and that he wanted to expand into the United States. Garza could tell within five minutes of the meeting that Carillo knew how to run a business. He quickly deduced that Carillo had the money and contacts to fund a large-scale undertaking. Frankly, Garza had never heard of anyone arriving in unfamiliar territory and setting themselves up as a paramount supplier so quickly. Swift had told him earlier that morning that Carillo had gotten to know all the small-time dealers in Dallas; and it was through them that Ulysses Carillo's cocaine trade matured. With such acceleration, switching from heroin to cocaine had been a minor hurdle.

Carillo talked a tough, clear-headed game. It was a no-nonsense approach and Garza quickly sensed that Carillo could deliver. Carillo surely looked capable enough. He stood just under six feet three inches tall and weighed more than two hundred thirty-five pounds. His long, straight, black hair fell below his muscled shoulders. He was cleanly-shaven, with a beak nose, and predominant forehead. His brown eyes were small and angry. His face did not carry a natural smile. He looked mean because he was mean. He made a formidable impression. As he spoke in that deep slow tone, he was very articulate. He sounded very confident, matter-of-fact and demanding. And he did not mince words. One knew immediately he could back up what he was saying. In Garza's mind, Ulysses Carillo was a pro. Immediately, instinctively, Garza feared the man.

Swift and Garza supplied cocaine to Carillo during those infrequent times that Carillo's own pipeline ran low. This loose arrangement worked both ways. When needed, Carillo helped out Garza and Company when their supply was low. No questions were ever asked about Garza's hierarchy, nor did Garza ever ask questions about Carillo's.

The merger, however, was not long lasting. One night, a runner did not arrive to transport fifteen pounds of cocaine to a particular area in their East Dallas domain. Since Swift was going that way, he decided to take it himself. A marked police car appeared, seemingly from nowhere, and began following him. Losing his composure, Swift started trying to outrun the policeman. The chase ended ten miles across town when Swift's car skidded, hit a telephone pole and wrecked out. By then police cars were all around the place. When Swift tried to shoot his way out of the trouble, he died from bullets fired by several officers.

Soon thereafter, Carillo asked Garza to come work with him. The network was growing and Carillo needed a right-hand man who knew the local trade, a lieutenant to help manage the growing demand. The night that the offer to Garza was made, Carillo had already reviewed his books and records of transactions. In the previous nine months, he cleared an average of fifty thousand dollars a month. The offer had been simple. "I need someone to help manage my affairs. In exchange, I will give you a hundred and fifty thousand dollars a year and all the coke you want for your own use."

"Done," said Ramon Garza.

During the first month, Garza learned first-hand how vicious Ulysses Carillo could be. One of his customary buyers had ordered five pounds from Carillo when the weekly order had normally been ten. Since this meant less profit for Carillo, he was more than incensed. When the buyer came to pick up the package, he was confronted by Carillo. Garza watched in amazement as Carillo angrily produced a pistol from his belt. Quickly grabbing the buyer's right hand, and without saying a word, Carillo shot off the man's little finger.

The years of roaming the streets in Havana had instilled in Carillo the characteristic of reacting violently in all situations. It was a raging reflex. It was this approach that enabled Carillo to gradually rise in stature among the drug lords in Dallas. Whenever Carillo encroached into new territories, he acted and reacted with fury. And if it meant disfiguring, roughing up, or murdering, he made the move. And as Garza witnessed time and time again, it was always the last and final move.

Ulysses Carillo had only one confidant, Ramon Garza. Garza handled the orders, arranged the meetings with potential clients, scheduled the drop-off times, and made the transports and pickups. And as always, Ulysses Carillo was in the shadowy background. He watched quietly, still directing, seeing that business was done his way.

Chapter Three

His Rolex watch showed a few minutes before one p.m. Garza knew he was going to be right on time. He turned off bumpy Industrial Avenue and into the parking lot of a burger joint. Garza opened a beer and waited for the drop-off person. His contact, a pock-marked, wiry sort, called Stoney, was rarely late. Garza had just finished his beer when Stoney pulled his yellow pickup truck into the parking slot next to Garza. After hurriedly exiting his own vehicle, he turned and reached for Garza's passenger car door handle.

"How are you?" he asked Garza as he slid into the car seat.

Garza leaned over the front seat and pulled up a satchel that had been lying on the back seat floorboard. "Here's your order. One fourth kilo of this sweet stuff. You got the money?"

"Yeah, sure do, my man," replied Stoney. "I have it right here," he said as he tapped his chest. He unbuttoned his shirt, exposing two money belts around his stomach. The bills, all of them $100's, were neatly arranged and wrapped in cellophane and filled both belts entirely. Garza looked at the money as Stoney counted it out loud.

The exchange was made in less than 3 minutes. Stoney opened the door to leave.

"Wait!" Garza said quickly. His hand reached over and grabbed the forearm of his passenger. "There's something else." His grip remained tight. "Hey, man, I'm scared shitless! Let me tell you this."

"Well, my man, make it fast. I've got to roll on out of here."

Garza excitedly told the events of the night before. He was doing a good job, or so he believed, of acting the part of the frightened worker. As he related the story, Stoney became uneasy. He had known Angela very well. He softly mentioned that he had even gone out with her a few times.

Both occupants were quiet for a few moments. Garza, letting the story settle in, and Stoney trying to regain his composure. Unexpectedly, Stoney's words came flying out: "Well, that's what the bitch gets for skimming money that's not hers." His voice was quivering.

"Look," Garza continued, "for our own damn good, you might better remember that he doesn't play around."

"No fucking shit."

"And listen, pass the word to others, if you know what I mean."

"No shit, man. I will. I will. But for what it's worth, tell him he doesn't have to worry about me. I play, I pay." Stoney opened the door to leave. "Later," he said as he walked away.

"That went pretty smooth." thought Garza. "I've got four more stops and four more stories to tell. I should be in the fucking movies."

It was after six p.m. when Garza finished his rounds. He related the events just as he had rehearsed; and knew the story would spread fast. He headed towards Carillo's house. "Just a quick hit, and then I'll be ready for action," he said aloud to himself. "Damn, it feels good!" he thought. Ramon Garza always needed his fix.

Chapter Four

Eleven forty-five a.m. Tony Medina knew he was early, but his errands had not taken as long as he had thought. Rather than go back to his house, he decided to go on over to his sister's house. He would just wait inside for her until she arrived home. Juanita got off work at noon and would normally be home by twelve-thirty. Once in the apartment's parking lot, he parked his white Datsun directly at the foot of the stairs leading up to her unit. Exiting his vehicle, he bounced up the outside stairs and knocked on her front door. No answer. He knocked again. Nothing. He tried the doorknob. Locked.

He did not mind taking her to the grocery store and to the other places she had mentioned. At one time, he too had been without a car and was forced to take the bus everywhere he went. After all, this was his little sister and little sisters needed looking after. Two more months of working at the plant and he would have enough saved for a down payment on a used car he was buying her. What a great surprise this present was going to make for her twenty-first birthday!

As he was lumbering back down the stairs, Tony heard loud rap music coming from the upstairs apartment located at the other end of the building. The door and windows were closed but the music was so loud that it was easily traveling through the walls. Kicking an empty beer can out of his way, he wished his sister would move out of this complex. He and the rest of the family had spoken to her many times about the conditions that surrounded her. The neighbors were practically all drunks or drug dealers and that area of the city was full of thieves, hookers and criminals. The family wanted her to move back home with them, at least until she could save up enough money to move to a better place. But Juanita Medina gave the same answer over and over again. Since she rode the city bus, she wanted to be close enough to her job to get there quickly, even in rush hour. The city bus service stopped just in front of her apartment. And the apartment complex was the closest one to the hospital that she could afford on her salary. She was steadfast in wanting to be able to pay her own way. Although she conceded that her apartment was not much, it was something that she had wanted to do for herself.

The prostitute had been given a hundred dollar bill up front and the trick had lasted maybe twenty minutes. This was seventy-five dollars more than she had bargained for. Afterwards, she quickly put on her wrinkled clothes, got the last wine cooler from the sack and opened her front door to leave. The John was still inside her apartment, practically passed out. The music coming from her apartment woke Tony Medina as he napped in the front seat of his car. Medina watched her as she walked from the apartment and down the metal stairs. Directly in front of his car, she stepped to the ground and then walked past him. With the driver's window rolled down, he was able to smell the loud perfume that was commingled with alcohol. Looking back up to her apartment, Tony saw a dark figure peering out from the slightly opened door and then it disappeared. After a few moments, the figure reappeared at the front window that faced the parking lot. He lifted the curtain and looked out again. Now Tony Medina was awake. He turned on the car radio and fumbled the dial until it landed on a sports talk radio station.

From Ulysses Carillo's position inside the apartment, he did not recognize the person seated inside the car. He had not noticed the white Datsun parked there when he and the hooker had entered her apartment earlier. Carillo, already high, shot himself up with another speedball. Since before noon, speedballs had been all that he had taken. After a few minutes, Carillo looked out the window again at the man who was still sitting in the car.

"Why is that guy following me?" Carillo asked himself. "He must be following me. Who is he?" He was swaying so much that he propped himself against the wall for support. "He must be trying to kill me." The thoughts and questions ran through his mind as fast as the drugs ran through his body. "He's waiting for me to come outside, and then he's going to shoot me." Carillo cracked open the door for a better view. The man was still there. "Still waiting," he said. Carillo did not recognize him. "He's wearing those damn glasses to try to fool me."

"I don't know who you are, shit head, but I know what you want. You want to kill me," he muttered under his breath. The drugs and alcohol had already taken hold of his body. Large doses of paranoia filled his mind.

Tony Medina looked at his watch again. It was twelve-thirty. Maybe, he thought, he had made a mistake and his sister had told him a different time. But she was only thirty minutes late, and so he decided to give her ten more minutes.

Moments passed. By now Carillo was pacing the floor like a caged, angry wolf and talking aloud to himself. "You are waiting to kill me. You fucker! You are waiting for me to walk right past you and then you will try to kill me." His rage filled the room. He was out of his mind. His body tense, "Who do you work for? You fucker, you faggot! Are you trying to move into my territory?" Carillo walked past the window and again looked out. The white Datsun was still there and the sole occupant still in it.

Ten minutes were up, and Tony decided he would go to Parkland to see if there had been some kind of mix-up. But first, he wanted to hear the rest of the sportscast on the radio.

"You fucker, you fucker! I will kill you first, you little maggot!" screamed Carillo. Now in an uncontrollable state, steeped with the drugs, he got his pistol from the coffee table and pulled back the hammer. "I will blow your fucking head off! I will blow your fucking head off! I will blow your fucking head off!"

Hearing footsteps running down the stairs, Tony looked up from the radio. The long-haired man, dressed only in pants, was carrying a huge gun in his right hand. Tony had just leaned his head out of the car window when the first bullet struck his ear and shot it off. Grabbing where his ear once belonged was the last thing Tony remembered.

Chapter Five

The police radio message was short: "Shots heard in area." After hearing where the gunshots were heard, Dallas Police car element 529, already close by, began driving around in that sector looking for the trouble. Turning down Maple Avenue, the patrolmen saw a crowd of people waving at them. When the patrol car, the first one on the scene, stopped in the apartment complex parking lot, onlookers pointed toward a nearby white Datsun. The patrolman riding in the passenger seat quickly exited his vehicle while the driver stayed behind and radioed their location to the dispatcher. The first officer drew his gun and approached the crowd on foot. The spectators parted as the officer neared the Datsun. Inside this vehicle was the bullet-riddled body of a young man. The officer made a quick glance around the area for any apparent danger. Seeing none, he holstered his gun and opened the car door. He checked the vital signs of the victim and thought he detected a faint heartbeat. He yelled for his partner to call an ambulance.

Seconds later, a half- dozen cars arrived on the scene and began to secure the area. The crime scene was quickly cordoned off and limited only to policemen and ambulance attendants. The paramedic unit of the Dallas Fire Department responded and transported the gunshot victim to the hospital. He was barely breathing but at least he was still alive. Alive, but fading fast. It was shortly after 1:00 p.m. when police detective Frank Barnes sat down at his desk to eat his extra thick bar-b-que sandwich and fried onion rings. The ringing of the telephone interrupted his meal. He looked around hoping another detective would take the call. The offices that housed the Homicide Division of the Dallas Police Department were empty except for him. "Crap," he muttered between bites. "Where is everyone?"

He picked up the phone. "Homicide. Yeah.......Where's the ten-twenty? ...... Where?........ 1400 Maple Street?........ Got it. How many are down?...... Has PES arrived?...... Call and make sure they have been called. I'm on my way." As he hung up the phone, Barnes' fresh, young partner walked through the main door. "Saddle up!" said the veteran detective as he hurriedly munched the last few bites of his sandwich and grabbed the brown paper sack of onion rings to take along with him.

In less than five minutes, Detectives Frank Barnes and Bobby Gallagher were in their unmarked police vehicle and on their way. The excitement of working in the Homicide Division had not worn off for Bobby Gallagher, even after six months. For five long years he had worn the blue uniform, patrolling the streets of Dallas. He had always wanted to be a police officer, ever since grade school in Oklahoma City. Two years after joining the police force he had passed his corporal examination. Then, two years after that, he made the highest score of those taking the sergeant examination. No sooner had he sewed his new sergeant stripes to his patrol uniform than he immediately applied for transfer into the Homicide Division. It took four months and a couple of retirements in the division before the move came through. This was where he wanted to stay. The Homicide Division was everything Gallagher had thought it would be. For the twenty-eight year old detective, who looked like a young Tom Selleck, life was grand. As he drove to the crime scene, Detective Gallagher thought about his passenger. How lucky Gallagher had been to have been partnered with Frank Barnes who was sort of an icon in the DPD.

From all accounts in the entire police department, Barnes was the most respected detective on the force. He was twice selected as Police Officer of the Year by the statewide Texas Association of Peace Officers. He had repeatedly turned down numerous requests from the Police Chief to promote into the Administration Division of the police department. A desk job was not something he envied. "I belong in the field." was his standard reply. A slim, bespectacled, handsome man of fifty, Barnes had been a police officer since the mid eighties. After graduating from high school in Waco, Texas, he had joined the U.S. Army. Honorably discharged five years later, he moved to Dallas. During his last two years in the Army, Barnes had worked in recruiting. It was during this time that he occasionally traveled to Dallas for recruitment drives. Single and unattached, he found that Dallas was a haven for pretty girls. Unmarried females from the surrounding farming communities traveled to Dallas seeking fame and fortune. More importantly, they were also looking for a husband. After bouncing from job to job for about a year, Barnes applied and was accepted with the Dallas Police Department. Nine months later he proposed to the red-headed girl who lived in the duplex next door to him. They did not have much of a honeymoon, because Barnes had no vacation time. After a weekend honeymoon trip to Fort Worth, barely thirty miles away, he was back patrolling the streets on Monday morning.

As a rookie police officer and a newlywed, life was hectic. The shift work of police duty was hard to get used to. Slowly his life settled into a routine and, when it did, Barnes became restless.

It was after his third year on the police force that he decided to enroll in college. Barnes had to obtain special permission from the police chief to arrange his police work around each semester's classes. Fortunately, the police department was willing to accommodate him. It was not unusual for police officers to take several college courses in police-related studies and normally these were the only classes taken by them. But Barnes wanted a full college degree so this meant taking all the basics: Freshman English, History, General Science, and all other curriculum in the degree plan. He became a full-time college student, attending morning classes and occasionally night school. Four and a half years later he walked across the stage and received his Bachelor of Arts diploma, with double degrees in Police Science and Psychology.

Gallagher looked at his older partner as they continued driving toward the crime scene. Barnes had not changed much from those pictures of him receiving commendations and civic awards adorning the walls of various substations. He still had that full head of wavy brown hair. It had, however, quite a few--make that a lot--of gray streaks running throughout. Since Gallagher was almost six-feet tall, he guessed that Barnes was maybe five feet ten. Gallagher was an exercise freak. Barnes was just the opposite–no exercise at all except lifting a beer bottle to his mouth. Even when Gallagher was still a patrol offer, Barnes' reputation in the 3600-man police force was huge. There was not a better, more thorough, professional police officer.

And that reputation had existed from the front office on down to the patrol ranks. Gallagher smiled, "I'm glad to be on board."

The scene of the shooting was as typical as they come to Frank Barnes. He had seen hundreds during his career. He went about his work--methodically. After talking to the uniformed patrol officers, Barnes checked the individual apartments. In that particular building four separate apartment units were located upstairs and four were located downstairs. It came as no surprise when he was told that no one was at home in any of them. But he double-checked them himself--knocking on each door. No answer. From talking to the numerous bystanders, no one had seen anything. They had only heard the shots.

"Looks to me like a typical drug deal gone sour," Gallagher told one of the uniformed officers.

Overhearing the comment, Barnes rebutted, "Can't tell yet." Then he raised both eyebrows and added, "But who knows, you may be right. Maybe PES will be able to tell us something." He turned to an officer dressed in a blue coverall jumpsuit, "Pat, what do you have?"

Pat Jenson had been in the Physical Evidence Section for five years. Barnes knew how good Jenson was in processing a crime scene. 'Processing' meant allowing PES to photograph the scene, discover and preserve any fingerprints, collect hair fibers, bloodstains and other items of evidence that might be connected to the case. Jenson had been a patrol officer for five years, then applied for transfer to the Physical Evidence Section-PES for short. Since techniques and methodology of crime scene preservation were constantly updated by the evolution of modern science, continuing education was a necessity. Pat Jenson's professional credentials read like a Who's Who in the field of Police Science having been schooled by the state police and the FBI.

A couple of hours after arriving on the scene, Jenson approached the detective with news that Barnes did not want to hear.

"I'm through with the car. Nothing." bemoaned Jenson. "The inside of the car was kept clean; not purposefully wiped clean to remove evidence, just a clean-kept car. It was spotless--like your grandmother would keep it. I wasn't even able to pick up a smudge from a fingerprint, much less one that I could compare.

There were no loose objects, such as books, papers, or glasses inside the car. Like I say, it was a well-kept vehicle. Looking at the blood splattering, it appears -- unofficially, of course -- that the victim was just sitting behind the wheel. His door was closed and the window on the driver's side was rolled down. The key was in the ignition and turned in such a way that the power was on, but not the engine. The first patrol officer on the scene told me that the radio was playing when he arrived. So he was probably just sitting in the car and listening to the radio. I have to do some measuring and calculating back at the office, but it appears as if the victim was facing the gunman when he was shot. A few minutes ago, I radioed and talked to both of the paramedics and was told the victim's right ear was completely shot off. And get this, the ear was found in the back seat. There was a typical amount of blood in the car. Some in the floor-board, some speckles on the inside of the roof, and some on the front seat. We've collected some of it and will be sending it to the Crime Lab to determine if all of it came from the victim. But from the way it was found in the car, to the naked eye it appears to have come from the same individual. Fortunately, before the victim was transported by the paramedics, the patrol officers requested the victim's hands be bagged so we might be able to detect if any gunpowder residue exists on his hands. Of course, that's if he dies. But if he lives, hell, the nurses will scrub him down until he's raw. And then there goes any hope of detecting anything. By the way, what's the condition of the person?"

Barnes exhaled deeply. "A patrol unit met the ambulance at the hospital, the officers stayed with the victim. They just called and said that, according to the emergency room doctors, the guy has an outside chance to live. Shit! They said he had about half a dozen gunshots in him. No one around here saw anything, as usual. Some kids down the street heard the shots, and by the time they ran up here to see, everything was over and everyone was gone. We've knocked twice on all the doors in the apartment unit. No one's answered. It appears to be empty at the present time. Now that's not to say that it didn't become empty after the shots were fired, if you follow me."

"No shit."

"But anyway, right now, I have no witnesses and no suspects. The damn computer is down so we can't even run a registration on the car. The officers at the hospital collected some identification papers from the man's wallet and will hold it until we get there. We've got the owner of the complex on his way over here right now to let us inside all of the units. Hell, we don't know but that the son of a bitch that did the shooting might be inside. Unlikely, but who knows? If he is inside and tries to shoot his way out of here, he is one dead motor scooter," cracked Barnes as he surveyed the fifteen to twenty officers that were surrounding the crime scene and the apartment building.

For a moment, no one spoke. Barnes gazed silently at the numerous policemen who were along the apartment walkway. "What a waste of precious time," he thought. "We could have already searched those damn units and gone about our business. Instead, we have to sit on our sweet asses until someone with a key arrives to let us in. But before they do they'll want to see our search warrants." He yearned for the old days, just kick the doors down and go in.

Ten minutes later the apartment manager drove up. He had been grocery shopping. He was a little apprehensive about opening the entire apartment building. He finally consented, but police found no one.

"Do you want me to process any particular apartment?" asked Jenson. Before anyone could answer, he added, "But, hell, I can't do them all. I would be here a week."

"No, we searched all of them." Barnes responded. "Nothing turned up in any of them. Tell me, what's the bottom line?"

Detective Jenson had been scribbling some notes on a small note pad.

"Well, the best I can tell at the moment, it's not much. We have one victim that has approximately six to eight bullet holes in him. We know he was sitting in this car and the suspect was standing outside next to the driver's side door. There were no empty shell casings found, so the shooter either picked up all the casings from the automatic weapon after he shot, which is highly unlikely, or he was using a revolver. From the size of the blood drops, I'd guess the gun was nothing smaller than a .32 or a .38 caliber. No drugs were found anywhere, nor did we find money anywhere in the car to indicate that this was a drug deal." Jenson paused."Of course, I haven't heard from the hospital yet advising if any money or drugs were found on the person, but I know the paramedics didn't find any. Other than blood inside the car, there was nothing else. No ricochet marks, no bullet fragments. No guns were found inside or outside or around the premises. We're in the process of towing the vehicle to the auto pound and will keep it for possible evidence. The area surrounding the shooting produced nothing. Oh, and by the way, no fingerprints were lifted." Jenson's tone took on a facetious ring, "That's all my good news. And what about you, Doc?"

Barnes had nothing to add. "The search of the apartments yielded absolutely nothing. Nothing and nobody. The closest thing that we have to a bona-fide witness is a twelve-year old boy from down the street who heard the shots, and then saw a light-colored car leave the scene in a hurry. But he doesn't know what kind of car, or anything else about it, other than it was light in color. He was a fairly long way away from the crime scene and can't really add much. After the gunfire a lot of people appeared on the scene, but none of them saw anyone leave. That's not too surprising. No real car description that's of any use. No one-arm man running from the area. Zero." Tossing a pad of paper into his car, Barnes was ready to leave. "There's nothing more we can do here. Let's go."

Gallagher climbed behind the wheel of the car. "Do we even know the name of the person that got shot or anything about him?"

The passenger side car door closed.

"Not yet, but we soon will."

Chapter Six

"I wish they'd hurry and tell me something." Juanita Medina was sitting in the hospital waiting room --waiting and worrying. She glanced at the wall clock. It was 5:05 p.m. It seemed like hours had passed since she had first arrived. But, actually, it had only been twenty minutes. She had just walked into her apartment when the telephone rang. She did not recognize the hospital spokesman when he spoke, "Miss Juanita Medina, please."

"This is she."

"Ma'am, my name is Charles Stone, and I work at Parkland Hospital. There has been an accident involving your brother, Tony. He's okay. He's being treated now in the emergency room."

"What? Is he okay?"

"Yes, he's going to be okay."

"What happened?"

"Ma'am, I don't know any of the details, but he has been shot."

"Oh no. No. Not Tony. Is he alive? Is he going to be okay?"

"Ma'am, that's all I know at this time. He is in Emergency Room B at Parkland Hospital."

That was all the conversation that Juanita Medina could remember. She quickly picked up her purse and ran out the door. She looked at her watch. The next bus going towards the hospital was due. As she ran across the street in front of her apartment, she saw the bus turning the corner coming toward her.

"Oh, thank God," she thought. "I haven't missed it."

At the hospital emergency room, Juanita flagged down the first nurse she saw, recognizing her as a friend. Juanita explained her situation, and the nurse passed on the necessary information to the attending physician and emergency team that had been assigned to Tony Medina. Juanita did not know the doctor working on her brother but she knew most of the nurses. She wanted to barge into Emergency Room B, but her professionalism kept her out. Moments later the nurse returned and approached Juanita.

"All I know, Juanita, is that he's been shot more than once. He's alive, but very critical. The doctor will be out in a minute. I told him you're a Parkland nurse. He'll be out. You stay put."

Juanita leaned against the hospital wall as her friend went toward the nurse's station. "Thank goodness they were able to reach me," she said to herself. It was only then that she remembered she was to have met Tony hours ago at her apartment. She had stayed late at work, completely forgetting about going to the store with him.

Her spirits rose a little when later she saw her father and younger brother and sisters come through the door of the waiting room. She spoke first: "I don't really know much yet, except that he's been shot and it looks bad. I've only been here about twenty minutes. The hospital called me at home and told me that Tony had been shot but that he was alive. Do you know any more? What happened?"

They had no more information. At that moment Juanita saw a doctor whom she knew walking down the hall and told him of the situation. "I'll find out something," he said, and disappeared into Emergency Room B.

Moments later, a paunchy, middle-aged man clad in gray surgical gear appeared from behind the double doors of Emergency Room B, and glanced around the waiting room. Juanita Medina and her father took a few steps toward the physician.

"Hi. I'm Dr. Lucas. As I understand from your friend, Dr. Middleton, the patient is your brother, right?"

Juanita nodded, gripping her father's arm.

"Here's what I found. He has multiple gunshot wounds. I count five, mostly to the chest and stomach area. One hit his outer ear. One, possibly two bullets, hit the spinal cord. At this point in time, I don't know the extent of that damage. The other bullets have been removed. We've stopped the internal bleeding for the time being. The bullets against the spinal column are now our primary concern. We are moving him into the surgery room as we speak. The neurosurgeons are on their way. Dr. Middleton tells me you work here, and I appreciate your staying out here in the hallway." He viewed the older man standing next to Juanita and also the three kids sitting together on the waiting room sofa. "Are these family members?"

"Yes, sir," she answered.

Dr. Lucas turned to her father. "He's alive, but he's in very critical condition. I can't say if he's going to make it or not. But right now we're attempting to get him stabilized. Also, he had most of his right ear shot off." The physician touched his own right ear. "It's the outside part that's gone. No damage, that I could ascertain, was done to the inner ear."

Turning once again to Juanita, "One of the nurses in the emergency room found your name and some more family names and phone numbers in your brother's wallet. She knows you, from work. But at the time, in the midst of all the confusion, did not associate you with the patient. She gave all of your names and phone numbers to the hospital admitting personnel as soon as she could. So it was only when that other nurse came in a few minutes ago that she realized that you worked here. If we had known that you worked here we could have tried to notify you at your station. Were you on duty?"

"Yes, but don't worry about that. Tell me, do you know anything about how it happened?"

"Your brother was brought in here about 1:00. I briefly talked with some officers about an hour ago. Maybe it was a little longer. Anyway....uh.....they escorted the ambulance here. All they know, or all they would tell me, is that he was shot as he sat in a car. That's all they knew. They said they would stay a few more minutes, and then said they had to leave but that an investigator would arrive shortly."

"Is he going to live?" one of the younger children asked.

The physician looked down, "I hope so, son." Returning his look to Juanita, "Like I said, it's going to be touch and go for a while, maybe lasting all night or even a few days. I don't know the extent of the damage of the wounds around the spine. They are very dangerous wounds in extremely dangerous locations. And there was some damage. Any more than that, the neurosurgeons will have to answer. I'll tell them that you are here so they can talk to you when they've finished."

It was a long and seemingly endless wait at the hospital. Juanita, though tempted to move around, stayed with the rest of her family. No one was speaking. She reflected. She looked at her father, Juan. She loved and admired him. On his next birthday, he would be fifty-seven years old. As an unskilled Mexican laborer, he had worked construction for Brown and Root for almost thirty years. After her mother died seven years ago, Juan Medina never remarried. Instead he funneled all his efforts into holding his family together. How he made the house payments, and provided food and clothes for the five children, while all the time giving money to the church, still amazed Juanita. Now, as she stared at him, Juanita could plainly see the fear covering his face. The long lines on his ruddy face, put there by years of grueling work, now looked like long lines of mental torment. He had been through enough difficult times already. As he sat in the strange, unfamiliar and sterile hospital surroundings, Juanita knew she would now have to become the strong one. Her father had done so much up to this point; now it was her turn. The small man sat there with his head down. His tired eyes stared at the tile floor. His short black-and-gray hair was neatly combed straight back. He wore a faded khaki shirt. His faded khaki pants were frayed on the ends. Both were cleaner than clean.

Her mother's death thrust Tony, the eldest, in charge of running the household while his father worked in construction. From the time Tony was fifteen years old until he was eighteen, he had cooked, cleaned, and supervised the housework. When Tony started working at various jobs around his seventeenth birthday, the housework was still his responsibility. Juanita helped, especially involving the younger ones. And even now, seven years later, she thought, they were still just kids. Hosea just turned sixteen, Rose was twelve, and Mercedes was ten. They were good kids. Here in the hospital waiting room, Juanita thought of the last time all of them had been together in a hospital setting. It was when their mother had died after a car accident. At the time everyone was so young. The youngest, Mercedes, was not even three years old. A few days after the funeral, the elder Medina called all of them together. He sat them down on the sofa in their small living room and told them how their lives had to go on. Right now in the hospital waiting room, Juanita vividly remembered the details of that time. And why she started thinking about it now, she could not explain.

A hushed sound brought Juanita back to the present. She turned and looked to see who it came from. It was her younger brother. "It's all right to cry, Hosea." she said, as he fought back the tears. You know Tony is tough, and he will be okay." Hosea continued to sniffle, hiding his face in his father's lap. Mercedes and Rose cried themselves to sleep. Now they lay side by side on the sofa in the waiting room. The exhausting two-hour wait was beginning to affect everyone. Her father sat quietly, his eyes blankly staring straight ahead. His rough hand gently stroking Hosea's head. A worried look stil on his face. The waiting continued, and still no word.

The neurosurgeon finally emerged from the operating room. Juanita noted that even he looked weathered, with perspiration coming through his cap and shirt. The news he delivered was both good and bad. The two bullets had severed parts of Tony's spinal column. The damage, undeniable, was going to mean some paralysis, but it was far too soon to tell the extent of it. But, he was alive! He was alive and the doctor believed that the patient would live.

"Keep fighting, Tony! Keep fighting!" she found herself saying out loud as she watched the doctor disappear.

The five of them had had the waiting room all to themselves. However, when four other people came, the room suddenly became crowded.

Juanita took her family from the crowded room to the cafeteria.

An hour passed with no further news from the doctors.

"Why don't you take the kids back home?" she said to her Dad. Call Uncle Joe and tell them what happened. I'm going to stay here until they move Tony. If I get sleepy I can lie down at my work station. If Aunt Yolanda wants to come here for a while, tell her to check first in my ward. I'll leave word there of my whereabouts."

"I think that's the best idea".

"Take them home. They've had enough for the day. If Aunt Yolanda comes, she can take me home; if not, I've got taxi money."

"No, come stay at the house tonight. The kids need you." His voice was clear and unbending. At that point, she knew better than to argue with her father.

Alone, she sat down and looked at her watch. Eight o'clock. It had been almost four hours since she had first been notified of Tony's injuries. And still, she had not seen nor spoken with the police. A hundred questions filled her thoughts. Between the worries about her brother's condition, she wondered what had happened.

Earlier, when her father had started to call the police, she had stopped him. She did not even know why. She knew the police had been there right after Tony had been brought into the hospital. They had stayed awhile. At least that is what one of the doctors had said. But that had been hours ago. Why had they not come back? Just as she was getting up to call the police station, she saw two uniformed officers coming toward her.

The older of the two asked, "Are you Miss Medina?" As she nodded, he continued, "I'm Sgt. Francis and this is Corporal White. We have been assigned to work on Tony's case. Let's go to the hospital security office, and we can tell you what information we have obtained."

The four minute walk ended behind strange doors. She had never been in Parkland Hospital's security offices. The blue sign next to the doorway read "Dallas Police Department and Hospital Security." As the three entered, another man, wearing a coat and tie, approached them. "Hello, I'm Detective Frank Barnes. You must be Juanita Medina."

"Yes, I am."

"First, let me apologize for not being able to contact you sooner. After the hospital spokesman called you and your father, that hospital employee got off work and inadvertently took with him the piece of paper that had your name and your father's name and addresses on it. We had trouble locating him, but we finally ran him down and obtained your names and addresses. Again, I apologize." Barnes gestured with his hand to another room. "Please be seated." Everyone moved a few steps to a side conference room and sat down around a long rectangular table. "About your brother, I assume you don't know anything concerning what happened."

"No, I don't. When I got home from work about 3:30 this afternoon--I work here at the hospital--a man from the hospital called and told me that my brother was in the emergency room and that he had been shot. I came directly here. That's all I know."

Looking intently at Juanita, Barnes began, "Let me start at the beginning, if I can," his voice controlled and resolute. "About 1:00 p.m. today we received a telephone call concerning some shots being fired at 1400 Maple Street ...."

She gasped, "That's my address. What..."

"Yes, that is what we later found out." Barnes slowly nodded his head.

Suddenly, she began to softly cry. He paused momentarily, then continued. "The police found your brother sitting in his car parked in the parking lot of the apartments. He had been shot numerous times. That was between 12:30 and 1:00 o'clock this afternoon. No one claims to have seen it, nor was anyone at home at the complex when the police arrived."

The detective then briefly narrated the continuing investigation. "It wasn't until a couple of hours ago we learned that you lived at that complex. Did you know your brother was coming over?"

Finally Juanita was able to control herself.

"Yes and no," she said. "I usually get off work at noon. I'm a nurse's assistant here in the children's ward. But this morning my supervisor asked if I wanted to work some overtime, and I said yes, so I worked until three o'clock. But a few days ago I asked Tony if today he would take me to the grocery store and some other places to shop. See, I don't have a car. He was going to meet me at my apartment today at noon when I got off work. I forgot that Tony was coming over, and then I didn't call him to tell him that I was working overtime and wouldn't be getting off at noon. I guess that when he got to my apartment and I wasn't there, he decided to wait for me. I worked until three, then got on a bus and went home. I had only been in the house for a few minutes when I got the phone call from the hospital."

"Evidently, we had just left your apartment when you arrived. I think we left about three. We just missed each other. From the way it looks at this point, ma'am, someone just walked up to your brother and shot him at point-blank range. There is nothing to indicate that he was involved in a fight or anything." He paused to let the information sink in before he continued.

"Could you give me some background information on your brother? If he went to school? Where he worked? That sort of thing. You know, what he does or what kind of a person he is."

Juanita was crying softly, but she composed herself the best she could. She felt weak, but answered.

"Tony is my big brother. He is twenty-two. I am twenty. He is the oldest in our family. I have a younger brother and two younger sisters. Tony and the others live with my father in Oak Cliff." She was puzzled. "Is this the kind of information you need?"

"Yes, that's fine. Go ahead."

"After Tony graduated from high school he started working at the Farmer's Market. He was a meat cutter at the meat market there. About two years ago he started working a second job at night. He was cleaning and sweeping offices in the building where Bell Telephone is located on

Young Street." Big tears were beginning to roll down Juanita's cheeks.

"Wait, Miss Medina. Want some coffee or something?" the officer said softly.

"Yes, please. Some coffee. Thank you."

The detective cast a look toward one of the uniformed officers who quickly stood and left the room.

"Go on. I'm sorry," said Barnes.

"Well, anyway, let me back up a minute. Before he started cleaning the buildings, he tried to join the Army. He took the tests, or whatever. But when he went to take his medical examination they discovered something was wrong with his heart; he had a hole in one of the valves of his heart. He had had it since birth. As a result, they wouldn't take him. After that, he got the second job cleaning. About a year and a half ago Tony started taking some college courses at El Centro Junior College. And he was still working at two jobs. He was going to school in the afternoons. He worked and studied, worked and studied, and worked and studied."

"Good gosh, how did he manage all of it?"

"Tony has a goal, sir. He wants to better himself. He isn't married and any money that he makes is spent helping my dad and my brother and sisters. The meat market owners allowed him to shift his working hours to accommodate his school hours. I don't know how is able to keep it up. He begins working at the meat market at six in the morning and works until his afternoon classes began around one or two o'clock; then he starts cleaning about six or seven that evening. He arrives home somewhere around ten at night."

Barnes was impressed. "And he's done this for a year and a half? That's a credit to him." Barnes was also impressed with Juanita. She was smart and articulate.

"He would have done it for two years next month. That's a long time. Perseverance is his strong suit. I admire my brother. I'm proud of him. His life has not been an easy one. See, my mom died several years ago in a car accident. While my dad worked, Tony was the one who looked after us kids. I was able to help a little, but my younger brother and sisters were still babies. And I've never heard him grumble or complain about doing any of it. I guess he saw how hard my dad had to work to support us. He's majoring in history and even made the Dean's List. Get this, he wanted to be a college professor. And he would have made it." She started crying again. She was beginning to ramble.

"Don't give up on him too quickly. He can still become one."

"Mr. Barnes, I understand that Tony's spinal column is severed. I also know that the chances of him ever being able to walk again are virtually zero. I am a nurse, you know."

"Well, it may not be as bad as you think. Let's wait and see." Barnes changed his tone. "Juanita, does Tony have any enemies?"

"None. Tony is not the kind of guy that makes enemies. He's too easy going. He's outgoing. He smiles a lot, laughs a lot. He goes out of his way to be helpful and friendly. Oh, and I forgot to tell you, every Sunday he goes to St. Emmanuel's Catholic Church on Jefferson Street. He works with the youth minister. He doesn't put on any airs. What you see is what you get. No, sir, Tony has no enemies."

"Does he ever do any drugs?" Barnes was almost too embarrassed to ask.

"Hell no." Juanita nearly shouted the words. "Don't you see? He wants to better his life, and he was working hard to get it--working night and day. Mr. Barnes, if you go to my father's house, you can see it is not in the best of neighborhoods. The house is not the best in the world. But we have love in it. But anyway, now much of the neighborhood is overrun by druggies." She was rambling but Barnes knew enough to let her go. She continued, "Tony, and anyone else who's got half a head, can see what drugs are doing. He used to sit all of us down and lecture us over and over about drugs. I have never even seen him smoke marijuana. Now, how many people his age have never done that?"

She had a point, thought the detective. "I didn't mean anything by the question, Ma'am. I just have to cover the bases." He had scribbled some notes as she had been talking. Referring to them for a moment, he finally said, "We are just starting the investigation. Tomorrow I will go back to your apartment complex and around the area and ask again if anyone saw anything. Sometimes that produces results. When there is a crowd with a lot of police around, sometimes people are reluctant to come forward with information. But if we talk to them individually, many times they will open up to us. Also tomorrow, maybe Tony will be able to talk to us."

"So you're saying there aren't any leads as to who did it or why?"

"That's right. But we'll know soon." He paused a long time as he was skimming his notes. "Juanita," he concluded, "that's all I need for the moment. Do you have any other questions for me?" Having none, the detective was finished for the night. The other officers walked Juanita back to the waiting room, Detective Barnes sat back and reflected. Not a typical family. Certainly Tony seemed to be above average, an impressive young man. Good family.

Chapter Seven

While Tony was in the hospital, Juanita checked on him during her working shift. After her workday was complete, she went home, ate a quick meal, and returned to the hospital for a few hours. After a few days of this routine, hope for her brother's complete recovery began to fade. The doctor's daily report had not changed from the first conversation. Though Tony had regained consciousness, he was, at least for now, paralyzed from his chest to his toes.

One week after the shooting, Detectives Barnes and Gallagher obtained the doctor's permission and spoke at length with Tony Medina. After he had told them everything that he knew about the shooting, the police were left with only one lead. But it was significant! They now knew the particular apartment from which the shooter exited before the shots were fired. The next morning they drove back to the crime scene.

"Yeah, but don't get too excited" said Gallagher, "Remember we have already talked to the whore that stays there. She saw nothing, as usual. In fact, remember she said she was not even present at the time."

"But she doesn't know that we now have a witness who can place the shooter coming out of her apartment. Her apartment!" Barnes emphasized, "We didn't know that when we talked to her the first time. By the way, did you check to see if she had any warrants out for her arrest?"

"No outstanding warrants. Just convictions. Nine convictions for prostitution; four convictions for public lewdness. Gallagher smiled and added: "Just an old fashioned gal. My type."

They parked their unmarked Ford police car in the complex's lot and Gallagher looked around, "Not much shaking here at eight o'clock in the morning.

"Yeah, that's right. But if you want to catch these whores, you have to catch them in the mornings while they're still asleep. If she was working last night she probably went to sleep about four or five o'clock this morning."

Barnes knocked long and hard on the apartment door. No answer. He knocked again. And again. And again. After some minutes they heard some movement coming from inside. "Police, open up," he shouted.

The door, painted purple, cracked open a few inches. Gallagher saw a sleepy-eyed black female on the inside. He barely recognized her from their conversation a few days earlier.

"Selma, hello. I'm Detective Gallagher. Remember me? We talked the other day about the shooting that happened in the parking lot last week. Can we come inside?"

Selma Hale opened the door and stepped back without saying a word. Both policemen walked into the living room. "You remember Detective Barnes. We want to talk to you some more about the shooting."

"Okay. But you woke me up. Let me have a few minutes to get dressed." She walked down the hallway with the police following. "You guys want to watch me get dressed?"

"Nope. We just want to make sure you're alone."

"Shit."

They quickly scanned the one-bedroom apartment. Seeing no one, they retreated back to the front door area.

"Sit down and make yourself at home," she called from the bedroom.

Barnes obliged and sat down in one of the two chairs at the dining room table. Gallagher wavered and hesitated momentarily before taking a seat on the stained, smokey-smelling sofa. He felt uncomfortable, yet eyed Barnes' apparent ease.

They looked around. Cheap furniture, dirty walls, even dirtier carpet. A faded 8x10 black-

and-white photograph of President John F. Kennedy hung on the wall over the sofa. A 2' x 3' poster of soul singer James Brown was tacked on the wall above the dining table. A high school graduation picture of Selma Hale was framed and placed on the coffee table in front of Gallagher. Lying on the floor, underneath the table was a worn copy of Fashion magazine. In the corner was a brand-new, expensive, high-tech music and stereo component system. Barnes began to flip through an edition of the National Enquirer that he found on the crumbly dining table. As Gallagher sat waiting, he detected the smell of stale marijuana smoke.

"Ain't life great?" muttered Barnes.

After a few minutes, Selma reappeared in a red chenille robe. Without even being dolled up, she looked like a hooker as she walked across the room.

"Anyone want coffee?" She asked as she walked into the kitchen. While she was busy pouring the water into the grungy Mr. Coffee, Gallagher observed the resident. "Typical lady of the night", he thought. "Tall, thin, flat ass". The robe she was wearing was tied in such a way so that she could proudly expose her body. "Her kind are always on parade," he mused.

Gallagher did not wait for her to re-enter the living room. "Selma," he began matter-of-factly, "we found a witness that says the shooter came out of your apartment seconds before he fired the shots. We know it was not you, dear. It was a man. This witness saw you come out and leave fifteen or twenty minutes earlier. We know that it was you, because the witness has picked out your photograph. You want to talk here, or do you want to come downtown to talk with us?"

"I can talk here, Mr. Police, because I don't have anything to hide."

"That's fine. Then why did you lie to us the other day?"

"Look, you probably know that I 'date'; I can't remember every one of them."

"Girls like you", Gallagher interrupted, "don't take their clientele to their own place. We know you work off of 'The Boulevard.' You normally use one of those shitty hotels over there."

"I usually do. Yeah, that's right. That's right," her voice containing a degree of sarcasm. "But I was walking back to my place from the store when he drove by and picked me up. He said he was in a hurry. And so was I at the time."

"That shit is a lie," he said forcefully. "Then why did you go off and leave him in your apartment?"

"He paid me. That's why." Her voice rising a few degrees, "After the trick, he gave me a fifty to go get him some beer at the store. He said I could keep the rest. I was gone about fifteen minutes. On the way back, the bastard nearly ran over me with his car, he was leaving in such a hurry. I thought that he had ripped off my stuff here, so I ran the rest of the way home. I didn't know the dude was shot until I heard the siren from the ambulance and came out to see."

"You didn't see the man sitting in the car bleeding?" asked Gallagher pointedly.

"Not when I was going back into the apartment. Like I said, I was in a hurry to see if the dude had stolen any of my shit. So, hell no, I didn't stop and look at the cars in the parking lot before I went inside."

"What kind of car did he drive? What was his name?"

"The dude say his name was Ray. He drove a white Cadillac, brand-new looking."

Suddenly the sound of glass breaking outside the apartment startled everyone. Barnes jumped up and hurriedly opened the door. Gallagher was right behind him with his pistol drawn. As the apartment door flew open and the three occupants ran outside, they saw two young boys about ten years old throwing rocks at the detective's shiny police car. Both kids were laughing. Upon seeing the two men coming out the door, they scampered behind the building and disappeared. By the time Barnes had run to a stairwell at the end of the building, the rock throwers were long gone.

"Damn little shitheads!" he breathed.

"Did you see which way they went?" asked Gallagher. "I couldn't see."

"Around this way is all I could tell."

"I'll head this way looking for them."

"Don't waste your time," puffed Barnes. "Hell, by now they're across town." The senior detective was angry. Back at the car, both men surveyed the damage. Every window was broken. Numerous dents along one side were obvious to the eye.

"Now, why would they do that?"

"Because they're young punks, that's why. Little thugs on their way to becoming bigger thugs. They see a shiny new car and figured they have to mess with it. Let me radio the office and relay what happened."

Gallagher and Selma reentered the apartment while Barnes remained outside by the car radio. A few minutes later he came inside. "Let's go," he said hurriedly. "The captain wants us back downtown. Pronto."

"What? We're on a case. We can't just jump up and leave now." Amazed, Gallagher stared at his superior.

"Yes, we can, and we will. We'll have to continue this at a later time. A Deputy Chief was on the horn trying to reach us when I called in. There's been some kind of shooting downtown. One officer has been killed, maybe two. Let's roll."

Turning to Selma Hale, "We're coming back tomorrow to talk. You be here. You better be here. You're not going to be arrested. I just want to tie up some loose ends. I believe you. But if you are not here, you are going to be in deep water. Understand what I mean?"

She nodded. "I'll be here all morning. I ain't hiding nothing."

With that they left. In the car on the way to their office, Gallagher asked, "What happened downtown? What's going on?"

"They didn't tell me much. Some crazy man grabbed an officer's revolver and shot him. The Deputy Chief said a crowd of people standing nearby encouraged the crazy man to shoot."

Five minutes after the officers left, someone knocked on Selma's door. Just as she reached for the doorknob to open it, Ulysses Carillo kicked it open with his foot.

"Dumb bitch," he bellowed as he crossed the threshold and stood in the living room. "What did you tell them?"

She let out a small shriek. She was too frightened to scream. "I lied to them. I lied. I did. I really did." Selma Hale, leaning against the wall, had both hands covering as much of her face as she could. She was horrified.

"What did they ask? I know they were cops. You better convince me, or you're a dead whore." Selma Hale was petrified. He pulled out a pistol and placed it between her eyes.

Stammering and crying at the same time, she related the conversation as best she could. The gun never left her head. When she finished, Carillo put the gun into the waist of his pants, and then he backhanded her. Her body slammed against the wall and then slid to the floor. Dazed to the point of being nearly unconscious, she remained on the floor. The next thing she knew, Carillo was ripping off her robe, literally tearing the fabric, and biting her breasts. Completely nude, she tried to escape. But he was too strong and she was too weak. He raped her on the filthy, linoleum floor. When he was finished with her he bragged: "Sometimes I pay you, sometimes I don't." She was still in a fetal position still lying on the floor as he stood and pulled up his pants.

"I was just driving in," he began, "and saw the cops getting out of their car. I could tell who they were. Watched them as they came straight here. I turned around and drove down the street to where I saw some kids playing. I paid them twenty dollars to come up here and throw those damn rocks. Figured after that they'd leave. And I was right."

"They didn't leave because of you," she groaned while still on the floor. "They went back to their office because of something else. Not because of you."

"Shut up. You better not have told them anything."

"I didn't tell them anything. But they said they were coming back tomorrow morning."

"If you tell them who I am, you are chopped-up fish food. Understand?"

Chapter Eight

Juanita Medina heard that Dr. Royce Strickland was the best neurosurgeon on the Parkland Hospital staff. Luckily, he was on call when Tony had been brought into the surgery room. At least her brother had the best specialist during the operation. Twelve days after the surgery, the doctor had called and arranged a time that he would meet with her family to discuss Tony's situation. She thought it best if only she and her father were present. The days were dragging on and still no clear answer as to Tony's condition.

She was nervous as she and her father waited in the doctor's reception room. She looked at her Dad. He seemed calm. Soon the doctor walked in and ushered them into his office. "Please sit here," said the doctor gesturing toward a leather sofa. The doctor avoided the high-backed leather chair behind his mahogany desk and sat in a much-used, old-timey rocking chair alongside the Medinas.

The neurosurgeon got straight to the point. "The situation involving Tony's paralysis has not changed," he began. His tone solemn. "Initially, we knew that there was some damage to the spinal cord. But because of the swelling, we did not know to what degree. That was last week.

Now most of the swelling has subsided and we are better able to see the extent of the injury." The doctor drew a deep breath and slowly continued. "The spinal cord is completely severed. The damage and the paralysis is permanent. In our medical opinion he will remain paralyzed. That is terribly bad news, I know, and I am sorry."

Juanita looked at her Dad. The sadness on his face would be ingrained in her mind forever. But this expression faded just as quickly as it had appeared.

"But thank God that he's alive," responded the father. "He is still alive. He will live, won't he, Doctor?"

"Yes, he will."

"Thank God. Thank God," said Mr. Medina as he bowed his head.

The doctor continued. "He will have to stay in the hospital at least three or four more weeks. After that, if things progress okay, he can go home but he will have to continue physical therapy. I will need to tell Tony about this therapy as soon as I can."

Looking again to Juanita, "I feel he will eventually be able to move about in a wheelchair if his therapy progresses sufficiently. The partial numbness that exists in both of his arms will go away, we feel, in a few weeks. He will not be able to function physically from the chest downward. The paralysis will not go away."

Chapter Nine

Ramon Garza's phone woke him suddenly from his nap. Looking at his watch, he saw that he had been asleep for three hours. Ulysses Carillo was calling.

"Hello...... Hell, I've been asleep," said Garza. "What's up?"

After a few moments, he continued. "Yeah, okay. Yeah. I'll be over in a few minutes."

Forty minutes later, Garza entered Carillo's house.

"Selma, that bitch, may blow our entire operation," announced Carillo. "The damn police were talking to her today. Tonight I want you to take her to your place. When you are there with her, call me. I want to talk to her."

"How did the fucking police link her with us?"

"I'll tell you the details later. Right now, I'm going to take a long snooze. See you tonight."

The telephone rang just as the ten o'clock news was coming on television. Carillo immediately answered it.

"Is she there with you right now?" Carillo asked. Pause. "I'm on my way over there."

Ramon Garza lived downstairs in an end apartment. For precautionary reasons, Ulysses Carillo also paid the rent for the apartment adjacent to Garza's and also for the one directly above. Both were intentionally kept vacant. Carillo did not want nosy neighbors too close.

A half hour after the phone call, Carillo entered the apartment without knocking. Garza and Selma were just finishing some fried chicken dinners.

"Want some?" asked Garza.

"No." Carillo closed the front door and walked inside. "We've got some serious shit that we have to talk about." Before anyone else could say a word, Carillo abruptly produced a small caliber chrome-plated pistol and pointed it toward Selma. The end of the barrel was within a foot of her head. He fired once. She fell to the floor without ever having uttered a word.

Immediately, Carillo straddled her limp body, placed the end of the barrel into her left ear and pulled the trigger. Her head bounced sideways on the floor as some drops sprayed into the air. When Carillo placed the pistol on the dining table, Garza noticed that a green-colored hand towel had been wrapped around it to help silence the noise from the gun. It worked since the gunfire had not even been heard outside the apartment. Neither Garza nor Carillo were talking.

Carillo entered the bedroom and returned shortly with a white bed sheet. He quickly and expertly rolled the body into it, making sure that the entire body was covered and tucked away. Garza was still seated at the dining table. He had not even had time to move and was too numbed to speak. The shots had taken him by surprise. While Carillo finished putting the wrapping on the body, Garza was busy wondering: "If he was planning on doing this, why didn't he tell me? And why, for Christ's sake, did he have to do it here?"

Finally Carillo looked up at his lieutenant. "You have a job to do tonight," he said. "Find Hector. Both of you take this dead bitch to Houston and dump her in some part of the 'hood'. And listen, before you dump her, cut off her hands. That eliminates the fingerprints."

"And do what with them?"

"I don't give a shit. Just get rid of them. I don't care how you do it. Just make sure that afterwards they can't be found. I took everything from her pockets, so there's no identification on her. You should be able to get down there and back by nine or ten in the morning. I'm going over to her apartment and wipe it down. My fingerprints may be plastered all over that place.

Let's get this chunk loaded up so you can get on the move. Any questions?"

Ramon Garza quickly shook his head.

Chapter Ten

Juanita’s work at the hospital was becoming nonproductive. It was the stress. She had to force herself to smile. She had to force herself to be friendly with her patients. During work hours she was at the hospital. After work she stayed at the hospital. She caught herself becoming unusually short-tempered. She realized all of this. She needed someone to talk to, but the person that could supply this need was the person who had it equally as tough: her father.

Through it all, he had remained the constant. And yet, this did not surprise her. For some reason she had known that he would react this way. She had the professional training, but he had something else. He had also always been the family's sails. Pushing and pulling ahead. Through the adversity, through the tough times, through the set-backs, her father never ran. He never hid his face. He never buckled or broke. In all things he was constant. Juanita saw it clearly during the crisis of her mother's death and during her raucous teenage years. And now, especially now. The soft-spoken patriarch welded his family into a stronger unit. Throughout this ordeal, his voice was sturdy. His spirit was indomitable. Every day when she got off work and made the three minute walk to the other wing of the huge hospital complex to be with her stricken brother, the first glimpse of her father gave her renewed strength.

Four eternally long weeks after Juanita Medina and her father had met with the neurosurgeon, Tony was released from the hospital. The weeks following Tony's arrival home were not easy. His gunshot wounds were healing slowly. The slightest movement caused pain to shoot through his body. Juanita bought a used television set for Tony's room. She then brought over her own music system. The doctors at the hospital told her, and she already knew, that it might be weeks or even months before Tony would be ready for a wheelchair. For now, he was confined to his bed.

She was surprised at the way Tony had accepted the situation. But then, not so surprised. He was always the positive one, the cheerful one. Yet she knew he really had to ache inside, regardless of the way he appeared on the outside.

By the end of the fifth week at home, Tony settled into a routine.

"Your bullet wounds have almost healed," Juanita told him one night.

"What about my ear?"

"Well, we're going to get plastic surgery done. I don't know exactly when, but I'm looking into it. As you can probably see, it's not too pretty now, but just be glad that you can even hear out of it." She could not bring herself to tell him how unsightly it actually appeared.

"Do you think they'll ever catch the guy that did this?"

"I don't know, Tony. The police keep telling us they will; for us not to lose hope. But I know they don't have much to go on. I really dislike having to say that, but ... but ..." Her voice trailed off.

"In my mind, I go over how it happened," he lamented. "First in regular speed and then in slow motion. I do this over and over and over. I'll never forget that face." His tone suddenly changed, picking up speed and emphasis. "The evil and anger that was in that man's eyes. He looked right at me. He knew I wasn't doing anything. I didn't even move." For the first time his sister detected some hostility, and she could not blame him.

"Say," Tony continued, his voice having resumed a conversational tone, "turn off the television for a minute. Let's talk. Did you ever see the composite drawing that the police made? It looks just like the guy. I mean, it really does."

"I know, I know. I saw it, but I didn't recognize the person. I thought I might recognize him, if he had been in the area before, but I didn't."

"It looks as if that prostitute completely vanished into thin air," Tony exclaimed. She was our only break. I think she knows the man's name, but just isn't talking. Didn't you say that you didn't even recognize her?"

"Yea, that's right. Never seen her even though we lived in the same complex. When the police showed her photograph to me, I still didn't recognize her. But you have to know that her disappearance is somehow connected to this. I mean, after you identify her photo and the detectives talk to her, she suddenly disappears."

Frowning, she shook her head. "Unless that girl comes forward ...... I'm sorry, Tony." Juanita, suddenly depressed, had to leave the room.

The next day Tony awoke to a tingly sensation in his right arm and hand. He was euphoric. Since the shooting he had had no sensation in either arm. Though he still could not move them, the tingling remained in his arm and hand all day.

Each day thereafter, more and more feeling returned to his arm and hand. Every new day brought more and more movement. His therapy was progressing. Eventually the use of his right arm and hand was restored. Suddenly one day, the left arm and hand started tingling. Seven weeks to the day after he was brought home from Parkland Hospital, Tony dialed the numbers on his telephone.

"Could I speak with Juanita Medina, please?" Pause ... "Hey, it's me. I dialed the number." He was exuberant "I did it all by myself. I can use both of my arms and hands." Tony did not have to express the joy, it could be felt through the line. It was a huge accomplishment. His rehabilitation had seen its first positive result. On the first day that Tony left the hospital, his father brought home a used wheelchair–bought from a lady who lived down the street. It was dirty and needed cleaning, but Juan Medina felt he could make it usable again. Besides, it was all he could afford. New or used, it did not matter to Tony. When both arms were lifeless, he did not feel like sitting in it. It was only after he regained the use of one arm that he asked to sit in the wheelchair.

With his body weakened, his ability to get around by himself in the wheelchair was hampered. At first, someone had to help him get in, push it around, and help him get out. It was slow going. But the weeks passed, and his body-- especially both arms strengthened. Four months after the injury he was able to accomplish maneuvers all by himself. He had regained complete use of both arms and hands. At first he was apprehensive about being seen in public. At least Juanita thought so. With time, she noticed he was beginning to overcome this.

Now Tony was able to get into and out of the wheelchair without help. He sat on the front porch enjoying the view. The early mornings were special, the awakening of the day. Watching the people going about their daily lives was somehow satisfying to him. By actually being able to watch his neighbors begin their daily tasks made him feel like a part of society. Though confined to his wheelchair, more or less on the sidelines, he was still in the game.

"Now listen Hosea, my son," said the elder Medina, "even though you don't have your driver's license, I'm going to let you drive anyway." Hosea suppressed a smile but he still picked up the sternness in his father's voice. "I have no other choice at the moment. You've driven before, but it's always been just up and down the street. You know how to drive safely and you've got to do it now. I'm giving you some responsibility so don't waste it." The authority in the voice corresponded with the look on his father's face. The recipient of the lecture, the sixteen year old youngest son, was standing straight and solemn. "Juanita can't come over right now, and I've got to catch the bus to go to work." Touching the boy's arms, the older Medina repeated an earlier question: "Do you have the grocery list that I made?"

"Yes sir. Yes sir. And I promise to drive safely."

"Go straight to the supermarket and straight back. Straight there and straight back. And nowhere else." Slowing down his speech, he continued, "I understand that Tony is going with you. Is that right?"

"Yes sir. He said he wanted to look at some new video movies."

"Okay, then, I'll help Tony get into the car," said the father. He was trying to determine how long it should take the boys to drive the three or four miles to the grocery store and back.

Hosea pushed Tony through the automatic door of Kroger supermarket. Tony said, "I'm going over to the movies. When you are finished and ready to go, come get me. Okay?"

"Alright. It'll only be about five minutes," Hosea predicted. They split up.

At first Tony was alone as he viewed seemingly hundreds of movies. He scanned the many movies located in front of him row by row, oblivious to people walking around him. Every now and then, he would pick up one and read the back cover. "Too many good ones to choose from," he thought. Finally he narrowed it down to three. Holding them in his hand, he studied them some more. He could not decide. At that moment, he felt the presence of other people. They, too, were shopping the selections. Tony started to move out of their way as they began talking to one another. Making a final selection, he turned his chair to leave. As he raised his head in their direction, his eye focused on the one standing closest to him. Suddenly his whole world completely stopped! His eyes locked on the man, and he could not move them away. His eyes grew larger than saucers! He could not believe who he saw! "It's him! It's him!" raced through his mind. The man that shot him was standing within three feet of him! Tony's eyes stayed glued on him. His heart was beating fast. He would never forget that damnable face. Tony could not move. He tried, but it was as if he was frozen. Petrified, he tried to speak, but he could not do that either. He opened his mouth, but his voice was gone. He again tried to move, but his body had suddenly become completely immobile. His gaze was still fixed on the person that was within an arm's reach of him. "I know that's him.....The face, the eyes, the expression. It's all the same," he whispered to himself. His body began to feel cold. His pounding heart was running totally wild. His rapid breathing shook his entire body. Mentally and physically, tremors consumed him. Ulysses Carillo and Ramon Garza were looking at the science fiction videos. They were unaware of the stares coming from Tony Medina. After making a selection, they turned to leave. Carillo's eyes met Tony's. At that exact moment, the man in the wheelchair yelled, "You're the one! It's you! It's you! You shot me, you bastard! It's you! You shot me! You shot me!"

Garza made a vain attempt to quiet him. "What are you talking about? What do you mean? S-h-h! S-h-h! Be quiet!!"

But Tony continued. His voice blasting, "He shot me! He shot me!" Still looking directly at Carillo, he yelled "You shot me! You shot me!" He began to yell louder and louder. "Help! Help! Someone call the police! The Police! Call the police! He shot me!"

People were running to the hysterical voice. Panic struck Carillo and Garza at the same time. They turned to run down an aisle in the store. As they approached the front door they could hear the voice in the background: "Stop them! Police! Help me! He shot me! Stop them! Stop them!"

Running towards the door as fast as he could, Garza stumbled and turned over a shopping cart full of groceries. Carillo was fighting his way past the people that were coming toward the sound of Tony's loud screams. Carillo was pushing the onlookers out of the way and running over others. He believed Garza had made it out of the store ahead of him. "He better not have left me. He better be waiting on me," Carillo thought. "Shit!" Carillo, uncharacteristically, was becoming terrified.

He cleared the store's front door and was running as fast as he could. Ten feet into freedom, an unknown force threw his hulking frame onto the hard asphalt pavement. Someone had tackled him from behind. Two giant arms gripped him around the waist as he was being wrestled to the ground. He tried to break the lock that was holding him but his arms were tightly pinned against his body. It was impossible to use his fists. Kicking with his boots was the only "weapon" he had. But the person holding him was too close to kick. Moving back and forth and jerking his body in an attempt to free himself was also futile. Someone, and a big someone at that, had him. And that person was not coming close to letting him go. Carillo twisted and stretched and tried to reach his pistol. He finally did, but it was not there. It fell out when he hit the ground. Garza was nowhere around. No one could hear anything above the shrieks and screams of the scared patrons in the grocery store. Finally, from exhaustion more than anything else, Carillo stopped squirming and moving.

This giant of a man who had the prisoner slowly said, "Easy now, easy. Easy. Easy does it! Now, see that man over there?"

Carillo's eyes focused on a Kroger-employed security guard wearing a uniform. The officer had his blue steel revolver drawn and pointing in their direction.

"He has a gun on you and will shoot if you try to move."

Carillo turned his head around and looked over his bruised shoulder at the person who had prevented his escape. He too was a private security guard employed by Kroger. He placed the prisoner's hands behind his back and handcuffed them.

"You can't cuff me," said Carillo. He was defiant. "I haven't done anything! Hey, you can't arrest me, you shit-head! Let me go! Let me go!"

"We are going to let the police sort this thing out. In the meantime you are under arrest for unlawfully carrying that pistol."

The prisoner was taken to the store's security offices located in the back of the supermarket. In a matter of minutes, the police arrived. Tony Medina was kept in the front of the store in the manager's office. He was explaining to the assistant manager what had happened when the police arrived. After getting the story from Tony, one of the patrol officers radioed the central station and asked to be patched to Frank Barnes, Homicide Unit. Another patrol officer was talking to Carillo. "What were you doing with the pistol?"

"That ain't my pistol you mother-fucker. You better let me go or I'll sue your tin-star ass. I'm going to sue this mother-fucking store, too. And I'm going to sue that shit in the wheelchair. He started all of this shit."

The officer continued, "Why were you carrying this pistol?"

"I ain't got nothing to say to you mother-fuckers."

Shortly, the police officers at the store received word that Detective Barnes wanted to see all of the people involved at the police station.

Tony and Hosea Medina were driven downtown by some of the patrol officers, while Carillo was transported in another police vehicle.

Barnes instructed the patrol officers to bring Tony and Carillo to his office. And, of course, to keep them separated and out of each other's sight. The detective was waiting in his office when Tony came in. Tony seemed to be moving around better than the last time Barnes had seen him.

Immediately upon seeing the familiar detective, Tony cried out. "We got him! We got him!" It was the first time Barnes recalled he had ever seen Tony's smile. The detective did not have to tell Tony where to begin; he only had to tell him to slow down. Numerous times.

Minutes later Barnes stepped into the police interrogation room. Carillo had been there the whole time, still handcuffed with two officers keeping him company. As Barnes took a seat in a chair opposite Carillo, he just looked him over for a short period of time. Gently rapping his fingers on the black wooden table, the homicide policeman did not say a word.

Eventually he slowly spoke. "You're in a big mess."

Carillo did not even look up. With his head down, he stared at the floor, his long black hair falling into his eyes and covering most of his face.

The detective continued, his voice carrying that soft tone. "My name is Frank Barnes. Tell me about yourself."

The subject was still silent, still unmoved. The only sound at the moment was the humming sound being generated from the fluorescent lights overhead.

The detective gazed at the prisoner and tapped his fingers on the old table until Carillo spoke.

"What does this young man say that I did?" came the question, but the face and head was still pointing downward. The detective raised an eyebrow.

Barnes was somewhat surprised with the tone of the voice. It was very pleasant and very clear. It was a voice that did not fit the type of person that Barnes had before him. He had been expecting an incoherent, hardly understandable string of words that would be masked together. But not so. He also detected an accent.

"He says that you shot him."

"Anyone that would shoot a crippled man has to be sick."

"He says you caused him to be crippled."

"I've never shot anyone. Nor, sir, have I ever injured anyone." The suspect, still looking downward, had not moved or changed positions.

Barnes gambled: "We have some witnesses that saw you shoot him."

"That's either bullshit from you or they are lying." The responses were slow and unemotional, but very articulate.

Barnes was beginning to believe that it was a futile attempt to continue, but he decided to press the prisoner just a little longer.

"What if we found your fingerprints at the crime scene?" he asked. "The witnesses' testimony and your fingerprints make a convincing case against you."

Suddenly Carillo's head shot upright. Before he spoke he lightly shook his hair away from his face. Barnes viewed into a pair of violent, hate-filled, brown eyes.

"Hey, if you mean you got my prints from that whore's apartment, big deal. I know I screwed her."

The homicide man remained motionless. Gazing blankly and silently at the wall behind the suspect, Barnes was thinking where to go or what to do next.

It had worked! He slowly nodded to himself. It had worked. Barnes thought to himself, "I now know we have the right man."

Only the person who had actually been to the particular apartment and had sex with the prostitute could have known Barnes had been referring to an apartment and a prostitute. Only that person could have said that. The detective continued. Cautiously. Carillo did not know that he had slipped and made a mistake.

"Yes, and we know it, too," said Barnes. "She told us everything. She mentioned names and places."

Carillo suddenly began thinking how glad he was that he had killed Selma Hale. Even if she had told the police all she knew, he knew that she wouldn't be able to say it again.

"Bull shit. No one believes whores," he said. "I'm through talking. I have not done anything. Get me a lawyer to get me out of here."

Lt. Barnes knew then the conversation was finished.

He knew that the guy was not going to admit to doing anything. He had played a hunch when he had mentioned the bogus fingerprint and the witness, and it had paid off. At least the police knew that Tony had been correct in his identification.

"What do you want us to do with him?" asked one of the other officers.

"Take him to the county jail and book him in. You file the charge against him for unlawfully carrying a weapon, and I am going to file on him for attempted murder. Tell the book-in sergeant at the processing desk that I'll bring the paperwork on the attempted murder to him later tonight. Better yet, I'll call over there right now, and tell him what I'm going to do. I'm going to ask for a high bond on this guy, and they may want to know what is happening."

It was a ten-minute ride to the Lew Sterrett County Jail. As the transportation officer led him through the county jail entrance doors, the musty smell of human body odor hit his nostrils. "I ain't staying here too long, you fuckers. This is not for me. I'm better than this."

"You don't have much choice for now, hot dog," noted the officer. "So get moving."

At the book-in desk, the desk sergeant was in the process of fingerprinting Carillo when he noticed the marking.

Between the thumb and forefinger on the web of the hand there existed a series of small tatoos. On each knuckle were some more markings. The tatoos did not spell out any words. They did not have to. Though he did not know exactly what they meant, the deputy knew their significance. The prisoner was a "Marielito."

In the spring of 1980, when thousands of Cubans protested and made it known to Fidel Castro that they were dissatisfied with their way of life in Cuba, he announced they could leave. He instructed them to gather at the Port of Mariel for emigration. What he did not expect were the more than one hundred thousand people that converged on the port city. Placing them on whatever floating vessels were available, from huge tankers to private boats, the "Marielitos" were permitted to sail to the United States. President Jimmy Carter and his administration were caught by surprise. Initially, President Carter indicated that the United States would accept the "Marielitos" with open arms, thinking it virtuous to live up to the writing inscribed on the famous statue located in the New York harbor: "Give us your huddled masses....." Such a decision rocked most of the citizens in America and especially the Department of Immigration and Naturalization. But the executive decision had been made, so the INS followed directives. During the summer of 1980, approximately 125,000 Cuban refugees entered the United States. President Carter eventually saw that this "freedom flotilla" was political suicide, so in September of 1980, he abandoned the policy. The growing resentment in the United States was heightened when it became known what types of Cubans were being released in America.

Castro was embarrassed, politically, by the large number of dissidents. Along with these dissidents, he purged his prisons of the most violent criminals, and placed them on the boats leaving Mariel.

For many years, Castro had been uniquely identifying criminals when they had been placed in Cuban prisons. When a convict entered the prison, the prison authorities placed a tattoo, and sometimes more than one, on the web of the hand and the knuckles of the fingers. By this means the authorities could readily identify each person, his crimes, and especially, his propensity for violence.

Barely three years had passed since Carillo had been sent to a Cuban prison camp for murdering one man and cutting off the right hand of another. When the United States refused any more refugees, Castro, still embarrassed, had arranged a special deal with Mexico. Castro and the Cuban government agreed to pay the Mexican government ten million dollars in exchange for Mexico's agreeing to permanently house a certain number of prisoners. After the Mexican government had safely banked the money, the authorities allowed the boats of Cuban convicts to land. Rather than transporting the prisoners to a Mexican prison, these same authorities simply turned the prisoners loose. Ulysses Carillo, then 20 years of age, found himself free in Mexico wandering and living off the streets.

The deputy made a mental note of the tattooing so he could pass it along to his supervisors and to the Magistrate who would be setting the prisoner's bail. Only for the crime of capital murder, a crime that carried the possibility of the death penalty, could a judge refuse to set a bond.

After being apprised of the special tatoos, the Magistrate decided against the normal bail amount for attempted murder, $100,000.00, and set it at $500,000.00

"That bondsman was a real jerk," Garza remarked as they drove away from the jail. Less than an hour had passed since the amount had been set. Drug money paid the bondsman's fee, and Carillo walked out of jail.

Minutes later they pulled into Carillo's driveway. Once inside Garza popped open a beer. "Well, chief, what's the game plan?"

"First, gimme a cold beer." Carillo grabbed the beer bottle from Garza's hands. "Second, a small hit of the white dust," he continued as he sniffed some cocaine into his nostrils. "Now, we can get down to some business."

"Tell me," Garza stated, what in the hell is this guy talking about? He claims you shot him. I don't remember it."

"I was coked up at the time. I was at Selma's place about two or three weeks before I shot her. While I was there I noticed this fucker waiting on me. He was in his car and I was in Selma's apartment. He kept waiting for me to come out. He was going to shoot me, I know. So as I walked past him, I shot him first. I intended to kill the shit-head. I don't know how he lived, because I shot the shit out of him. Anyway, the police started questioning Selma. Lucky for me, I happened to show up over at her place one day after the shooting just as the cops got there. They didn't see me but I saw them. I knew they were pigs so I paid some boys who lived around there twenty bucks to bust the windows on the cop car. It worked. They left soon afterwards. They hadn't been there too long, so I knew they'd probably want to talk to Selma some more. I figured that sooner or later she would start talking and...."

"And so you zapped her," interjected Garza. "How do you know that she had not already finked on you?"

"I didn't at the time. But the pigs never came by my house, so I figured they didn't know. But we took care of Selma, didn't we?" Carillo laughed. "I put a bullet in her nappy head. I understand from some of my friends the police still come by her apartment periodically to check and see if she has ever returned. That tells me that the police have never connected the body dumped in Houston with our Selma."

"And now," said Garza, "we just happen to bump into the guy at the store. Shit, what luck."

"Before we do anything, let's find out who this guy is. He may have a weakness or two."

"How are we going to find out who this guy is?" asked Garza. "Ask the police?"

"It may not be as hard as you think. Think a minute. Do the people who live in the rich part of town drive all the way across town to grocery shop in the poor section?"

"Huh?"

"Listen, skillet head, we happened to be at that fucking store because you live close by. People don't drive across Dallas just to go shopping for groceries. They go to a store close by where they live. Just like you. I figure he lives somewhere in the area. We can put out the word there. You know, ask around."

"Yeah, sure. What are the chances of us finding him? I say 'not much.' "

Unexpectedly riled, Carillo yelled, "Look, my ass is in trouble! I run this show, and I am going to do something about it. I've got too big of an operation established here in Dallas to run off. Dumb shit-heads do that. And they eventually get caught and are brought back. I say that we nip this thing. If we can't do that, then I might leave."

"Okay Chief, okay. I'm with you. No need to get flipped out."

For the next few days they covered the area around the supermarket talking to people on the streets or anyplace else they found a group of Hispanics. Spreading the word was easy enough. The question was simple: Do you know of a Mexican in a wheelchair? For an incentive, Carillo said that any person would be paid $ 500 bucks for good information. It did not take long before some teenager collected the money.

"His name is Tony Medina," the teen responded. "And he lives on Manana Street."

Chapter Eleven

"Has the jury reached a verdict?" the judge asked.

"We have," the foreman answered.

The judge began reading from the verdict sheet: "We, the jury, having previously found the defendant guilty of murder, now assess his punishment in the Institutional Division of the Department of Criminal Justice for 99 years without parole, and we further assess a fine of ten thousand dollars. Signed J.T. Brown, foreman of the jury."

Turning to the jury, the judge asked, "Members of the jury, if that is your verdict, would you so indicate by raising any hand?"

Each juror raised his hand.

The judge continued, "Members of the jury that completes your jury service. Let me thank you for your patience and your consideration in this case. You are now free to go. The Bailiff will show you out."

Seconds later, as Assistant District Attorney Roy Mitchell walked into an office adjacent to the courtroom, someone slapped his back and said, "Great job." Turning, Mitchell saw it was the prosecutor that had assisted him in the trial.

"Thank you, Andy. That was a hard one. I'm glad to get that headache out of here. I appreciate you trying the case with me."

"I like trying cases with you. You never lose. I counted them up. That's the fifth straight murder trial in which you've gotten the maximum punishment of ninety-nine years. We're going to start calling you Agent 99." Both laughed as they rode the elevator up to their offices on the eleventh floor. As they walked into the District Attorney's office, filing past the receptionists, they met Fred Peppers, one of the senior investigators in the District Attorney's office.

"Say Roy, I sat in and listened to your final arguments. Wonderful! It was tremendous. I don't think there was a dry eye in the joint."

Mitchell's face turned a shade red. "Thanks Fred."

Before anyone could go, Fred continued, "What was it you said? I liked it so much. What was it? Let's see. You were referring to the dead woman's three little girls. You said, 'Who will take them from crayons to perfume?' Mister, I nearly cried myself. Even the court reporter teared up. That was great. Better than anyone could do on TV. But I've heard that line before, I think. Or have I? Where did it come from?"

"I got it from the song "To Sir With Love."

The investigator snapped his fingers and nodded. "Okay, Okay. Hey, great delivery."

When Mitchell closed the door in his office, a cubicle that measured nine feet by nine feet, he arched his back until he heard his vertebrae pop. Sitting down in his chair, he exhaled loudly. Thankfully the case was over. It had been a hard case from the beginning. Two women had gotten into an argument over an empty parking space. After the defendant shot the deceased, she pointed the gun to her own head and fired. Although she blew out a portion of her brain and skull, she miraculously lived. The defendant's history of mental problems prompted the insanity defense at her trial. But the defendant was also known for her bad temper. Not to mention her past assault convictions. The prosecution not only overcame that defense but also the sympathy factor for the defendant, who appeared at trial with part of her head missing. Mitchell thought the jury would convict her and give her about twenty-five years instead of the ninety-nine she received.

As he leaned back in his chair, he closed his eyes and realized how tired he felt. The murder trial had lasted eight days. It was not only the length of this case that tired him, but the constant barrage of case after case, crime after crime, that passed across his desk for prosecution. Every now and then he wished for a simple shoplifting case, where the Assistant District Attorney would learn about the case on the same day he tried it. As it was now, Mitchell tried only murder cases that usually lasted one or two weeks. As soon as one case was finished, he would start working another.

Mitchell had actually dozed off in his chair when Andy pushed open the office door to give him some phone messages. The noise had not disturbed him. Andy thought about waking him but decided against it.

When Andy Kindred was promoted into the Major Felony Crime section, he was lucky to have been placed on Roy Mitchell's trial team. Most of the two hundred attorneys who worked in the Dallas County District Attorney's office considered Roy Mitchell one of the best prosecutors in the office. Now, after working with him for nearly two years, Kindred agreed. He saw first- hand how good a prosecutor Roy Mitchell was. Kindred couldn't find a single weakness in his friend's trial ability. Young prosecutors categorized their co-workers into 'the best in giving closing arguments' or 'the best cross-examiner' or 'the best person in selecting juries.' Most people in the office said it was a toss-up between Mitchell and another trial attorney in effectively cross-examining a witness.

Both were excellent and equally devastating in ripping a witness to shreds or neatly setting a trap for a lying witness. However, most observers agreed that Roy Mitchell gave the best, most effective closing argument at the courthouse. Co-workers and other courthouse personnel would fill the gallery when Roy Mitchell stated his case.

After watching and working with his supervisor, Kindred thought he knew what it was that made Mitchell so convincing, so believable, and so likable with the jury. It was certainly not his physical stature, since Roy only stood about five feet, eleven inches, and weighed not more than one hundred and seventy pounds, dripping wet. His voice did not have the piercing and riveting tone that some Hollywood celebrities had, nor did he have the 'drop dead' handsome look that swooned audiences on the big screen. Instead, the soft-sounding voice coupled with the East Texas drawl gave Roy Mitchell a voice that was easy to listen to and pleasant to hear. He had the unique ability of being able to shout, if need be, at the top of his voice during closing summations to the members of the jury and yet not offend anyone with the volume he used. Many jurors, thought Kindred, did not enjoy attorneys shouting or yelling at them. Kindred knew that with Mitchell, juries enjoyed hearing him speak, loud or soft. For Kindred, however, the most poignant, positive thing that Mitchell possessed was his talent for accentuating a word or 'coining a phrase' that was needed at that precise moment.

During the ten years that Kindred had been an assistant district attorney -- five years in Houston and five years in Dallas -- he had seen his share of good attorneys. Some had specialized in civil cases, some in criminal law, both defense lawyers and prosecutors. Regardless of which area of law they had practiced, Kindred had observed that all of the good ones had a special rapport with the jury. While each one might not have the particular talent of effective cross-examination or dramatic closing summations, they each had that unique ability of getting jurors to believe in them. A likable personality could win more cases than anything taught in law school. And Roy Mitchell was in this category.

As Andy Kindred quietly closed the door without waking Mitchell, he turned and nearly stumbled over Bragg Buchanan, the larger-than-life District Attorney for Dallas County, Texas.

Chapter Twelve

Born on June 1, 1949, Bragg Buchanan grew up on a ranch in Abilene, Texas. After graduating as Valedictorian of his high school class, he enrolled in Stephen F. Austin State University in Nacogdoches, Texas via a football scholarship. When his college and football days were finished, he joined the Marines and was sent to Vietnam. He wanted to fight. And fight he did, earning a silver star and a bronze star for bravery. After two tours in Vietnam, he discharged and enrolled in Texas Tech University Law School in Lubbock. His first job as a new lawyer was as an assistant city attorney in Abilene. Quickly bored, he started looking for a job in Dallas. The lanky, ever-smiling Buchanan landed a job in the Dallas County District Attorney's Office as an assistant prosecutor. Three years later he resigned and began practicing probate law. But the excitement of big crime lured him back to criminal law. The District Attorney was the top crime-fighter in the county and the most illustrious. It did not take much for Buchanan to be talked into running for the high office. Tall and country, "Bucky" as his buddies called him, beat the other two candidates flat out. In 1988, he was elected District Attorney for Dallas County.

Choosing his assistants, Buchanan began to build his office of top-flight, tough, and fair prosecutors. He hoped to produce cracker-jack trial attorneys. Soon representatives from metropolitan areas all over the United States came to Dallas, surveyed his layout, and patterned their offices likewise. But it was the trial division that garnered the most attention.

Within the trial division, an elite, blue-ribbon group of prosecutors were assigned to the Major Felony Unit. In the early years, Buchanan purposely designed this unit so that this group of five to seven assistant district attorneys handled the most dangerous, most publicized type of cases. This unique and much envied trial unit tried only those severe cases which were usually labeled by the public and the press as 'heavy-duty.' Each assistant, selected by merit and ability, had an investigator that worked only with that prosecutor. An assistant district attorney in the Major Felony Crime unit answered only to Bragg Buchanan. It was here that Andy Kindred learned how to prosecute criminals. He learned from the best.....Roy Mitchell.

The week following the trial involving the two women found Roy Mitchell starting to work on yet another murder case. He had hoped to have a longer break between cases but things simply hadn't worked out that way. With his handkerchief, Mitchell wiped the sweat from his face as he walked up the long steps that led to the Homicide Division of the Dallas Police Department. He hoped this next case would be easier. He would enjoy the luxury of having a case that had fingerprints, confessions, and numerous good eyewitnesses. However, such niceties always seemed to elude him.

"Good afternoon," Mitchell greeted the pretty receptionist at the front desk. "My name is Roy Mitchell from the DA's office. I'm supposed to meet Detective Frank Barnes."

"Sir, I'm sorry, but Detective Barnes has been called out on a shooting and is not here right now. I've been trying to reach you for the last thirty minutes but the phones have been messed up. I'm very sorry and I have no idea how long he will be gone. He just got the call and left around an hour ago. Would you like to wait for him? I can try to reach him by radio and see how long he might be gone."

"I might stay a few minutes," Mitchell responded, "just to cool off. But if he has gone to a shooting scene, he could be gone for hours. Go ahead and try to reach him. I'll be down the hall resting my heels."

He bought a drink from the large, red, Coca-Cola machine and sat down. As he sipped on the cold soda, another homicide detective walked by and saw Mitchell.

"What are you doing out here sitting on your butt?" The tall detective smiled at his friend of many years.

"I'm supposed to be waiting on Frank. I had a meeting with him but he's been called out. Actually, I'm just stalling. I don't want to get out in the dang heat again."

"Come on back here with me. You can rest just as easily back here in my office. You can tell me some more lies."

With that invitation, Mitchell trailed the long-striding detective into the offices of the Homicide Division. The offices of the Homicide Division always made Mitchell chuckle to himself. They looked just like the way it was portrayed on television. A large open office area, with numerous metal desks -- probably thirty or more -- situated side by side. The off-white tile flooring, the well-worn desks, and the chairs on wheels were standard in every police station that Mitchell had ever been in or had seen on television. The detective pointed to an empty chair. "Have a seat. Frank won't mind if you sit at his desk. As a matter of fact, the chief would probable pay you if you would clean it off a little."

For thirty minutes they talked baseball. The tanned, good-looking detective had pitched in professional baseball for three years with the Minnesota Twins organization back in the day. Finally Mitchell stood up to leave. Just then Barnes walked into the room. Simultaneously the telephone buzzed on Frank's desk. Barnes waved to the prosecutor with one hand and reached for the telephone with the other.

"Frank Barnes, Homicide." Pause. "Hello, Tony!" Although hot and exhausted, Barnes face lit up as he talked. "Yes, Tony, we filed the case last week with the District Attorney. Someone from that office should be getting in touch with you within the week.....What's that? ..... Great! That's just great! Tomorrow, I'll come by to see you just to see how you're doing. Are you going to be home? ......Oh, I don't know, probably about two or three o'clock in the afternoon...... Okay, see you then."

Barnes plopped down into his worn out swivel chair and let out a low sigh. He looked across his cluttered desk at Mitchell, a good friend of many years. "Let me tell you about the guy that I just talked to. It's a sad story."

For the next fifteen minutes Barnes unfolded Tony Medina's life story. Every so often Mitchell would break in with a question or two. When Barnes finished, a peculiar look was on Mitchell's face. It was a strange look. Barnes noticed it. Mitchell suddenly stood and said that he had forgotten something and had to leave. As the attorney began walking briskly out of the office, he said to Barnes, over his shoulder, "I'll think I'll check into that case involving Medina. It sounds like that case was meant for me."

"Meant for him?" Barnes thought. "What does that mean?" He shrugged his shoulders as he watched Mitchell go out of sight.

At 9:05 a.m. the next day Mitchell picked up the telephone and dialed the police station.

When Barnes picked up the receiver, the voice began, "Good morning, Frank, this is Roy Mitchell."

"Well, it's nice to know that some lawyers get to work before ten-thirty."

"Damn right. Pass the word along upstairs. Say. That case that you told me about yesterday...."

"About the kid in the wheelchair?"

"Yeah, that's it. Well, listen. That case fascinates me. I've decided to look into it and maybe prosecute it myself."

"Sounds good to me. But it's not the kind of case you usually take. What's up?"

"Nothing, nothing. I just don't have anything really pressing right at this moment," said

Mitchell, though he knew that was false. "Are you still going to see the guy this afternoon?"

"Yeah, I'm planning on it."

"Can I go with you? If I am going to be the prosecutor on it, I might as well start on it ASAP."

"Sure. Hell yeah, come on. I'll pick you up in front of the courthouse at two o'clock."

Barnes replaced the telephone receiver. "Strange," he thought, "What's Roy Mitchell wanting a case like this for? It's not a famous murder case. No headlines or publicity."

Shortly after two p.m. Barnes and Mitchell were driving the tree lined city streets leading to Tony Medina's house. The Oak Cliff section of Dallas was once the prime residential area of the city. Once upon a time, it was crime-free with neat neighborhoods and pretty terrain. It was located ten minutes from downtown, making the area an enviable place to live. That was forty-five years ago. Now much of the area was just getting old and making its way to being run-down. Some pockets had already become crime-ridden and a haven for petty crooks, thieves, and drug pushers. However some neighborhoods were still vibrant. Homes of the blue collar working class people of Dallas. Mitchell thought how difficult it might be raising a family when two or three blocks away drug pushers roamed the street. From what information he had learned about the case, the Medina family was one such honest, working family. He pictured them as close. Struggling and working hard. They were less privileged than some, of course, but closer together than most families in Oak Cliff, or anywhere else for that matter.

When Barnes pulled into the driveway of 1220 Manana, Mitchell's thoughts came into focus on a white frame house, neatly trimmed with evergreen shrubs around the front and sides. A fresh coat of paint set the house apart from the others in the area. The grass had been recently cut, with a few potted plants hanging from the ceiling of a large front porch. Just from the appearance on the outside, Mitchell knew the type of people who lived on inside.

The detective knocked on the door. A young boy about ten years old answered. "Hello, Mr. Policeman." Without waiting for a reply, the child, grinning big, kept talking rapidly. "Did you bring your gun with you this time so I can see it? You said that you would bring it."

Barnes laughed. "Slow down, slow down. First of all is Tony awake? I told him yesterday that I was coming by today. And, yes," he said still laughing, "I brought my pistol. Before we leave I'll show it to you."

The youngster's eyes became as large as saucers and he disappeared running back into the house.

As soon as they walked inside, Mitchell saw a nicely kept house. The well worn furniture neatly arranged. The floor and walls were spotless. The air smelled especially clean with just a hint of some kind of detergent.

The same youngster walked back into the room. "Cousin Tony is back here. Come on, I'll show you."

They walked down the hallway. Before they reached the back bedroom, Mitchell saw someone lying almost motionless in bed. His heart beat faster.

The policeman spoke first as they entered the small room, "Hello Tony."

"Well hello, Mr. Barnes. I've been looking forward to talking to you. I've been thinking about you for the last couple of weeks."

"Tony, I want you to meet Roy Mitchell. He's from the District Attorney's Office. He'll be handling your case."

Tony's eyes shifted to the other man, and he stretched out his hand to greet him.

"Hello. I'm Tony Medina."

"Tony, I'm pleased to meet you. Detective Barnes let me come with him. I hope you don't mind."

"Heck no. I don't mind. Pleased to meet you. I like company. I don't get out often so the more conversation I can get, the better."

Barnes sat in a metal folding chair near the foot of the bed, leaving Mitchell standing next to the bed. "Like I said," continued Barnes, "Roy is the lawyer that will be handling your case against Carillo. He is a prosecutor and he specializes in putting people into the penitentiary for long periods of time. He's the best in the office."

Mitchell looked from Barnes back to the person lying in the bed. "Tony, I'm going to do as much as I can to punish the person that shot you."

Mitchell realized that the mental image of Tony he had formed when first talking to Barnes was accurate. Something stirred inside of Mitchell. "Here lays a good boy." he thought. Probably raised with less privileges than a lot of people, struggling day in and day out in order to try to get ahead, and totally blameless in the predicament that he is in." The entire situation saddened Roy Mitchell. Briefly, and only briefly, maybe for an instant, Tony Medina's face became invisible, and another face appeared. Medina's voice shook him back to reality. He refocused. His mind and ears picked up on the ongoing conversation between the policeman and the victim.

"Tell me about the man that crippled me for life," he asked the policeman. There was a tinge of resignation in Medina's voice. But the calm, rehearsed question impressed Mitchell as they waited for Barnes to reply.

The police officer took a deep breath. "Well, here's what we know. Our Intelligence Division tells me that he is Cuban. He left Cuba and went to Mexico when he was 17 years old or so. He had been in prison in Cuba for murder. Fidel Castro put him and others on a boat and shipped them to Mexico. After he hit the shores of Mexico, he started selling drugs. Built himself quite a business. Then, for some unknown reason, he came to America. I mean, he was a rich man in Mexico with a lot of connections. Anyway, once in Texas, he started selling drugs. The business got big. Still is big. His name comes up often in the Narcotic Division, but they have never been able to put anything on him. As a matter of fact, he's been very elusive. He's smart, very smart. He's very dangerous and just plain evil. The Intelligence boys tell me that when he shot you, it was very out of character for him. That is to say, he's usually more careful about how he operates."

"But if he is so dangerous, why haven't you guys arrested him before this?"

"We don't have any cases on him. There are no warrants on him. We've just heard of him by reputation from others involved in drugs. He's very careful, Tony, and like I said very smart."

Mitchell watched Tony's face grow tense as the officer detailed the information known about Carillo. With each tidbit, Medina's anguish heightened. He had choked down as much as he could stand. Mitchell saw it coming. Tony could hold it back no longer.

"The dirty bastard. I didn't have much, but at least I was trying to better myself. And this bastard, a dope-dealing shit, ruins my life. He ruined my life," his voice trailing off as he slowly lowered his head. Shaking it back and forth.

Unexpectedly Mitchell's hand reached out and rested on the man's shoulder as Tony quietly sobbed. Barnes sat up and looked at the lawyer as if to ask: What do we do now?

After a few moments, Tony's voice gained strength, "I'd like to be alone. Please come back later. Please. I like to talk and listen. But just now, all of a sudden, I don't feel too good."

Barnes stood, and quietly said, "We understand. I'll call you in a day or so." With that, they left the room.

As they let themselves out of the house, Mitchell discreetly used his handkerchief to wipe tears from his eyes, hoping no one saw him do it. But Barnes did.

Both men were silent on the way back to the courthouse. As they neared the courthouse, Barnes summed it up, "Pretty unusual individual, isn't he?"

Mitchell answered, "I was genuinely impressed. He came across as just a good young kid... Well, let me say this: I'm glad you told me about this case. And I'm glad we are on it." His tone was resolute. "We are going to the max on this one."

The old cop stared at his passenger. His head nodding in agreement. From what he sensed, the brief encounter between Roy Mitchell and Tony Medina touched the prosecutor for some reason. "For some reason, and I don't know why, I thought that you'd feel this way," Barnes said. "Give me a call next week and we can start working on it."

"Next week, hell, I'm starting right now. As soon as I get upstairs I'm calling your Intelligence Division and asking them to send me everything they have on this Carillo."

All the way up to his office, Mitchell thought about Tony Medina. Why did this case intrigue him? He knew the answer. Even though he had just met Tony Medina, the feelings that he had suppressed many years before were creeping back. It was not just another case.... not just another shooting.... not just another victim. It was a chance for Roy Mitchell to redeem himself.

The Assistant District Attorney walked through his office door and plopped down into his chair. He was mentally drained. He leaned back, and looked out the window, daydreaming of other times. For half an hour he pushed criminal law completely out of his mind. Then he hurriedly got up and went home.

That night as he lay in bed, the Medina case kept surfacing. He could not put it out of his mind. But what weighed more on his mind was the opportunity to atone for what had happened years and years ago. This time he had the power to do something, and he would do it. He would not walk away. He would not close the door. Fate had finally given him one chance -- one opportunity to dictate the outcome. He would not let himself and others down. Roy Mitchell did not sleep well that night.

At breakfast the next morning, Mitchell told Beth, his wife, that he wanted to go to Linden for the weekend -- leaving as soon after work as he could.

"Is anything wrong?" She peered into his face. He shook his head. "No, I just want to go. Haven't been in a while."

After all the years of being married to him, Beth knew her

husband. And she knew from his expression that something was troubling him. To suddenly say that he wished to go to his hometown without having first talked about or planned it, was not like her husband.

"Are you OK?" she asked.

"Yes, I just need to go there. I haven't been in a while."

"Is anything wrong there?" she softly persisted.

"No. I just want to go, that's all." A slight edginess in his voice. The type of edginess that experience had taught her not to press any further.

"Do you and the kids want to go with me?" His voice shifted back to its normal tone.

"The boys have a birthday party to go to and they've been looking forward to it. It's an ice skating party. I'll stay here with them -- but you go on. You'll enjoy it. Like you said, you haven't been there in a while."

She smiled across at him as she sat at the kitchen table. But she could still tell something was bothering him.

Chapter 13

Linden, Texas. Population 2133. The census bureau road sign probably needed updating, thought Mitchell as he drove his car past the metal marker on the western edge of town. His small hometown had only grown by approximately 500 people since he had been a kid growing up in northeast Texas. But, he thought, that had been 20 years ago. Twenty years. That thought made it sound like it had been long ago. He guessed it had, but the 20 years seemed like only a flash to him. As he drove over the curvy roads, he saw the small farmhouses sitting back off the main highway. The area made Mitchell feel good–he was back in his element.

Driving along Texas State Highway 11 on the outskirts of town, he took in the sights. All of them old memories. The American Legion Hall, still in use. Events from long ago began to pop up into his mind—high school dances, reunions, various kinds of parties. On the outside, it still looked the same. A rectangular building, two-story red brick with a double door centered on one end. He was just as sure that the inside -- a large auditorium with a stage on one end -- also looked the same. That was good. When he approached the four-way stop sign of State

Highway 8 and Texas State Highway 11, he exhaled deeply. He felt the peace that always overcame him whenever he traveled back home. He wondered if everyone had that feeling whenever they went back to their hometown. He doubted it, but was ever thankful that he did.

The honking of a car behind him brought him back to the present, and Mitchell accelerated through the intersection. As he neared downtown, he passed a vacant lot between two houses where a group of kids were playing football. He slowed down because two or three dogs were chasing a squirrel across the highway.

With the fall season in full swing, leaves were turning multi-colored. Trees were everywhere. There were several different types of huge oaks -- all with large, unusually shaped leaves. Hickory and sweet-gum trees stood elbow to elbow with the tall pine trees. With the cool fall air, Mitchell had driven the last 50 miles with his windows rolled down. The fresh air seemed to invite a stroll under the arching limbs of the big shady trees.

Linden sat atop one of the many rolling hills. The downtown area consisted of four city blocks surrounding the courthouse. This courthouse--a three story antebellum building-- was the oldest courthouse still in use in the State of Texas. Dating back to the pre Civil War days. The outside surface, looking like some type of plaster, appeared as if it had been recently painted. This afternoon its white paint was shining brightly. The grass surrounding it looked as if it had been cut that day. The evergreen shrubs that hugged the base of the structure were closely pruned back, which made the historical building appear even larger. The cement benches, placed around the square gave it the genuine character one saw on picture calendars. How many times as a youngster had he ran the sidewalks that girded the courthouse. Played chase, shot water pistols, and hung out on these grounds. Too many to count. Too many good times, but overshadowed by one bad time. Sometimes when his mind was flowing like a stream, the happy scenes were endless in their coming. But regardless of how nice they were, they all abruptly stopped when he reflected on that one event. The wonderful memories of the courthouse lawn quite often surfaced in his mind, but he never, ever looked at or thought about that courthouse without the despondency of a broken heart from that one occurrence. Somehow, through the years he had grown accustomed to this competing feeling. Maybe as time went on, his feelings had dulled to the pain -- or so he had thought. It encompassed his entire childhood and adolescence.

The downtown still thrived. Stores were located on the streets of all four sides of the courthouse square. Most of them had been there for more than 25 years -- having entrenched themselves in the community and then having persevered the test of time. The two department stores were still open. The lumberyard and the hardware store were both independently owned. The grocery store's marquee sign promoted the pep rally to be held downtown Thursday evening. Mitchell could walk into all of them, knowing almost everyone who worked in them, and spend hours talking with friends. Here he felt at ease. Here he could let his guard down. Growing up, he had never lived anywhere else.

Roy Mitchell had come to believe that these people -- the people who worked and lived in Linden -- were the main-stays of the country. These people were his bona fide friends; elsewhere, everyone was somewhat of a stranger. For Mitchell there was comfort in knowing almost everyone around the town; not just knowing their names, but knowing about their lives. They had all been a part of each others' lives. Of course, there was the flip side. As he grew older, Mitchell came to understand that some people were meddlesome. It was hard to maintain any high degree of privacy. Good or bad, people knew their neighbor. They took walks in the neighborhood, watched the sun set from their backyard, and still dropped by unannounced to visit their friends. People spoke to one another and looked after and helped one another. If the feeling of community spirit was fading in general society, it wasn't in Linden. The townspeople knew the police -- one constable -- as their friend, and most people still left their houses unlocked.

When he stopped his car at the four-way blinking red light, he was in the heart of the town. It was not even a standard traffic control signal light with red, yellow, and green signals. It was one red light intermittently flashing in all directions. The light had been there as long as he could remember.

As he looked around the town, he noted the grocery store was crowded, foot traffic busy at the lumberyard, and quite a few cars parked around the courthouse.

Seated in his car, he arched, popping his back, and then rolled his head from side to side. Mitchell could hear his neck joints cracking. The tensions and problems that came with him from Dallas were drifting away; it was excess baggage that would soon be discarded. Some of it was gone already. He was glad he had gotten away.

Turning left, he slowly drove north along Houston Street, headed to his father's house. Less than thirty seconds later, he pulled into the gravel driveway of a familiar place. The red brick house -- still pretty in color -- at 804 Crockett Street, was nestled underneath the tall elm and sycamore trees. His father's tan Chevrolet Impala was not in sight, and Mitchell hoped that his father had not gone away for the weekend. He knew otherwise when he saw the water sprinkler shooting water across the front yard.

He did not knock before he walked into the house. The sound of the radio playing music came from the next room. Mitchell had not telephoned to tell his dad he was coming. The surprise, he thought, would be fun. Standing in the kitchen, he did not see anyone.

"Hello." Silence. "Hey, anyone here?" No voice except his own was heard. Entering the den, Mitchell saw the old, ever present RCA radio that was playing the music. He reached and turned it off. The overhead light was off, making it darker than normal. But the reading light on the lamp pole next to the recliner was turned on and an empty coffee mug sat on the small, wooden table next to the chair. A very familiar sight. He made a quick sweep through the rest of the house. No one was home, but he knew that his dad was somewhere close around town.

These days it was a quiet neighborhood, where all of the people were older and mostly retired. These large homes, all at least 40 years or older, were once home to crying babies and noisy teenagers. These kids had since grown up and moved on. Now, just the parents remained. All were good neighbors. If the crazy world existed; it was somewhere else. Minutes later, Mitchell sprawled across the sofa. It felt good to be home. He leaned his head back onto a couple of throw pillows, closing his eyes. Momentarily, he opened them and looked around again at the well-known, fixed settings. Many of the items and objects that he saw were permanently vested in their own spot.

He heard the clock strike four times. Cocking his head sideways, he watched the grandfather clock as its pendulum made its constant swing. That clock, said to be over 75 years old, will never belong anywhere else but right up there in the middle of that bookshelf. That was the place where it had always been, and it need not be any place else. As it ticked and ticked and ticked, not another sound could be heard. His eyes stared at the ceiling. His mind in neutral. The time spent here...endlessly happy.

His eyes opened suddenly. He hadn't realized he had fallen asleep or how long he had napped. But the undeniable sound of someone's footsteps in the next room alerted him. Immediately he recognized those footsteps and the person who was making them.

"Dad, it's me!" he said.

Through the kitchen door a man appeared. A smile already on his face. The older man spoke. "I knew that was your car. I'd been to town."

They shook hands and then hugged one another.

"Roy, my boy, I sure am glad to see you. Have you been here long?" His father sat in a nearby chair, while Roy returned to the sofa.

"No, just a few minutes. I wanted to surprise you, and that's the reason I didn't call."

"Did you come alone? Where's the family?"

"They stayed in Dallas. I've been real busy at work. Beth thought I could use a break; so I took off today and drove in for the weekend."

"Well, Dad, tell me what's up? I haven't talked with you in about two weeks. Been feeling okay?"

"Yeah. Sure have." His father did look healthy. The seventy-one-year-old had managed to stay trim during his older years. His black hair, combed back and parted, was just now beginning to have some gray speckles. His dad walked over and raised the window shade on a window. Roy observed that his dad was walking well. It had been five years since Roy's mother had passed away. After the sudden loss of his mother from a stroke, Roy was ever so concerned about his father—his health and disposition. But both looked fine. His father seemed to be doing remarkably well.

"How's Toby?" asked Mitchell with interest.

"He's is doing the same. I just got back from there. He was resting well. Say, I haven't talked to you since he got a new television. Or have I? Anyway, our Sunday School Class pitched in and bought him a brand-new one. Bigger, newer, better." His voice perked up a beat as he was detailing the new set.

"Well, that was nice. I'm sure Toby appreciates it."

"Oh, he does. You should have seen his face and eyes when we plugged it in and turned it on......"

"Now, Dad," Roy interrupted suddenly and pleaded, "don't start in on it again."

"I don't care what anyone says, I can see these things from his eyes."

Roy did not feel like arguing the point. It would not do any good, he thought. It never had.He stood up and then asked, "I'm going over to see him; want to come with me?"

His father glanced at his watch. "No. Go ahead. I just got back."

A hefty, balding, black man was cleaning the window glass on the front door as Mitchell walked up the sidewalk to enter the one-story building. As the man opened the door for him, Roy smelled the fresh odor of a window cleaner. The man's uniform consisted of a starched, long-sleeved, white shirt, and starched white pants. The one-inch, black leather belt that he wore made the white uniform look even more official. Mitchell smiled as he approached the door.

"Hello, Bennie. Working hard or hardly working?"

The man grinned at first, then a big smile appeared. "Good afternoon, Mr. Money-bags." The husky voice carried a playful tone. "I haven't seen you for weeks. You're looking good." They shook hands as old friends.

"Well, thanks, Bennie." He thought Benton Brown still looked like he did in high school -- tall, stocky, well proportioned, with a smooth complexion. Though Mitchell was a few years older, he remembered Bennie had been a good football player in high school and had gotten some offers to play college ball. He tried it for a year, got homesick and returned to Linden. As soon as Bennie returned home he had started working here at the Westend Nursing Home. He had connections. At the time his mother had been employed here as a nurse's assistant for more than 20 years. Although his mother retired last year, Bennie had worked steadily here for more than fifteen years. He was the top orderly and headed a staff of six people who worked around the clock.

"Toby's doing just fine today," remarked Bennie, still smiling. "Say, you haven't been here since he got the new TV. I believe it makes him rest better. I really do." Mitchell knew Bennie took extra care in looking out after Toby. Bennie had constantly said so himself. He had been working at the nursing home less than a week when he called Mitchell aside one day.

"Don't you ever worry about someone taking extra good care of Toby," Bennie had told him. "I'll see to it myself." And throughout the years, Bennie had reminded Mitchell of that promise. Mitchell stopped once inside the front door and put his arm around Bennie's thick shoulders. "You look the same now as you did in school. What's the secret?"

Bennie laughed in that deep coarse voice. "Clean living, and Coors beer."

Mitchell walked alone down the wide corridor in one of the wings. With Thanksgiving less than three weeks away, the walls were already decorated. He had been so immersed in the workings and dealings in Dallas that he had almost forgotten.

He slowed down and then stopped in front of Room 104. He stood still. Everything was quiet. The door was closed. His heart began racing. He reached to push open the door but stopped. Over a thousand times he had walked into Room 104, but this time seemed different. This time something was different; the difference was in Roy. Tony Medina's face instantly crossed his mind.

He quietly walked into the medium-sized room. It was dimly lit. The curtains, pulled shut, blocked out most of the daylight. Both the Sony radio and the Panasonic television set were playing. The body lying in the bed was still. Roy walked softly to the side of the bed and looked down at his brother. The heavy breathing told him he was sleeping. Roy's gaze lasted a long time. He had not really changed much over the years, thought Roy. The body was still that of a young boy, but the face had aged. Instinctively, Roy turned and picked up a comb that was lying on the stand next to the bed. He combed the flock of hair that had fallen onto Toby's forehead. Then moving a chair close to the bedside, Roy sat down.

The deep breathing had stopped, and so he knew that Toby was "awake" even though his eyelids remained closed. He had never opened his eyes since the accident nearly 30 years before. Nor had he ever moved. At the time, the doctors said they did not believe he would live three years. The specialists had told them that he would probably never awaken. Roy remembered that as a boy he had come to understand the situation was like someone who was asleep and could not wake up. The periodic trips to Houston to retest the brain activity always produced the same results: brain waves were present and responded to stimuli. His brother, Toby, was in a coma.

For the first few months, and even years, the family maintained vigilant hope he would just one day come out of it; just wake up and be normal. But as the years ticked by, the entire family seemed to have lost hope for this kind of recovery. Keeping him comfortable, letting him exist the best he could, and never losing their faith, was the family attitude.

Roy turned off the radio and the television set. He sat back down quietly, staring at his younger brother. This was his only brother. He knew that he loved Toby more than he loved anyone in the world. Toby had given up his life in saving Roy's. The older brother also knew that it had been his own fault for what lay before his eyes.

It had never been easy for Roy to push the accident out of his mind. After it happened, the counselors said that as time passed he would think less and less about the incident. They suggested that in Roy's situation, as he grew older, he would one day be able to realize that he was not to blame for the accident. Roy sighed. Just when would that happen, he wondered. "But see, it was not just an accident. I caused it. I didn't mean to, but I'm still to blame." He startled himself when he realized that he was speaking out loud.

The person in the bed did not move. Slowly shaking his head, Roy felt tears rolling down his cheeks. He thought about long ago. Something from a long, long time ago..........

Chapter 14

He was not quite sure what had awakened him. However, the pillow in his face and a boy's laugh coming from above gave Roy a good clue. He had wanted to sleep till noon. As a matter of fact, he had told Toby the night before that he was going to do just that. As he propped himself up on one elbow and looked at the kid on the top bunk, Roy said to Toby, "I'm going to beat your butt after breakfast. I told you I wanted to sleep late. I'm going to tell Mama."

Turning his head, he saw the sun rays coming through the windows. It was still early morning. As Toby climbed down from the top bunk bed, he said to his older brother, "Let's ride our bikes to town. I know where we can find some bottles to turn in. I think they're paying five cents now."

This was only the second week into the summer vacation, and it was already hot that June morning. It had rained every day the previous week, and it appeared that this was going to be the first day they could roam around outside.

Roy slowly got out of bed and was putting on his clothes when Toby hollered from the kitchen, "Do you know how to make pancakes?"

"Maybe. But if I do, I ain't making you any," as he sat down at the kitchen table.

"If you make us pancakes, I'll show you where those bottles are."

Roy scratched his head -- a recent burr haircut still made his head feel funny -- and yawned, "Where's Mama?"

"She's hanging clothes on the clothesline."

"Forget pancakes. I'm going to eat that new cereal."

"Yeah, me too," responded Toby.

After breakfast, Roy went out in the backyard and started spraying the already soaked garden with water from the water hose. He had been doing this for a few minutes when his mother called him inside.

"Do you and Toby want to go to town for me? I have a few errands for you to run. If you do a good job, I'll give you enough money for some snacks."

"Hey, great! Sure, we'll go." Roy tore out of the room yelling for his ten year old brother. Moments later both were peddling their bikes down the street. Since their house was located in town, it took less than five minutes to ride downtown. The first stop was the shoe repair store to deliver a broken high-heeled shoe. It was the smell of leather that made Toby linger longer than usual. Mike's Shoe Repair and Leather Shop sold handbags, wallets, and other leather items. But what interested the boys were the saddles. Shiny and looking exactly like the ones on cowboy shows, these polished new saddles were just what Roy and Toby thought they needed.

The grocery store was next on the list. Picking up the few items was quick, but deciding on the snacks took longer. Minutes later they strolled outside; each munching on some Fritos and a Pepsi. Pieces of Bazooka chewing gum had been sacked up for later. Neither boy trusted the other one, so each had his own sack of gum.

Roy handed Toby the small bag of groceries. "You take these." Toby placed the sack in the metal wire basket on the front of his handle bars.

Toby asked, "Well, what now?"

They grabbed their bikes. Still snacking, they slowly headed down the street. Roy exclaimed, "Let's go walking around town." They had no particular place to go and were in no rush. They stopped and looked at the display windows of the stores they passed. They knew and spoke with practically everyone they saw. They swung by the post office to see if there were any new Army or Navy pamphlets from the three racks of military brochures that solicited recruits. The boys liked the pictures.

They crossed the street and were passing in front of the town's only bank when Toby spoke,

"Go in here! Go in here! See if they have any free suckers."

Moments later they both exited the First State Bank, each licking suckers that had been offered by one of the tellers -- who was also Roy and Toby's neighbor.

"I've got to use the restroom," urged Toby.

"Hey, let's go to the courthouse and use the restroom in the basement. I like to read stuff that's written on the walls."

"Cool, man."

On one corner of the courthouse lawn, the boys laid their bikes next to a granite statue, a twenty-foot monument commemorating those from Cass County who had died in the Civil War. Sitting on the two-foot ledge at the base of the monument, the two gawked at the chiseled inscriptions. The bushes around the marker were loaded with some kind of berries. Roy started throwing the tiny berries at Toby. The other brother quickly returned fire.

"Let's go," said Toby.

Roy raised his pop bottle and looked at it. "We've got to finish these drinks first. They'll get onto us if we take them inside."

Aunt Opal does it all of the time. I've seen her."

"Let's see."

The first floor of the courthouse housed the District Clerk's Office, the County Clerk's Office, and the office of the County Judge. Numerous typists pecking away on the typewriters dotted the long, wide corridors.

Running inside, the two immediately saw their Aunt Opal sitting in front of a typewriter a few feet away.

Toby spoke first. "Aunt Opal, hi."

The short, fiftyish woman wearing half-rimmed glasses stopped typing and looked over the top of her specs in their direction.

"Well, if it's not the two outlaws."

Both boys were grinning widely as they approached their father's oldest sister.

"It ain't against the law to drink pop in here, is it, Aunt Opal?" Toby made it sound urgent.

"No. See, I've got one here," she said, motioning to the Coca-Cola next to her Underwood typewriter.

"Told you so." Toby looked at Roy.

At that moment, a telephone, sitting on a table a few feet away started ringing. "Excuse me, boys, and let me answer that phone," said their aunt as she rose to reach for the receiver.

Before she was able to pick up the phone, the two were off again. "Come on, Toby. See you, Aunt Opal." They were gone before she could answer. They were running down the hall toward the basement stairs.

A few moments later, when they reached the top of the stairwell, the big clock that was perched on the top of the courthouse sounded 10:00. But before the clock was through chiming, Roy spoke, "I saw some men working on that big clock the other day."

"So."

"I know how to get on top of the courthouse," he bragged. "No one can see me do it.

Toby stopped walking. "How far you can see if you are up there?" A quizzical look came across his face.

"I think about a thousand miles. Come on, let's go up there."

"No, better not. We might get in trouble."

"No one will know. I told you, I know the way. We can do it without anyone seeing us." Roy was tugging on Toby's sleeveless shirt.

"Come on."

Toby resisted. "I don't think we should." But the resistance in his voice was fading.

"Don't you want to see the Pacific Ocean? We can see it real good from up there. All we have to do is walk up these stairs." He pointed to a flight of stairs next to them.

Toby was still hesitant. "Will it be dangerous?"

"Heck no. I saw those men do it. And when I was here the other night for the 4-H meeting, I checked it out and found out how they did it. Come on!" Roy was already halfway up the stairs. As he looked over his shoulder he saw his younger brother tagging close by.

They climbed the stairs until they had reached the third floor. So far, thought Roy, no one had seen them. The third floor of the courthouse was originally designed to house jurors overnight in the event a jury had to be kept together until the case was over. It had not been used in years since the motel opened in town. Essentially, the third floor was vacant except for the janitor's closet.

"I'm getting scared," Toby said softly.

"Look, it's right here." Pointing to a hole in the ceiling, Roy exclaimed, "We climb through that hole using this ladder; then we're in the attic. That's it. We are on the roof."

"I ain't going up there."

"It's easy, Toby. You aren't going to get hurt. I saw those men doing it when they were working on the clock." Roy had already climbed the ladder and was going into the attic when he turned and looked down. Toby was at the base of the ladder, looking up. "Come on, chicken. You scaredy cat. I'm going to leave you here."

In the attic, an air duct opened directly onto the relatively flat roof. When Roy climbed out, he was standing next to the huge clock. He was overwhelmed with the sensation. What a feeling! The wind was blowing in his face. The many noises of town were coming from below. He heard something behind him. Turning, he saw his little brother following his course. "See Toby, ain't it great? I can see .... forever," he shouted.

Toby was standing close behind him in the center of the roof. "Wow! Oh, wow! Look at how far you can see."

"I want to look down and see if I recognize anyone," boasted Roy as he walked away from Toby. As he got closer and closer to the edge he got a better view of the town below.

"Don't go over there," hollered Toby. "You'll fall."

"Wow, come here and see." Roy turned his head and looked toward Toby. "Hey, I see your teacher, Mrs. Walker. I see her. Come here and see. She's walking toward the bank."

"Where?" Toby moved close behind Roy. They were standing about three feet from the edge. The ground, forty-five feet below, looked a thousand feet away.

Toby, standing behind his brother, craned his neck to see below, touching Roy's shoulder for a brace. The unexpected hand on Roy's shoulder startled him, and he flinched. He momentarily lost his balance. He looked over his shoulder at his brother, Toby, then reached back for him, but could not grab anything. Toby lunged to catch his brother, but tripped and missed completely, falling forty-five feet to the ground below. The visual image of Toby falling in the air was still crystal clear in Roy's mind. Even to this day, years and years later, Roy could seemingly feel the terror he had felt as he watched his brother falling and falling to the ground below. It still created panic inside Roy whenever he thought about it.

He was rushed by ambulance to Wadley Hospital in Texarkana, Texas. After a couple of hours, a medical helicopter flew him to St. Luke's Hospital in Houston. The boy suffered severe head and spinal cord injuries. The attending physicians prepared the family for the worst.

But Toby just slept. That was the only way that young Roy could understand it. He was asleep and could not wake up. After staying in the hospital in Houston for two weeks, Toby was transferred by ambulance back to Wadley Hospital. Three weeks later the doctors at Wadley allowed him to transfer via ambulance to the hospital in Linden. Linden's hospital had a staff of three full-time physicians, and was competent enough to handle the young comatose boy.

The parents consulted several major neurologists in Houston, Dallas, Shreveport and Little Rock. They were always met with the same diagnosis. The major head and spinal cord injuries should have killed him instantly. The full extent of the injuries was not determined until two months after the accident. It was during his stay at the hospital in Texarkana that the neurologists discovered a very active brain wave and dilating retinas. However, no words, sounds or movement came from the patient. The medical explanation given was Toby was suspended in an involuntary coma.

Roy, in the meantime, suffered constantly. Every day for hours he thought of Toby. And every single day Roy laid more guilt on himself. Months later, when it was painfully clear that Toby probably would not get any better, his mom and dad tried to talk with Roy about the enormous burden he was placing upon himself. Things like that happen in life, they said. Several professional counselors met with Roy for the next few years. Whether it did him any good remained unknown.

When the family's insurance ran out one month after he was transferred to Linden, Toby was moved to Westend Nursing Home, a private facility owned by their great-uncle.

Chapter 15

There was a soft knock on the door. Mitchell turned to see Bennie carrying a small carton of orange juice.

"I thought I'd bring you one of these before you had a chance to ask for one. You drink more of these things than anyone here." Bennie's presence was uplifting.

"Thanks, Big Ben. You knew that I'd be around to beg for one sooner or later. Hey, how's your mom doing?"

"She's doing fine. She likes the retired life. Grandkids running all over the place."

The light conversation was suddenly interrupted by a female voice coming from a speaker above: "Paging Bennie. Paging Bennie. Please come to the front desk. Please come to the front desk."

"That's me, brother. Got to run. See you later." He dashed out the door.

Roy's voice raised, "Thanks again, Big Ben."

Roy slowly backpedled to his usual gray chair by the side of the bed. All the while watching his younger brother. There was still no movement. After all these years, Roy still held a thin thread of faith that one great day he would see some discernible movement.

For a long time Roy just stared into the face of his younger brother. Finally, and unexpectedly, a smile began to crease Roy's face. "I love you. I love you more than you can ever know." The words were barely audible. They were the same words that had been spoken so many times before. "Do you know that you give me strength? You really do." Roy's voice was now clear and distinct. "Thinking of you lying here made me go on, even when I did not think I could go any further. You helped me hold on just when I was about to let go. You made me push ahead when I thought I had pushed out. And I don't mean just lately, either. Since God put you right here in this bed, you've been the person that I rely upon the most. That's right. I rely on you. No rah-rah speeches or pep talks, but somehow you told me what to do or how to do it. You were my best friend the day we walked up those stairs at the courthouse -- and you still are. Roy paused. He held Toby's hand in his. "I don't know if this makes sense to you or not, but it does to me. Thanks. Thank you for being with me. I have thought about you during every episode of my life. In some strange way you have been my life. I just wish I could give you life. Every time something good happens to me; I think about you. I wonder if you are able to know about it, or maybe even see it happening. I wish I could do something for you. I know that I am the reason you are lying there in that bed. If there was anything I could do to correct that, I would. If I could do something to help you or make it easier on you, I would. I wish, oh, God, how I wish that I could do something."

He left the room at a hurried pace and drove back to his father's house.

The next day, Sunday, broke fair and clear. He had to go back to Dallas that morning but he made one stop before he left.

Roy quietly entered Room 104. He did not know why he always tried to be quiet. Approaching Toby, Roy could hear him breathing. Without sitting down, Roy reached and clasped one of Toby's hands. "You're always on my mind."

He returned to his car and started driving away. However, rather than taking the highway that led back to Dallas, Roy started riding around town. It was a gorgeous Sunday morning. The entire sky from east to west was a picturesque blue, still and breezy. The downtown and residential areas seemed deserted. He knew most of the people in Linden were probably at church. Traveling in a vehicle on the same streets and side roads he had once traversed on foot and bicycle brought back, once again, almost forgotten memories. Driving past the houses of childhood friends, they looked the same. Then Roy strangely wondered why he even thought they would appear different. His schoolmates had long since moved away, but their parents still lived in most of the houses. That was one of the things he liked about his hometown. He felt comfortable here. He knew at instant he could stop the car, knock on the door and he would be invited inside. Like he had so many times before. For some odd reason, knowing he could still go there was important to Roy.

Roy looked at the car clock. He had been driving around town for nearly half an hour. He decided to drive around the countryside. As the farm roads curved through the pleasant terrain, the fall season was rapidly coming into sharp focus. Practically all of the leaves from the hardwoods had begun to change, and most were falling with the slightest breeze. But the tall stately pine trees that remained green year round swayed back and forth in the wind. It made a soothing, rustling sound. "This is what I like most of all," he said to himself, "this countryside." It had looked this way for as long as he could remember. For some inexplicable reason, he felt secure.

Mitchell lost all track of time. Driving past a small country church, he saw the congregation leaving and knew that it was close to noon. Glancing once again at the car clock, "Five after," he muttered. Turning his car around, he headed west towards Dallas.

Chapter 16

Mitchell hoped that someone would answer when he dialed the telephone number given to him by Detective Barnes. He was anxious. It had been three days since he had seen and talked with Tony Medina. At the end of the third ring a female child's voice answered. "Hello, Medina's residence."

"Hi." Mitchell suppressed a laugh. "This is Roy Mitchell. Could I speak with Tony, please?"

"Uncle Tony? One second, please."

Roy was still grinning as he thought of the sound of the voice of the young girl. It was full of precociousness. Soon a male voice spoke. "This is Tony." Mitchell could tell he was breathless when he spoke.

"Hi, Tony, this is Roy Mitchell in the District Attorney's Office. Remember me? I was with Detective Barnes a couple of days ago when we came by to see you."

"Sure, I remember."

"Well, I would like to come over today, if I could. We need to talk about your case."

"Hey, sir, that's fine with me. I'm not going anywhere." He laughed at his own little joke.

"Good. I'll be over about 1:00. Is that okay?"

"That's fine. Bye."

When Mitchell pulled up in front of the home at 1:00 he saw the same young boy as before. The boy was raking the grass into small piles. Mitchell looked at the other houses up and down the street. They were not as neatly kept as this one. Just as I remembered it from last week, he thought to himself. As he opened his car door, the boy quickly turned.

"Buenos dias, Senor."

"Hola, que pasa?" answered Roy.

"Nada. Just doing my chores.

"Good for you. Good for you." He paused. "I came to see Tony. Would you tell him that I'm here?"

The skinny young kid ran into the house, carrying the rake with him. Momentarily, he returned to the front door. "Come in. Come in. I'll show you."

Tony motioned the boy to turn off the television when he brought Mitchell into the bedroom. Smiling, he greeted the visitor with an extended hand. "Glad to see you, Mr. Mitchell. Welcome."

"It's good to see you too, Tony. I just wanted to come over and talk, not only about the case but to get to know you and let you get to know me." He paused, then sat in the folding metal chair. "I have found throughout the years of being a lawyer that the more I know about the person, the better I am at representing him."

For the next two hours they talked, laughed and told stories. Eventually, Mitchell felt he had stayed long enough and said so. When he stood to leave, he realized they had never talked about the facts of the case. He sensed that Tony did not want him to leave. But as Mitchell said goodbye, he added, "I'll come back over in a few days. We need to get to work on our case."

When the veteran prosecutor started his car to leave, he caught the sight of two faces looking at him from a window inside the house. Both faces were eager with hope. He recognized them both: the little fellow that wanted to be a real policeman, and Tony Medina.

It had been a week since Roy Mitchell had seen or talked to Tony. He stopped his car in the Medina's driveway, hoping someone would be home. The cry of an infant came from inside the house as soon as Roy stepped onto the rather large front porch. It was mid-afternoon.

Tony answered the knock at the door.

"Hello, Tony. I was in the area and decided to drop in to see if there was anything I could do for you."

"Man, I'm glad to see you." A warm smile crossed Tony's face. "You made my day!"

The time passed quickly. Never once was the case mentioned. Both were having too good of a time enjoying the company. The closest the conversation came to the criminal case was when Tony talked about drugs. "One of the biggest evils that face my Hispanic culture today is the presence of drugs." he said. Mitchell had heard that many times, but it was not limited to Hispanic culture. He knew the problem invaded everyone. Still he listened once more.

"Drugs ruin lives," Tony continued. "It destroys and tears down -- just look around this neighborhood. It decimates human beings. Just look at me. I'm a cripple. I'll always be a cripple. I can't walk around; I can't socialize; I can't date. All because of some drug head, my life is gone."

When Mitchell heard that last remark, he looked away. Realistically he knew that Tony was partially correct. He searched for something to say, but nothing came. He wanted to change the subject, but did not speak.

Tony broke the silence. "We want you to stay and eat with us."

"Not tonight. I haven't talked with my wife."

"We have a phone in the house," he responded. "Call her right now. My sister,

Juanita, is coming over after work. She said she wanted to cook supper for us tonight."

It did not take much pleading to convince Mitchell to stay.

At the sound of footsteps on the front porch Mitchell looked toward the door. The front door slightly stuck as an older man pushed it open. Once inside the man's eyes went straight to Tony Medina. "Tony, Tony," the man said. He smiled. "I hope you've had a fine day."

Mitchell had no idea who the man was that had just come inside. The person appeared to be in his late fifties or early sixties. He was carrying a light work jacket and a scratched up and slightly dented black lunch box. It was the type of lunch box that Mitchell had not seen in years: curved on the top for a thermos to be carried inside. The blue collar work clothes and work boots seemed unusual for a man of his age.

"Hello, Dad." Tony responded. "I want you to meet my new friend. This is Roy Mitchell."

Mitchell immediately stood and extended his hand. Tony continued, "Roy, say hello to my father, Juan Medina."

"Hello, sir," spoke Mitchell. "It's my pleasure to meet you."

The older Medina hurried over to the visitor. His smile was wide and his eyes friendly.

"Welcome to this house. Welcome. Welcome. Any friend of my son is always welcome here."

Tony quickly added, "Mr. Mitchell works in the District Attorney's office, Dad. He's going to prosecute the man that shot me. He's just over here visiting today. Sit down, Dad, and listen. He's a good talker," Tony laughed.

"Is that so?" The father grinned. "Well, it's my pleasure to meet you. It sure is. Sit down. Mr. Mitchell, sit down. If Tony says you're a good talker that must really mean you're a good listener. Tony does most of the jabbering around here. None of us can hardly get a word in edgewise." The father and son looked at each other, both chuckling.

Mitchell thought to himself, "Close bond, these two." Immediately Mitchell took a liking to Juan Medina.

An hour later all three were still talking–mostly telling stories. It was as if they were long-lost friends who had suddenly come together. Mitchell felt at ease around the Medinas. Strange, he thought, but here he could let down his guard. He could joke and tell stories. And even stranger still, he was among people he hardly knew. It was a perplexing thought; but one he quickly dismissed. As the evening wore on, a thought kept coming back to him. Stop analyzing everything, he told himself, just enjoy the moment.

That afternoon Mitchell met the entire household. The elder Medina had a big family. Surprisingly it did not take Mitchell long to remember the Medina siblings -- Tony, Juanita, Hosea, Mercedes, and Rose. After the evening meal, the grownups made their way onto the front porch. Mitchell got the impression that porch sitting was the routine. Fine with him. Situated about three feet above the ground, the porch had a somewhat scenic view of the outlying street and front yards.

Sitting on the large porch was restful. The visiting, the talking. All of it......enjoyable. Houses now were rarely built with front porches. Mitchell recalled his childhood wherein front porch gatherings were habit. An after-meal sojourn to the porch had been a ritual for most families. It still prevailed here at the Medina's house. He thought it was great. The sun was beginning to set; a slight wind began to cool. This front part of the house, with its porch swing hanging from the ceiling and three old-timey, high-backed wooden rocking chairs was a popular sitting spot. Juanita sat in the porch swing. Mitchell and Juan took to the rocking chairs. Tony, in his wheelchair, was parked next to his father. Mitchell surveyed the chairs and swing. The three chairs, all painted different colors, had some wear and tear. The curved rockers were so worn that a lot of the wood had been rocked off. However, they were still strong. Probably hold up another 20 years. The arm rests were as slick as glass. Only years and years of constant use could have made them that smooth. But it was the age-old porch swing that caught Mitchell's eye. It was the kind that his family had when he was growing up. The two small chains hanging from the ceiling allowed it to swing with ease. It was unpainted and showed its natural wood grain. Whether the wind was blowing it or someone swinging, it quietly squeaked as it moved. It, too, like the chairs, were rubbed smooth. If only it could talk, thought Mitchell, the stories it could tell. Mitchell felt it. It was peaceful here.

The next morning Mitchell called Barnes at the police station. "Frank, this is Mitchell, DA's office. Hey you don’t sound so good. You okay?”

"Not really. I don't know if it's my allergies or if I'm coming down with the flu. But either way, this old cop needs some relief."

They chatted for a couple of minutes about the upcoming game that weekend. A group of them, policemen and prosecutors and their families, had planned on going. A block of seats had been donated.

"Say, Frank, I asked Tony if he would like to go with us."

"Tony who?"

"Tony Medina. You know, the one that got shot by Carillo."

"Oh." Barnes was not receptive to the idea.

"Do you feel that lousy, Frank, or do you have some problem with him going with us?"

"Well," the officer began, "I've been needing to talk to you about that situation. And I mean this both as a friend and as a professional." Barnes was not completely sure he should continue, but it seemed as good a time as any.

"Roy, I've worked on many cases with you over the years. We've put a lot of people in the penitentiary. But I've never seen you as worked up over a case as the one involving this guy. I mean, being prepared for trial is one thing, but you've gone overboard. You call me about it every other day; you've been hounding our Intelligence Division."

Mitchell tried to protest, but the detective did not stop.

"Let me continue, let me continue. Now that's just a small portion of the problem; the bigger portion is this: Roy, I think that you are getting too involved with the players. Know what I mean? I feel that you are getting personally involved. Now, I don't have to tell you what problems that can cause if that happens. You've been around as long as I have. You know that is not good. It's not good for you personally, and it is not good for the office."

"I hear what you are saying, Frank, and I agree with some of it. But I think you are wrong in this case. I know what you mean about mixing the two -- business and personal -- but I have it under control. I was just trying to be nice to the kid. He doesn't have much."

"I know he doesn't, and I know that you are just trying to brighten his world. But I think you are going overboard with it. I mean, look at it this way. You call him nearly every day. You go over to his house more than once a week. On your previous cases," Barnes' voice hardened, "how many times did you ever go by and visit with the victim or next of kin? Once? Maybe twice?"

"Look, I'm professional enough to separate the two. I ought to know when it's beginning to affect my ability. And it is not." Mitchell's voice carried a touch of resentment.

"Okay. Okay. Don't get mad. Remember, I'm on your side."

The conversation quickly ended. After Mitchell hung up the phone, he sat silently for a while, digesting everything that his good friend had said. He knew that Frank Barnes meant well; however, in this case his friend was just mistaken.

After work that day Mitchell visited the Medina house. When he arrived he saw Tony sitting in his wheelchair on the front porch. The worried look on his face was obvious.

"Good afternoon, Tony. I was in the area on other business and decided to come by. What's up?", he asked as he plopped down into a rocking chair. Mitchell wanted to appear upbeat. But he also wanted to find out what was troubling. No answer. Mitchell could see that something was definitely on Tony's mind. Still, no response.

"Look, Tony, my good friend, I'm your partner, your friend. What's wrong? What's going on?" He was leaning practically into Tony's face, but Tony would not look him in the eye. Instead, his gaze was fixed across the street. Slowly, Mitchell settled back in his chair, thinking it best to keep quiet for a few moments. Whatever the problem, it was clear that he was not going to penetrate the shield Tony had raised.

After a few minutes Tony turned his head toward his friend. "I appreciate you coming over here all this time. But right now I'd just like to be left alone. Please go."

He turned his wheelchair around and started into the house. But before he reached the front door, a hand grabbed the wheelchair, stopped it, and turned it around. Tony looked into the concerned face of Roy Mitchell.

"I can see that something has you upset. Give me a call when you want to talk about it. Please let me help. Don't shut me out." Mitchell walked slowly back to his car, head down and his thoughts hundreds of miles away. He muttered to himself, "Not again, not again."

Down the street, the men in the car waited a few more minutes. Hostility was already in Carillo's eyes as he angrily watched Roy Mitchell's car disappear down the street. When he finally started his vehicle he could see that Tony was still sitting on the front porch, with his back facing the street. He drove directly to the front of the house and abruptly stopped in the middle of the street. Leaving the car engine running, Carillo walked up to the house. Tony turned his head and saw him. With no chance of escaping, Tony wheeled his chair around and faced him. The man stood at the bottom of the steps, glaring at the figure sitting on the porch.

Tony could feel his heart beating. It felt like his entire body was pounding! His head was spinning. His stomach felt as if it was lodged in his throat. He was nauseous. The parts of his body that were not paralyzed were shaking uncontrollably.

"What a coincidence." The voice of Ulysses Carillo was firm. "Just when I was coming to pay a friendly visit, so does the damn DA." Suddenly the tone became cocky. "I'm glad he got here first so I could watch what went on. Binoculars are a wonderful thing."

"You didn't say much to him." he snapped, "And he didn't stay long enough for you to tell him." He looked at his wristwatch. "Let's see, school started last week, didn't it? Hosea, Rose, and Mercedes should be getting out about this time. Right?"

Tony was frozen. He could not have spoken a word even if he had wanted.

Carillo laughed. "Do you want me to give them a ride home?"

That was all the listener could stand to hear. "Leave them alone. Please leave them alone," cried Tony. "I'll do what you say, just leave them alone. I said I would do it." Tears began to flow.

The smile disappeared from Carillo's face. "You have two days to inform the DA of 'our' decision. I mean, 'your' decision". He turned and walked toward the car. After a couple of steps, he stopped and turned back around. "How does that song go? ..... 'With every move you make, with every step you take, I'll be watching you.'" He returned to his car and sped away.

Chapter 17

Roy Mitchell unwrapped his sandwich for lunch. It was only 11:30, but he was hungry. The telephone on his desk rang. At first he did not answer it. But then, for some reason, he picked up the receiver.

"DA's office. This is Roy Mitchell."

The voice on the other end was a familiar one. "Roy, this is Tony."

There was a sound of hesitancy in Tony's voice. He had started to hang up when Roy answered. Mitchell stood straight up out of his chair. He sensed something was about to happen. He blurted into the receiver, "Tony, where are you calling from?"

"Huh?"

"Tony, tell me where are you calling from?"

"I'm at my house."

Mitchell felt a sense of relief after hearing the answer. He exhaled and dropped his shoulders. Still standing, he asked, "What's the matter?"

"I apologize for the way I acted the last time that you were here. A lot was on my mind." Tony paused. To Mitchell, Tony sounded as if he were reading from a script. Soon he continued. "I have had many thoughts about the long-term results. And I have concluded that it is best for me to drop charges against Carillo."

Mitchell was stunned. He was still reeling when the voice continued.

"I don't want to testify. My family has suffered enough.

Mitchell slowly regained his composure. "Tony, wait a minute. I'm coming over. This is too important a decision to make over the telephone." He spoke with authority, "Do you understand me?"

The frightened voice on the other end faintly replied, "Yes."

Minutes later, Mitchell pulled into the Medina driveway. Tony was alone on the porch. Surprisingly, he did not appear to be as upset as he had sounded on the telephone. Nor did his face show signs of crying. Mitchell thought Tony looked like his usual self. "Tony, start all over."

Tony had not changed positions and was still facing the driveway. He took a deep breath, looked straight ahead and began: "It's just like I told you on the phone, Mr. Mitchell."

'Mr. Mitchell.' Tony had never called him by that name.

Tony continued: "I don't want to prosecute. I don't want to testify." He stopped for a moment, turned his head, and looked Mitchell in the eyes. "It's up to me, isn't it? I'm the victim. It's my case and my decision."

"Not really, Tony. It's my decision." The voice was unwavering. "I'm the one who decides whether to prosecute. If the police decide to file charges against an individual, then the ball is in my court to decide what to do from there. I've made the decision to go forward and prosecute. Now listen to me! Listen to me!" Silence. "Are you listening? Even though that is what the law says, I want you to tell me what brought on this change of direction."

Tony Medina was not long in answering. "First of all, it was not just an overnight decision. I have been thinking about it for almost a month." His voice was calm. "I just don't want my family to have to go through the hardships of a trial. They have already been through enough, and I don't want them to suffer anymore on account of me."

Mitchell was puzzled. "How is going to trial on this case going to cause them any more hardships? It's not going to affect them if you go ahead with this case. What is the connection?"

Tony avoided answering. "Look," his voice rising, "I'm the one that is crippled. My life is over. I've got to sit in this chair for as long as I live. If I don't want to go on with the case, that is my right."

"But why? Why, Tony? Damn it, you owe it to me to tell me what changed your mind."

"I told you the reason. Don't you see?" His eyes were trying to read Mitchell's face. "No, you don't see, do you? There is no one on this earth who ought to care more about what happens to Carillo than me. I want to kill the son of a bitch. I don't want to send him to prison; I want to kill him. I would do it myself if I could get out of this chair. I'm telling you right now, if I could get a gun and find that bastard, I'd kill him. In a way, he's already killed me." Mitchell didn't interrupt. He could see that Tony was finally letting himself go. The feelings that had been locked up inside were finally working their way out. And Mitchell knew how he felt. Or at least he thought he knew. Having your dreams shattered and starting over was one thing. But to have your dreams broken, and never being able to rebuild them, was devastating.

"I wouldn't even care," he continued, "about going to the penitentiary." The Assistant District Attorney was motionless. Sadly he sat listening. The anger was coming out and Mitchell knew it was best to let it come out.

"I can sit in a wheelchair in prison just as easily as I can here. Any place I go, I'll be the same. Don't you realize that no one wants to punish him any more than me?" Tony's breathing was heavy. A few moments passed. His voice cooled down. "But there are things and people that are more important than me. My family is more important than my desire to rid the world of Carillo. They take priority. And for their sake, they have had enough. I want to put this behind us and move on."

Mitchell heard him, but was not convinced.

"Has he threatened you?" His voice was commanding. "Has he?" Mitchell was almost yelling. But Tony did not flinch. Looking directly towards Mitchell: "No, he has not."

The Assistant District Attorney suddenly decided not to press it any further. Frank Barnes had told him that he was getting personally involved in the case and that he needed to back off. As he stood, looming over Tony Medina, he thought for the first time that maybe Barnes was right. Why did this case touch him differently from the hundreds or perhaps thousands that he had handled previously? Deep down maybe he knew.

He decided to back off.Without so much as a word, Roy Mitchell walked to his car and left. As soon as the vehicle was gone Tony started to cry. Slowly he wheeled his chair around and went inside.

The prosecutor drove past the courthouse and did not stop until he reached 108 South Harwood Street. He pulled into the city-owned parking lot, and flashed his badge to the attendant. Hurriedly, he entered the building, took the elevator, and walked down a long brightly-lit corridor until he reached a set of double doors. "Homicide Division". Entering, he saw a familiar face at the receptionist's desk, but her name slipped his mind at the moment.

"Good afternoon. Is Detective Barnes in? I'm from the DA's office." Mitchell felt totally exasperated. He hoped that this did not show on his face or in his voice. However, the girl detected the sense of urgency in his manner.

"He sure is." She responded quickly, "Walk on back and I'll ring him to let him know you're coming."

Frank Barnes was reading a magazine when Mitchell walked in. "Frank, we've got problems."

"What's happened? The beer store burn down?"

"Seriously, Frank. Shit. Listen. Tony Medina called and told me that he wants to drop charges."

The policeman's eyebrows arched. "What happened?"

"I don't know. This morning he called and told me over the phone. I rushed over to his house as fast as I could. Tony simply says that he wants to drop charges -- that he does not want to testify."

"Do you believe him?"

The man thought for a moment and slowly shook his head. "Not really. But then again, I didn't want to press him very hard. I sort of let him say his piece, then I left. That's the main reason I am here right now."

"What do you want me to do?"

"I want you to talk to him. Maybe interrogate him about his reasons. I've seen you work in this area, and you're damn good. You know how to talk to them and how to make them talk to you. Would you talk to him and find out what is going on?"

Barnes knew that he could not refuse. After all, he was the chief investigator on the case. Any work needing to be done was his job.

"Sure thing. I'll do it. Did you ask if Carillo played any part in the decision?"

"Yes, I did. He said no."

Barnes rubbed his face with both hands and then exhaled. "You and I have both been around the woods long enough to know that the defendant normally has his hand in it -- either directly or indirectly.

"Yeah, I know that.

"I'll go over to his house right now. After I talk with him, I'll call you.

Mitchell was looking toward the ceiling.

"Thanks. I owe you one."

"No. You owe me a six-pack. I'll collect tomorrow. Budweiser. Bottles. Cold." Mitchell said good-bye, and walked out of the room.

On the way over, Barnes thought about what Tony had said. Regardless of what was happening, he still thought that the assistant district attorney was too personally involved in the case. But he could not figure out the reason why. If there even was a reason. As long as Barnes had been a policeman, he had seen both cops and prosecutors get too involved in their cases. Mitchell's situation was the worst he could remember.

He stopped the unmarked police car in Tony's driveway and honked the horn. No one was visible. The detective hoped that Tony was still at the house. Before he could get out of the car, Tony wheeled outside to the porch. Immediately, the detective noticed that Tony appeared upset. This, he thought, was good. He wanted the person that was soon to be interrogated somewhat rattled before the questioning began.

Tony tried to force a smile and say hello. But he had barely gotten the word out of his mouth when Police Detective Barnes cut in: "What's this shit about you wanting to drop the charges?"

The sharp voice took Tony by surprise and it made him jump. It actually scared him. The policeman did not wait for an answer.

"You ain't dropping nothing." A stiff index finger on Barnes' left hand was pointing directly in Tony's face.

Tony's face turned pale. His mouth dropped open, and his eyes began to bulge.

Barnes could see that he had struck a powerful first blow. So he continued to lay it on. "You may not want to prosecute any further, but I do. We've done too much work; and this defendant is too dangerous for me to just up and quit. I don't give a shit what you think." Barnes' body was bending over, his face barely two feet away from Tony's. As Barnes straightened up, he took a deep breath and looked around. He had not even bothered to see if anyone else was present. No one was. The hard-nosed detective decided to sit down for a few moments and let the words sink into Tony's head. For the longest time Tony stared straight ahead. He did not utter a word, nor make a movement.

Finally he spoke. "Why don't I have a say in this?"

To match Tony's tone of voice, Barnes dropped the volume a few decibels. "You normally do, but this case is special. We are dealing with one of the most dangerous individuals I have ever run across."

"He will get his reward." Tony paused a second. "He will get it in the end."

"Tony, I've been around for many years. Something is going on with you." His voice was rising again. "Something is going on with this case, and I am going to find out what it is." Barnes was standing again. And yelling. Pacing back and forth, he was enjoying his own show. But he never lost track of his main purpose. Rather than let up for a while, he decided to press the point even further.

"So, what is it?" he yelled. "I want to know what is going on with you; why you want to drop the charges. And don't give me any of that crap about you not wanting to put a hardship on your family. That may fool a fancy-pants lawyer, but I don't buy it."

Tony covered his face with his hands. Barnes could see tears rolling down the back of Tony's hands. The policeman knew the man was on the verge of breaking down. Immediately, Barnes changed his tactic. He waited a few seconds, sat close, and lowered his voice. It was a coaxing, pleasant tone. "Carillo has been in contact with you, hasn't he?" The detective placed his left hand on Tony's shoulder. "He's threatened you."

Slowly, Tony's head nodded in agreement. With his hands still covering his face, he cried, "Come back tomorrow. I am too ashamed for you to see me like this. Come back tomorrow and I'll tell you."

"No, son. We're going to have to talk about it right now. Compose yourself. Get a grip. Let me get something to wipe your face." Barnes went inside the house and returned with some tissues. Sitting back down, he handed Tony the tissues.

Tony wiped tears from his face and then looked up at the ceiling. For a long time he said nothing. Barnes, drawing upon his experience, also remained silent. The detective knew when to push and when to stop. He knew when to talk and when to keep quiet. Barnes had broken him, and he would begin to speak momentarily. It was best to let the boy speak at his own pace. If he was rushed, details sometimes were left out.

Slowly, Tony's head straightened. Looking at the policeman, "Do you blame me?" the young man asked.

"For wanting to drop charges? No, I don't."

"No one hates Carillo anymore than I do. But I believe that I have a greater duty than doing simply what I want to do. I have a responsibility to the children who live in this house."

Barnes nodded his head. Leaning towards Tony, the policeman positioned himself even closer.

Tony placed his hands on the wheels of the chair. Slowly, he began to rock the chair back and forth. "I am charged with protecting them and looking out for their safety. You're probably asking yourself: 'What does any of this have to do with the case?' I am going to tell you. About three weeks ago, a boy I had never seen, came by the house one afternoon. I was sitting out here by myself. He was about 15 years old. When he walked up I noticed that he had a weird look on his face. As he got closer, I could tell that the kid was strung out on some kind of drugs. He walked right up here on the porch and sat down. He looked at me and told me flat out that I was going to have to drop the charges. At first I didn't know what he was talking about, and told him so. Then the boy stood up and said bluntly, 'Either drop the charges against Carillo, or he is going to kill one of the kids who live here'.

"I didn't know what to say or do. I didn't know whether to believe him or not. After that, the boy turned and ran off. I was too afraid to tell anyone about it; and at the same time I didn't want to believe him. Two days later another boy shows up. He says, 'Carillo means business. He kills one of the kids if you don't drop the charges. Their names are Rose, Mercedes, and Hosea. He's watching them. He's watching you.'

"Then he runs off. They didn't ask me anything, and I never said a word to either of them. The next morning we found a dead dog next to the street with his head cut off." Tony's voice began to quiver and his body was suddenly shaking. "The kids in the house were horrified when they saw the dog. Of course they didn't know what it was all about, but I did. I believe he'll do it. Later that morning, Carillo walked up."

By now, Tony was shaking uncontrollably. Barnes could see the fear in his eyes.

"He's evil. He's the devil." Tony paused. "He said, 'That dog that I put in your yard is something that I did. But I'm going to clean it up; take the dog with me. Get rid of the evidence.' He told me that he would do the same thing to my brother and sisters, unless I dropped charges against him. When he left, he took the dog with him." Tony grabbed Barnes' arm. Gripping it hard, "He will. I know he will. You, yourself, told me how mean he is. You told me that he has killed before."

"You can't drop the charges." Barnes was quick in response. "Hear me? You and your family are going to be safe. I will put a police guard at your house if I need to."

"But what about my brother and sisters? You can't be with them all the time."

"Yes, we can. I've done it before. I can arrange to have them escorted to and from school. We'll protect them."

"You can't protect them from a madman. If he wants to hurt them, he'll find a way."

"Not if he is in jail, he won't."

Tony's face became angry. "You ... don't understand. If I drop the charges he will leave us alone. That is all he wants."

Tony was pleading. He extended both arms toward the policeman. "Don't you see?" he implored. The voice was strong. "I am willing to give up what he has done to me in order to save my family! It's not right, I know that, but I have no choice. They come before me. They are more important than me."

"Don't give in." Barnes was trying to get back in control of the situation. "I won't let you give in!" His voice was demanding.

"You don't have a choice," said Tony. "If you don't drop the charges, I won't testify. I will not testify. Without it you have no case."

The detective knew Tony was correct. He sat back in his chair, looking at the person in the wheelchair.

Tony exhaled loudly and began anew. "He was here again today. Carillo was here today."

Barnes' eyes widened. "What? He's been here today?"

"Just after Mr. Mitchell left, he came up."

Barnes' eyes quickly scanned the area as Tony continued speaking. "He's gone now, but they are watching me. I know it."

"What did he say?"

"He told me that I had until Friday to drop the charges.

"Okay. Listen. Here's what I'm going to do. I am going to call and get a uniformed officer over here ASAP. I'll stay with you until he gets here." Looking at his watch, he noticed that it was 3:30. "Your brothers and sisters will be here when?"

"3:30."

"I am going to post a bodyguard here at your house. And we'll escort them to and from school. Or, if you wish, I can put you and your family in a hotel for a while. No one will know where you'll be. Carillo will not be able to find you, and he won't be able to harm anyone. I will also go down and talk with the District Attorney today, and we will have a warrant immediately issued for Carillo's arrest. With him in jail and a police guard here at your house, you will be absolutely safe. No harm will come to any member of your family."

"No! I will not allow it. No!" He was screaming. "If the police are here he will know that I did not drop the charges ... and you can't promise me that he will be picked up."

Again, Barnes knew that the man was correct. An arrest warrant could be obtained quickly enough; but being able to locate Carillo and placing him under arrest were two different things.

Tony's body was still trembling violently, but his voice was unyielding. "I want to drop the charges. I insist on it! I will not testify, and that's it! If I hold up my end of the bargain, he'll hold up his end."

"But how in the hell do you know that?"

"I know it because, if I drop the charges, then Carillo will have no reason to bother us."

The cop peered at the crippled man sitting in front of him. Mixed feelings, thoughts, and emotions were circulating through his mind. But more than anything else, Barnes was angry --angry at everyone involved. He was angry at the actions and bravado of a common criminal, a criminal who was so arrogant in his actions, so open in his defiance of the law. He was angry with the victim. He was angry, too, at Roy Mitchell for becoming personally involved in the case.

Frank Barnes sat back and contemplated his next move. He shook his head in disgust. "Damn everybody!" He closed his eyes.

Tony's voice brought Barnes back to reality, like someone being shaken awake from a long sleep. "I'm firm in what I said. I am a grown man and can decide what is best for me and my family. There is to be no police bodyguard, nothing."

Barnes was tired. Tired and frustrated. He pulled himself out of the chair. "I cannot stop you from dropping the charges. If you want to do it, you can. But before you do, talk it over with your dad and Juanita. Ever since you started talking about dropping the charges, I haven't heard you mention them at all. They have good insight. You can trust their judgment. See what they have to say, then we can talk about what you want to do."

Tony, saying nothing, nodded his head in agreement. The detective left the Medina's house not knowing his next move. He thought about placing an unmarked police unit nearby to watch Tony's house. But if what Tony said about Carillo watching the location was true, then the police would quickly be spotted. That would be endanger everyone inside the house. Barnes was going to the courthouse. He had to talk with

Mitchell. "Damn everybody. Damn this whole thing."

At the DA's office, Mitchell got quickly to the point. "What did you find out?"

"Plenty." His tone answered the question better than the words. Dejection.

"Okay. What did he say?"

"Carillo has threatened his family."

Roy Mitchell's eyes narrowed. "How in the hell did that happen?"

Barnes massaged his temples with both of his hands. "Somehow he found out where Tony lives. He's been to see Tony and told him that unless the charges are dropped, some harm will come to Tony's brothers and sisters."

He related the remainder of the story. The Assistant District Attorney was dumbfounded beyond words. Every now and then he slapped the desk top and cursed. When the detective finished, Mitchell was quick to speak. "What is our next move? Obviously, we can't put up with this."

"What the hell are you talking about? We may have to. Tony is adamant about it. He's like cement. I mean, I really laid it on thick. Finally he broke down and told me. But afterwards he stood his ground. So, as it stands right now, we cannot move. On the way down here just now, I've thought of using every legal trick in the book. But unless Medina consents to or cooperates, we can't budge. And that seems to be the bottom line."

"Or charge him with witness tampering. And, we don't have to have his permission to raise Carillo's bail. Get an arrest warrant and pick him up. That's what I say." He picked up the telephone. While punching the numbers, Mitchell was talking out loud: "I am going to tell the Judge the entire situation and ask that the defendant's bond be raised. We can put him in jail. And I guarantee you, he won't get out to do any harm to anybody." After a moment Mitchell slammed the phone down, "Damn it, no answer."

"Hey, I have already thought about that. The only problem with that is that he might order something to be done from the jail. That sometimes happens. And with what we know about Carillo and his organization and his setup, he's more than likely to do it."

"Shitfire, man," Mitchell erupted. "We can't just sit around and do nothing. We have to move. What he 'might' do if we put him in jail can't deter us from doing the right thing. Hell, everybody that you arrest 'might' do something, but you arrest them anyway. I'm surprised at you, Frank." He sounded indignant as he glared at his friend.

"Time-out, don't get mad at me. Hell, we're on the same side."

Mitchell suddenly retreated. "Man, look, I'm sorry. I know we're on the same side. It's just that I want to do something." Sitting down in his chair, Mitchell sounded flustered. "Well, you talked to him, and I trust your judgment. What do we do now?"

""About Tony dropping charges, I asked him to talk it over with Juanita and his father. About us going ahead and getting a warrant for Carillo's arrest -- regardless if Medina knows about it or how he even feels about it -- it's touchy. Of course, I know we could charge Carillo with retaliation and about half a dozen other crimes. But with Medina's wooden Indian stance of not testifying on the original charge, I imagine his posture on any new charges would be no different. He would not testify. It seems as if he's got us over a barrel."

"Yeah, I see that. But I am talking about asking the Judge to raise the bond amount on the initial charge and placing Carillo in jail under that. There would not be any new charges; Carillo would just be picked up and held in jail because the Judge found that his current bond was insufficient."

Barnes thought for a minute before he replied, "We are not allowed to do that at the police station. But, of course, you know that I am not a lawyer. The lawyer for the police department -- you know, the legal liaison division -- tells us that unless we have some additional charges to put on someone we cannot ask to have their bond raised."

"Well, you're partially right, Frank. The law says that the only time we can ask a Judge to raise somebody's bond is if we have information that the person is about to flee and will not be present at his court appearance. It doesn't appear that we have any such information in this case."

"Why don't you call Medina and talk to him again? It might also do some good if you visited with his father or Juanita."

"Good idea." Mitchell picked up the phone. He knew the telephone number from memory.

"Hello, Tony? This is Bud."

A disjointed look came across Barnes' face. 'Bud?' He repeated it to himself. 'Bud?' Mitchell could see Barnes' eyes squint and his lips move. 'Bud'?

Mitchell continued talking. "Why don't I pick up some pizzas tonight and bring them over?" Pause ... "Yeah, we have a lot to talk about." Another pause ... Mitchell winked at his police friend. "No, I have not talked to 'that detective' today. By the way, his name is Frank Barnes." Another pause ... "Yeah, I know you didn't mean it that way. Okay. I'll be over about six. You favorite is mushroom, right? See you then."

He replaced the receiver. "Well, you heard. Pizza tonight at his house." Holding up a ceramic cup full of coffee, the prosecutor asked, "Want a cup?"

"Yeah, whiskey. Well, good luck, I guess. I hope you can accomplish something."

The aroma of pizza quickly filled the car. Mitchell was tempted to open one of the boxes and snitch a piece. And he would have done so, too, but the pizza box was too difficult to reach on the floorboard on the passenger side. As it was, his mouth watered the entire ten-minute drive from the pizza place to Tony's house.

Without knocking, he entered the front door carrying four large boxes for dinner. Standing alone in the kitchen, Juanita looked up and smiled.

"Hello, Roy." She did not mind the boxes of pizza in his hands as she gave him a hug.

"Hey, I haven't seen you in awhile. You been okay?"

"Fine. Oh, I'm so happy to see you. I really am. I wish you'd come over more often."

"Where's everybody?" He looked around seeing no one.

"Tony's in his room and the other kids are out back playing. My Dad will be here any moment."

Roy set the pizza boxes on the kitchen table. Juanita offered a glass of tea from a pitcher sitting on the cabinet. He accepted the glass and backtracked to the sofa.

"Let me tell you I appreciate you and your family letting me come over like this. It means a lot to me. You've got a great family. Don't ever lose sight of that fact."

"Oh, I won't. I know my family is special.

Just then Tony came into the living room. His siblings followed behind him. At first glance Mitchell thought Tony looked a bit piquish. Seconds later Juan arrived home from work. Mitchell was glad to be in the Medina house. He had not seen them in a while. As Juanita was setting the table, Mitchell went over to Tony and touched his back. Tony reached up and grabbed his hand. As their hands clasped, Tony would not let go. Looking into Tony's eyes, Mitchell noticed they were misty. The look sent his heart up into his throat. It was the face of someone who was beaten down; someone who'd given up hope. For an instant–a nano second-Mitchell's mind flashed back. He was a youngster, and something about this was familiar. Mitchell pushed aside the thought. "I brought you the best mushroom pizza in Big D."

Tony smiled. The senior Medina made a motion with his hands for everyone to get quiet. "Everyone listen," Juan announced. "Listen up everyone. We owe a big thanks to this man. He has been here many times, and every time he comes he brings happiness and joy to this house. His mood shifted. "And tonight," his eyes gleamed, "he brings us pizza."

Everyone laughed heartily and then attacked the pizza boxes. After the meal, everyone went into the living room. Someone grabbed the TV remote and flipped the channels until a football game appeared. The living room was full as Roy and the Medina family talked and watched whoever was playing. The next thing he knew, Juanita was shaking him awake. Hel looked around sleepily. Only Mr. Medina and Juanita were in the room.

"Roy, wake up. Wake up. Everyone's going to bed. Do you want us to make a place for you on the sofa?"

Quickly rousing himself, he stood up. "Where is everyone?" He looked at his watch. It was 9:00 and the entire house was quiet.

The elder Medina responded. "Tony just went to bed. I've been watching the game. You've had a short snooze."

"Hmmm," he rubbed his face with both hands. "Oh, Juanita, don't make me a bed. I've got to go home. My wife will soon have the FBI out looking for me. I told her that I'd just be gone for dinner."

Mitchell had not had the opportunity to speak to Tony about dropping the charges. Juan walked over to him and placed his hand on his shoulder. "I have been meaning to tell you this for a long time. Thank you for all that you have done for my son. You have gone out of your way, and I appreciate it." He paused ... "I don't know what Tony would have done if you hadn't been here all these times. You've had quite a positive impact on him. You are my friend and you are welcome here anytime. Someday I'm going to repay you. I don't know how, but I will."

As Juan Medina was talking, Mitchell got choked up and could not speak. He opened his mouth, but nothing came out. He finally nodded his head and told everyone good bye.

Chapter 18

It was a beautiful mid-fall morning. The air was cool from a slight breeze. The morning had been more hectic than normal trying to get the Medina kids up and ready for school. When Tony finally got the last one out the front door and heading to school, he filled his coffee mug and made his way to the front porch. Everyone else had left for work a couple of hours before. Since Juanita had stayed overnight, Juan dropped her off at her apartment to get ready for her workday. Tony was alone in the house. When his wheelchair came to a stop at the edge of the porch, he was already taken in by the quiet peace of the morning. There was not any activity or movement along the street. This kind of solitude in the neighborhood was enjoyable. And something about watching the day unfold always pleased Tony.

It was close to 8:00 a.m. when he noticed the white car turn the corner onto Manana Street and travel slowly towards his house. As the car pulled into the driveway, the tinted windows hid the face of the person behind the wheel. But when the driver stepped from the vehicle, there was no mistaking the cruel individual. Tony began to panic as Ulysses Carillo strode directly towards him.

"Stay right there," Tony rattled. "Don't come up here."

Carillo stopped walking, but continued his gaze upon Tony. Finally he said, "You had a visitor last night. Did you tell him the desires of your heart?"

"Don't come up here or I'll call the police.

Carillo put his hands into his blue jean pockets, rolled his head back and laughed. "You ain't going to do shit," he said, "unless I tell you to. I have a feeling they are trying to persuade you to testify. So, if you have suddenly forgotten that I mean exactly what I say, go inside your house and go back to Mercedes and Rose's room; then look out their window and see what you see."

Tony was petrified. Frozen. Fear gripped his body with such force that he could not move an inch. He could not even breathe.

"I said, 'Go look out their window.'" The tone of his voice and his facial expression were compelling. Quickly Tony wheeled and reentered the house. Moving as fast as he could to the back bedroom, he was oblivious to Carillo's whereabouts. When he reached the bedroom window he skidded to a stop. Splattered over the entire window, the ghastly sight outside made his stomach churn. There was no mistaking the blood that covered and ran down the window.

Looking past this sight, Tony felt more than queasy; he was near fainting. Lying on the ground underneath the window were two dogs; both of them were decapitated. Tony was becoming lightheaded. Dizziness, accelerating dizziness, was coming. He left the room and returned to the porch. His fright had transformed into a rage. But there was no one present. Carillo's car was gone, and so was he. Banging both armrests with his clinched fists, he voice was resolute, "I'm going to kill you. I've had enough. I swear, I'm going to kill you."

An hour and a half later, Tony was still on the porch. His anger had subsided somewhat. Unable to clean up the bloody site himself, Tony had paid a wino walking down the sidewalk to do it. The stranger, still drunk, did not seem fazed by the scene. As long as the blood was removed and animals carted off, Tony did not care what the wino thought.

When Mitchell arrived at work, he had a message waiting. It was from Tony Medina asking him to come over that afternoon. At 12:15 Mitchell walked without knocking into the Medina house. He smelled Mexican food. He had not eaten breakfast and his stomach was making noises. Tony was in the kitchen when Mitchell entered the living room. Glancing quickly at the door, he continued cooking. "I know you like it hot and spicy," Tony exclaimed. "That's the way it's going to be."

Ten minutes later, the meal was ready. Fifteen minutes after that each of them wolfed down five tacos apiece. Tony passed on the rice, but Mitchell mixed it with the refried beans. When each had packed down as much as he could, they retreated to their usual haven -- the front porch. The trees that lined the street blocked the sun's rays and cast a suitable shade.

Tony was first to mention the case. For some reason, Mitchell had hoped that the subject would not come up. "I know you're very much concerned about my decision to drop the charges. By the way," he added quickly, "that is still my decision. My mind is still made up." Tony, himself, was impressed with the grit in his voice. "I want to drop the charges today. I have talked it over with my family. They understand my situation and have left it up to me. I don't want to argue the point. So please, let's don't." He voice was inflexible.

Mitchell did not answer straightway. He was not really sure what to say.

"This morning," Tony continued, "after I left you my message, I called a lawyer friend who goes to my church and asked him about dropping charges in criminal cases. He told me that the complaining witness in any criminal case has the right to drop the charges. He said that the victim can make the decision of whether to proceed or not. So, since I am the victim, it is my choice to drop the case. Period. Today."

"We have been over this before," stated Mitchell, "and I don't want to rehash it again. You will have to sign some papers." Mitchell had resigned to the fact. "I'll draw up the paperwork and bring it out for you to sign later this afternoon after work." Having nothing more to say on the subject, Mitchell quickly got up and left.

He returned that afternoon bringing the necessary paperwork.

"This," said Mitchell, pointing to a particular paper, "is called an Affidavit of Non-Prosecution. Read it over and if that is what you wish to do, then sign it." Mitchell had already passed the point of exasperation.

Tony picked up the paper. The one page document basically said that he, the complaining witness, wanted to drop the charges and not prosecute. At the bottom of the page there was a line for the signature of the Affiant. Tony quickly signed his name.

"That does it," said Mitchell. "As soon as I get back to the courthouse and file these papers, the case will be officially dropped. But as a friend and as your lawyer, you're doing this against my advice."

"Roy, I know what I'm doing. Just tell me we can remain friends. I still want you to come over. I still want to see you. I value our relationship. Don't cut me off."

"I'll never do that. We'll be friends forever, Tony. I frequently talk to people that want to drop charges. Normally, it doesn't affect me in the least. Usually, I look at it this way: It's just one less headache for me to worry about. But in your case, well ... I felt that here was the chance to actually help you. I was finally going to be able to make a difference in someone's life who had an unlucky hand dealt to him. And I don't mean that disrespectfully. It's just that you are in that chair and......and, well, I am not. I was going to be the one through whom you could get retaliation. Retaliation against the person responsible for putting you in that chair."

He continued, "And now, I feel that I've let you down. See, in my work I represent the 'system'. And the 'system' has let you down. That's what tears me up. If there was anything that I could have done to right the wrong I was going to do it. That is what bothers me."

Tony nodded, "I understand. And it makes me feel good to know how you feel. You were trying to be 'Big Brother' to me."

Hearing that, Mitchell's head dropped.

Chapter 19

The District Attorney's Office officially dropped the charges against Carillo the day after the papers had been signed by Tony Medina.A week passed before the prosecuting attorney felt like talking to Medina. By now, Mitchell was sure that Carillo was aware that the charges had been dropped. A queasiness formed in his stomach when he thought about the sequence of events. It was repulsive. Never once in his career had he ever conceded a case because of the threats of a criminal. And this criminal had gotten away with it. It was sickening. He had even thought about investigating other avenues of prosecuting Ulysses Carillo, in the dim hopes of maybe developing another case -- a different case -- against Carillo. The ideas evaporated, but anger was still there. Mitchell could not let it go. The feeling ran over and over in his head, "I've prosecuted every type of criminal. This man– Carillo– is the most dangerous. He's the biggest threat to society I've ever seen. Or even heard about. He needs to be put out of business. And I may never get this close to him again."

Tony Medina called several times during that week, but Mitchell had refused to return the calls. Once or twice Tony called Mitchell's home. Nothing. The battle with Medina over dismissing the charge against Carillo had cut deep into the soul of the prosecuting attorney. The nasty wound had not completely healed.

One afternoon a few weeks later, Mitchell was thinking about Tony Medina and Ulysses Carillo. On an impulse, he dialed the Medina's. Tony's voice was upbeat. It brought pleasure to Roy Mitchell. When he was asked to come over and visit at the Medinas' house that afternoon, he was happy to go. It was only within the last week had he even wanted to see or talk with Tony Medina.

As he left the office a little after 4:30 p.m. that afternoon, Mitchell felt good. The previous events had upset him greatly, and the wounds were still there. Nevertheless, he was looking forward to spending some time with his friend.

Juan Medina quickly answered the knocking. Gesturing with his right hand, the elder Medina beckoned Mitchell to come in. Once inside, Mitchell first noticed that Tony's face was beaming. Such joy. And then he saw some papers clutched in his hand.

"We have missed you at this house," stated Juan. "We have all missed you. I hope nothing is wrong."

"Oh no. Nothing's wrong. I've just been swamped at work."

"Listen, I have to go to the laundromat and will be gone an hour or so. Get Tony to play some cards or something with you, and when I return, I'll cook up one of my favorite Mexican food dishes -- chili rellenos."

"You've got a deal! I haven't had any of that good food you cook in a long time. I'll be here and hungry," Mitchell said. He handed Juan a twenty dollar bill. "Get us some of your favorite beer."

"Yeah, get some beer. It's time to celebrate," Tony added.

Mitchell thought that that was a curious thing to say, but he said nothing.

As soon as his father left, Tony gushed with excitement. "Look what I've got! Look. Look at this!" He had in his right hand several pieces of paper that Mitchell could not see well enough to recognize.

When Mitchell looked at the young man seated in the wheelchair he saw one of the biggest smiles on the man's face that he could ever remember. Tony looked good. But Mitchell had not the faintest idea what made Tony so excited.

When Tony Medina began spreading the papers across the dining room table, Mitchell recognized them. Each page was laid out individually. When he had finished, there were seven court documents in front of the two men on the table.

Looking at them more closely, Mitchell instantly knew them to be legal papers relating to the criminal case involving Carillo and Tony. Tony lightly nudged him. "Here's the most important one of them all."

Mitchell looked at the piece of paper. As he picked it up, Tony laughed: "We have him! We've got him now!"

The lawyer focused on the document and immediately saw that it was a copy of the bail bond that Carillo had posted upon being arrested.

"Where did these copies come from?" he puzzled.

"I got the Judge's clerk to send them to me."

"Why?" Mitchell asked.

"Why? I'll tell you why. I wanted to get a copy of the Affidavit of Non-Prosecution. I thought I might need it later on as proof that I actually dropped the charges. Well, I didn't know exactly what to do or how to do it. So, I called your office, and you were gone. My father suggested that I call the Judge and ask him. That sounded good to me, so I did. I then called and talked to the Judge's clerk or secretary or someone like that, and told her what I wanted, and she said that she would send it to me as long as I paid for the copies. I sent her the money, and she sent me all of this." Tony waved his open hand over the papers sprawled across the table. "All I wanted was a copy of the Affidavit of Non-Prosecution, but she sent me all of this." Mitchell nodded his head, "Okay. I'm glad you have it. But what's the significance?" He was still perplexed.

"This is the significance." Picking up and shaking a copy of the bail bond, "This is the piece of paper that I did not know existed up until now; I didn't even know its importance. And now I have it. I've got a treasure." Mitchell squinted his eyes and shook his head. He was still at a loss.

Tony saw the puzzled look. "Look, Mr. Big-Time Lawyer," he said, "Look right here." His left index finger pointed to a place at the bottom of the document. "You know what that is? Do you? Look!"

Mitchell looked. "Yes, I do. It's just the address of Carillo."

"Just the address!" Tony's arms were waving in the air. "Just the address!" he mocked Mitchell. "I stumbled onto where this Mr. Carillo lives. Now, I can find him. Now I can search him out."

It suddenly hit him. Roy Mitchell felt like a freight train had just smacked him. He sensed at once the importance that Tony was giving to Carillo's address. It made him sick to his stomach. From way back in his mind came a small voice saying: Surely not. Surely he is not thinking about hunting him down. Tony broke the silence.

"Don't look so shocked. He found out where I lived, and tormented me. Now, it is my turn."

Roy Mitchell stood dumbfounded. "It's your turn to do nothing. You had your turn to do something according to the law, but you chose not to."

"I didn't have any choice on that. But what I did is over and done with. And now, I've still got to protect my family."

"Stop the car! Stop the car!" Carillo yelled.

"What the hell for?" Garza's foot eased off the accelerator.

"I said, stop the damn car. Right now." The driver complied. Garza looked over at the passenger. The car was in the middle of the road, but that did not seem to bother Carillo. The other vehicles travelling along the business street were forced to change lanes in order to avoid ramming the back of Carillo's car.

"What the fuck do you want me to stop for?" Garza had become irritated.

Without answering, Carillo quickly exited the car and ran to the side of the road. Bending over, he picked up the carcass of a dead animal. To Garza, watching it all in his rearview mirror, it looked like a dead dog. A big one at that. Holding it with both hands, Carillo -- dodging cars -- ran to the rear of his vehicle. Carillo started hollering to open the trunk.

"What the hell is going on?", Garza muttered out loud as he pushed the button that released the trunk lid.

The huge black animal, still intact, landed with a thud as Carillo slung it into the back of the car. Slamming the trunk, he hurriedly re-entered the car. As he was shutting the car door, he was laughing extremely loud.

"Let's go. This is for our friend Tony!", Carillo said, still laughing as the car barrelled down the street. "The mutt wasn't even stiff yet. Still kind of warm."

"Well, I don't get it," responded Garza. "He's already dropped the charges. Why jack with him?"

"Why not? He's a wimp. He needs to be fucked with, just to let him know I'm still around. He needs to know what can happen to him if he ever starts talking again."

"Hell, then, just do him in. Why not just kill him outright, and be done with it? Then you won't have to worry about him anymore."

"If I do that, you idiot, the fucking police will be hounding me. And they don't let up. I've got too big of a set-up here without the damn police following me around everywhere. But this way," nodding his head back towards the trunk, "I can keep my grip on his ass. I'll keep him quiet and the police off of me at the same time."

Tony thought the caller might have hung up before he could make it to the telephone.

"Hello," he puffed. He had been in the far room of the house when the telephone started ringing.

"Tony, this is your favorite friend."

The voice was immediately recognized. Tony's eyes closed tightly as his heart beat faster.

"I said this is your favorite friend. Talk to me, mother fucker! I'm just at a pay phone down the street." Tony could not breathe. Finally, after several seconds, he was able to speak.

"Why are you calling me? I've done what you wanted. Please, leave me alone."

"I'll leave you alone, if you continue to keep your mouth shut. You were smart in dropping the charges. You saved your life and your family's. But it ain't over. No, mother fucker, it ain't over. You'd better keep on keeping your trap shut. I've left you a reminder of what will happen to Hosea, Rose, Mercedes, and even Juanita -- who works at the hospital -- if you start blabbing."

Tony was still holding onto the receiver long after Carillo had hung up. He was too terrified to move! Too frightened to do anything, except stay where he was. Suddenly, his upper body began to shake. Shaking so hard that it was moving his paralyzed legs. Tony's head began to spin, and he felt nauseous. He began to stammer ... "He'll kill them ...the bastard will kill my entire family ... he means it... Oh, God, he means it... Oh, God, please don't let him kill them."

Boom!

The sound brought him back into reality. Whatever it was shook the walls. Tony wheeled as fast as he could into the next room to where the sound had come from. He stopped his wheelchair next to the window that faced the street. Looking down at the ground a few feet away, he saw it. A dead animal, a dog. At the sight of it, Tony gagged.

Mitchell handed the teenage cashier a ten-dollar bill. The smell of hamburgers and fries was coming from the red and white paper sack. It had been four days since he had been at the Medina house. It had taken all those days for him to get over the storm and disappointment. Maybe he had been too judgmental or too critical. Hopefully, he was now more in control; at least he was prepared to try. But taking the law into his own hands was obviously not the right answer. It was one answer, all right, but it was not the right answer. Or was it? Mitchell suppressed the thought.

Without bothering to knock, Mitchell walked into the house. "Tony? Anyone at home?" No response. "Tony, you here?" While standing in the dining room, he barely heard a bed squeak in one of the back bedrooms. "It's me, Bud. Are you here? Tony, it's me, Bud." He walked towards the bedroom. "I brought us some hamburgers. Where are you?"

When he approached the bedroom door, he was not at all prepared for what he saw. Lying in the rumpled bed, Tony was crying. He had been crying for some time. His face was red. His face was soaked with perspiration and tears. Tony did not even look up as Mitchell walked into the bedroom. Quickly, Mitchell moved to the bedside.

Tony mumbled, "Hosea drove me by his house, and I saw him."

After some seconds Mitchell drew a deep breath. "Don't do anything," he pleaded. "I beg you. I --"

He was cut off.

"I have to kill him. I owe it to my family -- to protect them. I'm going to kill him; he should be killed. He must be killed." The earnestness in Tony's voice was frightening. Tony was talking now as if he were talking to himself. "He was sitting outside just like nothing had ev....er happened. Oh, I'm going to do it. Even if I have to do it alone, I must kill him. My family will always be in danger with him alive."

Still looking down, Mitchell turned his back. He just stood there. Not moving. Not speaking. He really did not want to say anything. He was tired of constantly trying to fight it. He slowly walked out of the bedroom. He stopped briefly in the living room and looked around. Tony had been right, one life was ruined. The sound of the young man mumbling still echoed in Mitchell's ears as he let himself out the front door. It stayed with him as he drove away. The echoes stirred up the weighty, burdensome memories that Roy Mitchell had long since tried to forget.

Chapter 20

Tony looked at the clock. It was nearly one o'clock in the afternoon. "The postman is here early today," he said to himself, as the sound of the mailbox next to the front door clanged shut and the footsteps leaving the front porch faded. Moments later, he rolled outside. Lifting the metal cover, he reached in to retrieve the day's mail. It was not a letter he grabbed, just a piece of paper. He read the words, "Juanita worked late last night. She is pretty. I like watching her. Maybe she will like me--when we meet.

At two-thirty p.m. the following Monday, Mitchell left his office. He wanted to pay a surprise visit to Tony. Spending time with Tony Medina was as much fun for Mitchell as it was therapy for Tony.

He thought about calling the Medina household to let them know he was coming. Mitchell needed to be cheered up. Lately, he had been thinking of Toby.

As Mitchell neared the house on Manana Street, the Medinas' car backed out into the street and headed in his direction. Mitchell steered to the right to allow the car to pull alongside. Sixteen year-old Hosea was driving with Tony in the front seat. Roy did not like the arrangement. Their car eased to a stop alongside of Mitchell's. As soon as he saw the wild-eyed look on Tony's flushed face, Roy became alarmed. Mitchell rolled down his window, "Hosea, what are you doing? You don't have a driver's license."

"Uh...uh..." He quickly looked over at Tony. Hosea's eyes signaled that something was not quite right.

"I know. But don't turn me in," Hosea pleaded. "I'm a good driver, just ask Tony. He knows. He's seen me drive. Dad lets me drive sometimes. We're just going to the store. I've driven there before. Honest. Don't turn me in."

"The store?" asked Mitchell, raising his voice.

"Yeah, yeah, that's where we're going." Tony's tone was totally false. "You know I can't drive. So who else can take us if I want to buy something? Yeah, the store. How else can we get there?"

Everyone was silent for a moment. Then Tony explained that he had indeed promised Hosea that he would get some snacks if Hosea would then take Tony to run a short errand.

"Pull back into the driveway, and I'll take you." Mitchell did not know what to think about the story, but he knew he did not like the way it was unfolding. He waited for Hosea to back up and drive in first so he could pull in behind them. Mitchell got out of his car and approached Tony's side. The smell of alcohol was in the air. The passenger window was rolled down, and when Tony turned to face him, the odor was distinctly coming from Tony's breath. More than the smell of alcohol, the look in Tony's eyes disturbed Mitchell. No one in the vehicle had moved; no one was talking.

"What's going on here?" Mitchell asked everyone.

"We were going..." Tony was not allowed to finish.

"Get out of the car, all of you." Mitchell's voice was sharp.

Less than two seconds passed. "I mean right now. Everyone out." Mitchell grabbed the door handle on Tony's side and opened it. Hosea got out on the other side and ran inside the house. The wheelchair was in the back seat with a gym bag lying on top of it. Mitchell grabbed the large bag and moved it over so he could get the wheelchair. As Mitchell was helping him into the chair, Tony's eyes avoided his. Mitchell pushed him onto the front porch and then sat opposite him.

"Look at me. Where were you going?" Tony's head remained down. "Were you going over to Carillo's house?" Silence. "Were you? I think you were. Tell me, were you?" Mitchell's voice was controlled but steady. He was not going to get into another shouting match with Tony again. The last time was enough. He could not take a second one.

Tony's head was still down. "He was just going to drive me by Carillo's house," he finally said. The tone was flat. "We weren't going to stop. I don't even know if he is at home." He raised his head and focused his eyes across the street, still refusing to make eye contact with Mitchell.

Mitchell placed his hand under Tony's chin and turned his head until he was facing Mitchell. "What difference does it make, Tony? Let him be." The voice was soft. "Look at me a minute. Let the law handle it. We're closing in on him." Mitchell could not believe he had just said that. He had lied. No one had been doing anything in regard to Carillo since the case had been dismissed. For some reason those words just came out.

"I did let you handle it," Tony said dejectedly, "and I still am."

Mitchell did not like the way that sounded. No one was handling anything.

"All we've ever done is drive by his house. We've never stopped. He's not seen us."

"Well, it's not good for you. Put it in the past. Bury it." Mitchell's voice was heating up; the calm tone was now gone.

"Like he tried to bury me? Let him keep on going and living it up, despite the fact he ruined my life?" Tony's voice was rising. "Just think how many other lives he's ruining with his dope."

"You're right," Roy agreed. "We had a chance to stop him, but you're the one that dropped the charges." He did not really want to resurrect that topic again, and now he regretted mentioning it.

"You know the reason why I did that. It was to save the lives of my brothers and sisters." Tony's arm was extended and his finger pointing. "He threatened to kill them, and you know that he would have," said Tony unwaveringly. Mitchell knew that there was some truth to what he had just heard.

"Will you drive me by his house?" asked Tony.

"Certainly not."

"Why? What could it hurt?"

"Well, why do it?" questioned Roy emphatically. "What's the purpose?"

"Please. In my own strange way, it helps me," pleaded Tony, his voice beginning to falter.

"That's a bunch a crap." Mitchell's voice was biting. But the contradiction in Mitchell's mind was the fact that he wanted to help Tony. The tiny voice inside Mitchell kept repeating itself: Help Tony. Help him. Redeem yourself.

"Please," he appealed, trying to hold back his sobs. By now his breathing was loud and unnatural. "Roy, I didn't have much, and now I have even less. I hardly ever ask you for anything. Just do it, please. If I could get down on my knees and beg, I would. If I could crawl to you and ask, I would. But I can't even crawl. I'm helpless." The voice was from a man who had given up.

The request had become more than a simple one. Tony was genuinely reaching out for help. Tony was grasping, and it created even more inner turmoil for Mitchell. Conflicting thoughts, battling each other, were playing through Mitchell's mind. All the time, above it all, he could hear Tony's voice begging for help.........

"I've just got to go. Just this one time, and I'll never go again. The man took away my legs. Can't you see? I can't walk, I can barely move. You don't know what it's like to be where I am." he implored. "My life is ruined. I'm just asking you to do this one thing. Just let me see him. Don't stop the car; just drive by."

Mitchell only heard the part about not knowing what it was like to be in Tony's situation. Actually Mitchell did know what it was like. He had caused it and was forever unable to do anything about it. He could not help Toby. He could not erase the mistake. But, how he wished he could. Hundreds of times he had wished there might be some way in which he could help Toby. Somehow, some way, he had wanted to do something -- anything.

".....Roy, what more can I do? Help me! You're the only friend I've got! Help me! Please help me!" Tony begged as he pulled on Mitchell's pant leg.

"I want to help, Toby," Roy wished as he closed his eyes and put his hands over his ears. "I want to help you, Toby," he muttered aloud. He shook his head violently.

Tony was still clinging to Mitchell's pant leg and was now crying uncontrollably. Mitchell placed his hand on Tony's head; for a few moments neither spoke. Mitchell was thinking about that limp figure in Room 104.

His thoughts were interrupted.

"I've always paid Hosea to do it," whispered Tony between breaths. "If you will not do it, we'll just wait until you're gone. What more can I do? What more can I say? You're my friend."

"Toby--I mean Tony--" Mitchell stopped himself. He was confusing the names more and more. "I'll help you. I will." Mitchell could not believe his own words. Something had made him say them, and he knew instantly that it was wrong. He should not do it, but still, some force pushed him onward. "I will help you. You asked me, and I'm going to do it." Mitchell found himself nodding his head as he was talking. Something caused him to feel good. His voice got strong. He felt relieved -- somehow liberated. Mitchell could not understand his feelings, but he did not want to rein them in. He let them go; he wanted the feeling to go on. And he seemed to gather strength and momentum as he kept his mind on that track. It was as if someone had lifted tons of weight off his shoulders. "I'll do it for you, my brother. I won't leave you Toby. Not this time. I can help you this time. It may be wrong, but I'm not going to leave you again." The burden had been lifted from Roy Mitchell.

"We'll just drive by," comforted Tony. "He may not even be home."

How quickly Tony's appearance changed. There was now a sense of urgency.

"We're not stopping, Tony. We're just going to drive by one time and come home. Clear?"

"Thank you, Roy. Thank you."

Mitchell was pushing Tony down the driveway to the car when Hosea came out of the house. "Hey. Roy is going to take me. You can drive somewhere else sometime." Tony's voice sounded positive. The tears were gone.

Mitchell helped Tony into the front seat of his car. As he closed the door Tony told him not to forget the gym bag in the other car. The two-foot long blue nylon bag contained medical supplies--mostly for his colostomy. It was a constant addition wherever Tony went. Mitchell walked up to the Medina vehicle, retrieved the bag and handed it to Tony through the open passenger door.

Neither of them spoke for a few moments.

"Don't go. Turn around. Stay," Mitchell heard the small inner-voice. But then, "I owe it to Toby. It was my fault it happened," said a larger more dominating voice. "This way I can make up for it." His conscience was still fighting the battle. The inner voices were pounding away at each other. But one side was more powerful. One side was more skillful. One side was more persuasive and more vigorous. And it was THAT voice that ruled and controlled. It demanded, "Go. And help him."

But even while that side of the inner conflict was prevailing, it had not made Mitchell outwardly euphoric, but only deferring. His mind in the lead had convinced his warring body to submit. He was resigned to follow the reigning power.

"Which way?" asked Roy, sounding defeated.

But Tony did not sound defeated as he gave the directions. His jubilation would have been easily detected if only Roy had been listening for it.

"The fucking batteries are dead. Son....of....a.....Bitch," said Carillo as he tried to get the cell phone to power up. Disgusted, he threw the phone onto the concrete. It shattered all over the garage. Getting into his Cadillac, he squealed the tires backing it out into the driveway. "We're going to have fucking music, one way or the other," he muttered to no one. He opened both front doors and turned up the volume on the car's radio.

"Can you hear that?" he asked as he stuck his head out the door. "I said, can you hear that?" he shouted. The woman, sitting in a lawn chair thirty feet away, turned and nodded. She began to move her feet, arms and head simultaneously in a dancing motion. Carillo walked over and slid into a reclining lawn chair. The speakers were blaring music loud enough to be heard far down the street. Leaning back, he lit a cigarette and blew smoke rings into the afternoon air. The weather was uncharacteristically warm for the first day of December. The sun felt good. Wearing jeans, a white T-shirt and no shoes, he was steadily getting drunk.

Earlier that morning, shortly after ten, Carillo awoke and fixed a Bloody Mary. He did not disturb the woman who had slept with him the past night. He took a hot shower and left the house at eleven. He walked into his house later that afternoon and saw the big screen television playing. The girl still there. He could not think of her name or where they had met. The last thing that he remembered was being at the home of one of Garza's friends. He was having major difficulty putting together the activities of the night before. He had just finished putting some beer in the refrigerator when she walked into the kitchen. He remembered her now—Wendy something.

Minutes later, they were sunning in the front yard, listening to the music from the car's speakers. Carillo had just finished a beer when he heard a car honking. Turning his head toward the street, he saw a car coming to a slow stop. Rather than pulling into the driveway, the car stopped in the street. The bright sun momentarily blinded him. Squinting his eyes, he stood and took a couple of steps toward the street. The car had come to a full stop, but no one had gotten out. Suddenly he recognized it as Garza's car, just as Ramon hollered through the window, "Hey, listen to this." He then turned up the music and smiled.

Carillo and Wendy walked toward the car. The noise from Garza and Carillo's car radios could be heard as far as two blocks away. Wendy laughed as Garza pantomimed the words to the song. She tried to open the passenger door, but the car was sitting so low to the ground that the door hit the curb. She walked around the vehicle and into the street as Carillo went inside the house for more beer. When he came out again, Wendy was perched on the vinyl roof of Garza's car, her tanned legs dangling below. Garza, now standing outside his car, was leaning against the door. Carillo returned carrying three beers in one hand and a small leather pouch full of coke in the other.

"We're going to have a partyyyy!" he sang as he passed around the beer.

"Oh, I forgot to tell you," mentioned Garza, "Serge is supposed to be over in a few minutes. He said he wanted to buy half a kilo. You have that much?"

"Yeah." He hoped Serge would not show. Carillo considered him a dumb, hot-headed street thug. But his money was all right. Ten minutes later a powder-blue Lincoln Continental crept down the street. Garza knew it to be Serge's pimp-mobile. When it got close to Garza's Camaro, it pulled up and stopped. A short, balding man got out from behind the wheel and came towards them smiling.

Serge was looking at both Garza and Carillo, and stopped approximately fifteen feet from them both.

"My home boys, you're looking casual." Serge's gold tooth was shining as he smiled, while he had both arms outstretched and opened wide. Looking at Wendy, Serge clamored, "My, oh my. She must be costing you some nickels."

"What do you want, Serge?" Carillo asked. "I'm busy."

"Yes, it looks like you are. It... looks... like... you... are!" Serge nodded his head as he looked around. "I need to buy a half a K."

"I've got some here at the house right now. You want it. It's all packaged up and ready for sale. It'll cost 10 grand."

"I have the cash in the car, my man."

"You get the money and I'll get the stuff." He wanted to dispense with this low life as soon as he could.

The money had been counted out by the time Carillo returned. He met Garza and Serge by the curb next to Garza's Camaro.

"Is that all of the money?" quizzed Carillo.

"Is that all of the coke?" asked Serge.

"Yes," Garza intervened, "that's the money. I saw him count it out."

Seeing some movement out of the corner of his eye, Serge looked up. A car drove by slowly, gawking at the trio, but passed on down the street. Wendy, shooting the finger at the person in the passing car, remained on the car's roof.

"Cut that shit out. This here's a 'family' neighborhood," Carillo snickered. She flipped him off, too, and they both laughed.

Chapter 21

Mitchell saw the people as soon as he turned onto Barrett Street. Roy Mitchell's mind was reeling fast -- real fast. His mind was still arguing back and forth. His foot left the accelerator and touched the brake, slowing the car to a crawl. Then he saw the desperate look on Tony's face. The passenger did not have to say anything. The silent stare said it all. And it was enough. It was more than enough. Mitchell knew what he had to do.

"I'm not running away this time," gritted Mitchell to himself. He had become defiant. "I can help him this time. This time I can show him I care."

The foot returned to the accelerator. For a few moments, Roy Mitchell was at peace with himself as they traveled slowly down the street. As they neared the party of people, Mitchell cut his eyes toward the group and instantly recognized Carillo. He stopped at the stop sign. To the left and in front of them were Carillo and friends. Mitchell straightened his eyes back toward the street. He began to turn left when Tony suddenly reached over, grabbed the steering wheel, and steered into Garza's car. Although they were traveling only twenty miles per hour, the collision caved in the driver's side of Garza's vehicle. Mitchell's vehicle stopped, then stalled.

"Oh, shit!" hissed Mitchell just before the collision. Immediately after the impact, he glanced towards Tony, but something else held his attention: Tony was pointing a sawed-off shotgun in Mitchell's direction.

"Shhhh," said Tony. "Don't move. Shhhh. Don't move or I'll have to shoot you, too," he whispered to his friend. The tension was such that he could barely talk. "I want them to come close."

"Don't. Tony don't, pleaded Mitchell. "Don't Tony. Let's go. Don't." Mitchell started to grab the end of the gun barrel, but he knew enough about guns to know that jerking it could cause it to fire. Everything was happening fast and yet, all in slow motion. Either way, Mitchell knew that he could not stop it. It was all happening clearly, and yet it was all in a fog. It was a dream - a horrid nightmare - and yet....thought Mitchell.....yet, was it deserving?

The wreck did not move Garza's automobile, but it knocked Wendy onto its hood. Carillo and Garza, standing on the curb almost ten feet away, were startled but not injured from the collision. Instantly, both ran toward the cars.

Tony mumbled and nodded to himself: "Yeah, that's right, come on over here, you fucker."

For a few seconds, Mitchell had time to do something -- if he had been willing --but he was frozen stiff. He was present and conscious, but someone else was in control; someone else had taken over the situation.

Tony held the gun below the dashboard, but still pointed toward Mitchell.

"Tony, I'm going to warn them." The faint statement carried no weight or authority.

"Don't try or I'll shoot you too," came the quick reply. From the anxiousness in Tony's voice, Mitchell believed him. He remained still and silent. Only a few seconds ticked by, but to Mitchell it seemed forever. It was surreal, and yet....yet it was happening! And Mitchell was suspended somewhere in the middle. Roy Mitchell had lost all control! He knew he should get out of there -- and quickly. What Tony was doing was incomprehensible, but then that was replaced with only one thought: What could he do? The muzzle of a shotgun was less than a foot away and pointing directly at him. He froze. Mitchell could not believe what was happening. Fear throughout his entire body. Fear and terror for his own life. And inexplicable horror for what he knew was about to happen........!.

As soon as Garza and Carillo stepped into the street in front of their cars, Tony pulled himself halfway out of the window with one arm; the other arm held the shotgun, aimed directly at them both.

"Good-bye." Tony's voice was full of vindication and triumph.

The first shot hit Carillo full in the face. Wendy caught him as he was falling onto the hood. The explosion scared Garza backwards. He tripped on the curb and fell down.

The second shot obliterated what was left of Carillo's face and struck the side of Wendy's neck. They both fell to the ground. Neither moved again.

Still hanging halfway out of the window, he braced himself with his chin on the edge of the roof. He saw a figure -- Garza --running to his parked Camaro. Garza reached through the open window and grabbed his gun. The shotgun was already loaded, jacked and ready to fire. With one hand, Tony tried to steady himself and get a better position for a shot at Garza. But he had trouble balancing himself on the window ledge of the car and kept teetering.

Mitchell had been thunderstruck until the second shot jolted him back to his senses. Self-preservation and panic set in as he tried to restart his car. But it would not crank.

"Help me keep still, help me keep still," Tony was yelling as he tried to maintain his balance and brace himself for another shot.

Mitchell was ignoring the as he attempted over and over to start the engine. It finally started! Slamming it into reverse, he stomped the accelerator. He looked up just in time to see a flash from Garza's car and instantaneously heard another shotgun blast. The explosion did not come from Tony's weapon. It came from Garza firing his. Tony groaned

Mitchell crammed it into drive, and furiously turned the steering wheel, and the car screeched forward down the street. The moving force of the vehicle plopped Tony out of the window and back into the front seat. But as it did so, Tony's pants' leg caught and pulled on the door handle and the door came open.

"You idiot! You idiot!" erupted Roy. "You stupid ...."

Tony was making a wheezing, gurgling sound. He was not trying to speak; he was trying to breathe. At each gasp, bubbles of blood and saliva foamed out of his mouth. Bright red blood was pouring through his shirt. Numerous shotgun bullet holes peppered the left side of his head. His glazed eyes stared straight ahead. Mitchell slammed on his brakes, stopping the car in the middle of the street. The car had traveled less than half a block. Mitchell was staring at his friend. Suddenly Tony's head fell forward and his body slumped forward to a still position. There was no more gasping. Mitchell knew that Tony was dead.

Roy's body flinched and he was in a state of panic. He glimpsed at the rearview mirror. No one was coming.

"Shit." He shuddered. His mind was clicking a thousand frames a second. He had no idea what to do, but he knew he better do something real quick. Grabbing pieces of a newspaper that was lying on the floorboard, he shoved some of it under Tony's left leg and some of it behind his back and neck. Blood was seeping out onto Tony's clothing, and the newspaper absorbed what rolled off. The car's tires burned rubber as Mitchell floored it. The weight of Tony's body shifted and pushed open the car door. Tony was falling out. But with one hand on the steering wheel, Roy reached over with this free hand and grabbed him. Tony's body was heavy, and it was all Roy could do to just hold on for a few seconds. Roy could feel his grip slipping from Tony's arm. The car, still being driven one handed, was weaving all over the road. Roy was looking back and forth from Tony to the street. Simultaneously, he was trying to drive and prevent his friend from falling out. He was able to get a better grip on Tony just in time before the car spun around, coming to a complete stop perpendicular in the street. But as it did, the door flew open and the shotgun skidded across the pavement with the gym bag rolling behind it.

Roy leaned his head back and gave a sigh of relief. Luckily, he still had ahold of Tony. Then the pain hit him. His arm felt on fire. Immense pain on his right side. Looking at his right arm he saw blood on the upper part of his shirt. Mitchell knew then he had been shot too. During the excitement of the moment, he had not realized he had been hit. When the adrenaline began to subside, the pain took over. He could still operate the car with his left hand, but the pain was becoming too strong. Animal instinct of survival took control. He knew he had to get out of there. The door closed itself and instantly the car was gone.

"Where to now?" Mitchell mumbled over and over. What to do? 'Uhh, the pain. Oh, this hurts.' Mitchell was becoming light headed. But he had to do something. Go where? Do something. Did anyone see it happen? He was driving aimlessly down the freeway. Finally he concluded he must get to a safe place ... but where? Once there -- wherever that might be -- he could plan what to do next. The pain in his arm was tremendous. But he had to think. Thinking was the key. Realizing he was closer to the Medinas' than anyplace else, he drove straight to their home. But when he turned down Manana Street, self-preservation again took over. He decided to go on and not stop. Yet when he was in front of the Medina home, the draw like a magnet seemed to steer the car into the driveway. Mitchell was physically weak; he stumbled and staggered as he slowly made his way toward the front door. He felt himself passing out ......

His eyes would barely open. Then they would close again. Then they would open, and then close. He awakened slowly. He had no idea how long he had been out. He saw only Juan and Juanita. The pain in his arm had lessened. His first thought was of Tony. Tony? Tony .... in the car. In spite of the haze, he still knew he had to tell them what happened. But how? Beginning where? Just tell them all of it, he thought to himself.

"Tony's dead," he blurted. "He's dead. They shot him." Mitchell was more delirious than lucid. Slurring his words and speaking incoherently, he told them what happened. He passed out again. When he came to this time he had been moved to a recliner. He realized his right arm was wrapped in white bandages. He saw bloody rags and towels on the floor next to him. Amidst the blur, he thought he saw Tony lying on the sofa.

"Tony?" he mumbled. "Tony?" Looking at the lifeless body, Roy saw some bandages lying on his chest. He heard the voice of someone crying.

Everything seemed surreal. It was as if he was watching all of it on tape and he was alone in the audience. Juan Medina appeared at his side. Once more, he wanted to hear what had happened. Juanita came close just as Mitchell was beginning to tell it again. When he was finished, Juan and Juanita conversed in Spanish.

Both had absorbed the situation. Both had brought Tony into the house. Luckily, the other children had previously gone to Juan's sister blocks away. While both were in an extreme degree of shock, neither was out of control. Mitchell was gradually beginning to understand the fact that he had been shot. The sharp pain was the reminder. While he saw the bandaged arm and the bloody rags, the puzzling events were still not all in place. Juanita and her father were still speaking in Spanish when Mitchell asked what was going to happen next.

"First, we're going to get you out of here." Mr. Medina's voice was firm, and the answer somewhat numbed Mitchell. "Juanita's going to take you over to her apartment. Tony's dead, and I'm calling Detective Barnes. Before they come you need to be out of here. What has happened, has happened. We'll talk more about that later. But now, right now, our concern is for you. The police will not know you've been here. Like I say, Juanita's driving your car over to her place. When the police arrive they will tell us what they know, but we will not tell them about you. You need to go. Now."

"Help him to his car," he said, motioning to Juanita.

Mitchell did not respond. There was no will in him to resist. It was like he was letting the swift current take him wherever and whichever way it wanted. Juanita helped him out of the house and into his car. She was moving with precision-like quickness as she scouted the house and the front yard for any telltale signs of Mitchell's presence.

In the car Mitchell became faint again. Leaning his head against the car window, he was going in and out of consciousness. By now, he vaguely remembered the shooting and subsequently going to the Medinas. He knew he was weak. "I must have been shot," he murmured.

Two hours later he was awakened by the sound of the telephone. Juanita answered it and in a hushed tone began speaking in Spanish. Speaking into the cell phone, she was looking at him as he was lying on the sofa in the living room, with his bandaged shoulder exposed from underneath the covers of a blanket. He still felt sharp pangs in his right shoulder and arm. Cocking his head for a better look he was able to see torn white sheets wrapped and tied around the portion of the arm where it joined the shoulder. His arm was stinging.

"When did I get shot?" he reflected. It must have occurred when Tony got shot. One of the bullets must have hit me. Mitchell tried to replay the shooting scene in his mind. He slowed each frame down as it flashed across his mind: After he had been told to turn at the stop sign he remembered Tony telling him that Carillo's house was located where all the people were gathered at the end of the block. As their car approached the house, Tony had indicated that Carillo was out front. Mitchell recalled seeing two or three men standing on the sidewalk. He was not sure of the number. He saw a girl sitting on the roof of a car. He recognized Carillo by his long hair. He did not know the other two men, and he only got a glimpse of the girl. After Tony steered the car into the parked car, he then pulled the shotgun out of the gym bag. And moments later the gunfire started.

From where Roy had been sitting behind the steering wheel, the people that had been shot were ... Mitchell was having a difficult time remembering exactly where everyone had been standing. He was not even sure how many people were out there. Everything happened so fast. 'Everything had happened so fast' ---

Mitchell had heard that statement hundreds of times before. Invariably every eyewitness used that same expression when describing a shooting. Just now, when he had said it to himself, he realized what a true statement it was. Everything had happened so fast that he had not had time to act. What was especially upsetting was that he had not been able to take control of the situation. If he had taken control, these things would not have occurred. Maybe, maybe not, he thought. The conflict was still present. Part of him felt that he had been in control and he had done it for Tony. Or had he done it for Toby? Maybe, and that was why he had felt good when he finally gave in to Tony's pleadings.

"Damn." Mitchell shook his head trying to erase the confused and competing thoughts. He had exceedingly far more important problems at the moment. At that instant, his body jumped. "Hell," he said excitedly, "I've got to call my wife." Then he slumped back on the sofa. He had forgotten that she took the kids to Houston to visit her sister for a few days. They would be back in about a week.

Mitchell rubbed his forehead with his good arm. His head ached; so did his arm and shoulder. "Tell me about my arm," he asked Juanita.

"The police just left my father's house," she said. "That was him on the telephone. He didn't tell them about you, and from what he said, the police don't have you connected with it at all."

"About your arm, well, you know you got shot. You got hit about right here" –she indicated a place on her upper right arm. "It's the size of a small pellet, and the bullet is still in there. You are going to have to get a doctor to remove it."

"Why can't you?"

"The bullet hit your arm and lodged fairly deep in your muscle. It may be up against a nerve. If it is, the pain will be greater. I don't know. I can't dig that deep. There may be nerve damage. That's the reason you need to see a doctor. Even if there is no nerve damage, infection will soon set in."

"What did your father tell the police?"

"Only that Tony was found somewhere outside our house."

It was the fourth time that Serge had cleaned and wiped down the pistol. But he was taking no chances on any fingerprints being found. He had even held it under the water faucet and washed it with dish soap. Serge hated to get rid of the almost new .32 caliber revolver, but he had to. He had heard of how easy it was to trace bullets back to particular guns. Though he did not really understand how it was done, just knowing it could be done was enough for him.

Serge was running scared. He had not been outside his apartment since the gun battle two days earlier. He had not seen anyone or talked to anyone. He was worried that someone may have seen him; someone who knew him or had gotten just a glimpse of him, or someone that recognized his car. When he had finally made it to his vehicle amidst all of the gunfire, the gunman's car was blocking the street. The only way out was to turn around and leave the same way he had come. That, Serge worried, may have taken too much time. Someone had time to see him.

Serge could only believe that someone had been trying to kill him and Carillo, and the others. Maybe, he thought, some rival was trying to make an impression. Killing two competitors would do it. For two days he replayed in his mind what had taken place. It seemed everyone was shooting everyone. The people in the car shot first. After two shots, Garza came up from somewhere holding a shotgun. Garza fired at the shooter's car. He then turned and was facing Serge, shotgun in hand. Chaos. Not clear as to what was happening, or to whom, Serge had drawn his pistol and fired once. The bullet had struck Garza in the upper chest. Garza went down. Serge did not wait for anything else. He ran around the back of the Camaro to his own vehicle. The man, shooting from the window of the car, evidently did not see him because he never looked in that direction. Starting his car, he quickly turned it around, and left as fast as he could.

When he was finished wiping off the revolver, he placed it in a discarded McDonald's food sack. The next day he drove 15 miles out of Dallas to the Lake Ray Hubbard reservoir. He drove around to all of the accessible parks that bordered the lake. He eventually found a deserted one. He walked to the water's edge and surveyed the area one more time. Seeing no one, he side-armed the revolver as far as he could into the lake.

"End of problem," he said under his breath as he headed back to his car.

Chapter 22

"It was not a pretty crime scene. Dead people were lying everywhere. Evidence found all over the place. Drugs, money, and death -- and a lot of each." Detective Barnes was talking on the phone to the local press.

By the time Barnes arrived at the grisly crime scene most of the work had already been done. Barnes saw Victor Russell and walked in his direction. He had trained Russell when Russell first moved into the Homicide Division. That was five years ago. From what information Barnes had received over the radio, Barnes was glad that Russell had gotten the initial call.

Turning to his mentor, Russell smiled and said facetiously, "Glad you're here. Welcome to the party." Barnes, with both hands in his pockets, faced Carillo's house. Russell continued, "Big-time drug dealer meets big-time death." Frank Barnes turned towards his friend.

"Victor, somehow this ending does not surprise me," he said mater-of-factly, as he was surveying the area.

"When the units first got here, three people -- two males and one female -- had been shot and were lying next to this Camaro. Some physical evidence was located here, and some was found down in the middle of the street." Russell was pointing to an area half a block down the street that was taped off. One male and the female were already dead. The other male was taken to the hospital. We got a report from the hospital about five minutes ago that he was barely hanging on. It was evident that both dead people were shot with a shotgun, but not the wounded guy that was taken to the hospital. It looked like he got hit with some kind of small caliber handgun. But who knows, really? That may have been just a stray shell shot. Anyway, when we found out that Carillo was one of the dead men, I thought you'd like to be in on this one. I know that you had had some big dealings with him recently."

"I appreciate the invite. Yeah, I'm glad that you called me." He paused. "Tell me, Victor, how do you think it went down?"

"As usual," he sighed, "no one saw a damn thing. We've got some people who were in their homes and heard the gunfire. When they looked out, it was already over. We have a witness that lives down the street who knows Carillo. He said that he saw Carillo, the girl, and another male -- presumably the one that is wounded -- standing around the Camaro earlier this afternoon. Since a shotgun was found down the street, I'm guessing that somebody drove over and got into a shoot-out, and left. Probably the shotgun was either thrown out or fell out as they made their getaway. No one saw the shooting, but one person who lives a few blocks away remembers seeing a light-colored car racing down the street immediately after the shots. She heard the shots and then saw the car a few moments later."

"Is that the best she can do?" Barnes quizzed.

"Small car, and light colored."

"Who's the dead female?"

"Don't know yet. She didn't have any I. D. on her and none could be found in the cars or in the house. The one that was taken to the hospital has been identified as Ramon Garza, one of Carillo's men.

"Say, Lieutenant," a voice called some feet away. Turning around, Russell and Barnes saw a young officer standing by a police car with a radio microphone in his hand. "Lieutenant, that guy at the hospital just died. The hospital personnel want to know if you want them to do an autopsy?" Yes, Russell slowly nodded his head.

"What have you discovered here?" asked Frank. "Anything?"

"Some narcotics. A big package of cocaine was found around the bodies. It was on the ground. Some small packages were found in the house. We found a large haul of money –about

$10,000 -- also lying on the ground. A little marijuana in the house -- not much, though."

"Excuse me again, Lieutenant," interrupted the young patrolman. "I got a call from the 911 operator. She said that a Mr. Juan Medina called looking for you, Detective Barnes. The operator said that this Mr. Medina indicated that his son had been shot and was at their home."

Both veteran detectives looked at each other.

"Do you want the Medinas' address?" continued the patrol officer.

"No. I know it," replied Barnes. "Victor, can you come with me? I think I know what happened."

When the unmarked police car stopped in front of Juan Medina's residence, it was 6:30 p.m. An ambulance was in the driveway. Barnes noticed that there were no strange cars present. Barnes did recognize the Medina's family vehicle parked in front of the ambulance in the driveway. As soon as the policemen opened their car door, the porch light came on. Before they reached the house, Juan Medina opened the front door and walked outside.

"Mr. Barnes, Tony's dead! He's dead! He's been shot!"

Entering the house, he saw the EMS workers standing over a body. He quickly looked around the room for any signs of danger. Seeing Tony lying on the sofa, Barnes went directly to him. Immediately, Detective Russell entered and made a quick search of the house. When Russell came back into the living room, his partner was slowly rising from the body.

"He's passed," Barnes murmured. The medical attendants slowly nodded in agreement. He then looked at Juan Medina. "I'm sorry."

Medina had his head lowered as he heard the detective speak the words. Closing his eyes, the father raised both hands until they covered his face. Barnes looked at his partner.

"I'll call for back up, and PES," Russell said softly. Facing the medical personnel, I'll call the Medical Examiner, if you haven't already done so."

Juan sat down and Barnes did likewise. The quiet sobbing from the distressed father was the only sound in the otherwise silent house.

It had been months since Barnes had last seen Mr. Medina. After a few moments, Medina raised his head and wiped his eyes. Barnes saw Mr. Medina was regaining some composure. The detective was silent for a moment. Looking at the floor, he was groping for the right way to express himself. He concluded that the direct approach was the only way.

"Mr. Medina, tell me what you know."

Medina's mouth came open. He stared straight ahead. A moment passed; then he broke down again.

Russell re-entered the room and stood next to Tony's body. Visually examining the corpse, he could make out several shotgun wounds on the side of the head.

"Tell, me, Mr. Medina, if you can, what you know." Barnes broke the silence.

Medina nodded. He still had his face buried in his huge hands. "How did it happen? I wish I knew. I had just been home from work about five minutes, when I heard a car horn honk in front of the house. It honked several times. And then a sound up against the front door. Like something hitting the door. I looked outside. Didn't see any car. But ... but ... I saw ... Tony ..." his voice cracking ... "lying on the porch by the front door."

"Did you see anyone else?" Barnes asked faintly.

Medina shook his head. "I was here alone, and when I ran outside to Tony ...He had blood on him. I got him in the house, that's when I saw he had been shot. I called 911 and then I called you." He placed both of his hands together, as if praying, and raised them to his lips.

Barnes hesitated a second, then he spoke. "Mr. Medina, late this afternoon -- about the same time you found your son -- someone killed Ulysses Carillo. He was shot, too. Do you know anything about that?"

With his eyes still closed, Medina shook his head. "I have not heard anything about that, Mr. Barnes," he finally spoke.

"Do you think," pressed Barnes gingerly, "that Carillo shot Tony or Tony shot Carillo?"

"I don't know, Mr. Barnes. He was just shot when I found him. I've been at work all day, and when I got home, this happened. Tony had been home alone all day. My other children -- the little ones -- were going straight from school over to my sister's house, and I was supposed to pick them up later."

"Do you know how Tony could have gotten around? Was someone supposed to come by and take him somewhere?"

"No, not that I know of. He hadn't mentioned it."

"Have you talked to your older daughter ... Juanita? I believe that's her name."

"You say Carillo was killed?" asked Medina, ignoring the previous question. "You think ... you think ... that ... that somehow, Tony was involved?" Frowning, Juan Medina began shaking his head. "I hope it's not true, Mr. Barnes. I hope it's not true. I don't believe that Tony could hurt anyone. Much less shoot someone. I ... I ... I told him to stay away from there. But he kept going anyway."

"What do you mean?"

"Somehow Tony found out where Carillo was living, and he started getting people to drive him by the house. I don't know why he wanted to do that. But he would. They would drive by, but they would never stop. I told him that it was not good for him; that he needed to stop. But he never listened." Pause. "He needed to get on with his life. What has happened, happened. He needed to put it behind him, but he would not do it."

"Who would drive Tony over by Carillo's house?"

"I don't know. He never would tell me. They would just drive by and look. Never stop." Medina paused, and the policeman let the silence linger. Finally, Medina began again.

"Tony had changed. He was acting so different lately. I tried to talk to him, but he would not listen to me."

"How was he acting different? What would he say?"

"I don't really know. It seemed like it was eating at him." Medina was talking barely above a whisper. The lines and wrinkles on his face -- put there from years and years of backbreaking work -- seemed to be growing even larger and deeper as he spoke. "You know, him being paralyzed and all. Carillo ruined Tony's life, and Carillo was still going strong with his. Tony ... Tony seemed scared lately. I knew that he had dropped the charges and all, but still, Tony seemed edgy. You know," Medina paused. "Well, scared is the word that I'd use."

Two uniformed officers had appeared at the house as Medina had been speaking. Just as he had finished talking, the PES officer entered. Russell had been walking around the room gazing at the family photographs while listening to the father speak.

"The ME's office is here to take the body, Mr. Medina. I think we should go into another room." Barnes was rising from his seat as he was speaking. He noticed that Medina was looking down at his son. The expression on the father's face was as sad as Barnes could ever remember during his years as a policeman. Placing a hand on the father's shoulder, he led the man away. As they were walking into the kitchen, Russell eased along side of them and gently reached out and stopped them.

"Do you mind if we look around," he asked?

"What for," Barnes thought. The question took him by surprise. "There's no need to," he answered. "Is there?"

"No, no, no," interrupted Medina as he looked at the older policeman. It was perfectly all right; there was nothing to hide. Turning then to the other detective, "Go ahead. I want to help. Go on and look around."

The veteran detective felt uneasy. He did not think Russell's question was appropriate. He shot a look to his colleague.

"Nothing's wrong here." Russell tried to make the inquiry seem disarming. "I mean nothing by it. I'm just trying to get a handle on this. That's all."

Medina answered solemnly, "Detective Barnes is my friend. If y'all think it best, go ahead."

Barnes looked at Detective Russell, "Can you stay here with Mr. Medina for just a minute?" He then excused himself and left the room. When he walked into the living room again, the personnel from the Medical Examiner's Office were transporting the body out of the house. Barnes was relieved to see that they had not left any indication of having been there. From previous experiences, Barnes knew that the ME's office often left towels, bandages, and assorted medical items at the scene. Just for Juan

Medina's sake, he was pleased that the living room was not littered. Luckily, there was no blood on the sofa.

"Any particular instructions?" asked the newly arriving PES officer.

"The body was found on the porch. You might look around outside for something. From what I can gather, the body was just lying up against the front door. Let me know if you find anything.

"Nothing to fingerprint?"

"No. The victim lived here. He was already shot. There's no evidence of foul play here," motioning inside the house.

Back in the kitchen, Barnes resumed, "Mr. Medina, let me tell you what I think. And this is only a guess. I'm guessing that someone drove Tony over to Carillo's house. They got into a shoot-out. Tony and Carillo got killed as a result. Right now, my only question is who drove Tony over there? Because that person may be involved in the murder and in trouble himself -- facing murder charges."

Juan Medina shrugged his shoulders. With watery eyes he looked at the detective, "Mr. Barnes, that's all I know."

Ten minutes passed. Barnes was through, but was just politely waiting around until the PES officer finished up with the photography. Medina walked into the living room to call his sister to ask if she would bring over his children. Barnes, who had followed him, noticed that nothing was mentioned about Tony. After he hung up, he turned toward his police friend.

"I thought it best to wait and tell them in person. And I want them to be here when Juanita gets here. Now," he paused, "more sadness. I've got to call Juanita."

Like the call to his sister, Medina did not mention anything about Tony. He only told her that he needed to see her.

"They'll all be here in about thirty minutes," he breathed aloud, his head hanging low.

Looking up, he saw Russell emerging from the kitchen. The detective held up some damp pieces of cloth, as he walked from the kitchen into the living room.

"Can we have these?"

He gripped some torn blue and yellow fragments of cloth. Laying them on the coffee table in front of Barnes and Medina, he unfolded two pieces of a cloth that had been ripped. One of them had a stained red splotch on the end. Barnes' eyes widened.

"I saw these in the kitchen sink," Detective Russell announced.

Medina tried not to show any anxiety. "Sure, you can have them. What is it?"

"It looks like homemade bandages, with blood on one of them," answered the detective.

Medina kept his composure. His true feelings and emotions still came from his speech and actions: true listlessness. The rags had been used to stop Mitchell's bleeding. He had promised Roy that his name would not be mentioned. "I used them on Tony, but keep them if you want."

Barnes quickly suppressed the idea that the father may have been the one that drove Tony to Carillo's house. A remote possibility, he thought, but highly unlikely, given the character of Juan Medina. Medina's whereabouts during the time of the shooting would be easy to ascertain and verify. Medina's explanation sounded reasonable to him.

"One last question, then we'll leave before the others arrive. Is that all you know about Tony's death?" asked the senior officer.The face was tired, and the eyes watery and red. The elder Medina was sitting on the edge of the recliner, with both hands placed on his knees. He was looking straight ahead -- but nothing was in focus. The police detective next to him could hear the deep breaths coming from him. Medina closed his eyes and gritted his teeth. Barnes could see the man's jaw as it hardened. For the longest time, no one moved or spoke. Finally, he said, "Tony's dead. Tony's dead." The words were hard to say for the elder Medina. It was even more difficult for him to believe. "Please, no. No!" Opening his eyes and looking up at his police friend, he slowly answered, "I wish I did. I wish I did know something. Tony did not deserve this to happen to him."

The two detectives walked towards the door. Russell had placed the pieces of cloth in a plastic bag he had retrieved from the police vehicle.

"When can I see Tony? What do I do now?" asked the father.

The man was resigned.

"His body was taken to the county hospital. They will have to do an autopsy on the body. When they are finished they'll release the body to a funeral home. You need to decide which one is going to handle the arrangements. Let me call them right now and find out when they'll release the body."

Barnes used his cell phone and called the Medical Examiner's office.

"They said that it may be tomorrow or the next day before the autopsy will be completed. I gave them your name and phone number. They'll call you when they can release the body."

"Thank you, Mr. Barnes.

"I will keep you posted on anything that I come up with. Here's my card. You call me if you need anything."

The two policemen walked toward their cars. Victor Russell spoke first.

"There's something fishy about these rags. I found them under a bowl in the sink. The bowl was turned upside down on top of them. It looked to me like a half-ass job of trying to hide them. Like whoever did it was in some kind of a hurry or something. They look like they're homemade bandage strips," Russell paused... "And you know that this is blood."

Barnes knew that he was probably right. They drove through the neighborhood streets toward the downtown station. Detective Frank Barnes was letting the facts settle in. From some reason this case bothered him, and he did not know why. Something told him that this was not going to be a typical murder case.

Chapter 23

The sharp pain in his right arm was still present. Through the curtains in the living room, he could tell that it was daylight. Roy Mitchell looked at his watch. It was 11 a.m. He had slept soundly all night and most of that morning, although he had not really wanted to sleep that long. He pushed up from the sofa on his left elbow, and called for Juanita. No answer. As he doggedly tried to get up, pain shot down across his entire back, down his right arm to the fingers. It was staggering and pushed him back down onto the sofa. And it was only an arm wound, he thought. But he knew he needed to see a doctor. He knew all Dallas hospitals reported any gunshot wounds to the police. For that reason, he realized going to a local hospital was out of the question. He could not even take the chance of going to any hospital in the area. They might have the same policy of calling the police as those in Dallas. Then an idea hit him. He would go to Linden. It would be a tremendously long drive in his condition. And the one in Linden might have that policy, but he would have to take that chance. In any event, the hospital personnel in Linden would more likely believe his story. Mitchell was not certain what the story was going to be. He would think on it on the way to Linden. Since his wife and kids were away for a few days, at least that was working to his advantage. Moreover, nothing was pressing at work, so he could take some vacation time without raising anyone's suspicion.

He needed to call his office and saw a telephone across the room. It seemed to take forever to stand and walk the fifteen feet. The pain was excruciating. He was glad his secretary was away from her desk. She sometimes asked too many questions about things, and he didn't feel like doing much explaining, or lying, or both. He left a voice mail and was relieved that it went that smooth.

Afterward he slowly returned to the sofa and sat down. His eyes focused on the handwritten note that had been left by Juanita. She had gone to her father's house and would be back around 2:30 p.m. The Medina's home number was written on the paper. The keys to his car were lying next to the note. Thank goodness, he muttered. Thirty minutes later he was on the interstate heading east toward Linden.

The plan was quickly hatched and would work if any amount of luck at all was with him. It was not foolproof, he thought, but nothing was. He drove more than a hundred miles, and still could not come up with a better story.

During the three-hour drive he was in constant pain behind the steering wheel. Fortunately, he did not have to stop; and he was glad that someone -- he guessed Juanita -- had cleaned up the large amount of blood that had been inside the car. While on the highway to Linden, he phoned Juanita. He only told her that he would get medical attention in Linden and possibly try to get his car repaired. He told Juanita to pass this information on to her father.

As he entered the city limits of Linden, he had already decided to travel the back streets to his father's house. Slowly he drove his car towards the house. From two blocks away, he was able to clearly see into the opened garage. His breath quickened when he saw that it was empty. His father was gone, at least for the moment! He quickly drove into the driveway and into the garage. With pain shooting through his body, he was barely able to carry himself into the unlocked house. He had to gamble that no neighbors were watching. The inside of the house was quiet except for the grandfather clock ticking. No one was at home. Once inside, he went straight to the gun closet. Opening a new box of Federal-brand 12-gauge shells, he jammed a handful into his pocket; then he grabbed a 12-gauge shotgun. He closed the door behind him as he left the house, estimating that he had been inside less than three minutes. He left the house driving along the same route in which he arrived. He saw no one. Thank goodness the weather had turned damp and chilly -- the light sprinkling of rain may have kept a few people inside their houses. In less than ten minutes he parked his car at the family's secluded lake house.

Johnson Lake, four miles east of Linden, was a 250-acre lake privately owned by individual shareholders. Ordinary wood frame cabins spaced around the lake area -- some on stilts near the shoreline and others hidden back in the tree line.

It had always been called "The Cabin". Sitting beneath two mammoth hickory trees, it was just a two-room wooden shack that was used mostly for fishing and hunting. The Mitchell family had owned it for as long as Roy could remember. Roughly furnished with mismatching furniture discarded from home, it had provided a great vacation retreat for Roy Mitchell. He had spent days as a child and young boy playing around the cabin and wading barefoot in the water. He and Toby -- always together -- had protected the planet earth from many invading aliens, and held off marauding Indians in the makeshift forts built nearby. As a teenager, the lake house -- partially hidden from the others -- had been ideal as a hangout and for unchaperoned parties. He unlocked and pushed open the front door. It unleashed conflicts that Mitchell did not want to deal with. He stood in the doorway and looked inside. He almost turned and walked away to face the truth. But he lingered ... and lingered some more. And then he walked inside carrying the shotgun. The plan must go on. He must go through with it. It was ... it was, he thought ... his duty. At the moment he was not aware of any pain. He was so absorbed in his actions that his mind would not allow the pain to interfere. All he could think about was his plan; nothing else mattered at the moment.

He looked over the familiar interior of the place, which he had seen a thousand times before. It had always looked this way. Nothing had changed. But this time, he was playing out a part, thinking through a particular scene. One scene of a bigger play. That play involved murder. He only wished it was a play -- some amateurish production -- but no, it was for real. It was real.

He made sure the shotgun was empty. The he leaned the 12-gauge against the backside of the slats of a wooden chair. He moved swiftly. So far, it was still workable. With just a slight push with his left hand, the gun fell to the floor, pointed in the direction of the entryway door. He repositioned the shotgun as before. Gently, he pushed it again. And like the first time, the gun fell to the floor with the end of the barrel pointing toward the door. And again, he set the gun. And again, after tapping it, it fell towards the door. He practiced one more time, with the same result. After the fourth time, he loaded the shotgun. Positioning his body behind the chair, he got down on both knees. With both hands on the shotgun, he gradually lowered the gun in the direction of the door. When the end of the gun's barrel was about two inches from the floor, Mitchell pulled the trigger. The explosion shook the entire house as the sound reverberated off the wooden walls and ceiling and rattled the windows. The pellets from the gun blasted into the door and wall. Leaving the shotgun on the floor, he left the cabin as it then appeared and returned to his car. Luckily, there were no other cabins nearby. He breathed a little easier. So far, so good, he thought. He then drove straight to the emergency room of the Linden Municipal Hospital.

As he passed through the emergency room entrance, he made a conscious effort to put more stagger into his walk and more slump in his body. He recognized the woman at the nurses' station as a friend from high school. Mitchell relaxed a little when he realized she was probably going to be the nurse that attended him. He was not certain what was next. Seeing a familiar face somehow was more comforting. He faked the appearance of more pain than he actually felt. "I'm playing out a part. I'm playing out a part," he repeated as he approached her.

"Hello, Sandy." He lowered his voice and spoke more slowly, "I'm glad you're here." The name tag on her nurse's uniform read Sandra Wommack, R. N. Everyone called her Sandy.

"Well, hello, Roy Mitchell," she said as she looked up from a hospital chart she was studying. "I haven't seen you in a while ..." She paused, and suddenly saw that he was injured. "Oh, you're hurt, Roy!" she gasped. "Let me help you right over here, and you sit down." She eased him to a nearby chair and eased him into as he felt the pain in his shoulder recur. "What happened?"

"Hunting accident at the cabin," he hurriedly told her the story. Moments later, she assisted him to a nearby examining room, and called for the physician on duty. While waiting for the doctor, she started cutting away the white gauze bandages around his arm. He watched her as she made the cuts. "You're still giving orders just like we were back in school." She smiled but her attention was focused on washing and cleaning the wound.

The doctor arrived and Mitchell, again, was relieved that it was someone he had known all his life. By coming to the Linden Hospital, Mitchell had counted on being treated by someone he trusted. This gamble paid off when Dr. Henry Gann entered the room. Dr. Gann had been the family's doctor since Mitchell was in junior high school.

The doctor examined the wound. With his head tilted back and his eyes partially squinting the doctor tapped around and felt of the injury. "Roy, what happened to you? The nurse told me that you had gotten shot, and, sure enough, you have. Let me see here. Let me see here," he said as he peered into the wound with a hand-held magnifying glass. "How did this mess happen?"

Before he began, Mitchell thought about his make-believe answer. He had practiced it over and over and over. "It's got to work," he said to himself. "It has to. Mitchell briefly hesitated before he spoke.

"I was out at Johnson Lake. About to go hunting. You know we have a cabin out there." He began to talk as the doctor prodded further into the wound. "Anyway, I leaned the gun up against the back of a chair to turn on the lights. The gun slipped off the chair, fell to the floor, and went off. Some of the shot hit me. Luckily, I think it was just one or two pellets that penetrated. It tore up the wall pretty good." Mitchell stopped. So far, so good. "It sounds believable to me," he said to himself.

"When did it happen?" groused Dr. Gann.

"Yesterday afternoon. I thought the pellet would work its way out, but it started hurting too much. So, here I am."

"Bullshit."

Mitchell quit breathing. He was caught. The story did not sell. The doctor was about to call his bluff. But Dr. Gann only smiled as he said, "Bullets never work themselves out on their own. That only happens in John Wayne movies."

"Well, how does it look, Doc?" The breathing started again. "In a minute we're going to take some x-rays of it. We've got to find out how deep it is and where it's actually located. If it's not too deep and easily found, I can take it out right here. If not, we'll do surgery on it tomorrow. Since it is from a shotgun, I presume that it is a pellet and not an actual bullet. Is that correct?"

"Yes, it's a shotgun pellet."

The doctor continued examining the wound.

"If I can take it out right now, you want me to do that, don't you?"

Fortunately, the X-rays revealed that the small pellet was not too far embedded in the arm. Moreover, it was not touching any nerve or bone, just lodged in the meaty portion of the upper arm.

When he was told this good news, Mitchell's anxiety dropped a notch or two; at least that is how he felt as they wheeled him back into the examining room. Fifteen minutes later a steel pellet smaller than a BB fell into the surgical pan. Its removal had not been as difficult as Dr. Gann expected. The path of the shotgun blast had been easily traceable. It had entered the right arm about three inches below the top of the shoulder and traveled evenly and in a straight line, stopping in the middle of the arm. With a set of long tweezers and the help of a long needle-looking thing, the doctor retrieved the single pellet rather simply.

Prior to leaving, a young man who worked hospital administration arrived for some signatures from Mitchell. Under the category "type of Injury", someone had written, "Accidental Injury". In his mind, Mitchell replayed the afternoon's events. I got the gun out of the house undetected. The cabin scene went perfectly. The hospital scene went perfectly. Still, so far, so good.

With some reserve, Roy pulled into the driveway of his father's house. Lying to his father was going to be the hardest part. But he would perpetuate the story as rehearsed. No car in the garage. Like before, the absence of his father's car more than likely meant no one was there. Such was the case. He leaned back in the recliner again and closed his eyes. Again, he re-enacted the afternoon's events. Then he noted the things he had to do next. 'Think ... think' ... he kept repeating ... 'think'.

Think it through. The shotgun holes in his car had to be patched. Some of the blast had struck the door; and the outside mirror had been shattered. For this job, he knew instantly the person to do the body work on the vehicle–Mr. Jackson. Three miles south of town, Theodore Jackson owned and operated a car repair and body shop business. He lived in the white frame house that was situated next door to his repair shop. It was completely isolated from anything or anyone else. The woods surrounded his place, and it could not be seen from the highway. No other houses or buildings were even in close proximity. Jackson's ability in body shop work was superb. Mitchell had used him several times over the years. The body work needed to be done discreetly with as few people knowing about it as possible. People wagging their tongues about Mitchell's car being shot up was not desired. Because of their past relationship with each other and its location, Mr. Jackson's Paint and Body was ideal.

Ten minutes later, Mitchell went outside the house. He surveyed the damage to his car. Surprisingly, there was not that much damage. Six or seven shots had penetrated the door. Each hole was the size of a BB. He knew already the outside mirror on the passenger side would have to be replaced. Fortunately, there was nothing else. No damage from hitting that parked car. Since he had been moving slow, the impact had not damaged Mitchell's bumper or fender.

Jackson was closing the huge shop door just as Mitchell drove up. "Roy Mitchell. Long time."

"Yes, it has been. Probably about two or three years," he said, holding out his right hand to shake. The pain in the shoulder and arm was constant, but he masked it well. "Say, I'm glad that I caught you today. See what I have?" asked Mitchell as he pointed to the car door.

"I see. I see. What happened?"

I was at our lake house on Johnson Lake about to go out hunting. I accidently dropped the gun and it went off. And, well, you can see what it did."

Jackson looked at Mitchell intently. His eyes got big and then he nodded as he spoke. "Someone could've got shot bad!"

Do you think you can fix that by tomorrow night?"

"I don't know if I can do it by tomorrow." His eyes narrowed and he slowly shook his head from side to side. "We have one or two cars ahead of you."

Mitchell sized up the situation quickly. He pulled out a hundred dollar bill from his wallet.

"That's extra," he then said, "and it's just for you. Can you do it?"

Theodore Jackson smiled. "I gotcha. I can handle it."

"Listen," Mitchell concluded, "run me back to town, and then you can drive it back out."

The drive back to Dallas a few days later was considerably more comfortable than the drive to Linden had been. Most everything had been completed thought Mitchell. All had gone quite well and according to plan. Except the broken rearview mirror on his car. He would have to replace it in a week or two.

A little more than three hours after leaving Linden, Mitchell pulled into a McDonald's parking lot not far from his home. After eating, he found a pay phone and called the Medina's house. It had been four days since the shooting and Mitchell hoped that by now the police had considered the case closed. While the phone was ringing, he wondered what he was going to say. What could he say? What could they say to him? They knew what happened. Had they told the police? How much did the police actually know? Should he just call the police and tell them everything? In Linden he had been absorbed in other things. Little time had been left to worry about what was happening in Dallas. But now was that time.

He was just about to hang up when the familiar voice of Juanita spoke faintly, "Hello."

"Juanita. It's Roy."

"Oh, Roy, we've been worried about you." Her voice sounded concerned. Mitchell overheard her as she spoke to someone inside the house: "It's Roy! It's Roy!"

He waited a moment; then he continued. "Well, I had to leave and get some first aid. I called and told your dad. But I'm all right. Tell me the situation. I have not spoken to anyone since I left. But first, is it okay for you to talk? I mean, can you talk now?"

"Yes. Yes. I can talk." She paused.

"We...we...we are having the funeral tomorrow." She paused again. The sadness in her voice was so heavy that Mitchell could almost see it coming through the phone. "It's going to be at ten o'clock in the morning." She paused, trying not to break down. "We want you to come to the house and go with us."

"I will."

"Roy, Tony looks so natural..." her voice began to falter.

"Listen, we can talk tomorrow. It might be better if we waited until tomorrow."

"The police..." Hearing that, Mitchell tensed.

"The police," she continued, "have been here three or four times." Juanita regained some of her voice, but it was still very flat. "We have even been down to the police station and given statements to them. Lieutenant Barnes has been assigned the case."

Mitchell winced. He had known, inevitably, that someone would be assigned to the case, but he had not wanted it to be the best detective on the force.

Juanita slowly continued, "He said that because he was connected with the other case, they felt that he should be on this one too."

As if she could see Mitchell's reaction, she asked haltingly, "Is.....that good?"

"I don't know." This information caught him off guard and troubled him. "I'll -- uh, uh, --see you tomorrow morning."

Chapter 24

"Hell, I'm glad the son of a bitch is dead." The chief's voice rose with ire. Frank Barnes looked straight ahead. Rarely did the Chief of Police allow himself to make such risky statements.

"Society is better off," he pursued. "Me and you and this entire community are better off. Everyone benefits by Carillo being dead. He was evil personified." Looking toward Victor Russell, he continued, "Tell me, how many people was he suspected of killing?"

"We have information of ten separate homicides. All of them unsolved. All of them are believed to be drug-related."

Detective Barnes was hoping that this briefing session would soon be over. The chief was about to make a press release. The news media had been hounding the police department for two days. Everyone wanted to know if the event was a bona fide drug war between two rivals. Barnes felt relieved when told the police chief would field the reporter's questions.

The chief rose from his chair and leaned across his desk. He handed a bulging file to Barnes. "This is the Intelligence Division's file on Carillo. It's massive, isn't it?" he snarled. "Return it to them for me, please."

He then handed Barnes another file. This one was not as large. "And here is the file that you had on the previous incident between Carillo and Tony Medina. The bottom line seems to show it to be a simple case of retaliation. The only piece missing is the driver of the car. Right?"

"Yes, that's right." Barnes nodded as he spoke. "The family's still shook up and rightly so. After they bury the boy, we can talk again. We have to be very delicate. I sure as hell don't want to alienate them. I'm on their good side from the prior incident. I'm also waiting on the test results from the items found at their house. The funeral is tomorrow and I'll probably go over to their house afterwards."

"Just keep me informed. These press hounds are asking about an open drug war, or at least that's the impression they want to create. On your way out tell my secretary that I'll be in the press room for a while."

Lieutenants Frank Barnes and Victor Russell rose to exit.

"And thanks for the briefing," added the chief.

Barnes looked at his watch. He realized the funeral had long since been over, and he decided to go over to the Medina's house. When he approached Manana Street, he had to park two blocks away because of all the cars present. As he walked down the sidewalk toward the Medinas', the sun's rays reflected off some object that lay ahead. Whatever it was, it was shining brightly. He noticed that the reflection was coming off some vehicle parked in the street down from Medinas' house. The closer he came, the stronger and brighter was the reflection. When he was approximately fifteen feet from the car, the light was so bright that Barnes could not see anything except the brightness. It was as if someone at night was shining a large flashlight directly into his eyes. It was blinding. Holding up both hands to shield his eyes from the all-encompassing glare, and squinting, the policeman distinctly saw that the outside mirror on the passenger side of the vehicle was beaming the sun's rays toward him. He thought it highly unusual, if not eerily strange, for the glare and reflection to cast such a bright light. It was as if, he often thought afterwards, it had been purposefully done to gain detection. It was only when he stood directly next to the mirror, shielding the sun's rays, that it was not blinding. By then, his natural curiosity had peaked to a point where he was determined to find the reason for it.

He placed his hand on the metal frame that held the mirror. And observed nothing more than a typical, outside rearview mirror. With his attention glued to the mirror, he had not even noted the make or model of the car. The mirror itself was broken. It was missing some pieces, but there were still some small fragments inside. The surrounding metal frame was scratched and dented. But, so what, he thought. The brightness was coming from a broken piece of mirror. All that reflection caused by nothing more than a small piece of a mirror. He grinned to himself: "I thought I'd found King Solomon's lost gold and diamond mine." Turning, he walked toward the front porch. The penetrating and powerful glare from the sun via the mirror -- as intriguing as it had been for a couple of minutes -- was quickly forgotten. There were quite a few people standing on the lawn and on the porch. None of whom Frank Barnes recognized. The front door was open and he hesitantly peered inside. The Medinas -- the entire family, thought Barnes -- were all sitting at the kitchen table. Not thinking it proper to barge in at that particular moment, he turned and sat in one of the many gray metal chairs that decked the porch. He looked around at the people in the yard and on the porch. Barnes recognized no one. Two or three small groups of people were talking among themselves. The rest of the dozen or more people were sitting or standing alone in the yard, the driveway, and the porch. With no one attempting to converse with him, Barnes remained quiet. He looked up and down the street and tried to count the number of parked cars. His vehicle was almost out of sight, parked about a block away. Then he thought about the interesting walk up to the house and the incessant glare coming from the broken mirror. It had been like a spot light. A light that near blinded him all the way to the Medina's house. He turned his head and gazed at the vehicle. It was a fairly new car. Not more than a year old. It sort of looked familiar, but then again it didn't. His mind wandered to other mindless things. Then, as if a bolt of lightning struck him!! He remembered! The crime scene officer had collected bits and pieces of a broken mirror from the street where the gun battle had left Ulysses Carillo, Tony Medina, and the others dead. Broken glass.......from someone's shattered rearview mirror.

Barnes practically leaped from his chair. This might be it! This might be it! This might be the break we've been waiting for! He stood up on the porch and stared at the vehicle. Barnes did not want to draw attention to himself. But while he was slow to move, his brain had been ignited:

This could be the car! Hot damn! Hot damn! We need a lucky break! His thoughts were reeling. Slowly, he moved off the porch. At the base of the steps, he stopped and looked around. No one was watching him. He meandered around the front of the house and eventually came to a stop at the vehicle.

He scrutinized the mirror with the eye of a police detective. The major portion of the mirror was definitely missing, except for a few shards lying inside the metal frame. He could readily discern some type of small indentations -- possibly made by shotgun pellets. He counted four, maybe five. It did not take Barnes more than a minute to digest what he had discovered. His professional hunch was that this vehicle transported Tony Medina to Carillo's house. The driver of the vehicle was accountable for murder. But it was only a guess, and Barnes knew he needed a lot more evidence to prove this was indeed the car. His experience told him he could not get a search warrant and seize the vehicle based only on a broken mirror.

Intuitively, he placed his hand on the door handle and started to open it. But he stopped, knowing that if he found any incriminating evidence inside, without first having authorization to open it, the items he found would be suppressed. The items could not be used at trial. What Barnes was doing -- standing alongside the vehicle and inspecting it --was not considered a search. Consequently it was legal. He had a lawful right to be standing where he was standing. And with the knowledge he had about the broken mirror found at the crime scene, he could take photographs of the mirror. Photographing it would not be a search. He could not physically remove the mirror as evidence -- that would be a "seizure" and fall under the same law as obtaining a search warrant --but he could photograph it. He thought about calling the crime scene officer to photograph the mirror. But he was concerned that all the police activity would upset the Medinas and would definitely scare off the driver of the car. If the driver thought he might be a homicide suspect, any hope of seizing the vehicle in the future would be diminished. The best avenue to take was not to alarm the owner.

Barnes raised his head and nonchalantly observed the people milling about. No one was paying him any attention. He eyed the license plate and committed it to memory. Still standing next to the vehicle, he peered inside. Nothing. The car was clean. Nothing on the seats or floorboard. The outside of the car was clean as well, and Barnes could tell that it had been recently washed. He had done all he could do for now. He eased away.

He returned to his unmarked police vehicle. Radioing the dispatcher, he asked her to run the registration on the license number he had memorized. Barnes tried to recall the vague description given to the police of the vehicle that had been seen in the area immediately after the gunshots were heard. Only one account had been given to the police: a small, late model car, light in color. Barnes looked in the direction of the Medina home. He could not see the car from where he was seated, but it was a late model Nissan. A small car, light gray in color. The description was a close enough match for him.

It seemed like an eternity but the dispatcher's voice finally broke across the radio waves. When she told him the registered owner, Barnes wished she had never answered. He wished he had never asked. He wished he had never heard of Tony Medina and Ulysses Carillo. It made him sick. Lt. Frank Barnes requested that she run the license plates again. Again, the information was checked and relayed. He felt as if someone had taken a baseball bat to his stomach. The car's tags were registered to a Roy Mitchell from Dallas, Texas. Barnes could not move. Several moments passed. Somewhere, somehow, he hoped it could all be explained. For the next several minutes, Frank Barnes tried to formulate how Roy Mitchell could have been drawn into the murder scene. The most obvious and most plausible explanation was that someone other than Mitchell had driven Mitchell's car.

Several cars passed, bringing Barnes back to reality. Some people were leaving the Medina house. Barnes knew he had to go back. Earlier he had not seen Mitchell, and maybe he was not there. This would fit with the idea that Mitchell had loaned out his car; and the person who drove by Carillo's house was at the Medinas. Barnes wanted to believe this story, and that his friend had not been involved -- but yet...! He shook his head and walked for the second time up the steps and knocked on the door. An unknown woman invited him inside. The woman led him over to Juan Medina. Just then Mitchell walked into the living room from the back of the house. Barnes thought Mitchell seemed a little stiff in his movements. His gait appeared abnormal. An incriminating thought quickly filtered through Barnes' mind. Could it be that Roy had also been shot? From the many gunshots that had been fired, could Mitchell have caught a few pellets? Possibly. Really possible. The detective kept wondering and watching as Mitchell walked by and nodded to him. That, too, was strange. Why not stop and talk? It was more than strange, thought Barnes. It was telling. Mitchell kept walking, however, and went outside. Barnes finished his conversation with Juan Medina and excused himself. He eased over to a window and peeked outside.

Mitchell, alone, walked over to his car, and stopped by the broken mirror. "My plan," he thought to himself, "seems to be working. It has worked." He rubbed his hand across the paint job. "What a good job Theodore did."

Barnes had not moved from the window; he was just watching. Less than two minutes later his friend was coming back toward the house.

When he reentered, Mitchell's gaze first picked up Barnes.

Barnes spoke first. "Hello, Roy. Sorry I missed the funeral." He deliberately thrust out his hand to shake Roy's.

"Good to see you, Frank."

The detective keenly watched his friend's face as he gripped his hand and shook it harder than usual. The escalating pain shot through Mitchell's arm and shoulder and across his back. But he had been ready. His expression remained constant. Barnes followed his friend to some chairs located against one wall.

"I have been away for a few days, Frank, but the Medinas tell me that you have been over quite a bit. What gives?" Mitchell knew very well why the police had been asking questions, but he wanted to hear it firsthand from the person doing the investigating.

Barnes decided to play along. He was already convinced he had found the last link to the shooting. Maybe he was wrong. He hoped he was, but he did not think so. Before he could answer, his friend spoke again.

"I mean," said Mitchell, "I've talked a long time with the family." Lowering his voice, "It appears that Tony just could not cope with it anymore. He wanted to even the score." He was speaking barely above a whisper. "I hate to talk about it that way because he was such a good, good friend of mine, but that seems to be the driving factor. I hate it, Frank. This hurts. This entire case has hurt me. And now, it ends up this way. I keep asking where I went wrong; what I could have done differently." Mitchell threw a hand up in the air. "I don't have an answer. I don't know if anyone does. I tried, Frank, I really tried to help him. I talked to him almost like a brother. And now, this. I felt sorry for him. I feel sorry for what happened to him, and I feel sorry for the type person that, I guess, he turned into."

Barnes kept silent and did not intervene since his friend sounded as if he wanted to talk. He kept silent. But he, too, was sorrowful. But for a different person: Roy Mitchell. For as each second passed and as each word came from Mitchell's mouth, Barnes knew. He knew he had found the last piece of the puzzle.

"We had talked and talked about it," his friend continued. "I could tell it was mounting up inside of him. I had hoped talking about it was a release valve from the pressure that was building." He paused and then looked at the ceiling, "I guess not."

Mitchell wanted to talk, Barnes could see that. And he could tell his friend was speaking from the heart. He could see Roy trembling, and could hear his voice quivering.

Mitchell was quiet for a few seconds. "I just cannot believe it," he resumed. "He talked about doing it. He said he wanted to do exactly what he did. And I just let him, I guess." There was a long pause. "I tried to steer him away from it. Hell, we got into some hollering matches. But in the end, I guess it had just eaten away too much of him." There was another pause. "Say, I'm going to get some more coffee." Holding up a cup, he asked, "Want me to get you some?"

"Yeah, please."

Mitchell stood up...slowly. This did not go unnoticed by Barnes. When Mitchell returned, he sat down....slowly.

Mitchell regained his composure. "Why are you still asking questions?" He wanted to know how much information the police actually possessed.

Barnes was candid; no use lying about it. He realized that the man asking the questions was smart enough to get the answers one way or another.

"It seems practically everyone involved is dead, plus one or two are dead that were not involved. When I say involved, I'm going all the way back to the initial incident between Carillo and Tony. The motive on Tony's part is fairly clear. Everyone's better off with Ulysses Carillo dead. The chief feels that we should practically close the investigation right now. But I know -- and the chief also knows -- that there is one missing link to the chain of events. And that's this: Who drove Tony over there? That person is an accomplice to murder." Barnes was watching Roy Mitchell as he spoke, looking for a reaction. "And who knows, that person may have actually pulled the trigger." Barnes raised his eyebrows as the two men's eyes locked for a second. "After all, Tony had limited mobility. If that person pulled the trigger that killed one or more of the victims, that person is guilty of murder. But even if that person didn't actually shoot anyone, he's still guilty of murder, because he helped the person who did shoot the people. So he's guilty, either way. You know that."

Roy Mitchell was well aware. He was trying to remain stoic; keep a straight face. It nearly worked.

When he finished, the policeman shot a glance toward his friend to check his reaction. Did a faint grimace cross his friend's face? It had been quick and barely detectable. But it had been there, and Frank Barnes saw it.

"Where have you been?" asked Barnes, changing the subject, as he sipped the black coffee. "I haven't seen you around here the past three or four days. I tried to call you, and so did my partner. We wanted to let you know about..." his voice trailed off "...what happened."

"I went to Linden on the morning that Tony was shot; just to visit and see my dad and brother. I called the office yesterday, and that's how I found out about the shooting. No one at the office thought to call me. Beth and the kids are visiting her sister, so no one was at our house. I guess if I hadn't called, I still wouldn't know about it because I was planning on staying about a week."

Barnes determined that it was time to leave. "Well, I have to get back to the office." Rising from his chair, he added, "Let's go and say goodbye to the family."

"All right. I'm going to stay a while longer. I'll meet you outside. I need some fresh air."

Roy Mitchell was standing on the porch when Barnes came outside. As they walked together toward the steps, the detective broke the silence.

"Roy, give me a call if I can help you. I know you were close to Tony." He waited a second, then added, "See you around." Barnes intentionally gave him a lighthearted but semi-forceful slap on the right shoulder just before he turned away.

"Ooohhh," exhaled Mitchell. The pain reverberated throughout the entire right side of his body and then traveled to the other side. "Ooohhh, ooohhh." The pain would not stop. Barnes abruptly pushed the metal chairs aside in order to step in front and keep the man from falling. It was evident Mitchell was in pain. After about twenty seconds, it subsided, and he straightened up and caught his breath.

"What the hell happened?"

"I hurt my shoulder." His thinking accelerated: "I slipped and fell on some wet concrete in Linden. I thought at the time I had broken it, but I didn't. It's just real tender; I'm all right now. I'm not as agile as I used to be."

The detective looked at the injured shoulder. Mitchell was rubbing it lightly. The homicide detective had other thoughts as to how the shoulder got hurt.

"See you later." The policeman walked away still refusing to believe what the evidence was beginning to show.

Chapter 25

Barnes was cursing to himself. The Exxon road map of Texas, which lay unfolded on top of his desk, was at least ten years old.

"Son of a bitch!" he suddenly said aloud. "They've built entire cities and interstates since this damn thing was printed."

He had been studying the map for at least ten minutes. He had known Roy Mitchell was from somewhere in east Texas. But where, he had not known exactly. That is, until Mitchell told him the day before at the Medina's. He finally found Linden and the best route to get there. Then the good-natured detective perused the map for another five minutes.

He had not told anyone about what he had discovered. Until he had more evidence, he was not going to breathe a word to anyone. Something as volatile and explosive as this would be printed as special editions and sold as "Headlines" before the ink was dry. Even if the information was later determined to be totally unfounded, it could ruin a person. And worse still, the person involved was one of his best friends. He asked himself if someone else -- someone not as close -- should be investigating the case. He asked the question repeatedly, and he always came to the same answer: No. No other detective was more capable of doing this job. No bragging, just fact. He felt confident in his ability to remain objective. But more important to him, if his suspicions proved groundless, no one, but no one need ever know any of this.

Barnes wrapped up a few office matters unrelated to the Medina case. He then straightened his desk before leaving his office at 10 a.m. One more detail to see to. The police detective left word with the chief's secretary that he was taking a few days vacation.

That morning, before looking at the map, the homicide detective called his Report Division and obtained all the hospital and clinic reports in the area of all shooting victims treated on the days immediately after Medina's death. After pouring over the numerous quasi medical/police reports, he determined that none of the gunshot victims even remotely matched Mitchell's physical description. He was playing a hunch -- actually it was nothing more than a flat-out guess -- that Mitchell may have traveled to Linden to obtain medical attention in the far-reaching event that he had even been injured at all by a gunshot.

It was early afternoon and a warmer than usual December day when Barnes checked into the locally-owned and -operated Tall Pines Motel in Linden. He got a quick bite to eat from the adjoining restaurant and then settled into his motel room drinking coffee and looking in the telephone directory for any kind of medical treatment facility. There were only two: the Linden Municipal Hospital located at 405 Hiram Street, and the Linden Medical Clinic at 403 Hiram Street. Well, it won't take long to checkout both places, he thought. "Hiram Street," he said aloud, "now where in the hell can that be?" At the front desk, he asked directions to the hospital. Less than five minutes later he pulled into the hospital parking lot.

A woman was sitting at a desk just inside the front door. She was wearing a special kind of red jacket that indicated to Barnes she was a volunteer helper.

"May I help you?"

"Yes ma'am. I'm looking for the hospital administrator."

"Go right through that door and his secretary will help you."

"Thank you. Could you also tell me his name?"

"Surely, it's Gilbert Perkins."

He pushed open the glass door, and walked over to a younger woman with short-cropped hair sitting behind a large desk, typing.

"Miss, hello."

She had not seen him approach. His voice startled her and she jumped slightly.

"Oh," she laughed, "you scared me. I didn't hear you come in. Can I help you?" She looked up at him and smiled.

"My name is Frank Barnes, and I work for the Dallas Police Department. Could I see Mr. Perkins?"

The woman's smile vanished, and her eyes grew large. "Oh, gosh," she slipped. "Yes sir. Just have a seat and I'll tell him you're here."

Barnes took a seat in one of the three nearby chairs. The secretary scurried to an office in the back portion of the area. He grinned slightly, knowing that unexpected visits from the police usually shook people up.

Moments later the woman returned with a well-dressed, long striding man in his fifties right on her heels.

"Sir, I'm Gilbert Perkins," as he extended his hand to shake. "Come this way to my office."

The friendly-looking administrator ushered Barnes into a very spacious and paneled office and politely offered him a chair. He closed the door behind him.

"My secretary informs me that you are with the police department in Dallas."

"Yes sir. My name is Frank Barnes. I am a detective in the Homicide Division." He handed the administrator his business card and simultaneously showed him his badge. Barnes allowed the administrator a few moments to study and take it all in.

"Mr. Perkins, I am investigating a homicide that took place in Dallas last week. I am here in Linden looking into a very delicate matter. It's a touchy situation because one of the suspects is from Linden and a very high-ranking and highly respected prosecutor in the District Attorney's office in Dallas. I'm talking about Roy Mitchell."

The hospital administrator looked both disturbed and perplexed. He took off his glasses and laid them on his desk in front of him.

"Well, I've known Roy Mitchell all of his life." A troubled expression appeared on his face. "I'll help you, though, any way that I can. What can you tell me about the matter?"

Without delving into all of the details, the policeman related some of the facts. Mr. Perkins sat quietly, nodding occasionally, and was still visibly troubled.

"I have reason to believe," explained Barnes, "that Roy was shot during the episode. I am here to find out if he came here to be treated for injuries. Here's a subpoena for the records if they exist." Barnes handed the administrator the subpoena and allowed Perkins a few moments to process the papers.

"Excuse me for a few minutes and let me pull his charts and the emergency room logs." The hospital official put his glasses back on and rubbed his forehead with one hand. "It might take me a few moments to put my finger on it since it was so recent." The man looked down at his desk top and thought for a few seconds. During the silence, Barnes could tell that the person in front of him was thinking about something else. Finally the administrator stood and looked at Barnes. "Can you tell me again the dates that you're talking about so I can pull the correct logs? This is such a small hospital and I know Roy so well that I should have heard something about it." The man scratched the back of his head and then explained as if answering a question. "But I've been out of the office for a few days.... In any event, excuse me and let me get these records."

After writing down the needed dates, Mr. Perkins left his office.

In less than ten minutes, Gilbert Perkins returned to his office with a handful of papers. His face, once reddened, was now drained white.

"He was here! You were right, detective, he was here! He was here during that time, and he was treated for...a..a...a gunshot wound," he stammered nervously, as he handed the papers to the officer.

The homicide detective was deflated. He had propped himself up on the much too soft motel bed and was thinking over what he knew. The facts were shattering. The hospital official made copies of all of Mitchell's medical reports generated from the shooting injury and given them to him. The subpoena protected the hospital and hospital employees from being sued for revealing privileged patient information. Barnes had not spoken to any of the attending medical personnel, but had secured their names to be interviewed later. He stretched out over the bed with medical reports strewn all over. After glancing at all of them, Barnes laid his tired, aching head on a pillow. It was not long before he was asleep.

Someone sweeping directly outside his motel door awakened the sound sleeper. Lifting his head, Barnes looked at the radio/clock on the nightstand. He had slept an hour. He laid in bed trying to remember what he had planned to do next. Hearing a car's engine start up in the parking lot jogged his memory. As he sat up on the edge of the bed, he reached for the telephone directory again. Finding what he wanted, he made a few notations on a note pad. Once again at the front desk the same person as before supplied some directions and the detective was off. The first place he stopped produced nothing. Likewise, neither did the second, nor the third. The businesses could not supply the information he was seeking. Barnes had exhausted the places he had jotted down earlier. Pulling out of the last parking lot, he decided to ride around town before returning to the motel. As he was driving the streets, he noticed a place on the corner. Hey, he thought, I haven't thought about this. It's worth checking out. The three previous stops had been at automobile repair shops. While everyone at those places knew Roy Mitchell, no one had seen him lately.

The big-shouldered man behind the clean counter of East Texas Automotive Parts looked to be over seventy years of age and had on a pair of new Oshkosh overalls. He probably knows -- by memory -- every car part ever made, thought Barnes, amused.

The detective smiled and extended his right hand. "Good afternoon, sir. I don't need to buy anything today. But I'm trying to find someone. I am looking for Roy Mitchell. Do you know him?"

"Know him? I know his whole family."

"Have you seen him today?"

"No, I haven't. I haven't seen him since..." the nice man closed one eye and cocked his head upward, "...since around the opening of dove hunting season. That's been a while back, hasn't it?" The man grinned and chuckled.

"He was supposed to pick up a rearview mirror. He said he was going to do it two or three days ago."

"Well, he hasn't been in here for quite some time." The man continued, "I don't keep foreign parts in stock, but I can sure order you one."

"Well, no thanks. Roy may have already picked one up."

The policeman was turning to go out the door when the gray-haired man added, "That must be a hot item. Someone else was in here the other day asking for one."

He froze in his tracks. Careful to maintain a conversational tone he asked, "Is that a fact? Did you have one?"

"No. But I told him that I could order him one, too."

"Who was it?"

"Theodore Jackson."

"What does he do?"

"He works for his dad. They run a garage and body shop south of town."

Barnes was having to work to control his anxiety. How lucky could he get? After getting directions to the Jackson garage, he left.

The directions were right on target. When the policeman stopped his car, he saw a black man about his own age peer out from behind a raised car hood. Barnes, wearing a white shirt, tie, and sport coat felt somewhat out of place in the wooded surroundings and white sandy roads. They exchanged greetings. Barnes then identified himself as a policeman. "Sir, I received some information that two or three days ago you were trying to buy a rearview mirror. I was up in town at the automotive store." Barnes paused to let that information soak in.

"Yes sir, I was." Barnes could tell immediately that he wasn't going to have any trouble getting this person's cooperation.

The man continued, "I was trying to buy one for a customer of mine. I was doing some work on his car."

"That was Roy Mitchell!" The policeman smiled, hoping to put the man more at ease, but Mr. Jackson hesitated.

Theodore Jackson, Jr. got silent.

"You are not in any trouble. You aren't in any trouble."

"I know I'm not. But is he?"

"What kind of work did you do on his car?" asked the detective.

"He wanted me to do some body work on his car; to patch some holes."

"Did you do it?"

"Yes sir."

"What part of his car had the holes in it?"

"There were about six or seven small holes around his outside mirror. I bonded them."

The detective sighed deeply and lowered his head. The veteran cop now realized he had uncovered the evidence he had hoped he would not find. For a second, he thought about dropping the matter. Dropping it and keeping quiet forevermore. He recalled for some reason, his chief standing in his office proclaiming how society was better off with Carillo dead. Let society be better off, he thought. Don't destroy a good man who helped better the streets. A man who's given his entire career to ridding the public of criminals. Turn your head, leave right now, and walk away from doing this to Roy Mitchell. He wanted to leave, but he couldn't. After several seconds, Barnes rubbed his face and looked again at the mechanic. "What about the mirror?" he asked.

Mr. Jackson seemed to sense that something unusual was happening. He cleared his throat and continued slowly. "Roy wanted me...uh..he wanted me to...uh...to find a new or used mirror to...uh...uh...replace the one on his ...car. I...uh..." He cleared his throat again. "I...uh...asked around and tried to find one, but...but...I...I wasn't able to find one. He said he could order one in Dallas."

"Did he ever say what happened to his car?"

"No." Barnes had gotten all the information that he needed for the time being. Before leaving, he asked one last question.

"They were from a shotgun blast, weren't they? The holes in the car."

Jackson did not readily answer. Finally, he slowly nodded his head.

The next day, by the time Detective Frank Barnes had finished taking the last affidavit, it was nearly noon.

He was despondent and very depressed. He had not slept well the night before. It was only now that Frank Barnes began to second guess his earlier decision to be the investigator on this case. He had not really wanted to uncover what he had found. Somewhere, somehow, someway, he was hoping to prove his friend innocent. But instead, what came to light, was evidence of guilt. It lay bare evidence of direct involvement and participation, and then of an attempted cover-up. It completely dashed his hopes. And what unnerved him most were the feelings the day before when talking to Mr. Jackson. The chilling notion to walk away from it, keep quiet, and leave it alone. That caused him great unrest.

To seriously entertain such an idea scared him. Maybe he could not be objective. Maybe the friendship was too deep and too strong. But the facts were there and they could not be disputed. He thought of the blinding reflection from Roy's car. That incident had started it; started the wheels in motion that his friend Roy Mitchell was the one they were looking for. After that discovery on the sidewalk in front of the Medina's house, Barnes knew then -- as well as he knew now -- that he had a job to do. Barnes had uncovered everything he had hoped he would not find and learned something frightening about himself in the process.

With his business wrapped up, he checked out of the motel and walked across the parking lot to the nearby restaurant. As he waited for his meal, he wondered if there were any other places or things to follow up. Mr. Gilbert Perkins, the hospital administrator, had informed him of one thing, and he intended to look into just before he left town.

The investigating officer wrinkled his nose at the strong odor of disinfectant as soon as he walked into the brick building. A cork bulletin board four feet long, displaying notices of upcoming events and pertinent information, adorned a wall in the lobby. Numerous live plants -- some as tall as five feet -- decorated the entire place. A large screen television set, tuned to "The Edge of Night", was playing in the corner. Three residents sitting in wheelchairs were watching it but quickly turned toward Barnes as he entered the convalescent home. He smiled at them and said hello. Two ladies smiled back and the gentleman raised his hand and waved. He timidly walked up to a standard-size office desk designated "Information Desk" and lightly shook a hand-held choir bell. A middle-aged, fairly attractive attendant appeared and asked if she could help.

"Maybe so," he said softly. "I am a friend of Roy Mitchell. I'm from Dallas. I...uh...I understand that Roy's brother is here." Barnes felt a shade uncomfortable.

"Yes, he's here. He lives here." She answered quickly and matter-of-factly.

"Does he have visitors? May I see him?"

"Yes to both questions." Her voice -- deeper than most females -- had a rich quality to it. "But do you know anything about his condition?"

"Not really. I have just heard Roy talk about him." His voice and demeanor was picking up confidence. Strangely, this unknown nurse was making him feel more at ease. "That is...uh...that he has a brother and that he was involved in an accident of some kind may years ago. That's all I really know. Since I was in Linden I thought I'd come to see him. So I could tell Roy that I, you know, checked on him."

Her relaxing countenance rendered soft her words. "Maybe I should tell you then, sir, that Toby -- that's his name -- is comatose. He has been this way for about twenty-five years." Her pleasant demeanor remained as she went on, "He breathes on his own, but that's all. I had just started working here when they first brought him here. He and I arrived here the same week."

"Can I go see him?"

"Sure. This way."

The nurse led him to Room 104. The door was open, but she knocked before entering.

"It's a habit," she said, smiling.

They walked into Toby's entire world. Barnes was amazed at the person in the bed. He looked a lot like Roy, only smaller, sort of half-boy, half-man. He was clean, well groomed and looked healthy.

"Can he hear?"

The nurse shrugged her shoulders. "No one can tell. We talk to him as if he can. However, it may be only for our own benefit. Our therapy, if you know what I mean."

"I understand."

"He does get restless, believe it or not. He tosses and turns -- though not to a high degree -

- whenever we take his wristwatch off of his arm. See here?"

The nurse picked up his left hand to display a child's watch. She continued, "He had just been given this watch the day before the accident happened. I believe Roy had given it to him. If I have my story straight, Roy had won it somewhere. Anyway, soon after Toby's condition stabilized, Roy put the watch on his arm. It's been with him ever since. Stopped working long time ago. If we take it off though, he becomes, like I say, restless."

Barnes looked dolefully at the nurse. "What about doctor's evaluations? Surely, he's been examined..."

"By the best doctors in the country," interrupted the woman, "but they all say the same thing. They can't figure it out." Five or six seconds quietly passed. "So his dad comes here all the time, fixes his room up." She pointed and continued, Look, we even turn the radio and television on." Turning both off, she then straightened the covers on the bed. "Like I said earlier, it's probably just for our benefit. But we love him and try to maintain some normalcy when we are with him."

They both stood at the foot of the bed, staring down at the figure. Neither spoke for a while. The only noise was the rushing sound of the air being blown through the central heating unit. Her voice broke the silence: "I remember him before the accident. The two boys, Roy and Toby, were inseparable. Good kids. Real boys, if you know what I mean. I don't think Roy has ever gotten over it. Part of Roy is lying in that bed."

Chapter 26

Big Alan Parker, Chief of the Dallas Police Department, usually did not get to the office until around nine. Detective Barnes wanted to speak to him as quickly as possible. He asked the chief's secretary to notify him as soon as the chief arrived. Some critical information had to be relayed to him as soon as possible.

At nine-twenty his phone rang. It was the secretary advising that Parker was in his office. Barnes was not looking forward to this session. In fact, he was dreading it. It was making him sick thinking about detailing the information he had obtained over the last two days.

Parker was watering his ivy plant when the lieutenant walked in. Barnes was not even sure Parker knew he was present.

"Good morning, Chief."

Chief Parker continued with his weekly task as he spoke: "Well," boomed the voice, "I understand that you took a few days off, Frank. Go to the beach?" The chief talked too loud.

Barnes' voice was subdued. "No. I went to a small town in east Texas called Linden."

Parker's back was still facing the detective. "You did?" It boomed again. "I've heard of it."

"Chief, I have some bad news. It's...it's..." Barnes paused.

Chief Parker sensed the atmosphere was heavy. He turned and held up a hand signaling Barnes to wait. Closing the door, he stepped to his desk. He nodded his head when he was ready for Barnes to continue.

"I was in Linden investigating Roy Mitchell for murder."

For the next hour Chief Alan Parker was taken from start to finish.

Recounting the sordid events was not easy for Frank Barnes. He was investigating one of his closest friends for murder, and he had not even so much as whispered a word of it until now. The circumstances concerning Tony Medina and Ulysses Carillo were explained easily enough; the chief was already vaguely familiar with them. The briefing continued, and Barnes particularized how the faint suspicions of Roy Mitchell materialized into fact. Barnes' earlier disbelief during his investigation had become a resigned conviction.

Barnes had no earthly idea what effect this news would have on his superior; he only knew what effect it had had on him.

Chief Parker -- as big as a sequoia, and always too loud-- sat quietly with his arms folded tightly across his paunch. He felt as if he had been bulldozed. Every now and then he let out a low series of dismayed grunts. Of course, he knew Roy Mitchell. When Parker had been rising through the ranks of the force, he had tried a few cases, though not many, with the younger prosecutor. Most of them had been run-of-the-mill criminal cases. By the time Mitchell had reached near legendary status in the District Attorney's Office, Parker had moved into administration. He liked and trusted the easygoing prosecutor, as did everyone. Moreover, they were also friends on a first name basis.

When the deflated Barnes finally left the paneled office, the big man told him to leave the file. The domineering, bespectacled police chief wanted to study it some more. He also instructed the investigating officer that this case was top priority. Lt. Barnes was to suspend work on all other cases and to confide only with him. And he wanted regular updates.

Forty-five minutes later the detective was paged by the chief's secretary and the case file was returned. At the same time, Barnes was notified that at one p.m., he and the chief were to have a meeting with the District Attorney, and to rendezvous with Parker at his office at twelve-thirty p.m. sharp. They would ride together to the courthouse.

Barnes walked briskly away from the girl's desk. "Shit's about to hit the fan," he sadly mumbled to himself.

He spent the rest of the morning drawing up the search warrants he needed. One for Roy's car. Based on the information acquired from his trip to Linden, he had enough evidence to procure a warrant to confiscate and search the late model vehicle as evidence.

A separate warrant covered Mitchell's house. Because the physician recovered a single projectile from the body of Ramon Garza, the police -- in this case, Barnes -- were still looking for the unaccounted handgun. Crime Lab personnel had subsequently informed the Homicide Division the bullet was from a .32 caliber handgun, but the Physical Evidence Section had not recovered any pistols from the initial inspection of the crime scene. After receiving the single bullet from the attending physicians, PES had readily returned to the scene of the shootings two more times. They could not find a pistol anywhere. Actually, Barnes did not believe they would find the handgun at Mitchell's house. Nevertheless, he had to do his job and cover all the bases. And, of course, part of his job entailed searching for and collecting any evidence of a crime.

It took Barnes about an hour to draw up both warrants. He laid both warrants on his desk in front of him. Again he deliberated about removing himself from the case. Ever since he returned from Linden, the thought was on his mind. And even now, it would be difficult executing these blasted warrants. Roy's wife and kids might be at home. How could he face her in this process? He did not know if he could do his job. On the other hand, he probably should do it since it might be less sterile or painful for Mitchell's family coming from someone they knew.

Frank Barnes could not eat lunch; he had no appetite. Instead, he drove to a nearby city park, sat on a park bench, and focused on the dreaded upcoming meeting. He -- and not the chief -- was going to present the facts to the DA. Thankfully, Parker had informed him in advance. The chief was just going along because he wanted firsthand input and the DA's response. A case of this magnitude dictated highest-level involvement.

"Good afternoon," smiled Barnes. "We have an appointment with Mr. Buchanan. "We're from the police department. I'm Detective Barnes, and this is Chief Parker."

About halfway down the hallway to the DA's office, Bragg Buchanan emerged from his office.

"Hello, Chief," voiced Buchanan. "How are you?" They shook hands vigorously.

"I'm fine, Bragg. This is Frank Barnes, Bragg. He's from our Homicide Division."

The meticulously dressed District Attorney extended his right hand. "I've heard a lot about you over the years. You're one of the best we've got," Buchanan commented, shaking Barnes' hand. "Come on in." His baritone voice resounded off the painted walls.

Chief Parker looked at the District Attorney, a friend for almost 30 years. "You're looking good, Bragg. You must be enjoying yourself."

The cigar-chomping DA laughed --his whole body shaking with laughter --"I play as much golf as the law will allow."

They proceeded into the room. The elected DA's office was not as large and palatial as Barnes had anticipated. Three light-gray walls were adorned with autographed photos. A few were politicians, but most were sports figures. Some current, some from yesteryear. Against the fourth wall a bookcase standing seven feet tall stretched the entire length of the office over fifteen feet. Neatly arranged on the six shelves were probably a hundred knick-knacks, trinkets, joke gifts, and mementoes that a politician gathers over the course of 25 years in public office. On the wooden credenza behind him and also on his desk were framed pictures of children and young adults. Presumably, the man's children and grandchildren. The room was somewhat dark because the overhead fluorescent office light was turned off. Three lamps, two freestanding and one desk lamp, provided the lighting. It created a powerful atmosphere.

The DA closed the door and motioned them to the soft-backed, cloth armchairs directly in front of his desk. He edged around his desk. "Hell, boys, it must be something big for the chief of police to make a personal call."

Barnes only sighed to himself: "Big, huh? Just wait." The job of having to tell Mr. Bragg Buchanan the news of a murderous assistant district attorney was not going to be easy or pleasant, to say the least.

Twenty minutes later, when Frank Barnes finished talking, the shining patriarch of all the district attorneys across the country rubbed his cheeks with both hands. Throughout Barnes' detailed recitation of the facts, Buchanan had not spoken a word. Most of the time, he had been sitting with his elbows propped on the top of his desk. Every now and then he had taken his unlit cigar out of his mouth, looked at the chewed end, and returned it to one side of his mouth. He nodded occasionally and made one or two short written notations. But that was all. Otherwise, he sat motionless and listened. "That's it," concluded Barnes. After Barnes' last word, the room was silent.

Finally, Buchanan said, "Well shit! .... When I popped off earlier about it being big, you guys weren't fooling." For the next few minutes, the lieutenant fielded questions and comments from Buchanan about the case. Infrequently, Chief Parker asked a question or two. Barnes was astounded at the District Attorney's quick grasp of the case. Buchanan was questioning them as if it was an unknown typical lawbreaker instead of his close, personal friend and decorated prosecutor, Roy Mitchell. Not a hint of disbelief or wonderment rang in Buchanan's voice. Not even a simple "I can't believe it" or "It's a shame." Surely, reasoned Barnes, this would rattle the career prosecutor. But if it did, it was hidden from Frank Barnes. What a man to play poker with. Neither his voice nor mannerisms gave away his inner thinking. That was, to a degree, shuddering.

Buchanan rolled his high-backed leather chair away from his desk. He was in no rush. Leaning back and looking at the ceiling, he chomped on his cigar. Still staring above, he finally drawled, "We don't have many decisions to make." He paused... "Unfortunately." He paused... "I'll have to let him go.......or I could just suspend him until it's over." He looked at the men across his desk. Buchanan was unequivocal, "You fellows have no choice whatsoever. You have a case and you have to file it. We'll have to bring in a special prosecutor and that's the way it should be. Ethically, our office cannot do it."

Again, Barnes was aghast at the dicing way Buchanan spoke with no emotional attachment. This did not sound like the compassionate, fair-minded person that Barnes had heard was a sentimentalist. He was beginning to think the District Attorney was bordering on being ruthless, until he saw a glimmer of concern come over him.

Straightening himself in his chair Buchanan suddenly grimaced and uncharacteristically pounded his large meaty fist on the top of his desk. "Damn, how did this happen to him? How could it happen?" His voice now seeking answers -- became emotional. Buchanan let down his guard and was now floundering. "How can someone like Roy get involved in crap like that? Why didn't he come to me? What got into him?" Buchanan's eyes locked in on Barnes. Buchanan was devastated. Entirely empty and sick to his stomach. His mind kept conjuring up the image of Roy Mitchell's smiling face. "How? What? When?" Buchanan groaned out loud. "What came over him?" Buchanan's rueful expression was felt by everyone.

"I think I know," the investigating officer said solemnly. He then, professionally, ticked off the salient points involving the person that lay in Room 104. With emotions held at bay, Barnes heard himself supplying the motive to damn a decent man. When he had finished, Barnes' voice was barely audible. The whispering of his words unintentionally elevated the tense atmosphere already in the room. The air hung thick and still.

Chief Parker opened his mouth to say something, but his lieutenant spoke first. "We have two search warrants that need to executed. One is for his car that I told you about. The other is for his house. Both have already been signed by a magistrate. We're looking for that missing pistol."

"Do you all have an arrest warrant?" the somber Buchanan asked.

"Yes sir." Barnes reached into his suit coat's inner pocket and extracted some folded pieces of paper. "We have three. Three warrants pertaining to the three dead people: Carillo, Garza, and the girl." The homicide detective held out the search warrants and the arrest warrants.

"I don't need them," said the DA. "I just wondered if you needed some time to get them."

Frowning, Chief Parker bent forward and reached for them. "Let me have the ones for his arrest. You can hang on to the other ones. When do you want to search the car and house?"

Barnes exhaled, "I guess the sooner the better. After he's placed under arrest, I'll tell him what we are about to do. Fellows, I don't mind telling you that doing this...doing this is going to be...grim. He...he..." His long face revealed his feelings. "He might want to get the wife and kids out of the house before we arrive."

Seconds later, the DA was on the phone to his secretary, "Find Roy Mitchell and tell him that I need to see him. Thanks."

Neither Buchanan, Barnes, nor Parker felt like talking anymore. All three sat in silence - each to their own thoughts. For Barnes, the dark, silent office produced an eerie feeling. Quite different from the feeling of power it had exhibited earlier. After a few minutes, Roy Mitchell came in. Immediately, Mitchell's eyes met Frank Barnes'. Then he looked at the chief and then at Bragg Buchanan. Before anyone ever said a word, the assistant district attorney knew. He knew why everyone was present.

Buchanan cleared his throat and spoke first. "Roy, Chief Parker has something to say." His voice trailed off and he bowed his head.

"Mr. Mitchell, I have a warrant for your arrest for the murder of Ulysses Carillo, Ramon Garza, and Wendy Strutton. Let me inform you of certain rights that you have. You have the right.....Roy Mitchell did not hear anything else. When Chief Parker had finished, he looked up from the card that he had been reading. Tears were falling off Roy's face. A second ticked by without anyone saying anything.

"Do you have to put the handcuffs on me?"

"No, we don't," the chief said quietly. "Are you ready to go?"

The well-respected, quintessential prosecutor nodded. With his head bowed and looking downward, he turned and was escorted out the door.

Chapter 27

Barnes was awake lying in bed when the newspaper hit his driveway with a flop. He was normally still asleep at five in the morning, but not this morning. He had not slept well the previous night.The electric coffeepot had just finished percolating when he wearily picked up the stainless steel container and poured a cup. The smell off freshly brewed coffee lingered in the kitchen as he sat and looked at the unwrapped morning paper. The television coverage on the 6 and 10 o'clock news stations was over the top. He was slow and hesitant as he reached for the paper. He had been expecting a lot newspaper print pertaining to the case, but what he saw was just plain astounding. The Dallas Morning News displayed the largest headlines he had ever seen. Letters more than two inches high covered the entire width of the paper: ASSISTANT DA CHARGED WITH MURDER. On the front page was a gigantic photograph of Roy Mitchell being released from jail. The monster-sized headlines and corresponding article and photo covered more than 3/4 of the front page. Inside, the paper carried two more related articles. He read them all. Then he sat silent and motionless, staring out the kitchen bay window.

As soon as Chief Parker arrived at his office, he tried to locate Barnes. When he called down to the Homicide Division, he was informed that Frank had been in the office earlier, but left to go to the crime lab to check on some blood analysis work. An hour later Barnes knocked on Parker's door.

"Hello, Chief. I heard you were trying to reach me."

"That's right, that's right." Pointing to his subordinate's waist he said, "Doesn't that damn beeber work? I called twice."

"Yes sir, it works. But I was occupied at the time."

"What's the point in having it then?" the chief fumed. "I wanted to talk to you about some things."

"About the blood analysis?"

"Yes, I heard that's where you've been."

Barnes sat down. "On my way out to the crime lab, I stopped off at the County Health Department and got a copy of Roy's physical examination he was required to take when he first joined the DA's office..."

"Hey, good thinking."

"....hoping to use that to compare with the blood on the rags. The blood on the rags found in the Medina home has been analyzed. At one time, there had been quite a lot of blood on them. But herein is the problem. Before we found them, the rags had been soaking in water, and this diluted its strength, so to speak. Anyway, the only thing the lab can tell us is that it's human blood on the rag."

A few more minutes were discussed about the blood work. The detective then got up to leave. "Wait a minute, Frank," he said. "I meant to ask you yesterday, but, uh... I forgot. Uh...do you have any personal or professional problems working this case? You know what I mean? I don't know how well acquainted you were with Roy. I am sure you knew him. But are there any conflicts?"

Barnes frowned and slowly walked back and sat down. "I've thought about it, Chief. I've thought about it long and hard. Roy is a good, personal friend of mine. But if he messed up, he messed up. I can handle it."

"Good. I believe you. And you handle this case the best way you deem proper, but keep me posted." He paused, then asked, "By the way, have you heard anything from PES?"

"I went with them yesterday when they searched his house. They came up empty. Of course the car shows the bullet holes and the patch up job. But nothing else that we didn't know. I haven't talked to them this morning to see if anything else was found. I think I'll do that right now."

"Yeah, do it and let me know if they find anything."

Back at his desk, Barnes called the Physical Evidence Section. They had found quite a few stains -- which they thought were bloodstains -- in the front seat. However, it appeared that the seat had been thoroughly washed out and dried, leaving very faint impressions. The stains were not visible on the outside fabric, but were visible on the padding underneath. They removed the entire front seat and packed it off to the crime lab. They found the stains in basically two areas of the front seat. One group of stains -- the larger of the two -- was located on the passenger side of the seat, and the other -- the smaller group of stains -- was found on the driver's side.

They also detected what they believed was recent repair work around the rearview mirror. They scraped the paint and bonding compound away to emphasize the actual indentations in the metal.

That was all. The PES team had been expecting some fingerprints might be lifted, but they found nothing but smudges. And none with good enough quality to compare. Barnes requested a copy of all of their findings be sent to him. ASAP. He then went to lunch.As he passed by his secretary, she handed him ten telephone messages. All were from television news stations. After scanning them, he handed them back.

"The chief wants me to refer all messages like these to him. So whenever the media calls, 'patch them over to his office." He was glad.

Chapter 28

Beth Mitchell had rushed back to Dallas immediately. Her husband phoned from home after leaving the police station. Beth thought it would be better to leave their children in Houston for the time being. Her sister agreed, and she flew home alone as quickly as she could. The Southwest Airlines flight from Houston arrived at Dallas Love Field at seven-thirty-five p.m. During the entire flight, the words Roy said to her kept revolving around in her brain: "I've been arrested for murder." He had not gone into everything, and she had a difficult time remembering much of it. But she did recall him saying that Tony Medina and Carillo had been killed. Of course, she knew who they were, but she could not remember anything else he had said. Except, 'I've been arrested for murder.' That's all her mind focused upon. 'I've been arrested for murder'.... 'I've been arrested for murder.' Her mind countered with, 'There's got to be a mistake! There's a mistake somewhere! Roy will explain! He'll explain it somehow!'

It took only fifteen minutes for the Yellow Cab to pull into her driveway, although it felt like days. Fumbling for her billfold, she swore under her breath. The driver offered to carry her two suitcases up to the front door, but she declined.

As he was backing out to leave, she bolted for the house, running as fast as she could.

He met her at the door. And as they both sat on the sofa, she listened as he talked. Silently she listened while the man she loved told how he had gotten too involved in the Medina case. He had panicked, gotten caught and arrested. She still could not believe it. Surely they did not think he had anything to do with the killings....Him?..... Roy Mitchell?.....My husband?.....Murder? The hardest part was having to tell her what he had done in Linden after the shooting. But he had panicked -- gotten scared, he said. Beth broke down. Up to this point, she had been strong enough to fight it off. But no longer. Draping her arms around Roy's neck, she cried and cried and cried. Roy had been expecting her response and was emotionally prepared. He decided to let her cry herself out, so he sat in silence. They chose to put off telling the kids until they could be told in person and not over the telephone. It was after one a.m. by the time Beth fell asleep. She had lain in bed for more than two hours. Tossing. Thinking. Worrying. Crying. Roy had tried lying down, but could not stay. His mind -- drained as it was -- would not rest. It was all so totally frightening and unsettling. He paced all night. He tried lying down on the sofa, but that only made him feel worse. When darkness of the night started giving way to the early morning, he was sitting in a rocking chair in their bedroom. The rocking action had tamed his nerves somewhat.

The plan that he thought to be infallible and indestructible had blown up. What had gone wrong with it, he silently asked. But the question that played most heavily in his mind was how he had ever gotten mixed up in it. How? When? Why? He had no clear answers. Yes, he realized that he had become too engrossed in the Medinas' case, too immersed with the family personally. But at the time, he did not see the harm. He had just been trying to help a kid -- a good kid -- cope with a tragedy that had befallen him. How was that harmful? Where was the danger? Wasn't that the way it was supposed to be? He asked all of the questions, but he had none of the answers.

And now, he thought, my world is gone. My life, my family is shattered, broken, disintegrated. And Toby, what does he think of it? Somehow I think he knows about it.

Chapter 29

The north wind was blowing against Travis Payne's face. The sun's rays were already starting to filter through the white-barked Aspen trees that stood as if at attention-- thickly covering both sides of the stream. Daybreak was the best time to catch rainbow trout. Payne had been fishing his way up and down the rocky stream for several days. The morning air had been cold, but the slowly rising sun was bringing the much desired warmth to the wild and untamed outdoors. Days like these were a beginning and pleasant respite from the frostbiting depths of winter. Payne was standing on the rocky bank of the mountain stream as it swirled and rushed over the bumpy bed. The clear freezing river, just inches away, was lapping around the ends of his shoes. For a few minutes the solitary man just absorbed the raw surroundings and the hypnotic sound of the water running uncontrollably and noisely down the rivulet. The trees, some seventy-five feet tall, swayed and rustled their limbs against each other as the wind passed quickly through them creating a slumbering sound. The sun was shining down into the isolated valley. The mountainside was somewhat shadowed. He inhaled deeply several times. The air smelled so clean. Every now and then he caught a whiff of smoke from his small campfire. An airplane somewhere high above and out of sight was sending its sound waves down. That was the first unnatural sound he had heard in four days. When it eventually passed, only the sound of the wind and the rushing water remained.

Travis Payne had been going deep into the Rocky Mountains for several years. Always alone, he stayed for as long as it took to set his mind right. Hiking uncharted terrain into the rugged mountains, he was far off the usual camper trails. He was using only a topographical map and a Browning compass. Concerning orienteering, he was a throwback. No fancy gadgets for him. He was able to see things and places that few people -- maybe even none -- had ever seen. And during these pilgrimages, he rarely encountered or saw another human being. Complete isolation surrounded him. That was partially the reason, but not the only one, that he came. He planned to hike out that afternoon because he was running low on supplies. But he was also ready. The four days commingling with nature had cured the mental obstacles. Three, sometimes four times a year, forty-seven year old Travis Payne had to get away.

The hike back to his car took five hours. He estimated that he had been camping more than fifteen miles away. The rough terrain lengthened the walking time, but he did not care. That was all part of it. When he steered his black Cherokee Jeep back on the gravel road, he headed south, home to Gunnison, Colorado. Revitalized, he was ready for another nationally publicized case. This was the life of Travis L. Payne, the premier criminal defense attorney in the country.

At eight-twenty a.m. the next morning, petite Melody Gage, part Cheyenne Indian extraction, looked up from her monitor and burst into a big smile. She had not seen her boss in about four weeks. The trial in Chicago had lasted two weeks, and he had left the week before to prepare for it. When he returned to Gunnison on the Saturday after the trial, he had left for the high mountains the next day. As Payne casually strode through the office door, Melody ran around her desk and threw her arms around him.

"Congratulations! Congratulations!" she shrieked. The other members of the law firm -- lawyers and secretaries alike -- quickly crowded around the figurehead. Fellow barristers, grinning and jovial, shook his hand and happily slapped his back.

"I didn't know if you'd be able to do it," one said.

"No one really did!" said another.

Melody lightly chided them: "When my boss takes a case, he takes a case."

"You did well," one of the other secretaries exclaimed. "We're so proud of you. The whole town is proud of you."

"Yeah, you should've seen the papers," proudly said the newest and youngest attorney in the firm. "They built you up as if you were running for president."

"I'm not running for anything but the county line," laughed the trim, youngish-looking man. While the happy group was still chuckling, Melody slipped out of sight and then hurriedly returned with four dozen hand-decorated sweets, pastries, and doughnuts. Above the tray, a hand printed sign read "The Real Matlock". Painted on the sign was a picture of a wiry man showing a huge, toothy smile while holding a large caveman-like club behind his back.

After the impromptu victory party, Payne settled into his large office. A huge stack of unopened mail and telephone messages obscured the massive top of his beautiful red oak desk. He found it impossible that morning to set his mind back into the routine. The tedious trial in Chicago had zapped him of any interest pertaining to the law. The day before, while standing in the middle of the Rocky Mountain rapids, he had thought he was ready to get the wheels of the law moving again, but maybe not. The life train needed to stop and let him rest for a while. For the past ten years it had seemed more of an adrenaline-yielding roller coaster ride than a train excursion. The speed, the excitement, and the thrill of the journey just kept accelerating. It never stopped, never slowed down. His rise to the top of the criminal law profession placed him in select and limited company. Newsweek had recently named him one of the best criminal defense attorneys in the country. The fast-paced action of crisscrossing the country defending notables charged with crimes had an alluring charm to it.

But Payne's inclusion into the top flight list of criminal defense lawyers had been anything but planned. Upon graduating from the University of New Mexico School of Law with average grades, he joined the law firm of Jenks and Brown in Santa Fe, New Mexico. The seven-man firm had been looking for a young attorney to assist in their growing civil practice. Two years later, Payne was in Colorado defending a suit. The senior partner in a small firm from Gunnison, Colorado, was on the opposite side of Payne in the trial, and he was greatly impressed with Payne's trial skills. He made Payne a lucrative offer of taking over the defense of all their personal injury cases. Coincidentally, at the time of their offer, Payne had been mildly entertaining the idea of relocating to the area he loved the most -- the Colorado Rocky Mountains. Still single at the time and easily mobile, the outdoorsman jumped at the offer. For the next three years, he defended individuals, private companies and businesses sued by people claiming personal injuries. It was his seemingly magical ability in the courtroom that brought him into the potentially million-dollar lawsuits. But defending civil lawsuits quickly became boring. Going to jury trial in a personal injury case was rare. More often than not, both parties settled the lawsuit out of court prior to trial. So it was mostly deposition after deposition after deposition. Sure the money was good, but Payne wanted more excitement in his legal career. Somewhere along the way, he started defending individuals charged with crimes. At first, the cases involved defending people charged with minor offenses—shoplifting, possession of marijuana, driving while intoxicated. There was no shortage of jury trials for these types of crimes. The more of these types of cases he tried, the better he liked it. Gradually, the minor offenses graduated into major offenses. His trial skills were always excellent; he just shifted from lawsuits involving money to lawsuits involving a person's liberty. This, he found exciting and stimulating. And he was good at it.

His reputation became statewide when he successfully defended a female socialite from Denver on an intoxication manslaughter charge. Wealthy individuals charged with criminal offenses started seeking Payne for his legal services. He became a nationally known criminal defense attorney when he defended a person in New Mexico charged with murder. The defendant was the governor's son. He won, the son was acquitted, and Payne was soon recognized as one of the premier criminal defense attorneys in the nation. If they could afford his price, Payne would travel.

Payne was gazing out his office window, still feeling -- it seemed -- the morning mountain air against his face, and still hearing the rambling stream rushing over the mossy rocks. From the outset, the camping had been emotionally and physically rewarding. And even now, he still felt good. He was content.

Chapter 30

"I don't think I know anyone in Dallas, Texas," muttered Payne to himself. The phone message was almost at the bottom of a massive pile of other notes and the mail. The while-you-were-out note had been rather cryptic. He wished his secretary would gather more information about incoming calls.

Holding the telephone receiver in his hand, waiting for the line to start ringing, he wondered if there were any newsworthy crimes that had occurred in Dallas lately. None came to mind. When the phone was answered on the other end, he immediately thought he had the wrong number. A small child talking gibberish was the only thing that he could hear for the first few seconds.

Finally, a woman's voice spoke, "Hello."

"Hello, this is Travis Payne in Gunnison, Colorado. I'm trying to reach Mr. Roy Mitchell."

"Oh, yes, Mr. Payne, that's my husband. My husband called you. Let me get him."

The woman's voice had that pleasing Texas drawl, Payne said to himself. He pictured the voice belonging to a cattle baroness on a majestic ranch on the high Texas plains. While he waited, he thought about a quirk that he had not relinquished from his early law practice. Most firms, he knew, had the secretary place the call. Only when the called party came on the line did the secretary connect the call with the attorney. He had long believed that that method was too condescending and impersonal. So he patiently waited and studied the hieroglyphic note one more time.

"Hello. Mr. Payne?" a voice asked. "This is Roy Mitchell."

During the next few minutes Mitchell identified himself personally and professionally and briefly recited the reason for his call. Upon concluding, he asked very clearly, "I'd like for you to represent me, if I can afford it."

As the voice of this stranger was making his opening remarks, Payne immediately detected it as belonging to someone very articulate and very experienced in speaking. Payne did not remember having read about the case, but from Mitchell's brief recitation of it, it had already piqued his interest.

After many questions, the defense attorney saw the need for a meeting. A tentative arrangement was made wherein Mitchell would travel to Denver two days later. Payne would meet him at the airport, and they could use an airport conference room. Before Payne quoted a fee to any client, he wanted to know as much about the case as possible. Mitchell was to call back to the Gunnison office after he made flight arrangements, and with his estimated time of arrival. Payne reflected on the phone conversation. Although Mitchell had not mentioned it, Payne suddenly realized that he had once met Roy Mitchell. He vaguely recollected having met him years ago in San Francisco. Both of them had been featured speakers at a widely promoted seminar sponsored by the prestigious American Trial Lawyers Association.

After the phone call, the defense attorney from Gunnison buzzed his secretary. "Melody, could you call the District Clerk's office in Dallas and have them make us copies of the entire Court's file against Roy Mitchell. Be sure they include the indictments, and I want copies of the search warrants, arrest warrants, and the supporting affidavits. Those affidavits lay out the facts and information the police used in obtaining the warrants. It contains their probable cause evidence. It's all public record; we'll just have to pay for the photo copying. Also, call all of the local papers in Dallas and have them FAX or email us all of the newspaper articles–both current and dated on Mr. Roy Mitchell."

"Do you need them today?"

"Yes, I do."

Chapter 31

He knew it was a highly strategical move. And Marshall Logan, the special prosecutor from Houston, Texas, appointed by the governor to prosecute Mitchell, knew it could very well backfire on him. If it did, the chances of getting a conviction on Mitchell would be much more difficult. The State's Motion for Change of Venue was one of the first moves employed by Logan upon being appointed special prosecutor. However, it was made only after much deliberation. As far back as Logan could research it, he could find only a handful of cases in which the prosecuting attorney had filed the motion for a change of venue. Ordinarily, he knew that a defendant and his attorney were the ones wanting the case moved to another county because of adverse pre-trial publicity. Logan knew a Dallas County District Judge would decide the motion, but the prosecuting attorney did not honestly believe he would have much trouble persuading him to move the case. Logan was totally convinced he needed to get the trial moved to a different location. A stranger, he did not want to go into what he considered the enemy's camp to try Mitchell. The judicial and public environment, he believed, were pro-Mitchell. In fact, most of the newspaper and television coverage placed Roy Mitchell in a positive light -- some even going so far as to portray him as a hero -- and at the same time negatively show the type of sorry criminal Carillo and his followers had been. He had subpoenaed and photocopied every newspaper article from both the Dallas Morning News and the Dallas Times Herald. In addition he had obtained endless streams of television footage that had been devoted to covering the case. If there was ever a better case for a trial to be moved based on pre-trial publicity, Logan had never seen it.

To go into court and publicly suggest that the citizenry could not be fair and impartial would not sit well with the general public. But, if the motion was granted and the trial moved, Logan did not care about the public shellacking that might be aired in the Dallas community. After all, he did not live in the Dallas area and couldn't care less what the people thought about him, Roy Mitchell, or the trial itself. He was in it only for himself and whatever fame and power he could squeeze out of it. And that would come only if the verdict went with his side. But if the motion was denied, and the case stayed in Dallas County, the special prosecutor's insult might weigh on the jurors' minds when the case was tried. And that, he knew, would be devastating. So, therein lay the dilemma. Placing the special prosecutor in a bad light in the eyes of the prospective jurors would only serve to benefit Roy Mitchell. And Logan felt that the way things were going so far -- from the media's portrayal of the defendant -- Mitchell did not need any more fodder for his highly positive image. He did not want to meet Roy Mitchell on his home turf where the man was liked, respected, and well known. This factor alone had caused Logan considerable consternation.

Sipping coffee in the Dallas courthouse cafeteria that morning Logan thought about the upcoming day's activities. It had taken him a full day to present his evidence on the Motion for the Change of Venue. He concluded with his evidence late the day before. He guessed that the defense team would present at least a day of evidence in their efforts to keep the trial within the boundaries of Dallas County.

To show that an impartial trial could not be held in Dallas County, Logan had to present sufficient facts to prove that the populace as a whole had already formed an opinion on the defendant's guilt or innocence, and that such opinion was slanted in favor of the accused.

Slowly Logan stirred his second cup of lukewarm java. The metal spoon clinking rhythmically as it rounded the thick white porcelain cup. "How could any judge refuse to grant a motion to move this trial?" he thought confidently to himself. From all of the newspaper, radio, and television accounts this would be the biggest and most publicized trial since the Jack Ruby-Lee Harvey Oswald trial in the Sixties. And the added fact that Mitchell had been such a high-profile individual in the city for many years attributed to the prosecutor's position that, in this case, the State would not receive a fair trial. Logan was able to show hour after hour of television news accounts, and page after page of newspaper stories. But this was where Logan stopped in his presentation of evidence. He did not offer any testimony to show that such news accounts had already prematurely affected the ability of the jurors to be impartial.

Logan reflected for a moment about the defendant in this trial. He had never personally met Roy Mitchell; but he had certainly seen him and heard him speak at many seminars and conventions over the years.

"I've got to convict his ass!" he pronounced, half aloud to himself. "I must convict him. His ass will be mine. And it will be!" His lips puckered at the pleasant thought, as he ran his hand through his hair. Combed straight back and puffed-up, his brown hair had a touch of pomp to it. His head, slightly large for his six-foot, two inch frame, carried a tanned face that looked to some people like a smart-aleck. With half-sleepy eyes and pronounced lips, Logan looked the part of a wise-cracking womanizer. He was banking on this case -- this case and this conviction. He was blindly convinced and overly self-assured that a guilty verdict would boost him toward an appointment to a judge's position on the Court of Criminal Appeals, a statewide post. So wolf-like was his aggression in his appetite of this case, that less than two hours after the case was plastered over the statewide news wire, Logan sent an email directly to the governor's office asking to be appointed the special prosecutor. The unorthodox pitch was made even before the local District Attorney, Bragg Buchanan, had publicly stated he was going to remove his office from prosecuting Mitchell. Marshall Logan anticipated that the DA's decision was only a matter of time, since politically and ethically, Buchanan could not prosecute one of his own men.

Logan had sought and obtained a jump on everyone else in being named the special prosecutor in the most famous trial of recent years. The self-aggrandizing attorney was publicly seeking a feather in his cap -- a coup -- if he could convict the famous Roy Mitchell. Unabashed and proud, he conceitedly made his plans. It was going to be this case. This case! This case was the ammunition that he needed to be appointed a judgeship by the governor. After the initial message by Logan was sent, he shrewdly began the onslaught of politicking to his friends and former co-workers in the District Attorney's Office of Harris County, Houston, Texas. He began seeking their assistance -- their pull in getting the governor to appoint him as a special prosecutor.

"They'll hand me that damn judgeship on a silver platter," he thought. "Plus, Mitchell may be guilty on top of it all. But who gives a shit about that? I'm going for that judgeship."

Marshall Logan looked around the brightly painted cafeteria. The place was not nearly as crowded as the one he was accustomed to in Houston. Practically all of the patrons that morning appeared to be lawyers -- at least Logan thought they looked the part. It was partly rumor, but mostly fact that most attorneys in Dallas, the judges and high governmental officials within the county had rallied behind the DA's favorite son. "Shit on 'em," he muttered again. I'll take them all on!" Logan even expected some of them to testify during this motion on the change of venue. Logan knew from the outset that he would be portrayed as the villain -- the man wearing the black hat. "And that Roy Mitchell," reflected Logan for a moment, "was the golden boy. Shit on him, too."

It was merely incidental to Marshall Logan that the defendant Mitchell was represented by one of the nation's most prominent criminal defense attorneys. He had faced others of similar stature before. And truthfully, he had tried several cases -- and won convictions on them all -- against some of the best and most talented criminal defense attorneys in the South.

He looked at his watch and then scanned the many legal papers scattered all over the table. Bragg Buchanan had graciously offered him the full use of his District Attorney's offices during the trial, but Logan had felt uncomfortable using them. He had tried once or twice to blend in with the rest of the Dallas DA's staff, but it seemed that everyone was giving him the cold shoulder. The icy stares and the subtle rebuffs by Buchanan's personnel made him feel out of place. He knew their attitude was only natural. Since arriving in Dallas, he had done most of his trial preparation at the hotel, or in the county law library. He anticipated that the defense attorney would parade several lawyers, a few well-known citizens, and maybe even some of the media before the judge. All of whom, he was sure, would testify that twelve fair and impartial jurors could be assembled from the two million-plus population of Dallas County. Of course that is what they would say. He knew that from experience. Logan also knew that the defense witnesses would be friends and compatriots of both Mitchell and the judge. Friends of the judge, he conceded, made heavy witnesses. It would be difficult for the presiding judge to rule against the hometown cronies, but Logan was confident the judge's sense of fair play to both sides would override the hometown factor, and the judge would move the trial to a neutral site.

"All rise," announced the bailiff. "The 282nd Criminal District Court is now in session; the Honorable Wendall Carter presiding."

"Please be seated," responded Judge Carter. The hearing had concluded just before 4 p.m. Both parties had presented several witnesses.

The judge was succinct in his remarks. No fanfare. No speech. No lecture.

"The State's Motion for Change of Venue is denied. I tentatively set this case to be tried on August 1. That is approximately two months from today. Any questions?"

No one spoke from either side. Logan was too stunned to speak. But his thoughts raced on: "How could he do that? How could that damned

Judge have denied this motion? Something is not right. We cannot get a fair trial." Logan felt his face getting hot as it turned beet red. He was inclined to start arguing with the Judge, but he reasoned that would get him nowhere. And it might even damage him later during the trial. But still ... "That damned Judge is wrong. Wrong! Wrong! Wrong!" he muttered under his breath. "But I've got to get that appointment to the bench. That's the main thing. That's the most important thing. To hell with justice. And this is the trial that will get it for me." The thoughts were racing through his mind. "How could that bastard have done this to me? Me! Me, Marshall Logan!"

The judge resumed, "Then if there are no questions, this court is adjourned.

The special prosecutor quickly left the courtroom. The press flanked him on all side, pelting him with questions, as he hurried down the corridor. He quickened his stride. Looking straight ahead and thrusting his arms in front of him to move the mass, he headed for the nearest exit.

"No comment. No comment. I can't talk right now."

Back in his quiet hotel room, Logan digested the Judge's ruling. Slowly sipping an Old Milwaukee beer, he thought about the profound impact the ruling would have on the trial. There was no denying it, the Judge had dealt him a major setback. Moreover, he took it as a personal blow to his ability. He rarely ended up on the wrong end of a Judge's ruling.

"Damn, damn, damn," he cursed aloud. "I'm forced to try this bastard in his own backyard." He quickly drained the beer and opened another.

"But I'm the best there is in trying criminal cases," he vocalized. "Here I am deep in enemy territory, trying a major case, and being portrayed as the damned villain. But these damn idiots don't know how good I am. They'll see. After I convict the bastard, I'll shove it in their faces. And then I'll get the hell out of town, on my way to becoming a judge. I'm simply the best there is. I can beat these odds. Watch me. Just watch me."

In the center of his light-brown business card -- made from parchment paper -- appeared a king's crown. "Marshall Logan, Lawyer," was printed underneath the crown along with his address and phone number. Most attorneys' business cards made from white heavier-than-normal paper had the standard: "Attorney at

Law" under their name. But Logan had to be different. After leaving the District Attorney's Office in Houston, Texas, where he had practiced for ten years, his solo law practice had consisted mostly of court appointments on misdemeanor criminal cases, family law matters -- divorce cases and adoptions. The District Court Judges in Harris County would not appoint him many felony cases. They knew the man. His reputation as being shady and somewhat underhanded was well known. And in some cases, even documented. Though no one questioned his ability in the courtroom, he just was not liked nor trusted by his peers and the Judges who knew him. Most of them still believed there was some truth to the rumors circulating concerning his abrupt exit from the District Attorney's Office four years before. He officially resigned, he was actually about to get fired. In exchange for resigning, part of the "deal" that had been worked out included an agreement that the District Attorney's Office would not bring criminal charges against him. The Texas State Bar Committee on Ethics, had, however, privately reprimanded him. The unpublished events surrounding his departure had been hushed up as much as possible, and Logan was thankful for that.

But even now, years later, he still was curious as to what had prompted the woman to start talking. It was during one case -- actually his last trial as a prosecutor -- that he keenly observed an extremely attractive woman sitting as a juror in his case. One morning before the trial resumed, he parked his car next to the juror's vehicle by happenstance. As they both exited their vehicles on the way to the same courtroom, they exchanged morning pleasantries. During the short lunch hour, Logan returned to the vehicles and flattened one of her tires with his pocketknife. When the trial recessed that afternoon, he deliberately timed his departure to rendezvous with the woman at her vehicle just after she sadly noticed her airless tire. After much insistence that he be allowed to change her tire, they casually conversed for several minutes. Everything was going exactly as the handsome prosecutor had planned, with a final suggestion that they got to a nearby pub for a drink or two. The woman assented, and later that night they had sexual intercourse in his car in the parking lot. Logan had vehemently argued to the District Attorney that it has been entirely consensual. They were both single, he had stated, and brazenly continued that it was nobody's business. Neither the District Attorney nor the presiding Judge of the case saw it that way. A mistrial was declared, and Logan, the office playboy, had suddenly resigned.

Most of the attorneys and Judges in Houston who knew Marshall Logan had been utterly confounded when they heard that he, of all people, had been appointed the special prosecutor in such a highly-publicized, and immensely important criminal case. They, however, were not aware that the governor's aide in charge of such appointments was Logan's cousin.

Chapter 32

At 1:00 p.m. the jury was brought into the courtroom. The morning had been taken up with sundry motions and pre-trial hearings required by law. All of which had to be done outside the presence of the jury. Judge Wendall Carter looked at the twelve people in the jury box. "Would all of you please stand and raise your right hand? Do each of you solemnly swear that in the case of the State of Texas against Roy Mitchell, that you will a true verdict render according to the law and the evidence, so help you God?"

The jury affirmatively responded in unison. Roy Mitchell was viewing the twelve citizens from Dallas County selected to decide his fate. He had similarly surveyed countless other juries during his lifetime. What a world of difference it had made to Mitchell evaluating the jury from the eyes of a defendant and not as a prosecutor. Fellow workers always told him that he had the unique talent of quickly and accurately assessing others in their ability to be good or bad jurors. Whether it was a knack or just plain luck, Mitchell did not know. He visibly inspected the six-man, six-woman jury, and he had no particular feel for the twelve strangers seated in the box. Selecting the jury had taken four days, not like the normal one or two days in regular murder trials.

Finding twelve unbiased and fair jurors had been difficult for Judge Carter. A District Judge for seventeen years, he had observed many lawyers as they practiced law in his courtroom. And as the Presiding Judge with the most tenure in Dallas County, he knew almost all the local criminal lawyers, both prosecutors and defense attorneys. And they all knew and respected the balding, bespectacled, and amiable jurist. Logan had done his homework on Judge Wendall Carter. He found out that any time two lawyers squared off in his courtroom, while the outcome of the criminal case might be uncertain, Carter's fairness to both sides was never in question. But equity in the courtroom did not prevent Judge Carter from having his personal opinions.

"I've never seen a more arrogant and, at the same time, obnoxious attorney than Marshall Logan," he told his wife one evening after a long day of jury selection. Munching from an open can of Planter's cashews, he continued, "Arrogance is something I am used to seeing in lawyers. Others are sometimes irritating. But to have both characteristics rolled into one person is something that rubs me the wrong way. Of course, most of the potential jurors this week have heard of the case but not to the point of disqualifying themselves. But Logan, the damn fool, seems to take that as some kind of personal attack against himself. How he got appointed to this case is a confounded mystery to me." The near-retiring Judge looked wrangled as he shook his head. "You should see how he treats those people. He did not make any points with them, I'll damn sure tell you that." Then he added, "But, on the other hand, you should have seen Travis Payne in action!"

When the word got out in the legal circles of Dallas that the celebrated criminal defense attorney was going to represent Roy Mitchell, it became the hot topic of the courthouse crowd. For days before the start of the jury selection, Payne's stature -- always punctuated with war stories of his past cases -- seemed to dominate the cafeteria conversations. Late one afternoon six weeks before the hearing on the Change of Venue Motion, Judge Carter was alone in his chambers reading an Agatha Christie mystery novel, between dozes, when a light knock on his door interrupted him. Standing in the entryway he saw a man he thought he recognized. He was not quite sure, but his face seemed vaguely familiar. The rather thin man extended his right hand and introduced himself. The strangers grip was firm and warm.

"Good afternoon Judge. I'm Travis Payne from Gunnison, Colorado. I'm the person who is going to represent Roy Mitchell." Instantly, Judge Carter recognized the face from his photograph in several legal periodicals over the years. When the Judge invited Payne into his office, he noticed that he walked with a slight limp.

For some unknown reason, the Judge expected a more imposing figure. The small-framed defense attorney seemed to stand slightly less than the Judge's height of six foot. Weighing about 170 pounds, Payne appeared to be in good shape for a man in his mid-forties. His clean shaven face made him look younger. A long distance runner, thought Judge Carter immediately. He had short, neatly trimmed brown hair. His voice -- a very smooth modulation with a slight western accent -- matched his appearance. Payne had come to Dallas to introduce himself to the Presiding Judge before the trial started. And so, for the next hour, Carter and Payne spoke of major issues such as best-selling paperbacks, hunting, and homemade wine. It was against protocol to talk about the case. By the time Payne departed, Judge Carter had witnessed the charisma that had made Travis Payne such a renowned lawyer that he was. Here was a man, the Judge noticed, that could confidently and artfully sell his case. John Q. Public could easily identify with him. That trait, thought Judge Carter, could win many, many cases. And for Travis Payne, over the years and through case after case, it had done exactly that. "People like him. The jurors like him. And if you can get the critical-eyed jury to like you," Carter nodded toward his wife later that evening, "they tend to believe you."

After the jury took the oath, Judge Carter smiled and said to them, "Please be seated." He then looked toward the special prosecutor, "Mr. Logan, present the indictment."

Logan stood, unbuttoned his navy blue, finely woven wool suit, and approached the Judge's bench. There he was handed the Grand Jury indictment. Holding the one-page document in front of him, as if he were holding a church hymnal, he slowly and deliberately turned and faced the jury. As he took one step toward the jury -- poised and in character -- Logan spoke to them in a low and leveled voice.

"Members of the jury," he began authoritatively, "it becomes my duty to read to you the indictment in this case. It reads as follows:

In the name and by the authority of the State of Texas, the Grand Jurors, of the County of Dallas, State of Texas, do present that one Roy Mitchell, hereinafter called the Defendant, on or about the 1st Day of December, 1992 did then and there, in the County of Dallas, State of Texas, knowingly and intentionally, acting alone or as a party, cause the death of one Ulysses Carillo, hereinafter referred to as the complainant, by shooting the said complainant with a firearm, a deadly weapon, against the peace and dignity of the State.

Signed by Truitt Loving, foreman of the Grand Jury."

As he finished reading, Logan looked up and purposefully made eye contact with the male juror whom he figured would be the strongest State's minded juror.

For an instant, Logan stood perfectly still; then he turned, and with the same deliberateness as before, handed the legal document back to the Judge and returned to his seat.

Judge Carter broke the silence. "Mr. Payne, how does your client plead?"

"May it please the Court," began Payne as he rose to address the Judge, "and members of the jury, Roy Mitchell pleads not guilty."

The Judge nodded his head acknowledging the response.

Turning to Logan, he continued, "Call your first witness."

Chapter 33

The murder trial drew not only every local news outlet, but national syndicates as well. Four prime-time network television shows filmed and aired segments on the participants and the events leading up to the trial. Throughout the previous months, numerous articles describing the mind-bending saga appeared in monthly magazines and in cheap weekly tabloids. The excitement generated by the media's coverage about the case culminated that Monday morning with the start of the much-awaited trial.

Police Officer James Sears took the stand as the State's first witness. As a result of the pre-trial investigation by the defense, Mitchell knew that Sears was one of the first policemen to arrive at the scene of the shooting. The tall young officer described to the jury the battle-like scenario as it had looked to him as the first policeman on the scene. Bodies were lying everywhere. There was more blood than he had ever seen. It had not taken him long to determine that a drive-by shooting had occurred. He had also instantly recognized Ulysses Carillo. Having routinely patrolled that sector of the city for two years, he made it a practice to know the criminal element that lived in the area.

Carillo was obviously dead, narrated Sears. Continuing his inspection of the crime scene, he next examined the female. She, too, was dead. He detected some vital signs from the third victim, and the officer immediately called an ambulance. The inspection had taken less than five minutes. Once completed, his primary duty became to secure the area until help arrived.

Payne's cross-examination lasted less than one minute.

"Officer, my name is Travis Payne, and I have just a couple of questions for you. When you first got the call of the shooting over the radio, how long did it take you to get to the location?"

"Less than two minutes. That's just an approximation."

"I understand. But after you got there, there was no more gunfire?"

"That's correct."

"That's all I have. Thank you. Pass the witness."

The next few witnesses were the other officers that had initially converged on the crime scene. After detailing the evidence that had been seen and guarded by them, Rick Genovise of the Physical Evidence Section was called to the stand. Through him, the grisly-colored photographs taken by him of the crime scene were marked, identified, admitted into evidence, and shown to the jury. The original 8″ x 10″ photos had been enlarged, and now were huge 24" by 36" blowups. Mitchell sat passively as the crime scene technician proficiently explained each photo in detail. The numerous photos were displayed in front of the jury. Genovise next identified all of the physical evidence he collected at the scene. Logan -- like a good prosecutor should do -- paraded in front of the jury the narcotics, the money, and both guns. The witness detailed for the jury where each piece of evidence was found and also pointed out the particular photograph depicting the same. From his questions, he was deliberately setting the stage to depict a major drug deal.

However, when the PES officer began testifying about the gym bag and the shotgun found down the street, Mitchell took special notice.

"Did you collect the shotgun found down the street? And did you keep it as evidence in your investigation?" asked Logan.

"Yes, I did."

Rising to address the Judge, Logan asked, "Your Honor, may I have permission of the Court to leave and retrieve an item of evidence?"

"Yes, you may."

The prosecutor left the packed courtroom for a moment and returned carrying in one hand a long gun.

"Officer Genovise, I hand you what has been marked as State's Exhibit Number 30. Can you identify this?"

"Yes, I can." The officer took the gun and looked at it.

"What is it and where was it found?"

"It is the shotgun I found. It was about a block down the street and lying in the middle of the road."

"Okay. Your Honor, we'd offer into evidence, State's Exhibit Number 30."

From his chair, Payne said, "No objection, Your Honor.

"State's Exhibit Number 30 will be admitted into evidence," replied the Judge.

Logan then laid the gun on the jury rail directly in front of the twelve. "Officer, what kind of a gun is this?"

"It is a Remington-made, pump action, 12-gauge shotgun. A portion of the handle and barrel has been sawed off."

"When you found it, was it loaded or unloaded?"

"One empty shell was in the chamber. And one unfired or live shell was in the magazine."

"What's a magazine?"

"That's where the live shells are kept inside the gun -- once the gun is loaded. When the gun is ready to fire, the shell is injected from the magazine into the chamber -- or barrel -- and it's ready to fire."

"Detective Genovise, let me change directions for a moment. Are you familiar with lifting fingerprints -- how to do it and so forth?"

"Yes."

"In all of your years and years of experience, together with your schooling and training, have you ever seen, heard, or read about the fingerprint of any two individuals being the same?"

"No sir. No two have ever been the same."

"Never?"

"Never."

"Brothers?"

"Never."

"Twins?"

"Never."

"So, these little lines and ridges that each one of us have on the tips of our fingers are our individual calling cards?"

"Yes sir."

"Exclusive to that particular individual and no one else in the world."

"That's right, sir."

"Did you dust the shotgun for fingerprints?"

"Yes sir, I did."

"Were you able to lift any comparable fingerprints from the shotgun -- State's Exhibit Number 30?"

"Yes. I was able to lift three latent fingerprints."

"Officer, tell the jury where on the shotgun you were able to detect and lift these fingerprints."

"I lifted one print on the side of the front grip." Genovise gestured toward the barrel of the gun. "If you let me have the gun, please sir, I'll point them out for you as I go."

After the gun was handed to the officer, he continued. "Like I said, I found one print here," indicating a spot on the front wooden grip of the gun. "I found another print on the smooth part of the metal directly above the trigger; and I lifted the third print on the rear grip -- sometimes it is referred to as the smaller-ended portion of the stock, where the wooden stock connects with the metal part of the gun."

"Officer, have you ever shot a shotgun before?" inquired Logan.

"Oh, yes, many times."

"Were the prints that were detected on the front grip of the gun and the portion of the rear grip consistent with a person holding the gun and shooting it?"

"Yes, it is consistent."

The prosecutor laid the shotgun lengthwise on the jury rail less than two feet away from the jurors sitting on the front row. Twelve pair of eyes inspected the sawed-off deadly weapon. Logan quietly walked back to his chair and stood facing the witness. Silently he stood, until he felt every eye in the courtroom upon him. And for dramatics, he waited a second longer. He wanted everybody's ear before he continued.

"Whose prints were found on the gun?" he loudly and distinctly asked while still standing.

"They were the prints of Tony Medina."

The prosecutor paused for effect. He eyed the twelve jurors before he continued. "Officer, you told us earlier that you found this gun in the street down the block from the dead bodies. Did you find anything else in the roadway?"

"I did."

"What?"

"I found a bag, similar to what athletes use."

Logan reached underneath his table and pulled out a blue canvas gym bag. After getting the bag marked for identification by the court reporter, Logan again approached the witness.

"Detective, was the bag empty?"

"No. The gym bag contained two live shotgun shells."

The shells after being identified were also admitted into evidence.

Logan asked, as he returned to his chair, "What kind of shells are these?"

"They are 12-gauge shotgun shells. The brand name is Remington."

"Are these the same type of shells that were found in the shotgun? That is, the shells found in the shotgun were Remington 12-gauge, and these found in the gym bag are Remington 12-gauge, correct?"

"Yes sir.

"Detective Genovise, did you find some shotgun shells back down the street next to where the bodies were located?"

"Yes, I did. Back down the street, next to where the cars were parked, I found in the street two spent shotgun shells."

"What gauge were the shells?"

"Twelve gauge."

"What brand?"

"Remington."

"The same type as those found in the gym bag and those found in the gun found in the roadway?"

"Well, yes. Same brand and gauge."

"Where in the street were these two hulls found?"

"Carillo's house is located on Barrett Street, but looks down Rand Drive. Rand Drive runs into Barrett and forms a T-intersection. Carillo's house is located just off center of the top of the T-intersection of Barrett and Rand. The empty hulls were found in the street about two feet from the curb on Barrett Street where Rand Drive intersects with Barrett.

Again, Logan stood. Again, for effect, he waited a moment, until he was sure every eye and ear was on him. "Did you process this blue canvas athletic bag for any fingerprints?" The special prosecutor's voice increased its pitch.

"Yes sir."

"And what did you find?" His tone then rose even higher. Obviously, he was trying to garner some special attention.

"I lifted two identifiable prints."

"Where?" His voice was sharp.

"One print was lifted from the top. Right here." The policeman pointed to a two-inch leather strip on top of the bag that contained the zipper. "And another one was lifted from the luggage tag that was affixed to the zipper. Here." The officer so indicated.

Logan, still standing, the fervor ever-present in his voice: "Did you compare those fingerprints in an attempt to determine who left those fingerprints on that blue, canvas athletic bag?"

The officer responded in a low-key, businesslike manner. "Both prints were made by the defendant, Roy Mitchell."

Holding the exhibit with both hands above his head, "On this gym bag -- that you found in the street next to the shotgun -- you lifted this defendant's fingerprints?"

"Yes sir."

There was a small murmur in the courtroom by some spectators in the audience. Slowly, Logan turned his head and glared at the defendant. His "courtroom stare" was not unlike actors on the television shows But it was a bit too dramatic thought Payne. He sat impassively, trying to look unconcerned and unimpressed. He had long since known that his client's prints were found on the bag. Such information had been made known to him in response to pre-trial motions he had filed. Of course, there was nothing he could do to prevent the testimony. So he just sat motionless, trying to look unfazed.

"So," drawled Logan, "that shogun had Medina's fingerprints on it and this bag had the defendant's prints on it." Logan was holding both above his head.

"Yes sir."

Looking at some notes for a moment, he then asked, "Can this gun fit into that bag?"

"Yes, it can."

"Do it, please."

Handing both items to Genovise, the witness opened the bag and placed the sawed-off shotgun into the bag.

"Your Honor," Logan addressed, "that's all of the questions I have of this witness. I'll pass him for cross-examination at this time."

If the spectators in the courtroom expected a fiery, grilling cross-examination from Payne, they were soon to be disappointed. But the content of his questions did make his point.

"Mr. Genovise, when you processed the shotgun for fingerprints, did you find any prints that belonged to the citizen accused, Roy Mitchell?" he asked.

"No, sir, I did not."

"Did you find any fingerprints belonging to the citizen accused on the empty shotgun shells?"

"No sir."

"Did you find any fingerprints belonging to the citizen accused on the live shotgun shells found in the gym bag?"

"No, I did not."

"Mr. Genovise, how long will a fingerprint remain on an object before it evaporates or goes away?"

"It depends on a number of factors -- climate, surface area, quality of the print itself, things like that. Some prints placed on items have been detected years afterwards. Of course, that is rare, but it is not unusual to detect fingerprints left days or weeks earlier."

"So, concerning the gym bag, you cannot tell this jury how long my client's fingerprints had been there?"

"That is correct."

"They may have been there for a week or two, or even longer. You simply cannot tell?"

"Yes sir, that is correct."

"Furthermore, you cannot tell this jury if, when the prints were placed there, the bag was empty or had something in it, can you?"

"What do you mean, sir?"

"I mean, when my client's fingerprints were placed on the gym bag, you don't know and cannot tell this jury if the bag had a shotgun in it, or if the bag had jogging clothes in it, or anything about what was inside the bag whenever my client's prints were placed on it?"

"Oh, I see what you are asking. No sir, I could not tell."

"Pass the witness."

"I have nothing further of this witness, Your Honor," Logan responded.

"You may step down, sir," said the Judge to the officer.

Judge Carter looked at the clock located at the back of the courtroom. It was after 5 p.m. His back was hurting and he was tired. The afternoon's testimony had been long and sometimes cumbersome. He decided to adjourn for the day.

During the judge's thirty minutes drive home, he mulled over the first day of trial. The Judge's automobile was bumper-to-bumper with the rest of the cars along Central Expressway. He sipped a root beer and thought about Marshall Logan. The State had made points; Logan was effective in the courtroom. What a drastic change from the way he had acted during the jury selection. It was a complete "about face". A 180 degree turn in attitude and effectiveness. Judge Carter had a difficult time figuring out that change. The State's attorney appeared capable and was a good actor while in the courtroom. He knew how to make a point; he knew how to impact a certain piece of evidence. The Judge was impressed.

Chapter 34

Travis Payne took out a brand-new legal pad from his briefcase, and was searching for a pen, when the Judge entered the courtroom. Payne had slept well after the testimony the day before which revealed nothing he did not already know. He was amazed at the speed with which the case was progressing. Looking at his client, he noticed the bloodshot eyes and the haggard look on Mitchell's face. Payne had seen the before, and he knew that there was nothing he could do about it. Anticipation and fear of the unknown had wrecked many a defendant. And as good as Roy Mitchell was while sitting as the best prosecutor in the state, nothing could prepare him for sitting in the defendant's chair, charged with murder.

The Chief Medical Examiner from Dallas County was the first witness that morning. The older distinguished-looking physician calmly eased into the witness chair. Mitchell craned his neck to see if the doctor's bow tie -- his unique trait -- was in place. It was, as usual.

Mitchell had known Dr. Simon Butler for years. He was considered one of the best medical examiners in the South. It was an honor bestowed on him by his peers through the years. Dr. Butler was excellent at testifying in the courtroom. Having an uncanny resemblance to ""Doc" on the old television western Gunsmoke, Dr. Butler's appearance was as acceptable as his testifying ability. Vague answers or unclear responses were foreign to him. Both sides of any lawsuit appreciated his clear-cut and direct answers. Plus, his inimitable courtroom manner was akin to the good bedside manners juries wanted from their own physicians. Slowly and succinctly, the good doctor explained the procedure taken in performing an autopsy. Because of the number of dead bodies in the case, Dr. Butler had called upon a deputy medical examiner to assist him. Even with the help, the autopsies performed on the four individuals lasted an entire day.

Ulysses Carillo, the medical examiner testified, had died from a gunshot wound to the face. Because there was such a high degree of disfigurement, the doctor was not able to say exactly how many shotgun blasts had hit Carillo. In his opinion it had been more than one, but less than four. The numerous wounds had been caused by shotgun pellets fired from a shotgun. Several of the shotgun pellets found in Carillo had been retrieved and sent to the crime lab for testing.

Dr. Butler testified that he had also collected blood and tissue samples to determine the presence of alcohol or drugs in the body. Carillo had both -- and a lot of each. The amount of ethyl alcohol found in the blood of Carillo was more than twice the amount allowed for a person to be declared legally intoxicated to drive a vehicle.

Cocaine and amphetamine were also detected in the body. This, too, was in large quantities in the blood. How long the narcotics had been in the body could not be determined.

Smooth performance by the special prosecutor, thought Mitchell. Apparently the prosecution was going to air out all of the dirty laundry rather than allowing the defense to do so. The impact was lessened. But more importantly, it showed the jury that the State was not attempting to hide anything from the jury. "Let it all hang out," muttered Mitchell to himself.

The doctor's next testimony was about the autopsy of the dead girl. She, too, was killed by a shotgun blast. Because of the wound pattern discovered on her chest and neck, and the limited number of shotgun pellets found, the medical examiner testified that she probably received only one gunshot. And like Carillo, her body had been full of alcohol, cocaine, and amphetamines.

The autopsy of Ramon Garza, however, revealed something different. Judge Carter foresaw it because he detected a change in Logan's voice when he began his questions concerning Garza.

"Doctor, let's talk about the autopsy of Ramon Garza," suggested Logan.

"Okay," panned Dr. Butler.

"What did your examination reveal about his death?"

The doctor adjusted is wire-rimmed glasses and then placed both hands on his bowtie as if to straighten it. He paused before he spoke.

"Mr. Garza's external examination revealed a single gunshot wound to the stomach. The internal examination corresponded with the observations on the outside of the body. That is to say, that I found one projectile laying next to the spine and one bullet hole beginning from the stomach -- about two inches above the navel -- and traveling in a straight line to the edge of his spine where the bullet was found. I removed the bullet and sent it to the firearms division of the crime lab for analysis."

"Was that bullet from a shotgun?" asked the prosecutor.

"Objection, Your Honor." Payne was on his feet immediately. "Though I respect Dr. Butler's ability as a medical doctor, and his ability to perform autopsies, he is not qualified to testify as a firearms expert. He is not qualified to testify that the projectile was from a shotgun or any other type of gun."

"Sustained."

The prosecutor simply rephrased the question. "Doctor, was the type of wound that you found on Ramon Garza the same as the types of wounds you found on Carillo and the female?"

"No sir."

"What was different?"

"The bullet wound on Ramon was larger than the wounds on Mr. Carillo and the female."

"How so, Doctor?"

"The entrance wound was quite a bit larger. And the wound inside the body was larger."

"Were the projectiles that you found in Carillo and the female similar to the projectile that was found in Ramon Garza?"

"No sir. The bullet recovered in Mr. Garza was substantially bigger than the pellets found in Carillo and the female."

"Did you send the bullet and the pellets to the firearms division to be analyzed?"

"Yes sir, I did."

Logan stood to speak: "Doctor, do you have an opinion as to the cause of death of Ulysses

Carillo, the girl identified as Wendy Strutton, and Ramon Garza?"

"Yes sir, I do have an opinion. The cause of death of Mr. Carillo was a shotgun blast or blasts. More specifically, the cause of death was from a firearm being shot in the face of Mr. Carillo. The cause of death of the girl identified as Wendy Strutton was a shotgun blast. That is, she was shot with a firearm, and this caused her death."

The doctor went on, "And the cause of death of Mr. Garza was from a single gunshot wound to the stomach. It, too, was a firearm, but was different in all respects from the other wounds found in the other dead people."

When the medical examiner concluded, the special prosecutor nodded his head. He remained standing for a moment so the doctor's testimony could sink in with the jury. When he sat down, he continued with his direct examination.

"Doctor, were drugs or alcohol detected in Ramon Garza?"

"We checked, but nothing was detected."

The State's attorney poured himself a glass of water. He exhaled and then continued. His voice changed tones again.

"Sir, did you also perform an autopsy on a person identified as Tony Medina?"

"We did."

"What did you find?"

"Mr. Medina died from a gunshot wound to the body fired from a shotgun."

"Did you test for alcohol or narcotics in the body of Mr. Medina?"

"Yes, we did. No drugs were found; however, some alcohol was found in the bloodstream."

"How much alcohol, Doctor?"

"Well, he had 0.06 percent ethyl alcohol in his bloodstream."

"What does that mean? Was he drunk?"

"I can't say if he was drunk. In Texas, if a person drives an automobile with a 0.08 percent alcohol in his bloodstream, he is legally intoxicated. The deceased had not reached this level. He had 0.06 percent in his body. This would have been 0.02 percent less than the amount stated by law before one is legally intoxicated."

"Doctor, from all the wounds in all the bodies, can you tell in which direction the deceased persons were standing or facing when they were shot? That is, in which direction in relation to the shooter or shooters were they standing?"

"No sir."

"Why not?"

"All I can testify to are the paths of the wounds in the body -- front to back, or left to right, or going up or down. I have no way of knowing what position the body was in before it was shot. I can't say if the deceased was standing straight up, bent down, or turned to or away from the shooter. Nor do I know the position of the shooter. There are too many variables."

When Logan returned to his chair, he looked at the jury. "That is all we have of this witness. We pass him for cross-examination."

At that point, the Judge recessed for twenty minutes. A mid-morning break was in order, and most of the spectators who had packed the courtroom filed outside. For the first two days of the trial not an empty seat in the audience could be found. The bailiffs observed that some in the gallery had arrived as early as an hour and a half before the start of the day's trial. Some of the observers even brought a sack lunch. In their eyes, this was real life drama and delightful entertainment. For the media, this was the choice assignment to draw.

When the trial resumed, Travis Payne cleared his throat and began his questioning.

"Doctor, from all of your examinations done on all of the dead bodies, can you tell who got shot first?"

"No, I cannot."

"Can you even tell who first pulled out the guns? You know, who drew first?"

"No, I cannot testify as to who pulled out their guns first."

"Can you tell who first started shooting?"

"No sir."

"So, if Carillo and his gang --"

"Objection, Your Honor." The special prosecutor's voice was replete with contempt. "That is a mischaracterization of the people involved. There is no evidence that this was a "gang"."

Payne rose to his feet. "Your Honor, based on the facts adduced so far, this group can be characterized as such. Of course, Mr. Logan does not like it, but that is his problem. I can call them whatever the evidence has shown them to be."

A few chuckles were heard in the audience.

"Well," drawled the Judge, "rephrase your question."

"So, if Carillo and 'his friends' --" Payne purposely highlighted 'his friends' -- then he continued -- "had pulled their guns first and started shooting first, you would not be able to verify it, would you?"

"No. Like I said, I could not tell."

"So, if Tony Medina had started shooting in self-defense, that is something you could not refute?"

The question startled a subdued Roy Mitchell, but he retained his passive composure. "Where the hell did self-defense come from?" he wondered.

Payne shifted the scope of the cross-examination to another area. "Doctor, during your autopsy of Ulysses Carillo, did you find numerous punctures in the skin between the toes?" Payne asked the question while looking at a copy of Carillo's ten-page autopsy report.

The Dallas County Medical Examiner's office was a public office supported mainly by county funds, and, as such, any records such as the autopsy report were a matter of public record. A copy could be purchased.

"Yes, I found some."

Mitchell had read the autopsy reports of the deceased individuals but had overlooked any such reference to any punctures.

"Some? Doctor," Payne's voice rose, "your report indicates that, quote, numerous punctures were detected in the skin between each of the toes, end quote. That's what you wrote, isn't it, Doctor?"

The medical examiner shifted his body in the witness chair.

"Yes, I believe it is."

"Well, Dr. Butler, look at your report," the defense attorney gingerly poked. "Let's make sure -- for the benefit of this jury here -- that

that is what you found and that is what you put in your report. Isn't that a fact?"

The Judge was slightly enlivened. "... for the benefit of thls jury here ..." A neat little trick. From the very start, he thought, Payne was attempting to become the spokesman for the jury ... trying to be their advocate ... attempting to be on their side ... looking out for their benefit.

"Isn't that a fact, Dr. Butler?"

"Yes." The witness squirmed ever so slightly.

"Isn't the skin between the toes a common place for drug addicts to use when injecting themselves with drugs?"

"Yes, it is."

"Because after repeated drug use, a vein in the arm is sometimes difficult to find. True?"

"Yes."

Mitchell could tell by the expression on Logan's face this had caught him by surprise, too.

"That's all the questions I have at this time, Your Honor.

The Court recessed for ten minutes. On the way to the restroom Mitchell saw another familiar face -- Harry Johnson from the Southwestern Institute of Forensic Sciences.

The Southwestern Institute of Forensic Sciences was in the shadows of the sprawling

Parkland Hospital complex. The four-story crime lab served not only all of the police agencies in Dallas County, but most of the law-enforcement agencies in Texas. Its modern facilities and state-of-the-art equipment brought some of the smartest and keenest crime-fighting techniques to the Dallas area. The institute, comprised of twelve different departments, employed a staff of more than one hundred people. It was a diverse, yet tight-knit group of technicians, physicians, and scientists completely integrated under one roof. At first only the offices of the medical examiner and the drug analysis chemists existed. But in the early Seventies, the institute expanded with the Toxicology Department, the Intoxilyzer Department, the Sudden Infant Death Office, the Photography Department, the Environmental Department, the Trace Evidence Department, the Serology Department, the Document Examiner's Office, the Firearms Division, and the Crime Reconstruction Division. The overall administration of such a large secretive facility rested with Dr. Matt Hill. The politicians of Dallas County actively recruited Dr. Hill to head up the institute when he was still employed by the Federal Bureau of Investigation. His Ph.D. in both chemistry and law enforcement administration propelled him to elite status in the FBI's much revered criminal laboratory in

Quantico, Virginia. Because of his bulldog approach in overseeing Dallas' Crime Lab, the Institute was not lacking in funding from the county commissioners.

Marshall Logan was fortunate to have such a facility at his disposal. Indeed, a large part of the prosecution's case was developed from several of the departments.

When the trial reconvened, Harry Johnson, the firearms expert from the crime lab took the stand. Johnson did not look anything like an expert in firearms. Frail, stoop-shouldered and sickly-looking, the witness began his testimony by stating his qualifications that made him the chief firearms examiner over a staff of two assistant examiners. After receiving a Bachelor of Science degree in metallurgy from California Polytech, he joined the California State Highway Patrol as a firearms examiner. He worked there twelve years; and then was selected as the Southwestern Institute of Forensic Sciences chief firearms expert. Without much flair, Logan ably brought out from the witness the fact that the pellets taken from the bodies of Carillo, Medina, and the Strutton female were indeed shotgun pellets. Moreover, he reiterated what Detective Genovise had said earlier: The empty shell casing in the chamber of the shotgun found lying down the street was of the same brand and gauge as the live shells in the gym bag. The firearms examiner also testified that the pellets found in the body of Carillo and Wendy Strutton were consistent with the pellets found in the live shells in the gym bag. They were made of steel and not lead.

"Were two shotguns submitted to you for test firing to determine if they were functional?"

"Yes. I test fired the two shotguns; and both were operational. That means that both worked and were capable of being fired."

"Mr. Johnson, is it possible for you to take a spent shotgun shell casing and determine if a specific shotgun fired it?"

"Yes, it is. A shotgun has a firing pin. When the trigger is pulled, it releases the firing pin and the pin strikes the end of the shell. When the pin strikes the end of the shell, it causes the shell to discharge -- to fire. The firing pin strikes a portion of the shell that is called the primer. The primer is a piece of metal located in the metal end of a shotgun shell. When the firing pin hits the primer, the pin makes, and leaves, an indentation in the metal primer. The indentation sets off the gunpowder and the gun shoots." The witness paused a moment to let his testimony sink in. "Now, concerning this shotgun's firing pin, if you look at the metal firing pin under a microscope, you would see that it has scratches on the end of it. Of course, you cannot see these scratches with the naked eye, but you can under a microscope. When this firing pin hits this primer and makes an indentation in the primer, the firing pin transfers those same scratches onto the primer and leaves the indelible print on the primer. Similar to the way a fingerprint leaves the same markings onto another surface. So, if you have some spent shell casings and you want to determine if they were fired from a particular shotgun, all you do is test fire the shotgun. Then you take those shell casings that you know were fired from that shotgun and compare them with the other shell casings. You put them side by side under a specially made microscope that we have and look at the primers of both shells. If the indentations in both shells match up -- that is, if both indentations from the two shells have matching scratches -- then you can say that this shotgun fired both shells."

From the evidence table Marshall Logan picked up the shotgun found down the street next to the gym bag. Approaching the witness, he handed him the shotgun.

"Mr. Johnson, can you identify this exhibit?"

"Yes. It is a shotgun that was given to me by Detective Genovise."

"What did you do with it once you got it?"

"Well, like I said earlier, I test fired it to see if it was operational. And it was. Then I compared some spent shell casings to determine if this gun fired those shells."

Logan handed the witness a see-through plastic bag containing the two spent shotgun shells found in the street close to Ramon Garza's bent-in front fender.

"These were submitted to me by Detective Genovise. And I was asked to determine if this shotgun fired these two shells."

"Did you do that, and what did you find?"

"Well, I determined that this gun fired these two shells."

"Did you compare these two empty shells with the empty shell that was found in the shotgun?"

"Oh, yes. And they matched, too."

"Mr. Johnson, you told us that two shotguns were submitted to you by Detective Genovise."

His left hand held the gun found down the street. And then holding in his right hand the shotgun found next to Ramon Garza, "By appearance, can you describe these guns?"

"Okay. In your left hand is a 12-gauge shotgun. Made by Browning. It has been sawed off at both ends -- the barrel end and the stock end. It is a pump shotgun and can hold up to three shells."

"What does 'pump shotgun' mean?"

"That means that after the person shoots, he has to pump this grip or handle in order to eject that spent shell and to put a live shell in the chamber."

"Like so." Johnson pumped the grip, demonstrating his testimony. The witness nodded.

"What's a semi-automatic shotgun?"

"A semi-automatic ejects the shells automatically. The person doing the shooting doesn't have to pump it. After he shoots one round, the gun automatically spits that shell out and puts another one into the chamber ready to be fired again. Most people call it an 'automatic', but actually the technical name is a semi-automatic. An automatic allows a person to pull the trigger once and keep it pulled back and it would fire like a machine gun. A semi-automatic allows the person to pull the trigger one time and then it stops firing. If the person shooting wants to shoot again, he has to pull the trigger again. Automatic weapons are illegal for most people to own. Semi-automatics are not. Those are the kind you can buy at the stores. On a pump action, when I pull the grip down or pump it down, this action ejects the shell; and when I push or pump it back up, that pushes a live shell into the chamber. After the person pumps a shell into the chamber, he still has to pull the trigger. After that, he has to pump another shell into the chamber and then pull the trigger again if he wants to shoot it again."

"What happens if I shoot it and don't pump it?"

"Nothing. The spent shell stays in the chamber. And the only way to get another shell into the barrel is to pump it, like I showed you."

"Okay. Let's look at this other gun. The shotgun found next to Ramon Garza. What is it?"

"It, too, is a 12-gauge, pump action shotgun. It is an Ithaca brand -- made by the Ithaca Company. It, too, is sawed off at both the barrel end and the stock end. It can hold up to five shells."

"Of course, Mr. Johnson, you don't know if either of these guns were loaded or unloaded when they were found by Detective Genovise, do you?"

"Well, not of my own personal knowledge. But I have read his report."

"Now about the gun found next to Garza; you weren't given any spent shells to compare with this shotgun, were you?"

"No sir. One spent shell and four live shells accompanied the gun. They came with the shotgun."

"Yes sir," replied Logan, "only one spent shell?"

"Correct."

"Mr. Johnson, assume with me, if you will, that Detective Genovise found this gun next to a dead man, with one spent shell in the chamber and four more live shells in the magazine. What would that indicate to you?"

"It would only indicate that after a round was shot, the shooter did not pump it to eject the shell and put another live one in the barrel."

"That is to say -- and correct me if I'm wrong -- that for whatever reason, the shooter decided not to eject the spent shell and get another one ready to fire?"

"Well, I can't say that he 'decided' not to do it. I just know that the shooter did not do so."

"Then assuming what I told you, that is, that this gun was found next to a dead man having been shot, and that it had one spent shell in the barrel and four live ones in the magazine, is that setting consistent with the dead man shooting one time, and then himself, getting shot and killed before he had a chance to pump it and shoot again?"

"Yes it is."

Harry Johnson further testified that the shotgun pellets found in Tony's body were made of lead. The importance of this, explained the expert witness, was that the spent shell in the shotgun found within arm's reach of Ramon Garza had contained lead pellets. Not steel. Moreover, the four live shotgun shells found in this shotgun contained lead pellets; and the shells were the same brand as the one spent shell casing.

Logan began questioning the witness concerning the "mystery bullet" found in Garza's body. At this point, the theatrics started. The spectacle that Travis Payne initially thought would be forthcoming in the medical examiner's testimony concerning this bullet became a reality.

With an air of confidence, Logan casually walked to the witness chair and picked up State's Exhibit 47 -- the mystery bullet that had been found in Garza's body. With his right hand he vigorously shook the white cardboard box. The noisy rattling of the projectile inside could be heard all over the courtroom. While facing the jury, Logan suddenly tossed the cardboard box about a foot into the air and then caught it with the same hand.

"Shit," thought Travis Payne to himself, "enough of this Hollywood crap. Get on with it."

The special prosecutor tossed it into the air again. The quiet courtroom watched as he caught it a second time and then laid it on the witness stand in front of Harry Johnson. Saying nothing, Logan walked back to his chair and sat down. For 30 seconds there was silence.

"What is in that box?" he finally asked.

"It is the projectile that was removed from the body of Ramon Garza."

"What is the caliber of that bullet?"

"It was a single projectile from a .32 caliber."

"What kind of gun can fire this kind of bullet?"

"Only a .32 pistol can fire this type of bullet."

"Can a shotgun?"

"No."

"Only a pistol; and only a .32 caliber pistol?"

"That is correct."

"Sir, did you review the medical examiner's autopsy report?"

"Yes sir."

"And so you knew that the cause of death of those people was made by gun shots? That is, those pellets and this projectile?"

"Yes sir."

"So," paused the special prosecutor for effect, "what you are telling us, sir, is that everyone out there was killed by a shotgun except" -- Logan paused again and then continued in a raised voice while looking directly at the jury -- "except Ramon Garza?"

"Yes sir."

"And he was killed with a different weapon?"

"That's right."

While the expert answered, Logan was standing, cradling both guns in his arms. With a shotgun under each arm, Logan pranced for no apparent reason to the witness stand then back to the counsel table. He continued his volley of questions while standing with both guns clearly shoved into the jurors' view.

"Did the police submit to you a .32 caliber pistol to test fire?" A hint of disbelief shaded the question.

"No, they did not." The witness had a quizzical look on his face.

"Sir, you were aware, were you not, that two men and a woman were killed by shotgun blasts?"

"Yes sir."

"And you examined those shotguns, right?"

"Right."

"And as far as you know, this pistol.... has....never.....been....recovered?" His slow cadence at the end of the question dramatically emphasized the importance. Logan hoped the jury could see where he was going. This weapon's disappearance, by implication, was done by the person who used it. And since everybody else was found dead, except the driver of the car, was it the driver who fired the pistol? Marshall Logan let the question and implication stand.

The prosecutor was still cavorting around the courtroom, and Payne could take it no longer. He acknowledged the point had been made concerning the missing pistol, but he felt that he had to do something to stop the steamrolling effect.

"Objection, Your Honor," he bellowed. "The question calls for this witness to speculate. Also, the witness doesn't know what has or has not been recovered." But the brief interruption by the defense attorney did not slow down his opponent.

"Well," swaggered the prosecutor, as he simply rephrased the question with a voice full of sarcasm, "a .32 caliber pistol was never turned over to you for examination, was it?" The question, though proffered to the witness, was actually aimed at the defense attorney. The scowl on Logan's face made it clear to the defense attorney: Don't mess with me with meaningless and idiotic objections.

"No sir."

"Pass the witness."

The famed defense attorney -- trying hard to look unperturbed -- sat quite still. Feeling dejected, he said, "I have no questions." He knew the damage had been done.

The witness stepped off the stand.

The special prosecutor dramatized the existence of the "mystery" bullet as much as Mitchell thought he would. The single projectile found in the body of Ramon Garza had worried Mitchell since his attorney had first quizzed him about it. Payne had initially found out about it when the prosecution handed over to the defense all laboratory reports, and scientific evidence results and analysis.

What made the bullet "mysterious" to Mitchell and Payne was the fact that it could not be accounted for. How the bullet came into existence, who shot the .32 caliber pistol, where the pistol disappeared to, and how it disappeared were completely unknown and unaccountable. None of these questions could be answered by Roy Mitchell or Travis Payne. It was totally baffling to them. At first, Marshall Logan had shied away from discussing with Payne the existence of the bullet. Even Payne noticed the special prosecutor's reluctance to talk about it. The defense attorney interpreted this reticence as an attempt to downplay its importance---until trial that is. At which point Logan would vehemently declare its crucial importance and major indicator of Mitchell's guilt. In preparation for trial, Payne had grilled Roy Mitchell about it. Mitchell, confounded and befuddled, was at a loss for any type of explanation surrounding the "mystery bullet". He knew he had not had a pistol that day, much less fired that shot. He also knew, just as strongly, that Tony Medina had not fired it. Of the three dead people at Carillo's house, he had not seen anyone shoot a pistol. Nor could he remember seeing anyone else at the scene. Obviously someone shot Garza. But who? And how had the pistol vanished? Logan believed that Mitchell shot Garza with the pistol. Travis Payne was smart enough to see that Logan's theory made sense. And even though Mitchell denied any knowledge of it, other defendants had lied to Payne before. Maybe Mitchell was lying. Maybe Mitchell had shot Garza with the .32, then disposed of the gun. Maybe Mitchell was guilty. After all, that theory did make sense. And there was no other viable explanation. But in spite of the unexplained evidence, Travis Payne was a good judge of character. And he believed Roy Mitchell when he maintained his innocence. And Payne further believed him when he denied any knowledge of the pistol. It was, indeed, a "mystery" bullet. Payne had even obtained permission from the Judge to perform his own independent testing on the projectile. There was no doubt the projectile found in Ramon Garza was from a gun other than a shotgun. Roy Mitchell and Travis Payne had relentlessly pursued answers to the strange bullet. Regardless of how many times Mitchell went over the sequence of events -- both in his own mind and with Payne -- an answer or explanation for the existence of the "mystery" bullet was not there. And where was the pistol? All of the other guns at the scene were accounted for. The shotgun used by Tony had been found in the street; the shotgun used by Ramon Garza had been found near him. No other guns were found. And the likelihood that some stranger happened onto the scene after the shooting and swiped the gun was farfetched. The conclusion being drawn for the jury was obvious -- at least as far as the State's case was concerned: Roy Mitchell had possessed this gun. And it was this gun that Roy Mitchell had used when he shot and killed Ramon Garza. Afterwards, Mitchell disposed of the weapon during his attempt to cover up his role in the murder.

"How can it be? How can it be?" cried Mitchell to himself that night two months before the trial when he first became aware of the "mystery" bullet. Of course, he had by then been able to piece together the major point of the State's case: Mitchell's active role in the murders. But not only was this deduction untrue, but Mitchell and Payne were at a complete loss to explain that part of the State's theory. And both attorney and client knew that it was that piece of evidence alone that might convict Roy Mitchell of murder. Everything seemed to fit. The pieces of the puzzle all seemed to fit together. He and Tony had driven to Carillo's house. Tony had the shotgun; he had the pistol. Tony shot Carillo while Mitchell shot Garza. And while Mitchell was trying to cover his involvement in the crime he had hidden or destroyed the pistol. Since Logan had included on his list of witnesses the nursing home attendants where Toby lived, Mitchell could foresee the prosecution's strategy. The motive behind him getting involved, Logan would contend, was the fact that the assistant district attorney had gotten emotionally immersed in Medina's plight because of the similarities of the lives and fates of Tony Medina and his brother, Toby. And scariest of all, he was powerless and defenseless against it.

Travis Payne quickly left the courtroom at the day's end and eventually ended up at the hotel bar. It was here, alone with a draft beer, that the attorney reevaluated the day's testimony. The case was moving fairly rapidly. Since he was without much cross examination, Payne believed it was all going too smoothly for the prosecution.

Travis Payne thought about his antagonist, Marshall Logan. "That shithead was acting real cocky today. He had the jury members sitting on the edge of their chairs as he put on a real show for them." He finished off the rest of his beer and ordered another. "And the jackass is making headway with the jury." The day's testimony had been damaging, but he had known it was coming. Rolling it over and over in his mind, he still had nothing to fight it with. He just had to sit and take it. He slapped his hand on top of the table. "Hell, I don't like it," he growled, "It's not my style." The bartender cut his eyes toward the customer and flashed a grin. He was accustomed to customers talking to themselves.

"Another pull, please sir", he signaled as he held up his empty glass.

Payne just hoped the members of the jury would not make up their minds before the defense had a chance to put on its case -- a problem that existed in nearly all criminal cases. As the State plodded along laying pieces of evidence, it was far too easy for the jury to reach a conclusion of the defendant's guilt before the defense had an opportunity to present a case. And what made it even more intolerable for Payne was that he had known it was coming.

"Just hold on," he silently spoke to the jury, "just wait. He finally forced a weak smile, but it quickly left his face when the testimony about the so-called "mystery" bullet came to mind. So injurious and ravaging, he thought as he guzzled half of his beer, and yet so unexplainable -- unless -- unless his client had shot that pistol. The thought had crossed Travis Payne's mind before.

Across town, Marshall Logan was biting into a crispy taco. The extra large plate was once covered with them. Now only one remained. He had been starving. This was the first time he had eaten Mexican food since arriving in Dallas. It was really the first time he had wanted any, and he was celebrating a small victory. He could tell the jury was with him. Before the start of the trial he was not quite sure if he was satisfied with the final twelve jurors. But he could now tell, from reading their facial expressions and other body language, they believed in him. He sensed that they were already getting ready to convict. He figured he only had about a day and a half of testimony left.

The prosecutor glanced at the rectangular object hanging on the wall -- a beer advertisement with a clock on one side. On the other side, was a mountain range in the background and a cowboy in the foreground.

"I'm going to kick that cowboy's ass all the way back to Colorado." Logan left the restaurant and made his way back to his hotel room. It had been a good day.

The physician from Linden looked uncomfortable as he walked into the courtroom. He purposefully diverted his eyes away from his friend, Roy Mitchell. The doctor did not want to be here, it was plain to see. In fact, Logan had threatened to use the Texas Rangers to escort the witness to town to testify.

While the doctor related to the astonished jury the unusual events that had transpired at the Linden Hospital, Mitchell's face was stinging. Although very articulate, the physician's words were constrained. Mitchell felt sick to his stomach. A close personal friend had been forced to testify against him.

The weight of the trial was beginning to take its toll on the defendant. For months he had practiced smothering the worry and anxiety. He had been able to do it. That is, until now. This friend -- Mitchell hoped the doctor was still his friend -- was facing him and narrating events that, in part, were going to convict him of murder. The other witnesses had been Mitchell's friends in a professional setting. The assistant district attorney had been able to convince himself that they were simply doing their jobs -- as was expected and required of them. That had somehow been acceptable. But the present witness -- from his home town -- hit a nerve.

During the pretrial hearings, Payne had vigorously tried to prevent the doctor from testifying, citing doctor/patient privilege. Under the old law, the defense attorney had a point, but such privilege was now governed by the new rules of evidence and there is no doctor/patient privilege. The new rules of evidence -- adopted only two years earlier -- clearly prevailed. The Judge overruled the defense objections and advised both attorneys that he would admit the testimony before the jury.

Logan continued his assault on Roy Mitchell. It was relentless. The trial antics Logan used with the firearms expert were not needed with the doctor. The testimony alone was damaging. Each question to the physician was slow and punctuated. This different approach of direct examination, coupled with the doctor's noticeable reticence, only highlighted the testimony.

Payne's strategy on cross examination was going to be simple: Get the doctor off the witness stand as soon as possible. Nothing about the testimony helped the defense's case; and the less said on the matter, the better. Under the State's questioning, it took the doctor nearly an hour to relate the events. But on cross examination, Payne -- trying to appear stoic and unnerved by the testimony -- confidently announced to the Judge and jury: "Your Honor, we do not have any questions for this witness."

The same announcement was made by the defense attorney after the hospital nurse testified. The testimony of these two witnesses had taken up most of the morning. Both testified to the activities they had performed in the hospital. But, even more damaging, thought Payne, both testified about the explanations Mitchell had given. When the trial resumed after a 15-minute break, Theodore Jackson, Jr., the mechanic from Linden, began his testimony. The witness was obviously ill-at-ease in giving his account of what happened; but he did narrate what had transpired. He, like the doctor, was reluctant. But the alternative to not testifying -- going to jail -- carried the witness through. The witness was three-fourths of the way into his testimony when the Judge broke for an early lunch. After the recess was announced, Payne glanced at his client. Roy Mitchell looked frazzled. The jury, he surmised, had heard enough. How could he refute that testimony? He could not. How could he explain it? He could not.

It was there for all the world to see. He ruminated on the events that had taken place at the hospital. At the time it seemed so foolproof. Every detail had been worked out. Every detail had been carried out to perfection. But afterwards it had all blown up. Somehow, it had all gone awry. He held his head with both hands.

"I know how you're feeling," consoled his attorney, as he placed his hand on his client's shoulder. "But stay with me."

Payne stood from the counsel table and suggested that they go get something to eat. "I stumbled across a good burger place last night. Come on."

As they left the courtroom, the television cameras followed them. The news media had swarmed the trial, and the coverage had been non-stop since the trial had begun. The incessant questioning had started getting on Mitchell's nerves. He was thankful that Judge Carter had imposed a gag order prior to trial. The order allowed the defense to duck any questions, but it did not stop the coverage.

When the trial resumed that afternoon, Theodore Jackson, Jr. finished his testimony.

For what it was worth, Mitchell was proud the witnesses from his hometown had been conspicuously adverse to speaking out against him. Though they had told the truth in their testimony, they had done so begrudgingly. Yet, they were part of the net that Logan was attempting to throw over Roy Mitchell.

Long before the trial had begun, Travis Payne had decided not to question these witnesses from Linden. There was nothing he could ask of them that would exonerate his client. Mitchell had lied to them and had gotten caught doing so. Payne did not want to magnify the blight. After each witness was passed for cross examination, he coolly and impassively responded, "No questions."

But even the famed defense attorney from Colorado was beginning to get edgy. He was not used to keeping quiet as an opponent was flogging him with critical pieces of evidence. His nature said: "Fight back!" But realty answered: "With what?" For now, he was forced to simply sit and take it. Travis Payne kept saying over and over to himself: "Be patient, just wait. Just be patient."

As Theodore Jackson, Jr. left the courtroom, one of the jurors raised her hand to speak to the Judge. Slightly embarrassed, but obviously in much discomfort, she informed the Judge that she was feeling ill. After consulting privately with the attorneys, the trial was recessed until the next day. According to the list of States witnesses given to Payne, the State had only three or four remaining witnesses. The Judge had also been keeping track. After the jury had been retired from the courtroom, he told Payne he figured the State would rest sometime the next day and for Payne to immediately be ready to present his defense.

The next day the large headlines in one of the local papers read: JURY HEARS CONVINCING EVIDENCE. Roy Mitchell was prepared for this. The mass of evidence given at trial had surely been debilitating. At first, he believed the media was supporting him. Before the start of the trial, all of the news items -- articles and editorials alike -- had been pro-Mitchell. But now he wondered if they, like the jury, had heard enough. He wondered if the press heard what they had not wanted to hear. Even the expressions on the faces of some jurors had changed. It was not encouraging. What had not changed since the beginning of the trial was Marshall Logan's attitude. The bare exchange of cordial pleasantries to Payne continued, but his arrogance was ever present. Maybe it was because of the nature of the evidence; and then maybe it was because Logan was just that way. In any event, Mitchell realized that the special prosecutor was presenting a strong case. He also realized Logan had not yet presented the strongest of the evidence. Mitchell knew that the opposing counsel, like all good trial attorneys, was saving his best for last.

Chapter 35

"Tell us your name, please," the prosecutor asked when the trial resumed the following day.

"My name is Frank Barnes."

"And how are you employed?"

"I'm a police officer for the City of Dallas."

"How long have you been a police officer?"

"Twenty-three years."

"Sir, to what division are you currently assigned?"

"I am a detective in the Homicide Division."

Roy Mitchell had long dreaded Barnes' appearance as a witness. He could not begin to count the number of cases in which Frank Barnes had been his key witness. The thoroughness of his investigations was well-recognized throughout all of the Dallas County District Attorney's office. And Mitchell had known it for years and years. They had worked elbow-to-elbow on many cases. One of the most respected individuals known to Mitchell -- both on and off the job -- was now about to testify against him.

Their friendship, both in and out of the courtroom, had been the topic of many newspaper articles dealing with the charges against Mitchell.

When Mitchell first heard that Frank Barnes was the investigator on his case, he knew the detective's professionalism -- his never quenching thirst to know -- would dictate an exhaustive pursuit. Because of Barnes' task, the two had not spoken to each other since the prosecutor left the District Attorney's office. Mitchell suspected that Frank's wife had dropped out of the same bridge club as Beth Mitchell in order to avoid any potential embarrassing meetings.

The special prosecutor's piercing voice brought the defendant back from deep thought. As Logan began his direct examination, he started unveiling the whole story. For more than an hour and a half the attorney for the State questioned Frank Barnes. He asked about the criminal background of Ulysses Carillo and the first investigation involving him, Carillo, and Tony Medina. He asked about the initial shooting of Medina by Carillo, the charges that had been brought and the subsequent dismissal. Somberly, but yet pointedly, the detective particularized the relationship that developed between Mitchell and Tony, beginning as far back as Barnes' recruitment of Mitchell on the incipient case. He soberly testified that, in his opinion, the assistant district attorney took far too personal an interest in the situation.

Payne did not mind Carillo's criminal past being mentioned before the jury by Logan.

Payne himself wanted to use it in his case. He wanted to throw as much dirt on Ulysses Carillo's persona as he could. Travis Payne knew it always helped the defense's case if it was shown the deceased deserved to die. If society was safer or better off without this person on the street – good riddance. In essence, why punish someone who had done the community a favor?

On the other hand, Logan wanted to show the previous relationship between Mitchell and Carillo and how this prior relationship showed a motive for Roy Mitchell and Tony Medina wanting Carillo killed. Since the law allowed such evidence, either party would be able to show in the trial everything that had previously occurred involving Ulysses Carillo, Tony Medina, and Roy Mitchell.

During the morning recess, while Payne made a telephone call back to his office, Mitchell went to get them both a cup of coffee. Since the start of the trial, Mitchell had not walked around the courthouse. The reason stemmed from embarrassment. He knew almost everyone in the building and facing them was something he could not do. Once the trial started he quickly entered and exited the building, not stopping inside until he was in the courtroom or the defense witness room. However, Barnes' testimony began to upset him, and he needed something to calm him. He knew where a little-known coffee machine was located. It was partially hidden and rarely used, and he had often wondered why building services kept it there. Traveling down a few floors via the stairwell, his mind absorbed what Detective Barnes just said to the jury. Now, looking back, his friend was correct. He had gotten too involved with Tony Medina's case. Many times the homicide detective had warned him, but it never really sank in. He could separate business and personal. At least that was always his reply. Obviously, he concluded, he could not.

Reaching into his pocket for change for the coffee, he rounded the corner to the machine. He had only seen three or four people and, fortunately, had not known any of them. Suddenly, he nearly ran over Frank Barnes coming from the other direction. They both froze, neither knowing what to do or say.

The policeman regained his composure first. "Hello, my friend."

"It's been nearly impossible for me not to call," Mitchell replied.

"I've felt the same way, Roy. Regardless of what happens down here, you're still a good friend."

Enmeshed in the situation, Mitchell could only nod.

"I'll see you," concluded the officer as he stepped around Mitchell and went out of sight.

The tall, husky bailiff spoke in a commanding voice as he faced the audience: "All rise, please, the Court is back in session."

As the bailiff finished, Judge Carter appeared in the courtroom. The Judge's chair and the elevated podium were characteristically called "the bench". It was situated about three feet higher than the other tables and chairs in the courtroom. The job delegated to him by law was to preside over the matters below him. The high and mighty judge, so went the phrase, was just that: physically higher than anyone else in the courtroom and awesomely mighty. His job was to dispense justice -- usually adroitly done with just a slight movement of his hand across legal documents or the sound of his voice. The dignified setting was enhanced by the Judge himself. Wearing a black robe, and glasses, and carrying some law books, Judge Wendall Carter looked and carried himself like a Judge.

"Mr. Prosecutor, you may continue your direct examination of the witness," the Judge spoke casually.

"Thank you, Your Honor." Turning to the witness, "Detective Barnes, did you participate in the investigation of the deaths of Ulysses Carillo, Ramon Garza, and Wendy Strutton?"

"Yes, I did."

"Tell me -- or more importantly, tell the members of the jury what you did in that respect."

"I was called out to the crime scene by another officer. When that officer discovered that one of the individuals killed was Ulysses Carillo. He called me."

"Why did that other officer call you?"

"Protocol. I had handled the previous investigation between Carillo and Medina. Department policy said it was my case. I was familiar with the parties involved."

"So, once you arrived at the scene, what did you do?"

The witness recounted his movements in taking over the crime scene. Barnes testified that he was essentially overseeing the work of the other officers. He told the patrol officers to spread out among the crowd of bystanders to see if any of them had seen or heard anything. Conferring frequently with the officer from the Physical Evidence Section, he tried to piece together the facts.

"I had the advantage of knowing about the previous incidences," he testified. "With that knowledge, together with what I could see at the scene and....and what I later learned about Tony" -- he paused -- "I knew, or thought I knew what had happened. It was pretty clear to me."

"And what was that?"

"Tony Medina was seeking to retaliate against Carillo for what Carillo had done to him. And that Tony Medina was killed trying to carry it out."

"Was anything missing from that scenario?"

"I don't understand. What do you mean?"

"Well, from looking at the crime scene and what you already knew about the parties, could Tony Medina have acted alone?"

"Not entirely, no."

"Why was that?"

"Well, I knew Medina was paralyzed and could not drive a car. I figured that someone brought him over to Carillo's house. That car and the person who drove the car were missing."

"What did you do next?"

"Well, I was finishing up at the crime scene. I got a call from Tony Medina's father. I was still at the shooting location. Tony's body had been found in front of their house. He had been shot. I hurried straight over to the Medina home."

"Who went with you?"

"Another homicide detective, Victor Russell."

"Who was at the Medina house?"

"Mr. Juan Medina, who is the father of the deceased, and Juanita Medina, who is the deceased's sister."

"Were you the first officer to arrive at the Medina's?"

"Yes sir."

"What did you do? What happened?" asked Logan.

"Well, Tony was in the living room on the sofa. We checked for vital signs but he was already deceased. We called for additional police elements. We called for the Medical Examiner to come to the house. PES was also called. While we were waiting on those other units to arrive the other detective asked if we could look around the house. We were allowed to do so, and so we did -- or, I should say, he did."

"Did you find anything that you collected as evidence?"

"We found a rag with blood on it. Actually, the other detective found it, but I saw him when he found it. The rag was in the kitchen sink."

Reaching behind him, Logan pulled out a piece of cloth from a box lying on the floor. Walking up to the witness stand, he showed it to the witness, who identified it as the bloody cloth found at the Medina home.

When the witness identified the cloth, the State's attorney continued: "Detective, did you question anyone at the house about the rag?"

"No sir."

"What's that?" interjected the defense attorney. "I couldn't hear your answer." Travis Payne actually heard it. He just wanted to make sure that the jury heard it.

"I said, 'No'. I did not question anyone about the cloth."

"Why not?" asked Logan.

"About that time, Mr. Medina and his daughter were starting to break down and -- well, it was not or did not seem appropriate at that time to continue any further questioning. I knew the family, and I planned on coming back out when things calmed down and question them about it."

"What did you do with the rag?"

"We asked them if we could have it. They said, yes, so we collected it."

"Then what happened?"

"The back-up units arrived. The M. E.'s office arrived and transported the body away. When PES arrived later, they looked over the area and took photos of the sidewalk. Presumably they thought the sidewalk was the only area that needed their attention. And when they finished with the photographs, they left before I could give them the rag. I forgot to give it to them when they were there."

"What is the next thing you did on this case?"

"Well, sir, that night I became ill and was sick in bed with the flu for the next four or five days; so I did not do anything until the day of Tony Medina's funeral."

Detective Barnes detailed the events of the day of the funeral. He testified about the blinding reflection, the discovery of the broken rearview mirror and the pellet indentations on the car. He told of learning the car belonged to Roy Mitchell and that this was the first break in the case. He concluded his testimony with his trip to Linden and the things he found there. The dramatic testimony given by Barnes about the defendant's comatose brother stirred everyone. From all of the news that had been generated about the case, no one had uncovered those critical facts. Payne hoped that testimony about the condition of his client's brother would create a sympathy angle. But Payne also knew the reason Marshall Logan thought it important.

At long last, the jury had been given some evidence-a glimpse-into the mind of Roy Mitchell. And what would make him get involved in the murder. The jury was provided a motive, or at least some semblance of a motive behind Mitchell's participation. Roy Mitchell viewed Toby in the body of Tony Medina. He wanted to help kill the person responsible for putting Medina in a wheelchair. Mitchell had gotten caught up in the case, and wanted to help in granting his friend's only desire: Get revenge on Carillo. When Logan learned about Roy's brother and the condition of Tony Medina, the special prosecutor knew he had found the key to the case. It was a subtle connection. But Logan believed it. And if the impact that it had made on him was any indication of its degree of importance in the case, Logan had to show it to the jury. Marshall Logan finished questioning Detective Barnes after the revelation of Mitchell's brother. When the State's attorney looked at his watch, he noticed that it was 11:30 a.m. Barnes had been testifying all morning. Judge Carter recessed for lunch until 1:00 p.m.

Payne knew his cross examination of Frank Barnes would take quite some time. Over the noon break, he went over the many pages of notes he had written in anticipation of the lengthy cross examination of Barnes. One thing that distinguished Payne from the rest of the pack was that he wanted to know as much as he could about all of the persons involved -- their background, their habits, their pleasures. And no one was better able to supply this information about Frank Barnes than Roy Mitchell. Of all the things Mitchell told him about Frank Barnes, Payne had been impressed the most with the integrity of the veteran policeman -- even more than the high degree of thoroughness Barnes attached to his job. And it was through this witness that Payne was going to create his defense. Repeatedly, Payne had questioned his client about Barnes' knowledge of the prior affiliation among Carillo, Medina, and Mitchell. Barnes had knowledge that could help the defense, facts not known by Logan. And even some of the facts already elicited from Barnes would play into his defense.

When the trial resumed at 1:00 p.m., Payne began, "Detective Barnes, my name is Travis Payne, and I represent Mr. Mitchell. Sir, let me ask you, from your investigation and talking to the witnesses at the crime scene, do you know if the police were called immediately after the shooting had stopped?"

"Yes, they were. I spoke with a lady that called the police. She indicated she had called within seconds of the gunfire."

The attorney from Colorado delved further into the background of Carillo. The prosecutor had attempted to soften the impact by bringing it out first, but by Payne's standards he had not gone far enough. Whether Logan had intentionally neglected certain things, or had simply overlooked them, did not matter. Plus the jury got to hear some of this information twice.

Starting with Ulysses Carillo's activities in Cuba and then in Mexico, Payne showed Carillo's criminal life through Barnes. Payne had been able to subpoena the police intelligence files on Carillo. Every gritty detail of Carillo's sordid life was exposed before the jury.

"Detective Barnes, since you were the chief investigator in this case and in the previous case between Carillo and Mr. Medina, I assume that you have done an extensive background check into the life of Mr. Carillo." Payne's voice was low as he zeroed in on the criminal history of Carillo. "Is that correct?"

"That is correct. I have done so."

"You were aware, then, that Mr. Carillo had been serving time in the penitentiary in Cuba just before he was shipped to Mexico?"

"Yes, I was," answered Barnes. "He was in prison there for assault and murder."

"Murder?" highlighted the defense attorney.

"Yes sir."

"Did he go to Mexico voluntarily?"

"No, I don't believe so."

"Castro was emptying his prisons, and he was shipping the inmates to whatever country would accept them; isn't that correct?"

"I believe so, sir."

"He arrived in Mexico in about 1980, didn't he?"

"I believe so."

"He had been there less than a year when he was arrested and convicted of selling drugs and sent to a Mexican jail. Correct?"

"Yes, that's correct."

"After he was released from the Mexican penitentiary for selling drugs, wasn't he later convicted of murder and sent back to the Mexican penitentiary for five years?"

"Yes, that --"

Payne was on a roll before the jury, and he was not going to stop until he was finished making his point. Before the witness could finish answering the question, the defense attorney fired another at him. Travis Payne knew this was where his preparation paid off. He did not refer to any notes for the dates, places, or offenses. He knew them by memory. Taking time to refer to notes would break the smooth rhythm and flow of questions. Also, and maybe even more importantly, his rapid questioning did not give the witness adequate time to evaluate an answer.

"The first time he was in prison in Mexico for selling drugs, he received a sentence of five years. The second time -- this time for murder -- he only received five years." Payne's voice boomed to the jury: "How could he receive the same amount of time in the penitentiary the second time as he had received the first time? And the second conviction was for" -- he paused, lowering his voice to barely above a whisper -- "murder?"

Marshall Logan had to stop the steamrolling of Travis Payne, if he could. "Objection. Objection." Logan slowly rose from his chair before he addressed the Judge. "It calls for this witness to speculate."

"Sustained." The objection was of no consequence to the defense attorney; the question already had its effect.

Logan objected to the defense asking about every particular and specific bad act.

"Your Honor," responded Payne, "Carillo's past was initially brought out in front of the jury by the State. They opened the door on this evidence. Since they brought it up, we also should be allowed to go into it. They went into detail, and so we are allowed to go into detail. They -- the State -- just do not like the details that we are bringing out."

"Overule the objection," the judge ruled.

Payne wanted the previous crimes to make an impact on the jury before he continued, so he pretended he was studying some papers on his table. The courtroom was quiet. All eyes were on the defense attorney, as if they were expecting something magical. Even Mitchell did not dare move. Staring straight ahead, he was unsure what would happen next. But Travis Payne was not finished trying to paint a picture for the jury.

"When Carillo got to this country," pursued Payne, "and by the way, our country issued him papers to come to this country legally, didn't they?"

Looking at the jury and not at the witness whenever he asked the questions, Payne was not attacking the witness but attacking Carillo.

"Isn't that a hell of a way to run our country?" snarled Payne.

"That is a side-bar remark, an editorial comment, and I object to it."

"Sustained. Mr. Payne, I've warned you before. Don't do that," instructed the Judge. Payne nodded toward the Judge.

"Well," drawled the defense attorney, "isn't it a fact that when Carillo got to the United States, he landed here in Dallas?"

"Yes."

"And when he got here, he started selling drugs," said Payne.

"Is that a question?" asked Barnes.

"I meant for it to be one, yes, sir."

"Yes, you're correct. He started selling drugs."

"He got caught and convicted, and we sent him to our penitentiary, didn't we?"

"Yes sir."

"And when he got out of our prison, he wasn't deported was he?"

"No sir."

"Why not?"

"Objection," announced Logan. "It calls for this witness to speculate."

"Sustained." Judge Carter did not even look up.

"And when he got out of our prisons, he came right back here and started selling drugs ... again. Right here.....Dallas, Texas." The raw contempt in Payne's voice was evident. With his eyes fastened on the jury and not on Barnes, he continued.

"That's true, isn't it, Officer?"

"That's true."

"This man, Carillo, was becoming such a big person in the drug market that the Intelligence Division of the Dallas Police Department began keeping a separate file on him, correct?"

"Yes sir."

"But he was slick, wasn't he? He was able to avoid being arrested?"

"Correct."

Not wanting to alienate the witness, Payne quickly added while gesturing toward the witness, "Through no fault of the police department that is. I know you people wanted to arrest him as badly as anyone."

Barnes forced a smile. "You're correct there."

A few chuckles were heard in the jury box and scattered around the gallery.

"But my point is, Officer, the police were wanting to arrest him, but he was able to avoid being arrested?"

"Yes sir," Barnes answered emphatically.

"Officer, earlier in your testimony, when you were questioned by the Government lawyer, you reiterated that you were familiar with Carillo's shooting of Mr. Medina; the shooting that occurred some months prior to this case. Do you remember testifying to those facts?"

"I do."

For the next half hour, Payne took Detective Barnes through his involvement in the investigation of that case. By doing so, it enabled the jury to hear for the second time about the shooting of Tony Medina that left him paralyzed.

"I take it that during your investigation of the shooting of Tony Medina by Carillo, you had several interactions with the Medina family?"

"Correct."

"Did Tony Medina ever confide in you the fact that he wanted to get even with Ulysses Carillo?"

"Not directly."

"What do you mean?"

"On many occasions Roy told me that that is what Tony had said."

"Did you ever do anything to dissuade Tony Medina from such talk?"

"No."

"Why not?"

"I was going to several times. I mentioned it to Roy, but he said that he would handle it. He wanted to do it since he thought he shared the most rapport with him. I was confident he could handle it."

"Did you ever go over to the Medina house to make a social call? You know, just to visit?"

"Not by myself and not on my own initiative. I was with Roy once or maybe twice whenever he wanted to go over there and drop things off."

"What would he drop off?"

"Oh, food -- cake, cookies, that sort of thing."

"At some point you learned that Tony Medina wanted to drop the charges; isn't that true?"

"Yes sir. That's right."

"Did you ever attempt to dissuade Tony Medina from dropping the charges?"

"I think I did. I know Roy and I talked about it. I believe I did talk to him, once. Roy told me he had tried his best to talk him out of it and wanted me to try. But I believed that he was more capable of handling the situation -- both personally and professionally -- so I basically left it up to him."

"All during this time, Detective Barnes, did the citizen that is accused -- Roy Mitchell -- make any statements to you about wanting to get Carillo?"

"Certainly not! Certainly not!" The words gushed out so fast and earnestly that it momentarily took everyone by surprise. The emotional response had not been intentional. It had slipped out. For a second Barnes allowed his friendship with Mitchell to dictate his answer. For the first time he could ever remember, Barnes' professionalism slipped.

"As a matter of fact, sir, Roy Mitchell would never make such a statement because that is not the character of Roy Mitchell, is it?"

Logan was out of his chair instantly. "We object, Your Honor."

"I bet you do!" chimed Travis Payne, as he looked first at the prosecutor and then back at the witness.

"Now, wait a minute! Hold it!" burst in an angry Logan. He glared toward the defense attorney, his voice screaming and his arms flailing. "Wait just a minute! That's uncalled for!"

The hostile exchange between the lawyers brought out a buzz of chatter across the courtroom.

"Order! Order!" exclaimed the Judge in a loud voice, banging his gavel. "Everyone quiet, quiet." When order was restored in the courtroom, Judge Carter turned to the two lawyers. For a few seconds he said nothing, allowing his anger to subside. Staring down at the two men, he recognized them for what they were -- two gladiators fighting it out in the courtroom arena. At last he spoke.

"Mr. Payne, you know the rules of courtroom demeanor." Attorneys in trial can converse with one another. However, snide comments are not allowed. Judge Carter continued, "I will not tolerate any more comments like that. Is that clear?"

The defense attorney nodded. "Yes, sir," he said. But his tone was one of defiance.

Turning to the prosecutor, the Judge panned: "Counsel, contain yourself."

"The objection is overruled. Let's take a break. Better yet, I'm tired. We are going to recess for the day.

Payne was glad for the timing of the recess. He felt he had scored some points from the characterization of Carillo, and he wanted the jury to have some time to reflect on it. For now, though, it had been a productive day.

Chapter 36

Someone had already made coffee when Barnes entered the witness room the next morning. He was the only person in the room. Settling easily into a chair, he began to read the newspaper and sip his coffee. He intentionally avoided the story about the trial splashed on the front page. Actually, since the very beginning of the investigation, he had avoided reading news articles about the case.

The witness room was quiet except for the noise occasionally made from the turning of the sports page of the newspaper. Barnes relished these few quiet moments. Finishing the sports section, he set the paper aside and reflected on the past few days. He cupped both hands around the styrofoam coffee cup. Thinking about the trial. Like most others involved with the case, he was glad it had begun. The sooner it started, the sooner it would end. The unenviable position of being caught in the middle of the case was not comfortable; nor was it anything that Frank Barnes had wanted. Looking back on it, maybe he should have told the chief to assign someone else to the case. At least that was his feeling now. The only way that he had been able to cope with the idea of testifying against a friend was his belief in the judicial system. His professional career and practically his whole life had been spent working in "the system". And the judicial system did work. He believed in it. Sure, he knew there were aberrations, but, for the most part, it worked. It worked for the betterment of society.

Barnes' thoughts shifted to his testimony. So far, he grinned, he had not made an ass out of himself in front of the jury. The cross examination, while histrionic by Payne at times, had come out smoothly. So far, at least, the ranting by the defense attorney had not been directed at him.

After nearly ten minutes of solitude, other witnesses started drifting into the room. Barnes was glad all of the witnesses for the State were being kept in a conference room in the District Attorney's office and not near the courtroom. The courtroom had been packed every day. The overflow of spectators spilled out into the hallway; where they were constantly milling around. Added to the situation was the barrage of media representatives and cameramen.

He felt sorry for the bailiffs -- they had to control this mess.

He was looking at his watch when the Judge's intern came to retrieve him to the courtroom. It was exactly 8:57 a.m.

"Ready to go, Mr. Barnes?" asked the college student.

"You bet. Let's go. The Judge likes to start on time," Barnes replied. They went out the door and started the two-minute walk down the stairs to the courtroom.

It was standing room only as Frank Barnes entered the courtroom; it had been full since 8:00 a.m. With the large number of people talking, the noise had gotten quite loud. Twice the bailiffs had to call them down to keep quiet. However, as the homicide detective entered, all was silent. The Judge was on the bench, the lawyers in their spaces, with the jury already in the jury box. Striding down the aisle to the front of the courtroom, Barnes had the feeling of walking onto a stage for a theatrical performance. In a sense, it was true.

When he seated himself in the witness chair, the trial resumed.

"We're still on cross examination of Mr. Barnes," announced the Judge. "You may begin, Mr. Payne."

"Did the citizen accused ever tell you that he wanted to get Carillo, to get even with him for what he had done to Tony Medina?"

"No sir."

"A statement like that would not be characteristic of Roy Mitchell, would it?" Payne asked in a casual voice. It was quite a change from the way he had spoken the day before.

"Objection --"

"Overruled. You can answer the question."

"No sir. He would not say anything like that."

"Detective, have you tried many cases where Roy was the prosecuting attorney?"

"Yes, I have. Many."

"So, I take it -- and correct me if I am wrong -- you have a professional, working relationship with my client. You as the detective, and him as the prosecuting attorney. Is that correct?"

"Yes sir."

"So, Detective Barnes, when you say that Roy Mitchell would not make a statement like that -- that is, that he wanted to get Carillo -- are you speaking partly from a professional point of view?

"Partly."

"You also know Roy Mitchell on a personal basis, don't you?"

"Yes, sir, I do."

"You have been to his house; he has been to your house. Your family has been with his family; and his family has been with your family?"

"Yes, that's true."

"Knowing him personally, would Roy Mitchell make a statement like that?" Payne continued his low-key approach. It was too early in the morning for flair.

"In my opinion, no."

"From your personal and professional dealings with the citizen accused, he played -- as they say -- he played strictly by the book?"

"That's correct."

"Your Honor, may I have a moment?" Payne paused.

"Okay," responded the Judge.

Payne did not really need any time; he simply wanted the previous questions and answers to soak into the jury. After feigning looking at some papers for a few seconds, he continued. "Detective, I want to talk about fingerprints for a little while. A police officer does not get promoted to the level of a homicide detective without some knowledge of fingerprints; isn't that true?

"Somewhat. I know a little about them."

"I mean, we all know you are not an expert in the field, but in your experience working homicides and other crimes, you have been around cases where fingerprints have been deposited by individuals at the crime scene. True?"

"True."

"The fingerprint expert in this case has already told the jury that sometimes fingerprints can stay on an item for days, even weeks. You knew that, didn't you?"

"Yes, I did."

"Since you were the lead investigator on this case, I take it that at some point you were informed that Roy Mitchell's prints were found on a gym bag?"

"That's correct."

"You don't know how long those prints had been on that bag, do you?"

"No, I do not."

"Nor the circumstances as to how or why Roy Mitchell touched that bag, do you?"

"No."

"Those prints could have been on that bag for weeks prior to the shootings?"

"They could have been, yes, sir."

"As an illustration ... if, right now, I were to give you this fountain pen -- and, by the way, it is a real fountain pen," smiled Payne -- "and asked you to write your name on a piece of paper, and then I took this pen with me while I went and robbed a bank and somehow left the pen at the bank, when the police came to try to lift any fingerprints from it, your fingerprint might be lifted from it. See what I mean, Officer? That could happen, couldn't it, Officer?"

"Yes sir. That could happen."

"And your fingerprint might be on the pen, and you had no idea I was going to rob the bank. That could happen?"

"Yes sir."

"And then the police might think you were the robber, wouldn't they?"

"Probably so."

There was another lull, intentionally planned, before the next question.

"You said earlier that on a few occasions you had been over to the Medina house. I assume that after you got there, you sat down, like we all do when we go over to someone's house. And I expect that on the occasions that you were there, you touched a variety of things -- just normal touching or feeling of things?"

"Like what?" Barnes was confused.

"Nothing in particular. Maybe you touched the door as you entered; maybe you touched the arm of the chair as you sat down; maybe you picked up a drinking glass that was within your reach. Anything that would have been normal for you to touch while at someone's home. You know, you did not go over there with your hands tied behind your back."

"Oh, yeah. Now I follow you. Yes, I am sure that I touched some things,"

"Exactly. What I am getting to, Detective Barnes, is that your fingerprints may be on some things in the Medina house that belong to the Medina family; your prints that were just casually placed there by way of you having been over there. Isn't that correct?"

"Yes, that's possible." Barnes' eyebrows raised as he answered the question.

"And you know that Roy Mitchell had been over to the Medina house on countless occasions?"

"Yes sir. That's true."

"And as many times as Roy Mitchell has been over to the Medina house, you'd expect for him to have touched quite a few items. That's a fair assessment, isn't it?"

"Yes, it is." Without knowing it, Barnes' head was continuously nodding as he answered the questions affirmatively.

"So, Detective Barnes, knowing what you know about Roy Mitchell and the Medina household, in this particular case" -- Payne stressed the words 'in this particular case' -- "finding Roy Mitchell's fingerprints on objects belonging to the Medina family does not really surprise you, does it?"

Travis Payne was taking a calculated risk. Based on the previous answers given by the policeman, Payne believed that he had the officer boxed in to giving a "no" answer. It wouldn't really surprise Barnes if Mitchell's prints had been found on other items belonging to Tony and his family.

Frank Barnes also saw the paradox in the question. The question was similar to asking the old joke: "Have you stopped beating your wife?" For the first time since he had been on the witness stand, Barnes hesitated before he answered, "No, sir". And it was an honest answer based on how Frank Barnes actually felt about the matter.

His response caused some murmuring in the courtroom, which brought, in turn, a scolding look from Judge Carter. Silence resumed.

"Mr. Barnes," continued the defense attorney, "I am sure in your many years as a policeman you have had occasion to file a criminal charge against more than one person."

"That is true."

"That is to say, that more than one person can commit a single crime. For example, if three guys go in and rob a bank, all three can be charged with robbery, can't they?"

"Yes, they can."

"That is not new -- that is multiple people being charged with a crime. It happens all the time when more than one person commits a crime."

"Correct."

"Detective Barnes, in my example of the guys robbing the bank, if one had a gun, pointed it, and demanded the money; and another stood outside the door and acted as a lookout; and a third drove the getaway car; all three of these men could be charged with robbery?"

"Yes."

"With the exception of the man with the gun, before any of the others could be charged with robbery, they would have had to be knowing participants in the robbery. Correct?"

Frank Barnes nodded.

"In other words," continued Payne, "if they did not know that the place was going to be robbed and did nothing to assist the man with the gun, they could not be charged with robbery. Isn't that true?"

"Yes."

"On television, the people who knowingly help someone else commit the crime are called 'accessories'; but in Texas, these people are called 'parties' to the offense?"

"Uh-huh, that's correct."

"These people must aid, assist, abet, or help in some fashion the other person commit the crime. And they must do so knowingly. That's an accurate statement of the law, isn't it?"

"Yes sir."

"So, before anyone can become a 'party' to an offense, they must fulfill two requirements. One, they must aid, assist, encourage or help in some fashion the other person commit the crime; and second, they must do these things knowingly. That is to say, they must know they are assisting another person commit a crime. That's true, is it not?"

"Right."

"What I am getting at, Detective Barnes, is this. Just because a person is present when a crime is being committed does not necessarily mean he can be charged with the crime as a 'party'?"

"That's true. If he had no knowledge of the crime or did not assist in some way, you are correct."

"Back to my example. If, on the way to rob the bank the robbers pick up a hitchhiker, and they did not tell him they were going to rob a bank, and he just sat in the car with the getaway driver, he could not be charged with robbery, correct?"

"Right."

"And even if he decided to go in with the rest of them just to get a soda pop, if he had no knowledge of the robbery, he could not be charged with robbery?"

"That's still correct."

"Furthermore, if the hitchhiker had carried into the bank the bag to put the money in -- say he assisted the robbers in that fashion, he carried the bag into the bank -- if he had no knowledge that the bank was subsequently being robbed, he should not be charged with robbery. Correct?"

"You're saying if the hitchhiker innocently helped out by carrying the bag into the bank, and if he had no knowledge of the subsequent robbery -- is that your scenario?"

"Yes, that's the picture," responded Payne.

"Then you are correct. He shouldn't be convicted."

"Let's say that once inside the bank the main robber said to the hitchhiker: 'Here, hold onto this bag while I tie my shoe,' and then the main robber pulls a gun and demands the money. The hitchhiker should not be charged with robbery, should he?"

"Well, it would depend on what the hitchhiker did after the gun was pulled and he realized a robbery was going down."

"Okay, good. If the hitchhiker got scared, dropped the bag, and ran away --"

"Then he could not be charged," interrupted the officer.

"Even if his prints were found on the bag," concluded the defense attorney.

"In that example, that's correct."

"So, if a person doesn't assist the others in the carrying out of a crime, he can't be charged -- even though he's at the scene? Can he?"

"No sir."

"And even if he does assist the others by doing something -- if he doesn't know the others are committing a crime, he can't be charged and convicted of committing that crime -- even if he's helping them out?"

"That's true."

Finally, he stood and looked at his watch. It was 10 a.m.

"Your Honor, could we break for a few minutes?"

"Detective Barnes, just before we took a break, we were discussing the unlucky hitchhiker being picked up by a group of robbers on their way to rob a bank."

Judge Carter picked up on the word 'discussing' as it was used in Travis Payne's question. He thought it was a most appropriate. The question-and-answer session that morning had seemed more like a round table discussion than a cross examination of the State's most important witness. Judge Carter wondered if

Travis Payne had designed it that way. Travis Payne hoped the jury accepted it that way. The defense attorney did not need any questions on such a delicate subject being answered by a hostile and antagonistic witness. The Judge looked at Payne. The old adage 'You can catch more flies with honey than with vinegar' came to mine.

"And you had said that before a person could be charged with a crime as a 'party', two things had to happen. The person had to aid or assist the commission in some way, and he had to knowingly participate in the crime. That's where we were."

"I believe so."

"Detective Barnes, let me ask you one more question along this same line before I move on to something else. Is it against the law if a person does not report a crime?"

"Say that again."

"Is it against the law if a person does not report a crime? Let's say a person knows a crime has been committed -- but he did not participate in it -- is it against the law if that person does not report it to the police?"

"No sir. Sad to say, but it is not against the law."

"Let me move on to another area, Officer. Let's talk about this piece of cloth that was found in the Medina's home. Where exactly did your partner find it?"

"In the kitchen sink."

"Was there anything else in the sink?"

"Yes. There were some dishes. Not many, but a few."

"Were they submerged in water?"

"No, not completely. There was some water in the sink, but not very much."

"I think you testified that just as it was found, everything started becoming chaotic -- I mean, the death of a loved one was finally being realized by the family. Is that what you said?"

"That's correct. About that time, everyone started crying and basically losing their composure."

"Did you question anyone in the house about the rag? Where it came from? What substance was on it? How the substance got there? Things like that."

"No, I did not. Like I mentioned, the family became too hysterical for me to proceed with any more questions. The other police units had already gone. My intentions were to come back the next day and resume my investigation."

"But you got sick and were unable to do so," interrupted the defense attorney.

"That's correct."

"And you never went back to question them about this cloth?" asked Payne in a soft, low-directed voice. The stage was being set. Timing, timing, Payne was saying to himself. Go slow. Don't hurry.

Barnes did not like the question, and he liked his answer even less. "No sir. I did not."

Payne's voice rose a degree. "You have a bloody rag and you did not attempt to ascertain where it came from, did you?"

Barnes was aware how it appeared to the jury. When he became ill with the flu, he had left a message for his partner to return to the Medina house to find out about it. But evidently his partner never received the message, because he never went. When Barnes finally returned to work a few days later, he had forgotten to check with his partner. It had been his first day back to work when he made the discovery of Mitchell's car; and honestly, the previous finding slipped his mind. The detection of the broken and possibly shot-up rearview mirror had consumed him. But it was not good police work. It did not look good. And he realized that now.

"And even to this day you have never attempted to find out anything about this rag, have you?"

"That's not true," argued Barnes.

"Oh, it's not?" Payne stopped. The surprised look on his face was obvious for everyone to see. "Oh, it's not?" he repeated. "Well, what did you do?"

"We turned it over to our crime lab to ascertain if any blood was present."

"But, Officer," dug in Payne, "someone else did that work. And we already know about that. I'm talking about what you did -- or, better put, what you did not do."

Barnes soon realized it had been a mistake to spar with the defense attorney.

"I'm talking about what you did in trying to find out how this stain got here; by who, and when." The statement reached a high pitch. "Once you found Roy's car and the broken mirror, all questioning about the rag ceased, didn't it?"

Holding up the rag, Payne was parading it before the jury like a flag. With a look of disgust written over his face, Payne stared at the jury. Throwing the rag onto the defense counsel table, he persisted.

"That bloody rag," he shouted -- "that rag" -- pointing to it -- "that rag was critical, and you guys did not follow up on it, did you?"

There was nothing Barnes could do now. He knew he had erred. And the damage was being magnified in front of this jury. In layman's vernacular, Payne was eating Barnes' lunch. Breathing deep, he forced out, "No sir."

"I mean," Payne slowed, "you people were looking for the driver of the car. You find a cloth with what you think has blood on it, and you do nothing in an attempt to find out who put it there, or how it got there. Nothing!"

Payne was standing. He had been congenial with the officer all day long. But now it was time to play hardball.

"Is that a question?" shot back the witness. Barnes had taken all of Payne's blows and was now trying to fight back; but it only allowed the defense attorney another chance to rub it in the witness' face.

"Darn right it's a question."

"No sir."

Picking up the cloth and again holding it up in front of the jury, he contemptuously asked, "If you had asked anyone about this rag, you might have learned whose it was; you might have learned how it got where it was; you might have learned who put it there; you might have learned a lot of things."

"Objection." Logan had to break the barn-storming effect of the defense attorney. "First of all, it is multifarious; and second, there's not a question in it. Those statements are just that;

statements made by the defense attorney. They are not questions, and I object to them."

"Sustained."

Payne had made his point. The jury heard it. "Well, whatever you could have found out about it, you didn't, did you?"

"No sir."

"I have nothing further of this witness, Your Honor."

The Judge looked at his watch. 12:30 p.m.

"The Court will be in recess until 9:00 a.m. tomorrow. We have scheduling conflicts with some of the next few witnesses."

Payne had been pleased with his cross examination. He had only three or four areas in which he wanted to question Detective Barnes. He had covered them and obtained the answers he wanted. He packed his papers and materials into a worn-out leather satchel. Payne felt good. He had been in control; he had obtained the answers he had desired; and he had paced it for the jury very smoothly. He picked up a list of the potential witnesses that the prosecution might call in their case. After each witness had testified, Payne had penciled through the name. There were only two or three witnesses remaining. The State was winding down its case. He could see Marshall Logan had put together a finely woven case against Mitchell. As much as he personally disliked the prosecutor, he had to give him credit. The special prosecutor was a strong figure. His preparation was obvious. There had not been any kinks or wrinkles in the case styled The State of Texas versus Roy Mitchell. Travis Payne only hoped that the jurors had not already closed their minds. He knew what kind of defense he had to offer. Even though his client did not know it, Payne had some evidence of his own.

Payne smiled to himself when the witness said her name for the members of the jury. It had a pleasing sound to it -- conjuring up images of fairy tales and innocence. The voice of the young witness was accentuated by the deep tone of Logan. Olivia Vanheusen had been employed as a serologist at the Institute of Forensic Sciences for seven years. The smile and twinkling eyes of the witness made her name even more pleasant. Her educational background and qualifications that enabled her to work in the crime lab were beyond question. She obtained a Bachelor of Science degree in biology from Stanford University. She continued her studies at the University of Texas in Austin, where she received a Master's Degree in Microbiology. After graduation, she returned to her hometown where she started working in the renown Dallas County crime laboratory.

Specializing in blood analysis, she had become the head of the Department of Serology. She explained to the jury that serology was the scientific study of the properties and action of the serum of the blood. The testing of different objects for the presence of blood was a matter of routine work she did on a daily basis.

The jury heard that her primary job was to analyze a known blood sample and compare it to another blood sample -- usually collected at a crime scene -- to determine if the two samples had any common characteristics.

With the stained rag in his hand, the special prosecutor approached her and asked if she could identify that exhibit. She identified it as a cloth towel that had been sent to her lab for testing.

"Ma'am, did you perform any tests on it?"

After looking at the tag attached to the exhibit, "Yes, I did."

"What did you find?"

"This exhibit has some blood spots on it. The blood is human in origin, but it has been diluted in something. Because of this, I could not conduct any further testing on it. All I can say is that it has human blood on it. It had just been diluted too much."

"What do you mean? Why not?"

"This rag, I believe, was found soaking in water. And water breaks down the components of blood. As a result, I could not do any more testing.

"Ma'am, could you tell how recent was the bloodstain? And what I mean by that, could you tell if the blood had gotten on there within one day of it being found? Does that make any sense to you?"

"I think I understand what you are asking. You want to know if I could tell if the blood got on the rag the day it was found by the police or did it get on there the week or month before."

"Yes, that's it."

"No, I could not determine that."

"Why not?"

"Technology has not allowed us to go that far."

"So, the bottom line concerning this exhibit is that it has human blood on it, correct? That's all you can say?"

"That is correct."

"Thank you. Pass the witness."

Payne had already decided his cross examination would be relatively short. Actually, he believed because the police had bungled that area of their investigation, her testimony would not be that revealing. The police's failure in the beginning to pursue the lead had belied anything Vanheusen had to say, or so thought the defense attorney.

"Good morning, ma'am. My name is Travis Payne. Uh, of course, you don't know whose blood is on that cloth?"

"No, I don't."

"You just know ... well ... what you've already told us -- that it is human blood?"

She nodded her head.

"You cannot say whether it is Type A, AB, O positive? Can you?"

"That's true."

"Just that it is human blood. Is that right?"

"Yes sir." Again she nodded her head.

In an attempt to lessen any effect her testimony may have, Payne was deadpanning his questions, and also nodding his head after each answer, as if was agreeing with her analysis. He was hoping to silently signal to the jury that her testimony was not damaging in the least. It was a canny suggestion, noticed Judge Carter. It was also highly irritating to Logan. The discord on his face was noticeable.

"And you have already testified that," he paused, "uh, gosh, you don't even know how long that stain had been there," he nodded.

"That's right." Even Olivia Vanheusen was beginning to become silently annoyed at the attorney's attempt to lessen her testimony.

"And you can't tell if the stain came from a cut finger or a stubbed toe, can you?"Someone in the audience cackled at the question.

"No."

"Thank you for coming down. I don't have any more questions."

The attractive witness smiled at the jury as she stepped down from the witness stand.

"Call your next witness, Mr. Prosecutor," spoke the Judge.

Rising slowly and looking at the members of the jury, Marshall Logan replied, "Your Honor, and members of the jury, the State of Texas rests its case."

"Let's take a short recess," responded Judge Carter.

Travis Payne had discussed many times with his client whether he would take the stand and testify in his own defense. The decision had been relatively easy to make in this case. Nothing could be gained by him testifying.

The defendant could not explain away the damaging testimony given by the hospital personnel and the car mechanic from Linden. That evidence was clear and actually irrefutable. And the only logical and reasonable deductions that could be made from that testimony pointed only one way -- to Mitchell's guilt. So, why subject the defendant to being cross examined on a subject to which he had no defense? At least that was part of Payne's thinking behind the decision not to put Mitchell on the stand.

Also, the missing gun used to kill Ramon Garza could not be explained, not even partially. That missing gun evidence would convict Roy Mitchell. There was no way around it. The defendant had used that gun to kill Garza in an effort to help his friend, Tony Medina. Later the defendant made sure the gun would never be found. And as implied throughout the trial, Logan would vigorously cross examine that Mitchell disposed of the gun after the gun battle. Mitchell could only deny any knowledge of it. Such simple denial, thought Payne, would not be in the least bit persuasive.

Mitchell could not deny that he drove Tony over to the crime scene. He had already told his lawyer as much. The question that was most difficult for Payne to answer was whether the jury would believe Mitchell when he said he did not know that Tony was going over there to kill Ulysses Carillo. The theory of a person's mere presence at the crime scene had been thoroughly developed on the cross examination of Detective Barnes. Mitchell could easily testify that he had no knowledge that Tony was going to shoot, but the actions taken by Mitchell in Linden after the shooting did not coincide with that testimony. And then, again, there was the missing gun. The decision -- be it the right one or not -- had been made. The defendant would not testify.

Withholding information from his client was a cause of great consternation to Travis Payne. The defense attorney knew he had not so much as even breathed anything to his client about it. If Roy Mitchell had any previous knowledge about it, he had not spoken, or even hinted, about it to his lawyer. That, too, caused Payne much trepidation. He stared at the condensation that had appeared on the beer bottle, and then watched droplets slide down the side. It was totally quiet in the hotel room, and had been that way for nearly an hour. Ever since he had walked into his room, he had been completely immersed with the problem at hand. He had spent more time researching this point of the case than he had any other. And he was still bewildered. Uncertain. Perplexed. Confused. He was certain that his client did not know.

Payne closed his eyes and rubbed his face with his hands. When he finished the beer he leaned back in his chair and reached for the brown paper sack on the floor. The next beer was still cold as he twisted off the gold-colored cap. Setting the bottle in front of him, he stared at that one, too.

For the nearly thirty years he had been a trial lawyer, he had never been in this plight. He had reminded himself over and over again that his job was to zealously represent his client; at least that was what the lawyers' Canon of Ethics instructed. The Canons of Ethics -- a set of tenets, creeds, and dogma -- was something that all lawyers had pledged to uphold.

Someone knocking on a door down the hall awakened Travis Payne. He had fallen asleep sitting upright in the chair. He looked at his watch -- it was 10 p.m. The one hour sleep had been unexpected but restful. After setting his portable alarm clock radio for 6:00 a.m., he went to bed.

The bailiff had signaled to the lawyers that the Judge was on his way to the courtroom. Mitchell wondered if they would have final arguments that morning or afternoon. The Judge had not yet drawn up his instructions to the jury. But from experience Mitchell knew it would not take more than two hours to prepare. The mammoth case was practically over; at least the presentation of the evidence was nearly through. Though he had earlier agreed with his lawyer concerning the decision not to testify, he had some misgivings about it last night. Anxiety, like he had never experienced before, had overcome him. As he tossed and turned in bed, nothing could settle him. He wondered if this was how all defendants felt during a trial. He imagined it was. He was about to be found guilty by the jury. He felt it. But there was nothing he could have done differently. They simply did not have any evidence with which to work. Roy Mitchell had no defense. The missing gun puzzled him. Even with his own expertise involving criminal trials, it was a puzzle that had no resolution.

As Mitchell sat at the defense counsel table, staring downward, Payne leaned over to him.

"Whatever happens in the next hour, don't look astonished," his lawyer whispered. "You understand?"

"What?"

"Whatever you hear in the next hour, don't look surprised. Just sit there. No facial expressions. Nothing. Don't talk to me or do anything. You got that?"

"What are you talking about?"

The bailiff barked the announcement. "All rise. The 282nd Judicial District Court is now in session, the Honorable Wendall Carter presiding."

When the Judge took his seat, he looked up and smiled. "Thank you. Please be seated."

Looking at the defense attorney, "What says the defense?" he asked.

Chapter 37

"Your Honor, may it please the Court," answered Travis Payne as he rose from his seat. "We will call Mr. Juan Medina to the witness stand."

Mitchell quickly turned his head toward Payne as the defense attorney resumed his seat.

"I said, don't look," whispered his attorney.

As the deputy sheriff escorted Mr. Medina to the witness stand, Roy Mitchell felt like he was going into a stupor.

The small, sturdy-looking man walked slowly as he passed the members of the jury. His new khaki-colored pants were creased and rolled up at the bottom of each leg. His dark-brown work boots, worn and showing age, made no sound as he gently stepped toward the witness stand. A khaki-colored work shirt, also brand-new and matching his pants, hung loosely on his body. As he carried a straw cowboy hat with both hands, his head was bent. Before he reached his final destination -- the witness chair -- the Judge asked him to stop and raise his right hand. When he did, the jury was able to see a large, wrinkled, very brown hand -- clearly, a working man's hand -- calloused and strong for his age.

"Do you swear to tell the truth, the whole truth, and nothing but the truth, so help you God?"

"Yes, sir, I promise to do that," he slowly replied in a comforting voice.

As the witness seated himself, an anxious and wrought Mitchell was about to explode inside. A million questions were charging through his brain. What's he going to do or say? He was violently churning on the inside. He was calm on the outside. Years and years in the courtroom were surfacing this one last time.

"Tell us your name, please," Payne began.

"Sir, my name is Juan Medina."

"Mr. Medina, first of all I am going to ask you a few questions about your personal background --" Payne hesitated a moment -- "beginning with, how old are you?"

After placing his hat on the counter top before him, the witness gently responded, "Sir, I'm 59 years of age."

"Where do you live? What city?"

"I live here in Dallas."

"Have you lived here very long?"

"I came here when I was six years old. I've lived here ever since. My parents came from Mexico."

"Are you married?"

"My wife died eight years ago."

"Do you have any children?"

"Five. Three daughters and two sons."

"What are their names and ages?"

"Juanita. She turned 21 a few months ago. Rose is 13. And Mercedes. She's 11 years old. Hosea is 16. And Tony -- he died when he was 22."

Roy Mitchell was like a statue. His quick, shallow breaths shivered with uneasiness. His heart beat so hard and fast that he could almost feel it in his shoes. Sitting straight up in the chair and staring directly at his friend, Mitchell did not know what to expect. A hundred and one questions were flying through his brain.

"Where do you work, Mr. Medina?"

"I work for Brown & Root Construction Company. I've worked there for 33 years." The aged and wrinkled face agreed.

The pleasant, unassuming witness appeared comfortable up on the witness stand. His humble manner was quite obvious.

"Mr. Medina, back on December 1, 1992, where did you live and who lived with you?"

"I lived on 1220 Manana Street in Dallas -- and still do. My three younger children live with me; and back then my son, Tony, lived with me. My oldest daughter lives in an apartment across town."

The standing-room-only courtroom was eerily quiet, as everyone hung on to every word the modest witness was saying. Placing his hand on Roy's shoulder, Payne asked the witness, "Sir, do you know the man sitting next to me?"

For the first time since entering the courtroom Juan Medina looked at Roy Mitchell. "Yes sir. Mr. Mitchell." The soft tone of his voice was powerful. Payne looked at the jury. The facial expression on some of their faces was telling. They were receptive.

"You've known him very long?"

"Yes sir, a long time," Juan Medina solemnly answered as his eyes met Mitchell's. "I first met him when Tony was shot."

"Tell us about that, would you?"

"After Tony was shot, Mr. Mitchell started coming over. You know, being a friend to my son."

"Well, you knew he worked in the District Attorney's Office and was the prosecutor assigned to the case in which Tony was shot, didn't you?"

"Yes sir, I did."

"So, it started out work related? That is to say Mr. Mitchell was the prosecutor and Tony was the victim and Ulysses Carillo was the defendant. Is that the way it started?"

"Yes sir, it started out that way. But those two boys became buddies." An unexpected smile formed on Juan's face. Some jurors also smiled.

"Buddies, huh?" Payne looked at the jury. Let me back up for a moment. After Tony was shot, he was paralyzed, wasn't he?"

"Yes sir." Juan Medina's head dropped. His eyes were looking down at the floor. The slow even sound of his voice could not have been more sincere.

"What would Mr. Mitchell do whenever he came over to see you and Tony?"

"Sit and talk. Watch television. Sometimes he would take Tony to eat hamburgers or pizza. You know, just getting Tony out. Tony would get so lonely and down at times. But Mr. Mitchell would try to keep his spirits up."

"Could Tony drive a car?"

"No, he couldn't."

"Could he get around in a wheelchair?"

"Oh, yes sir."

"Mr. Medina, were you aware that Tony had dropped the charges against Ulysses Carillo for shooting him?"

"Yes sir."

"Did you have anything to do with that decision?"

"No. No, I didn't. I found out about it after he had already done it."

"Did you find out why he dropped the charges?"

"Objection, Your Honor!" Logan exclaimed. "The question calls for a hearsay response, and I object to it." So far, that had been the only thing the special prosecutor had found that he could object to. When the Judge sustained the objection, the State's attorney sat back down in his chair wondering what he could do next. Up to this point, thought Logan, the things the witness had said had not really damaged the State's case. What was doing the most damage was Juan Medina's demeanor on the witness stand. Juan Medina looked believable. He talked believable. Hell, thought Logan to himself, he is believable.

Payne was going extra slow, allowing the jury to soak up every question and answer. He thought the witness was impressive. Juan Medina came across as likeable. The defense attorney kept watching the jury. They still seemed receptive. Quickly glancing at his client, he noticed that Mitchell was doing a good job of being still.

"How had Tony accepted his condition?"

Mr. Medina hesitated a moment, and then he picked up his hat and very slowly rolled it around in his large, weathered hands. It was obvious that the question hit a sensitive area. The subdued witness tried to speak a couple of times, but no words came out. After a minute or two he regained his composure. Speaking, but looking down at the floor, the witness answered the question. "He had accepted it peacefully and better than I had thought he would. He was not sour." He paused, still looking down ... "Mr. Mitchell had a lot to do with that."

"Mr. Medina, let me direct your attention to the day that Tony was killed. Had you gone to work that day?"

"Yes, I had."

"After work did you come home?"

"Yes, I did, sir."

"When you got home, who was there?"

"Mr. Mitchell and Tony."

"What time was it when you got home?"

"Maybe 3 or 4 o'clock."

"Where was everyone? Inside or outside the house?"

"We were all inside the house."

"What were Tony and my client doing?"

"They were arguing," Mr. Medina quietly replied.

Roy Mitchell could not stand it any longer. He wanted to get up and walk out. He could not take it. His mind and body -- together -- were about to shake apart. 'Why is he doing this? Why?' For the moment that was all that Mitchell could think about. 'Of course, Juan Medina had not been at home at that time! He wasn't anywhere around! Why is he doing this? Why?' Again, he wanted to get up and walk out. But he found that he could not move.

"Had you ever seen them arguing before?"

Juan Medina silently shook his head for a long time. "Never," he finally answered.

"What were......" Payne knew the answer, but he wanted drama. He paused for a second before he continued. ".......What were they arguing about?" Softly, but confidently, Payne finished the question. The anticipation in the entire courtroom was thicker than smoke.

The witness drew a deep breath and then replied, "Tony wanted to be driven over to Mr. Carillo's house, and Mr. Mitchell would not do it."

"Were they arguing loudly or just casually talking?"

"Really loud."

"What was Tony's condition?"

"He was crying, begging for Mr. Mitchell to take him over there."

Payne continued to speak softly, but pointedly. "Did Tony say why he wanted to go over there?"

"He said he just wanted to see if Mr. Carillo was there. He said he just wanted to drive by and then come home."

"What did you do?"

"I tried to calm him down, talk some sense into his head, but it wasn't doing any good. Tony wouldn't listen."

Juan Medina began wiping tears away from his eyes as he spoke. He did not have a tissue; he was using the back of his hand. The courtroom was silent. Mitchell's heart was beating a thousand times a minute. His legs were shaking. To keep his head from shaking, Mitchell had both hands placed behind his ears with his thumbs under his chin. He dared not look around; his eyes were locked straight ahead. 'Why is he lying? Why is he doing this?' he repeatedly asked himself.

"What happened next?"

"Tony picked up a bag that was next to his wheelchair and pulled a gun out of it. A shotgun."

"Had you ever seen that gun before?"

Juan wiped his eyes and then said, "Yes -- that was my shotgun."

"What then?"

"Mr. Mitchell went for the gun and tried to get it away from him. They were wrestling over the gun and it went off -- hitting ....hitting Mr. Mitchell."

Roy Mitchell was becoming light-headed. His mind refused to believe what his ears were hearing. 'It can't be,' he said to himself. 'It just can't be happening.' Mitchell tried to move his arms and hands -- and couldn't. He was frozen, yet his whole body quivered inside. The trembling -- the throbbing -- the convulsing slowly began to show on the stoic Roy Mitchell. Payne noticed it. But the testimony was not only gripping Roy Mitchell. A couple of the jurors had eyes as big as saucers. Others were literally sitting on the edge of their seats.

"What happened next?"

"I rushed over to him," the witness was nodding his head toward Mitchell. "He had fallen down on the floor."

"What did Tony do?"

Mr. Medina pulled a white handkerchief out of his pants pocket and was wiping his eyes. He breathed deep a few times. Looking at the jury as he spoke, Mr. Medina finally continued. "He was still holding onto the gun. He pushed his wheelchair over to Mr. Mitchell. Tony started crying and saying that he did not mean to shoot him. He was really crying. I was trying to help Mr. Mitchell and so was Tony."

"What happened to the gun?"

"Well, at about that time, Tony was putting the gun in that bag."

"What happened then?"

"I was trying to call the police, but he" -- Juan nodded his head towards Mitchell -- "would not let me."

"I take it that at that time my client was still conscious -- he had not passed out, had he?"

"No sir. He never passed out."

"What did my client do to prevent you from calling the police?"

"Took the phone away from my hand and told me he didn't want the police called."

"Was he bleeding?"

"Yes sir. At first he was, but I got a rag and stopped it."

"At the time of the shot, it's just you three people at the house. That is you, Tony, and Roy Mitchell?"

When Juan Medina nodded his head in agreement, Payne continued: "When you were trying to stop the bleeding, were there still just you three people at the house?"

Again Medina nodded. Juan Medina's face showed the heartache he was having to relive.

"What happened next?"

Mr. Medina swallowed hard, took a few deep breaths, and finally regained his composure. "Well -- well --" he stammered, "I told Tony to go out on the porch while I tended to Mr. Mitchell. Tony was still shook up -- crying and carrying on -- saying he was sorry and all. So,

Tony went outside while I stayed with him." Juan pointed his hat towards Mitchell. "I wanted to call the police, but he" -- again indicating with his hat -- "wouldn't have it. I eventually got the bleeding stopped, and we were going outside to talk to Tony. As we walked outside, we saw Tony going down the street."

"When you walked outside and saw Tony going down the street, was Roy Mitchell with you?"

"Yes. He was in front of me."

"How was your son going down the street?"

"He was riding in Mr. Mitchell's car."

"How did he get into the car?"

"Don't know. The wheel chair was in the front yard."

Roy Mitchell closed his eyes. 'No! No! No! It can't be happening,' he prayed to himself. 'He can't do this! Why? Oh, God, why?'

"Let me back up for a moment, Mr. Medina. During the time that Tony was on the porch by himself, did anybody come to your house?"

"Someone came up and was talking to Tony, but I didn't know who he was. I was inside the house, tending to.....him" indicating Mitchell. But I heard some voices coming from the porch, and I looked out the window. That's when I saw a boy standing out in the front yard."

"Did you know him?"

"I'm not sure. I didn't recognize him."

"How old was this person?"

"Young man, early twenties. Don't know."

"Who was driving the car when you saw it going down the street?"

"This person that was in the yard."

"So, I take it that neither you nor Mr. Mitchell ever said anything to this young man?"

"No sir. Never did. When I heard the voices outside, I just looked out the window to see who was talking. Then I went back to seeing after --"

"Again, how old would you say this boy was?" interrupted the defense attorney.

"Oh, early twenties. Maybe a teenager. I can't say."

"What did he look like? Tall? Short? Heavy? Skinny? Beard? No beard?"

"Can't say. I didn't pay attention to him."

"What was he wearing? Coat? No coat? Hat? No hat?"

"He had a baseball cap on. That's all I can remember."

"Okay. After you saw Tony being driven down the street, what did you do?"

"I didn't know what to do. I -- I -- I guess I panicked. I went back into the house. He --" indicating Mitchell "-- was in a lot of pain. We talked about what to do." Pointing towards Mitchell, Juan Medina said, "He didn't believe that Tony would do anything. Me either. We thought that Tony would get scared and not do anything. So, we just waited. His arm had stopped bleeding; however, he was not able to move around very well. After about twenty minutes or so we heard a car horn. We looked outside and saw Mr. Mitchell's car in front of our house and saw the boy running away. I ran outside. Tony was in the car -- shot. The boy I saw running away stopped about a half a block away and was just watching us. Mr. Mitchell and I brought Tony into the house and laid him on the couch. He....." pointing to Mitchell...." told me to call the police. He looked outside and said the boy was now running down the street. And that he was going to go try to catch him. He ran outside, got into his car and drove off. I wasn't thinking very well. I didn't really know what to do. I tried to call Detective Barnes, but no answer. I was afraid to call any other policeman. I don't know why -- I can't explain it or anything. I just got scared. I sat down and waited. I don't know what for or anything. Maybe I was waiting on Mr. Mitchell to come back. I don't know. I can't explain it. I just sat and waited. I just waited at home. I don't know why. I didn't know what to do. I was too frightened to do anything except sit there. I called Detective Barnes again.

Finally reached him. And soon he and another man arrived and then more policemen came."

"Did you ask Roy Mitchell where he was going?"

"He just said he was going to look for the boy." Logan had thought about objecting to these hearsay statements by Mitchell. But he did not. He actually wanted to hear them himself.

"Did Roy Mitchell come back that day?"

"No, sir, he never came back. He did call. He did call me on the telephone. He said....." Logan again thought about making an objection to the hearsay testimony, but changed his mind. Hearsay testimony is a statement made by a person out of the courtroom but relayed in court by the person who heard it. Usually, these statements are not allowed. "....He said he was in Linden getting first aid on his arm. That he already had his arm looked at by a doctor. He also said that he had gotten his car repaired from the gun shots. He said he was doing this to protect Tony."

"Wait a minute." interrupted Payne. Payne wanted to break up this bombshell testimony. "He said he was wanting to protect Tony. That's what my client told you?"

"That's what he said. Yes sir."

"When the police were at your house on the day Tony was shot, did you tell them that Tony shot Roy Mitchell?"

"I thought I did. I think I did. Everything was going so fast. I don't really know. That's how Detective Barnes knew to go to Linden. I'm sure that's how he knew to go to Linden. How else would he know?"

"When did you next see him?"

"On the day of Tony's funeral, he came."

Payne held up the gym bag with one hand and asked, "Mr. Medina, have you ever seen this before?"

"It belonged to my son, Tony. It's the bag that Tony got the gun from."

Holding up the shotgun that was found in the roadway, he asked, "Have you ever seen this shotgun before?"

"Let me look at it." Payne allowed Juan Medina to visually check the gun. After looking at it up close, Medina nodded affirmatively. "That's my gun. That was my gun that I kept at the house. But the last time that I saw it, the barrel and stock had not been cut off."

"How can you tell this jury that this is your gun?"

"I scratched my initials on it years ago. See here." Medina pointed to a spot on the gun.

Payne took it from Medina and looked. Payne nodded and then held it for the jury to see. He pointed to initials 'JM'. These are your initials you carved onto this gun a long time ago, right?"

"Yes sir. Fifteen or twenty years ago. But like I told you. The last time I saw this gun, it was a regular looking shotgun. Regular barrel and regular stock."

"Who cut off the barrel and the stock?"

"I don't know. Last time I saw this gun was probably a year ago. I kept it in the closet. Sort of hidden."

"So you do not know who sawed off the barrel or stock?""

"No sir."

"Do you know when they were cut off?"

"No sir."

"We now know from earlier testimony that this gun was found at the scene of the shooting. My question is this: When Tony pulled a gun out of the gym bag at your house, did you recognize it as your shotgun that you kept in the closet?"

"No sir."

"And did you say earlier that it had been some months since you had last seen this gun?"

"Maybe a year."

"You didn't get it out or see it on a regular basis?"

"No sir. I just kept it in my closet, and that's where it stayed."

"Did you see when or how Tony Medina got this gun from your closet?"

"No sir. I don't know when he did it. He knew that we had it at the house."Travis Payne peered at the jury. The looks on a few of their faces were of pure astonishment. Some of them were staring down at the floor; others appearing bewildered, were staring back at the defense attorney. Payne sensed they had heard all that they wanted to hear. He had fired his only salvo.

Payne glanced at his client. Mitchell looked as if he was about to faint. Payne could not detect any breathing. His client's face -- expressionless and white as a sheet -- was looking straight ahead. Payne was now glad that he had not revealed Juan Medina's testimony prior to the trial.

"Mr. Medina, who shot Roy Mitchell?"

"My son did."

"You saw it?"

"Yes sir. I'm afraid I did."

"My client was at your house when it happened?"

"Yes sir."

"And then Tony left your house?"

"Yes sir."

"And Roy stayed?"

"Yes sir."

"And the next time you saw your son, he had been shot?"

Juan Median's voice cracked. Softly crying, he answered. "Yes sir."

Rising from his chair the defense attorney addressed the Judge: "Your Honor, we pass the witness."

Payne had detected from his peripheral vision that Logan was readying his attack. Squirming and feverishly writing notes on his legal pad, the special prosecutor appeared shell-shocked by the testimony. When he finally began his cross examination of the witness, however, Payne noticed a slight quiver in the voice of the special prosecutor. Hopefully, Payne thought, the jury picked up on that, too. Logan's cross examination went nowhere. As hard as he tried to shake Medina's testimony, no glitch or chink in his testimony was found. And this upset Logan even more. The special prosecutor was getting flustered. He was not able to make headway. The witness' testimony was not coming apart, and Payne knew this made the defense's case even stronger.

The final arguments were actually anti-climatic. The defense rested their case after their one and only witness. The State -- unable to alter or rebut Mr. Medina's testimony -- rested immediately afterwards. The final summations to the jury occurred the day following Juan Medina's surprising and dramatic testimony. However, the State was still rattled. In his final arguments Marshall Logan had not been able to overcome the explosive impact of the testimony of Juan Medina. Logan's aura of confidence had completely disappeared by the time he made his remarks to the jury. He was so unnerved by the startling revelations of Juan Medina that he only made a vague reference to it.

That testimony was riveting; and had come from an area that Logan had not followed through during his investigation. In retrospect, he realized he should have interviewed Tony Medina's father. He had thought about doing it, but with the evidence concerning what had occurred in Linden, he had disregarded it.

The bailiff was reading a magazine when a knock came from the jury deliberation room. The twelve citizens had deliberated an hour. The loud knock startled him. Glancing at his watch, he noticed that it was noon. They want to break for lunch, he surmised. When he opened the door, the foreman was standing, facing him.

"We have a verdict," he said.

The bailiff reached for the Court's Charge that contained the verdict sheet. He noticed that one or two of the female jurors were softly crying. From his 10 years as a bailiff in the courthouse, the deputy sheriff knew that tears in jurors' eyes were normally good for the State, and bad for the defense. 'They've convicted him,' he said under his breath. Taking the papers from the foreman, the bailiff said that he would return shortly. Closing the door behind him, he went to inform the Judge.

Judge Wendall Carter, feeling years older than he had a few weeks before, looked over the courtroom. He had expected most of the people packed into the courtroom earlier would have gone to lunch. Not so. Every seat was taken and the hallway was just as crowded.

"Has the jury reached a verdict?" he asked solemnly.

"Yes, we have," responded the foreman.

Looking down at the verdict sheet, the Judge began to read: "We, the jury, find the defendant NOT GUILTY."

The courtroom erupted. Cheers, clapping, hollering. Mitchell, sitting next to his attorney, bowed his head for a moment, while Payne dropped an arm around him. When order was finally restored in the courtroom, Judge Carter released the jury. While the defendant was still seated, Judge Carter addressed the citizen that had been accused: "Mr. Mitchell, I now release you from all embodiments of this case." Banging his gavel, the Judge, speaking to no one in particular said, "This Court is adjourned."

Chapter 38

Three weeks later, Roy Mitchell walked up the familiar front steps leading to the house. He had not seen nor spoken to Juan Medina since the trial. Frankly, he had not known what to say. Still unsure and hesitant, he knocked on the door. When Juan Medina opened it, the two men stood staring at one another for several seconds.

The morning air cooled Mitchell's face -- which, for some reason, had become reddened and flushed. Roy started to speak, but when his mouth opened, nothing came out. The words that he had rehearsed in his car driving over that Saturday morning were suddenly lost. Instinctively, Roy's left hand wiped his mouth as if it was wiping something off. He then tried to speak again. But like before, no words came out.

Juan Medina's facial expression was tranquil–complete peace.

Mitchell turned and partially faced the street. Gazing away. The prosecutor -- not known in the courtroom for his lack of words -- was speechless.

Still, neither had spoken. It was silent all around too -- inside the house, next door, down the street, everywhere. As Mitchell continued his wandering stare, the silence hit him. It was as if the whole world was watching this scene, waiting to see what happened, listening to hear what was said. "They" wanted to know "why".

Juan Medina's voice broke the silence.

"My friend, come into this house. You know you are always welcome in this house."

Mitchell turned and again faced the opened door. Juan had stepped back inside the house and was motioning with his hand for the guest to enter. "Come in, I say. My friend, come in."

"Are the kids still asleep?"

"Goodness, no!" exclaimed Juan. "They've been up and gone for an hour or so. They're already down at the park. They rode their bicycles down there with the neighbor's kids."

"How have you been getting along?" asked Mitchell as they both sat down in the living room. "Any problems?"

Medina shook his head and then smiled. "I'm doing okay. I will be fine. But the question is: How have you been?"

Mitchell did not answer immediately. And he noticed -- or at least felt as if Juan was staring at him.

Medina picked up on the hesitation. "It is going to take a while, maybe a long time, to....to move on. Eventually you'll move on. Don't resurrect it. Don't rehash it. Don't dwell on it."

Mitchell was looking at the floor. He felt uncomfortable. When he finally did raise his head, his vision locked on something he had not seen before. There, on the end table next to the sofa where Juan Medina was sitting, was a photograph. It was in an 8" x 10" wooden frame. It was obviously new, and it was one Mitchell had never seen before. At first, he could not make out where the photograph had been taken. Then he identified the familiar front porch with the familiar porch swing. He was within 15 feet of it right now.

Moments earlier, when Mitchell first approached the Medinas' front door, he had reminisced about earlier times in that very spot. The place where the Medinas had grown together. The place where family life in the Medina household had centered. Now, he was looking at a photograph of himself and Tony seated in that old well-worn swing. Both the man and the boy were laughing. At what, Mitchell had no idea. As he picked up the picture and drew it closer to him, he noticed how well Tony appeared. No hate. No revenge. No animosity. Just his smile and a look that conveyed, 'I'm just me' to any observer. Just that smile and just that look. That was how Roy Mitchell wanted to remember Tony Medina.

Then he noticed the photograph did not show the wheelchair. Strange, he thought. He could not remember ever seeing his friend without it.

The chair had become an extension of Tony. The wheelchair and Tony; Tony and the wheelchair. And it had been that chair -- that condition of the person -- that had initially drawn Mitchell to him.

Of course he saw that while Tony's face was captured in the picture, Mitchell had been substituting Toby in real life. Part of Mitchell had known that all along. But it was a part that he had been trying to suppress. Or, was it something he had been trying to purge? It was the latter, he finally concluded. He had tried to purge the guilt that had infected his body ever since the day of Toby's accident. But he never could. He had never been able to. That is until he met Tony Medina. And it was through Tony that Mitchell finally was able to do so.

This conclusion had been with Roy Mitchell since the day of Tony Medina's burial. He looked again at the framed picture.

"I did what I had to do." Juan's voice broke the silence in the room.

Roy knew what Juan meant. But unexplainedly, Mitchell asked, "What?"

"The trial. My testimony. I did what I felt was right."

Mitchell looked and noticed that Medina appeared to be wearing the same type of clothes he had been wearing during his testimony. Khaki pants, long sleeve khaki shirt, worn out work boots. As Roy Mitchell looked at his friend sitting across from him, Mitchell saw a common, everyday man. Humble. A man just trying to live life.

"If you isolate that trial," continued Juan Medina, "and look only at that trial and nothing else, then what I did was wrong." His voice was soft, yet clear and unwavering. "But if one has the ability to step back and look at the entire picture," -- Medina's extended arm swept the air from left to right -- "at the entire picture, one can see something else. I saw a boy whose life was probably ruined; a boy who had so much life to live and so much to give -- cut short by an evil man." Medina's hands clenched into a fist, and the voice became stronger. "An evil man who, unless stopped, would continue to do evil. Then I saw another person," Medina's voice was easing, "who came and extended this boy's life; a man who by his very presence breathed some life back into this boy's well-being. You were that person." His finger pointed at Roy Mitchell. "A good man doing right! You gave Tony life! I saw it and I felt it. In my view, you were doing right by Tony. As God as my witness..." wincing, he shut both eyes "... you were doing right by him. So, yes…" looking back at Mitchell "…if you isolate my testimony at trial, yes, that was wrong. But I look at the entire picture, and I also see that you were doing right." A twinkling appeared in his eyes. "And so in the overall picture of things, what happened was ... was ... was somewhere between right and wrong. Justice is sometimes blurred."

Roy Mitchell stepped down to the sidewalk as the front door closed behind him. He turned and paused. And looked at the front porch--the portion of the house where they had spent so much time. Everything was just as it had always been. The well-worn swing was gently moving in the breeze; but this time no wheelchair in sight.

CPSIA information can be obtained
at www.ICGtesting.com
Printed in the USA
FFHW010434200619
53029611-58672FF